I0593327

SUZANNAH ROWNTREE

Tall & Dark

Miss Dark's Apparitions, Volume I.

This one is for you (you know who you are):
the one with secrets
the one with burdens
the one who grows not weary in doing good.

Chapter I.

It is beyond a doubt far easier to conduct a séance when the dead are *not* trying to make their presence felt. *Qui s'excuse, se confond*, and all that, as they say in France—but in my defence, it *was* the first time I had been interrupted by a real, honest-to-goodness ghost.

I was already a little flustered that day. My half-holiday was supposed to begin at noon, but the life of a governess is very much at the whims of her employers; and after postponing Ada's French lesson so that she could be measured for new shoes, the Countess had insisted on my completing the lesson before I was permitted to depart. I had missed my tram, and had been obliged to walk all the way to the tiny flat in the Rembrandtstrasse; so that I had arrived warm and puffing despite the chill November air.

My newspaper advertisement, however, promised that in about twenty minutes The World-Famed Clairvoyant and Spiritual Medium, Fraulein Gwendoline Chant, would perform Marvellous Experiments in the latest refined Spiritualistic Phenomena along with Evidence that The Dead Do Return. I had gone to a deal of trouble creating Fraulein Gwendoline Chant; it was not easy to fabricate a World-Famed Clairvoyant on a governess' income in Vienna in those

1

days, but today I almost despaired of transforming a robust, glowing English governess into an appropriately wan and spiritual-looking medium. I accomplished it with a stark-white dress decorated with a quantity of hastily stitched white lace that *almost* washed out my complexion, a puff of rouge to each cheek, and a couple of drops of belladonna in my eyes to make them dilated and dark. By the time I had rendered my appearance suitably consumptive, the first of my guests had already collected on the landing, and after I had nearly tripped over an occasional table to get to the door, I found I had left the belladonna out in the open, by mistake, next to the mirror where any of my guests could see it.

So, it was a bad beginning.

In they streamed, mostly the solid, stout, middle-aged wives of bankers and doctors and lawyers. In a little while the room—which was small and shabbily furnished, though the old, faded wallpaper was a glorious pattern of dark and curling acanthus leaves—was full of their furs and feathered tocques. I smiled spiritually as I pocketed their *kronen,* but three of the faces gave me pause.

One was an extraordinarily striking young woman. Had her dark complexion and black hair smoother than a raven's wing fallen to my lot, I should have swathed myself in iridescent silks; but she had clothed herself severely in a grey wool suit. She did not speak, but she looked directly at the bottle of belladonna, and her full lips curved in a supercilious smile. I considered asking her to leave on some pretext, but then decided against it. Most mediums, being frauds, need to exclude sceptics from their séances for fear of discovery; but—well, reader, you shall see.

The next guest, immediately behind the dark beauty, nearly

caused my heart to jump up my throat: it was Frau Hofbauer—diminutive, golden-haired, famously lacking in tact, and an aunt of the two young girls I had come to Vienna to governess. The blood fled from my cheeks as I saw her, for I could not risk my employers discovering how their respectable governess was employing her half-holiday.

"You seem unwell, fraulein," Frau Hofbauer said with her customary directness, before glancing about the room. Her voice lowered. "What is it? Do you sense—a Presence?"

As a matter of fact, I did not—yet—but I did not like to disappoint her. Contriving to look paler and more interesting than ever, I murmured: "It may be nothing; time will tell." She nodded devoutly and pressed her twenty-*kronen* bill into my hand.

Last of all was a young man with ardent eyes and dark curls and the clean, neatly trimmed nails of a gentleman, though he was very shabbily dressed. He looked at his twenty-*kronen* piece almost hungrily as he laid it in my hand. I hesitated, wondering if I should accept it. I was doing honest work, of course—even if there isn't a word yet for exactly what I was doing, I *did* provide these well-to-do society ladies with genuine help—but I had an intuition that this young man had given me all the money he had. I searched the shadows behind him. It was to be hoped that some of my guests had come with unseen attendants—a séance tended to go better if I could piece together a suitably impressive reading—but I could see no memories haunting this man.

"My friend, what brings you here?" I asked gently.

For the first time, he tore his eyes away from the silver coin. When he saw me, he paled and startled, as though it was he, and not myself, who was seeing ghosts.

I had expected Frau Hofbauer to recognise me. This poetic pauper, however, I was quite sure I had never met in my life, and I did not like to fall into a dispute over my identity. Although I am a natural mimic, and after six months in Vienna my native accent had practically disappeared, I summoned as brisk an English accent as I could manage for my next words:

"Is there someone particular with whom you wish to speak?"

My voice must have done the trick, for he blinked and flushed slightly. "My wife," he said. "I wish to speak to my wife."

There was a world of tragedy in his voice.

"She has been dead—how long?"

"I don't know—some years." He was still watching me in visible confusion. "There's something I must ask her."

Despite my advertisement, I couldn't truly channel the dead. No one can. What I really did was provide a listening ear so that my clients could talk about their grief and lay uneasy memories to rest. Naturally I could not say so plainly: I would lose my clientele, and they would lose all the help I could give them.

"I am afraid the spirits don't usually answer direct questions in that manner," I said evasively. "Not through me, in any case."

He shook his head. "Please, fraulein, I have to try."

"But I can't—"

"Please, fraulein," he repeated, over my protest. After that, what could I say? I allowed him to move past me to where the small round table stood waiting, surrounded by chairs.

Tucking his twenty-*kronen* piece into my pocket along with the rest of the money, I went to join the party at the table. I

4

was halfway into my seat when Frau Hofbauer said, "Oughtn't we to shut the curtains?"

I should have done it myself: it was a crisp, clear November afternoon and the sun was shining brightly in at the window. "Of course," I said. The penniless young man jumped up and closed the thick velveteen curtains, plunging us into a cold semi-darkness with just a little sunlight filtering in around the edges; and naturally that was when I found that in my haste, I had forgotten to light the candles at the centre of the table. I was obliged to track down the matches in the dark: today, for a World-Famed Clairvoyant, I was not doing particularly well.

It proved to be an omen of things to come.

"Silence, please," I said, once the candles were lit. "I will commence the reading."

"Don't you want us to put our hands on the table, fraulein?"

The dark beauty spoke in very good German. I did not immediately notice the satirical note in her voice, for, I am ashamed to confess, I was rather surprised at the purity of her accent.

"Not particularly. It makes no difference, so long as you fix your thoughts on the departed. Put your hands wherever you like."

A banker's wife tutted. "Don't you think—"

"Hush," I said severely. "Clear your minds. Call to memory those you have lost."

An expectant silence fell. Most of my guests did place their hands on the table, except the dark lady, who was looking about the room with a reprise of the supercilious smile.

It was high time I shattered that composed scepticism, I thought with a sniff.

I glanced around the circle of tense, waiting ladies (and gentleman). Among the ten or fifteen guests of a typical séance, one or two could be counted upon bringing with them at least one imprint of the long-dead—or, with a little encouragement, summoning up the right sort of memory. This soon took place. Frau Hofbauer, having closed her eyes reverently, turned her head slightly, unconsciously, to the left. I fixed my gaze upon her left shoulder and was rewarded in time by the vision of a child in a sailor-suit, all big dark eyes and tousled golden hair. As he leaned up against her in a confiding sort of way, I felt a mood of entire stillness and trust settle gently over me and knew I was feeling what he had felt in that remembered moment.

Until now I had rather disliked Frau Hofabauer on account of her having reduced Steffi to tears over a broken tea-cup. Now, even as I gently disentangled myself from the memory, I found myself pierced by sympathy for the bereaved mother.

I touched her hand.

"Oh!" Frau Hofbauer's hand tightened convulsively upon my own. "Someone is touching me!"

"It's only me, madam. You had a child, I think. A son?"

Her eyes became large and luminous. "Heinrich! Heinrich is here?"

Everyone was paying attention now. I hesitated.

It is difficult to explain the things I have been able to see all my life. Heinrich—if that was the little boy's name—was what I have eventually come to call an *imprint*: a wispy, insubstantial thing that could neither speak nor deviate from actions he had taken in life. As far as I can tell, imprints are not spirits in the sense of that rational, emotional, and immortal part of ourselves that goes on living after our physical dissolution. *That* part never stays for long before being called away to whatever lies beyond this life—but which I suspect to be, quite prosaically, either Heaven or Hell. No: all that is left, if anything, is the imprint which fading memory leaves upon the world, a mere echo of memories and feelings. People who have died suddenly or violently leave the strongest imprints; but others remain with the people who love them, summoned up by affectionate memory, going unforgotten through all the habitual motions of their lives.

The answer to Frau Hofbauer's question, in other words, was no—Heinrich was not here; only his memory.

But Frau Hofbauer was paying me to give her—if not precisely the truth, then something she needed just as badly.

"He often used to lean against your shoulder," I murmured, sidestepping the question. "Such thick, golden hair! It's easy to see where he gets it from."

"Oh, that *is* Heinrich!" Out came a handkerchief. "Heinrich, *bärchen,* speak to your mother! Have you been watching over Papa and Mama?"

The imprint didn't move, only looking at us with great, unseeing eyes. He must have been an appealing little boy, rather wistful and quiet.

Once again, I evaded the question. "He was always so peaceful when he was with you," I murmured. The imprint was clear-cut and fresh; but given Frau Hofbauer's age, it must have been some time since the child's death: ten years, perhaps. The poor lady, she must have been grieving a long time without relief. "He asks if you miss him very much?"

"Unbearably," she replied, in a voice choked with sobs. "It is an unworthy thought, I daresay; but sometimes I wonder how I can bear to go on living without him."

"You were very kind to him," I said after a pause, looking into the wide, confiding eyes, and immersing myself once again in the emotion of trust that hung about him. "Perhaps you did not have him long, but you made his time on earth a happy one." And a tart little piece of me wondered why she could not have been as kind to Steffi, last week, over the broken china. "I think he is trying to tell you something, but I cannot quite make out what. Something about…crying?"

"Oh!" said Frau Hofbauer, dabbing at her eyes. "He would always tell me not to cry, if I was upset; he would run to the garden and pick me roses to cheer me up."

"That's it," I said, weaving a benign fiction. "He wishes he could bring you roses, so that you would feel better. But since he cannot, he asks you to find a garden with roses, and pick them yourself—as a gift from him, to remember that there are still good and lovely things in the world, even though he is gone. Can you do that, Mama?"

She beamed through her tears. "Yes—yes, of course I will, *bärchen.*"

I felt a glow of satisfaction: I liked to feel I had really helped my guests. I glanced around, thinking that there could not have been a dry eye at the table. There were: the handsome, flashing specimens belonging to the dark lady, who smiled knowingly to herself when she met my gaze.

"Let us proceed," I murmured, not allowing her scepticism to dampen my spirits. "Close your eyes and think on the people you have lost. Remember them as they were in life."

One or two more imprints appeared, and I continued with my work—observing, probing, revealing and soothing long-hidden wounds, as I had done every week for the past few months. At first, I had been reluctant to employ my gift in this way; for people who could see the things I could see had a way of ending up in lunatic asylums. But I had soon discovered that a governess' income, even in Vienna, was scarcely enough to support an ailing mother and three younger sisters who were still a few years away from being able to find respectable employment. Thus Necessity became the mother of Gwendoline Chant.

Perhaps the work was not quite as respectable as I would have liked, but this afternoon's séance had brought me nearly as much as I made in a whole week as a governess. After several months of steady work, word was beginning to spread; and although I did not yet quite have the nerve to hand in my resignation to Ada and Steffi's papa, the money I had already sent home had enabled Mother to pay a decent doctor to find out what was ailing her. Moreover, I had high hopes that my sisters—who were evidently destined to become great artists—would not be compelled to squander their talents as governesses.

I had begun to feel as though a great burden was lifting from my shoulders. Yet I could tell no one, not even my mother, because I did not think she would quite understand. Still, for the first time in my life, I felt as though I really knew why I had been made. In helping others lay their ghosts to rest, I had found my calling.

Having encouraged one of my guests finally to express her feelings of regret over an estrangement from a deceased sister, I asked the party once again to bow their heads in memory of their loved ones. This time, something changed in the room. We all felt it: a bone-deep chill, and a darkness that seeped into the room until the acanthus wallpaper loomed close, and the candles seemed to shed a small and oppressed light. No one opened their eyes, but the poetic young man shrank in on himself a little and the other ladies pulled unconsciously at shawls and wraps. Only the dark sceptic sat watching me impassively. After a moment, her eyes flickered to the window, as though she presumed it was simply a matter of the sun going in behind the clouds.

For a moment, I thought the same. Then the shadows resolved into a tall, pale figure, gaunt and stark—a formidable, choleric-looking old gentleman as solid and real-seeming as myself. He came up behind an old lady who, I now realised, wore fresh black crepe. As his shadow fell over her, she shivered; but it was upon me that he fixed his censorious glare.

"A *séance?*" he inquired, in deep disgust, as though he expected me to wither away on the spot. I glanced nervously about the room, but every head remained bowed save that of the dark lady, who watched me with an eyebrow half lifted. Evidently, I was the only one in the room who had heard his remark.

Once or twice in my life, I have stumbled across something that was capable of making itself audible, capable of interacting with the world of the present. This was no imprint, but a genuine shade—a dead spirit clinging to life.

Really, I ought to have put an end to the séance then and there. But the afternoon had been progressing smoothly, and I did not know the peculiar dangers of shades then so well as I know them now.

The old gentleman certainly did not seem to be of a friendly disposition, but the opportunity was too tempting to pass up: a genuine shade was material for a séance that would set all of Vienna beating a path to Gwendoline Chant's door.

Accordingly, I took the plunge.

"I see a new spirit is among us. Commune with us, spirit!"

"Certainly not; I am not in the habit of associating with young people of your sort."

"Is there a loved one here you wish to speak to?"

"Not particularly."

I pressed my lips together. If I kept my cool, I might surprise something out of him. "There's a gentleman here with—yes, side-whiskers and a black brocaded waistcoat. He's here to speak to a lady."

Frau Hofbauer seized the widow's black-gloved hand. "Brigit! It's Maximilian!"

The old lady paled. "Maxl," she whispered. "Please don't be angry."

"I'm not angry. Why do you always expect me to be angry?" the spirit retorted. Doubt crept over me, but I had committed myself. I relayed the message.

"He says he isn't."

"Because I have something to tell him." The widow's lips trembled. "It's about Irmentrud. I couldn't tell you during your life, Maxl, but…I must relieve my conscience. She…she isn't *yours.*"

Judging from the scandalised looks passed around the table by the living, this was News.

As for the ghost, he erupted.

"*Backpfeifengesicht!*" Maxl screamed. "I knew it! *Einzeller! Lustmolch!* Who was it? Who did you betray me with? It was that good-for-nothing Hans Hartmann, wasn't it?"

"My good man! *Language!*" I gasped, reverting momentarily to the governess.

"And now Irmentrud is to inherit all my money? Over my

dead body! Wait till I get my hands on that *kuckuckskind!* Tell her! Tell her, fraulein! I'm going to throttle the little imposter!"

Almost all the light was sucked from the room, despite the curtains shifting in a blast of air that could not possibly have entered by the tightly-closed windows. Now really alarmed, I realised the shade was becoming strong enough, in its passion, to affect the world of the living.

"Madam," I said to the widow very seriously, "you should send someone to see that your daughter is safe."

"Gott in himmel!" the old lady whispered, going as white as a sheet. The next instant she fainted dead away, toppling sideways in her chair. The young poet caught her with an exclamation. She returned to consciousness almost at once.

"Irmentrud!" she screamed. "My child! He's going to kill her!"

"I said I would, didn't I, if you played me false! I'll kill her first and you second!" The shade's voice boomed out loud enough to make me wince, loud enough to rattle the windows and set the neighbour's dog barking.

My guests must have heard *something,* for the séance broke up in disarray, the bankers' and doctors' wives starting from their chairs and flocking to support the hysterical old lady, oblivious to the enraged ghost. "Smelling-salts!" Frau Hofbauer gasped. "She needs smelling-salts!"

I was incapable of movement, transfixed by the drama unfolding around me.

"How dare you speak of smelling-salts! Busybodies! *Tratschtanten!*" the ghost yelled, clutching for his widow's throat. She actually choked; I started out of my chair to stop him, but my hands passed through the shade's arms without finding anything tangible upon which to fasten. The old lady's eyes were wide and staring; the ghost raged; I could feel the tension in the air like a plucked string, like the whine of metal on metal, high and agonising—until the crisis came. The glasses on the table shattered all at once, the room shook, pictures toppled from their place on the wall, a vase of flowers flew across the room and smashed against the opposite wall, the wives of the bankers and doctors and lawyers covered their heads with their hands and screamed, and the dark lady's eyes opened very wide indeed as she clapped her hands together, once.

With that—silence, blessed silence, descended.

I know now that angry poltergeists can be dangerous, but do not remain long, as a rule. The shades of the dead are only ever passing through on their way elsewhere, and kicking up a fuss about it normally only precipitates one's departure.

I arose from my recumbent position beneath the table to find the room full of shattered nerves.

"What is the meaning of this?" Frau Hofbauer said, turning upon me with indignation. "You've practically killed her!"

All eyes were upon me: I found myself the object of general censure. It really did take the muffin! Although these ladies had just witnessed events of the most impressive supernatural origin, they were dissatisfied?

How foolish I had been! I had, indeed, given all of Vienna something to gossip about; but it was unlikely to result in people beating a path to my door. Still, it was not in vain that I had endured the intrigues of St Alphege's Ladies' College, or five years dealing with the spoiled offspring of Continental nobility. I wrung my hands and looked as angelic as I know how.

"Madam, I really am *terribly* sorry. Please do accept my apologies. The spiritual world is a higher plane of existence, beyond our control or even our comprehension—"

"If it's beyond your comprehension, then what business do you have meddling with it?"

"Madam, we're all on a journey; one on which I freely admit I am merely a fellow-traveller. Here: some smelling-salts for your poor friend. Are you feeling any better, madam? I can assure you quite sincerely that it won't happen again; there was a *most* agitated and disordered presence here a moment ago, but it has been banished and I flatter myself it will not trouble us again. I feel quite sure," I added portentously, for the room was beginning to calm, "that you have just been cleansed of an oppressive—even a malign influence. Tell me: how do you feel?"

The old lady, who had listened to my words with bewilderment, said, "Very shaken, my dear! very shaken!"

"It's just as I thought," I said, nodding wisely. "The roots of evil are not plucked out without great disturbance. But take heart! From now on, I should not be surprised if you found quite a new lease on life."

"I think I can feel it already," said the widow, taking a deep breath. Frau Hofbauer, however, was made of sterner stuff.

"I don't know what you think you're doing, Fraulein Chant—if that's your real name—but in my opinion, you cannot be trusted with sensitive or spiritual matters. Now that you've half frightened poor Frau Kohler here to death, you should at least give her her money back!"

"My dear Frau Hofbauer," I began.

"And I want my twenty *kronen* back too," she added stubbornly.

After that, of course, it was all over. I was obliged to disburse all that hard-earned money, that would have made all the difference to my poor sisters, and be insulted while I did it. The ladies filed out in a twittering flock, poor little Frau Kohler supported by two of her friends. I really did feel sorry for her. A nice life she must have led with that man! I was glad his money had gone to this Irmentrud, whoever's daughter she was!

At last, only the starving poet remained. I felt rather relieved to be able to offer him his money back. "What did I tell you? The spirits don't always do as they're told," I observed gloomily.

But he wouldn't take the money from me. Instead he looked around the shattered room, rather embarrassed, and shook his head. "Keep it, fraulein. You need it more than I do."

Chapter II.

The door closed behind the last of my guests, sealing me in with what seemed to be the wreckage of all my hopes. I stared unseeing at that twenty-*kronen* coin. It was true that I was going to need it. The shade had surely caused at least that much damage to the apartment, which had come ready-furnished. I would be lucky not to owe money—money I could not recover on future séances, because the gossips in Vienna, none among them more indefatigable than Frau Hofbauer, would be tattling about this day for years to come.

Gwendoline Chant was all washed up.

That weight descended upon my shoulders again, more heavily this time. I had pawned my one possession of value—a pair of pearl earrings my grandmother had left me—to hire this flat; and now, of course, I should lose my deposit. It made me sick to think of having wasted the money. Money, the one thing we couldn't do without, not with Mother too ill to work, and the girls depending on me to pursue their own vocations. If I failed they, too, would probably be obliged to become governesses; and that meant they would be sent to a hole like St Alphege's. The days when one could become a governess knowing next to nothing were long past, and Lord knew none of us could take a leaf out of *Jane Eyre* and marry a brooding landowner—with or without a mad wife in the attic. In the drawing-rooms of Brixton, landowners are pretty thin on the ground.

In the meanwhile, at least I had twenty *kronen*—or no, I realised, as I went to return the coin to my pocket. There was a rustle of paper within. A banknote. Another of my guests had forgotten to reclaim her money.

I turned with a start and found that I was not alone.

The dark lady had risen from her seat and now circumnavigated the table, dragging a gloved finger through the shards of glass, pulling the curtains aside to inspect the window, and passing her neatly-folded umbrella through the air like a maid probing for cobwebs.

"I beg your pardon, Fraulein—?" I stammered. She did not at once acknowledge me, instead overturning the table to peer beneath it. Even with the curtains open, not much light entered the room: the short autumn day was over, the sun setting behind the Vienna Woods.

At last she straightened, removed a pair of steel-rimmed *pince-nez* from her nose and tucked them into her pocket. "Very impressive," she said, in English as perfect as the German she had previously spoken. "I can't for the life of me see how you did it."

"Indeed," I agreed, not bothering to explain that this was because *I* had not done it. I had learned early in life not to share the secret of my gift with the world. "Your twenty *kronen.*"

She took the money as calmly as she had taken everything else that afternoon, opened a small purse, deposited the money within, extracted a pair of small newspaper clippings, unfolded them, and studied my face with such attention that

I found my cheeks becoming warm. I was not accustomed to being scrutinised so closely, and by such a remarkably beautiful woman.

"I beg your pardon—" I hesitated, not quite knowing how to proceed. I only wanted her to take her money and go away. Instead, she said:

"I'll be frank with you, Miss Chant. Your little routine could use some work."

"Routine?" Indignation replaced admiration, and I felt once more in command of myself. "I'm not a charlatan, if that's what you mean. I earn my keep as honestly as you do."

"By charging old ladies twenty *kronen* apiece to be cleansed of malign influences?"

"She *has* been cleansed of a malign influence," I pointed out. "Her husband was a perfect beast, and she will almost certainly be better off without him."

She only looked contemptuously amused. "You really believe all this Spiritualism guff?"

"I'm not a Spiritualist," I said. It was true. I was not a Spiritualist precisely because I *could* see the spirits of the dead.

Spiritualism has three basic tenets: First, that it is possible to commune with spirits. Second, that spirits exist on a more advanced plane than humans. Third, that as such, spirits are capable of providing guidance on such moral and cosmological points as the nature of God and the future of human advancement. I have learned to be very wary of all three of these claims. After all, as Maximilian Kohler had proven that very afternoon, not all spirits *are* benign or better informed than the living; nor, being perfectly capable of lying like a bedspread, are they any more trustworthy on matters of cosmological significance. At best, shades are simply a burst of confused spiritual energy passing through on their way to a better—or a worse—place; a trip from which I have reason to know there is little or no return. And why should they return? One spends enough of one's days at the mercy of one's employers and masters in this life; what hope do we have, if not of repose after death?

In sum, it is my opinion that they had the right idea at my Infants' Sunday School. Attempting to summon or communicate with the dead is largely useless, occasionally perilous, and not entirely cricket. I had courted danger in attempting a conversation with Herr Kohler; from now on, I determined, I would only attempt to read imprints.

"Not a Spiritualist," my interlocutor said dryly, revealing one of her newspaper clippings—the advertisement in which I had promised displays of Spiritualistic Phenomena. "As you say. Still, the main thing is that you'd like to make some money, wouldn't you? I can help you with that."

That was a bait I could scarcely resist. "Can you?"

"I believe so. Your audience wants to be titillated, not terrified. Think of yourself as a stage magician—an entertainer, not a priestess. You need mirrors, puppets, masks." She produced a third neatly-folded paper and offered it to me. I beheld a perplexing diagram. "This, for instance. A little invention of my own, for lifting and turning tables. It operates by means of a pin and slotted ring."

Disappointment washed over me. "I'm afraid I'm not in a position to buy whatever you're selling, Miss—"

Once again, she ignored my attempt to learn her name. "I'm here to propose a trade of time and skills, not money. I need your help for a job. It would be more than worth your while."

I cannot deny I felt tempted. Yet: "I'm in regular employment, and don't have a great deal of time."

"Take leave of absence. There's a risk involved, but if all goes according to plan, I'll pay you double whatever you're getting now. And in any case, barring acts of God, or imprisonment, you shall have the inventions. Interested?"

I *was* interested—desperately—at least until she uttered the word *imprisonment.* At that, I shook my head firmly. "I can't take a risk like that. There are people relying on me."

"Very well. We shall split the takings, even shares. You'll never have to work again." My mouth must have dropped open, because she levelled a small, grim smile in my direction. "There's a fortune to be won, Miss Dark."

That pulled me up short. "How do you know my name?"

"I know a lot of things," she said evenly. She reached into her pocket and offered me a plain white card. "Think about it and call on me tomorrow."

She showed herself out, leaving me staring at the white card in fascination. *P. Nijam,* it read in the plainest, most unadorned type. Beneath the words were an address in Ottakring, Vienna's industrial district. I shook my head firmly and went to toss the card into the fireplace, but just then the sun must have set, for my father appeared.

He was a tall, thin, solemn-looking man with a cleft chin, which I had inherited, and a receding hairline, which I had not. He was dressed for travel with valise in hand and umbrella tucked under his elbow. As he leaned down to kiss my forehead, his lips moved with words I had long since forgotten. I closed my eyes. For a moment I almost felt the swift, fierce compression of his arms. When I opened my eyes again, he was gone.

A suffocating sense of abandonment swept through me,

followed by the prickling of tears behind my eyes. How I wished my father's imprint would fade! Sometimes I thought it only grew clearer and more unbearable with every passing sunset. It was intolerable, this nightly reminder of the last time I ever saw him.

He ought never to have left us. He ought to have provided for us. I ought not to have to work so hard, tending other people's children in such a desperate attempt to put food in my sisters' mouths.

If I had come to such a pass, it was his fault; but that his imprint haunted me was all my own, for it was my own mingled resentment and longing that kept this moment so fresh in my mind.

I looked down at Miss Nijam's card. A moment ago I had been about to toss it into the flames and poke at it until I was quite sure the temptation had disappeared. Instead, with an indecisive gesture, I propped it on the mantelpiece.

* * *

By the following morning, shivering barefoot before my mirror as I took my morning wash, I felt quite certain I ought to have destroyed the card. Miss Nijam might have an air of overwhelming competence and the nose that launched a thousand ships, but her scheme sounded like exactly the sort of thing I ought to stay away from, being the primary breadwinner of the family. I resolved to burn the card next time I returned to my hired rooms.

I was not, of course, actually occupying the Rembrandt-strasse flat, but a small bare room within the residence of my employers, the Count and Countess von Hügel. They were parvenu nobility, newly minted from the upper bourgeois, but they lived in style in a grand new house looking out upon the ghostly trees and graceful gas-lamps that marched along the Ringstrasse. On this sunny morning the great, raw, modern boulevard glittered with a deep frost, and stark shadows streamed away from every lamp-post; it was an unforgiving sort of light, in which there could be no margin for error.

I shook my head to rid it of such gloomy fancies. Today would be clear and sunny, perhaps the last fine day before Christmas. After morning lessons, I would take Ada and Steffi walking as far as the Volksgarten. Along the way there would be street musicians and hot, flaky sesame *böreks* from the stall of Uncle Hamit, who always made the time to ask a riddle or tell a joke or teach the girls a few more words of his native tongue. Ada had already declared her intention of running away to Constantinople to learn oil wrestling, and in pursuit of this goal she and Steffi were saving their pocket money for the expedition and learning all the Turkish words they could. A walk to the park would delight them immensely.

I was not particularly fond of the parents von Hügel, but let it not be forgotten that if I took up Miss Nijam's invitation, I would need to bid goodbye to the burgeoning oil-wrestlers. Being very fond of children, I expected to feel a pang at the thought, but a traitorous inner voice pointed out that if I did part from the future queens of the ring, at least I would have greater opportunity for rational adult conversation among people of my own class. Never again would I be obliged to take my meals alone in my room, being too elevated for the servants' hall and too common—or perhaps simply too dangerously young and pretty—for the family dining-room. And then I reminded myself that the opportunities for social interaction, let alone a comfortably wealthy marriage and the children of my own I so dearly wished for, would, in prison with Miss Nijam, be practically nil.

I sighed. Without Gwendoline Chant as an outlet, how could I endure this friendless, purposeless, soulless life? Perhaps I ought to run away with Ada and Steffi to become an oil-wrestler.

I did not have the chance even for that. My doom came upon me shortly after luncheon. Not, like the unfortunate Lady of the Lake, to the accompaniment of cracking glass as I plied my needle in an enchanted tower overlooking the river; but rather on the stairs, as I about to march Ada and Steffi off on their walk. A caller had arrived, and she and the Countess were standing tête-à-tête in the entrance-hall with their hushed voices pitched to the precise tone that informs everyone within earshot that a particularly toothsome bit of gossip is current. Even Ada and Steffi, children that they were, began to tiptoe as we descended.

"No!" the countess gasped. "What a scandal! Irmentrud?"—and at the same moment I realised what a terrible mistake I had made, for now I saw that the countess' visitor was none other than her sister, Frau Hofbauer.

I had half a mind to flee and take the children out by the back stairs instead, but before I could do more than congeal like Abram's wife into a pillar of salt, Steffi called out cheerfully.

"Mama! We're going to the *park!* May we have money for *böreks?*"

Frau Hofbauer looked up. There was no lack of recognition this time. Her eyes widened, her mouth set in a straight line—her accusing finger pointed directly towards me.

"That's the medium who frightened poor Frau Kohler half

to death!"

The reader will pardon me if I pass over the painful scene that followed. How I denied; how Frau Hofbauer insisted; how the Countess questioned; how the little girls begged me to teach them to talk to ghosts; how before you could say Robin Jackson I found myself trudging up the Schubertring with a valise in each hand and tears crawling up my throat, with no job, no character, and no *börek* to sustain me through it, the reader can imagine. It was the final straw when I reached the Aspern Bridge and was greeted by the sight of a suicide leaping into the waters below—the poor man must have done away with himself just last night, for the imprint was very fresh and clear, and I had crossed the bridge twice yesterday without seeing anything. For a moment, his sense of despair almost suffocated me; it was all I could do not to burst into noisy weeping. In the end, although it was within my power to walk, I paid for a cab to take me to the Rembrandtstrasse. What does half a *krone* matter when one's life is in ruins?

In Gwendoline Chant's flat, bits of glass still crunched underfoot despite the previous night's hasty attempt to neaten the room. Miss Nijam's card waited on the mantelpiece. I turned it within my fingers, considering. There was a chance of imprisonment, she had said. I threw the card into the cold, dead grate. Her "job" sounded either desperate or dishonest, and I was not yet reduced to such a pass. English governesses were much *en vogue* around the Continent—particularly in Saint Petersburg—and in a new city Gwendoline Chant could be revived. Then, too, I was not entirely friendless. There was Sir Humphrey, Daddy's old business partner. I hated asking for charity, especially after Daddy had nearly ruined him, but

Sir Humphrey had always been willing to assist us financially. He would, of course, deliver a fatherly sermon on a favourite text—*No wind is of service to him who is going nowhere,* or, *when hard work goes out the door, poverty comes in at the window*—and he would not make the terms easy, because as he always said we must learn to manage our money. But he *would* advance me the money for a train fare to Russia, and I would be able to repay him within a few months.

I resolved to walk to the nearest telegraph-office and send a telegram before the day was out. This reminded me that I had received a letter from England that very morning. I sank into an armchair and opened the envelope, feeling that a good, newsy letter from home was precisely what I needed to cheer me up.

The letter was a good deal shorter than I expected, and Mother didn't seem as talkative or encouraging as usual. The cat had had kittens, and the twins had already managed to convince Mrs Oakeshott next door to take one of them for sixpence once its eyes were open. Meanwhile, Emily was working on a really remarkable portrait, Lilias had begun writing a new novel, and Katie had sold her first poem—to *Blackwood's Magazine,* no less. Also, Mummy had consumption.

I had to go back and re-read that final paragraph before it made perfect sense to me.

Doctor Thorne says he has got to the bottom of my lung trouble at last. It is quite certainly consumption. He says that a couple of months at a sanatorium, perhaps in Scotland, before the winter is out, might make all the difference between—well, between life and death. Otherwise, with plenty of cod-liver oil and mist.gent.alk.

I may do very well, at least for the next four years or so. After that—well, it is consumption, and we all know what that means. I haven't told the other girls yet; I wanted to ask your opinion first. Sir Humphrey, of course, has been telling me for some time to stop Emily's painting lessons and have Katie and Lilias leave their writing to be educated for governesses; but I don't see how we can afford anything like a sanatorium even if I was to sell the house from over our heads. I won't do that to my girls, so I forbid you to suggest it or anything else of the sort. I can die happy so long as my girls have a place to live and some means of earning a decent living; only we must determine how we are to muddle along in the meantime. Write back to me soon, dearest.

I sat in the little armchair for a few moments longer, staring at the letter without quite seeing it. I had some idea of what a good sanatorium cost, and there was no point in asking Sir Humphrey for a loan of this size: we should all be trapped for the rest of our lives merely paying the interest, without making a scratch on the principal. My mother's opinion of *that* would be just as decided as her opinion of selling the house or stopping Emily's lessons.

For a moment, in the midst of my numb worry, I felt the sting of an old resentment. Before Daddy ruined us and died, I had been taking painting lessons, too. Art ran in Mummy's side of the family; she was something of a painter herself, having been taught by her grandfather, who had been a Royal Academician. Daddy himself had been very fond of storytelling. At Christmas-time, our amateur theatricals had filled the house with music and scenery-painting and hurried scribbling; Lilias was to be found debating with Daddy whether the fairy princess should be kidnapped by pirates or by cannibals in Act Two, with Mummy and Emily and me protesting that we could not possibly produce a convincing pirate ship merely out of the dining-table and half a dozen sheets. In those happy days, none of us doubted that the four of us were destined to become another set of Brontës or Rossettis. There was no question of our being sent to school: we were prodigies, and must receive specialised tuition at home.

I think I knew, even then, that I was not really a prodigy. I was a fair actress—the theatricals proved that—but in those days, acting was not exactly a respectable art. I was certainly not gifted to be a painter—or a poet, or a novelist. It wasn't that I didn't *want* to be. I took my lessons; I did my exercises; I ruined canvas after canvas, page after page, and never produced anything half so good as the careless sketches Emily scribbled in the margins of her workbooks, or the stories Lilias told her dolls before bed. But if I could not equal even the youngest of my sisters, at least I was happy in my efforts—at least I was surrounded by the people I loved, by the songs and sketches and stories that flowed from them.

Then Daddy died a ruined man, and we all knew that something had to change. My mother began painting landscapes to sell, by which she was able to provide a little of what we needed, but there was no escaping the fact that Art was no longer to be our sole master: one of us must be sacrificed to the god of Mammon. Katie was not strong, and like the twins was too genuinely gifted to be wasted in the role of governess. Farewell to home and family, Art and destiny: from then on I was to be an exile from my early Eden.

And almost, it had worked. Mummy's landscapes, eked out with the remnants of her diminutive "fortune", kept us afloat until I had got through four years at St Alphege's and taken my first position. After that we scraped along on our own efforts, and even managed to afford lessons for Emily once her abilities outstripped our mother's. By the time Mummy became too ill to paint, I had discovered my own particular form of genius and begun the séances.

Now I did not know if I would ever be able to hold another—and I had lost my employment to boot. It had fallen upon my shoulders to support my family, and I had failed in every way, and now my mother would die for it.

In that moment I made a vow to myself. I swore that I would *not* follow in my spendthrift father's footsteps; I would be a good and provident daughter, no matter the risks.

I folded the letter into my pocket, pinned on my hat, and fished Miss Nijam's card out of the grate.

Chapter III.

I had expected a shabby tenement; but the Ottakring address was merely a dilapidated warehouse, not particularly large. Its gate was shut, and the small loading-yard beyond entirely empty save for some tufts of dead, yellowed grass which grew in the shallow soil that had drifted between the cobbles. I narrowed my eyes at the card, but this was certainly the right place: 48, Thalhcimergasse.

The big brick factory next door must house a textile mill or similar, for it emitted a constant banging sound that drowned out my voice when I attempted to call a greeting. No Miss Nijam appeared, and a feeling of desperation came over me. I would *not* go away empty-handed. Moreover, after my initial surprise, I began to suspect that the person I had come to see—severe, practical, and unassuming—might indeed have chosen this place to conduct her business, whatever it might be.

I rattled the gate, and to my surprise, the chain looping it slithered away, allowing me to enter. Beyond, the door of the warehouse was also unfastened. When it did not open to my knock, I pushed in boldly to find myself in a cold, bare, open space illuminated primarily by means of opaque windows under the eaves. On the right-hand wall was a small pot-bellied stove, atop which a kettle puffed clouds of steam. Beside it was a narrow, almost military camp bed, neatly made, and a large wooden chest, atop which was perched a chipped but businesslike basin and ewer. It was the most depressingly practical and perfectly cheerless lodging I had ever seen.

As for the rest of the space, long benches stretched across the warehouse. Those towards the rear held shelves and drawers; others, a little nearer, held vats of liquid in which were suspended—I noticed with a shudder—what appeared to be prosthetic human limbs. Some were decently clad in flesh, while others were merely half-grown, so that their brass and steel inner workings, with cogs and cables, were still half visible. Upon the nearest bench of all lay something shrouded in canvas; all I could make of it was that it was sleek and sinuous and about twelve feet long.

Half fascinated, half repelled by this singular place, I ventured towards the shrouded object and found Miss Nijam herself seated at one of the workbenches beyond, wearing several layers of warm clothing and a sort of mechanical headdress that combined spectacles, several magnifying lenses, and a small and very bright electrical light all in one contraption. In the cage at her elbow were a quantity of white mice wearing what appeared to be tiny steel helmets, some of which were attached by wires to the roof of the cage. A neat array of tools lay on the table, ready to hand, and she was poring over what appeared, to my untrained eye, as a bewildering array of cogs, screws, springs, and moulds, besides any amount of thingamajigs and dooverlackies. I could not tell whether she was disassembling or creating something, or perhaps several things at once.

"Ah, Miss Dark," she said, looking up and taking off the

wonderful spectacles. I had to pay close attention to her lips, for she did not raise her voice, and the textile mill next door clanked on without let or hindrance.

"What are you making there?" I called, by way of breaking the ice—and the atmosphere, even near the stove, was extremely icy.

"I specialise in a specific type of prosthetic." Pulling a warm pair of gloves over her hands, Miss Nijam nodded towards the vats. "Anyone can grow a steel limb in a vat, even equip it with firearms or talons. My interests are a little more... subtle. Small implants, that can improve hearing or vision, or even regulate an erratic heart. Unfortunately there isn't much of a market for these yet. Those who can afford prosthetics naturally wish for something showier."

Prosthetics! A thrill of horror ran through me, and I took a second look at the mice. Their gleaming headgear covered their entire heads, twinkling with tiny pinpoints of light where their eyes ought to be. Two of them had had their tails docked and replaced by tiny steel appendages; I could see the pins going into their backbones.

For a moment I felt slightly nauseous. There was something monstrous in the notion of amputating one's body in favour of man-made limbs and enhancements, and doubly so in testing them on poor voiceless creatures like this. Of course, for some years the additions had been all the rage among the self-made millionaires of America; and if the impassioned opinion pieces in the papers were any indication, the fashion was quickly spreading among the moneyed classes of the Old World as well. I had never encountered a prosthete in the flesh, however, and it shocked me to discover an engineer here in the heart of Vienna.

I was still more shocked when Miss Nijam picked up one of the gadgets on her desk and advanced upon me, saying: "I've been working on a device for our job. Here, wear this."

I recoiled. "What is it?"

Miss Nijam only said, "Hold still; it won't hurt a bit." That was even more ominous; but then she only hooked a small but heavy device over my left ear, and inserted a small pea-sized whatsit into the canal; the latter being attached to the rest of the apparatus by a wire. She finished by pressing firmly down on the device until a click sounded. Abruptly, the quality of the hearing in that ear changed.

"What is it?" I asked again, nervously.

"A transmitter." Miss Nijam's voice rang tinnily in my left ear. "I've calibrated it to communicate with a subcutaneous implant of my own. Observe." She turned her head, drawing the hair back to display a neat scar just above the curve of her ear. Then she tapped gently against her temple.

I heard it in my ear as a clear *boom-boom-boom.* "Heavens! Was that you?"

"Anything I say or hear will be transmitted from my device to yours so long as both are operating and within range. And, of course, vice versa. At a pinch, we might resort to prearranged signals in Morse Code" and she tapped her ear again in a sharp, irregular rhythm.

"It's remarkable," I said weakly. Despite the racket from the textile mill next door, I could now quite clearly hear Miss Nijam's soft voice in my ear. It occurred to me at once that my grandmother, who had been as deaf as a post for the past ten years, might benefit greatly from such a gadget. There were other possible uses, too. Perhaps the mice were not so badly off, after all.

"It's a beginning." Miss Nijam scowled at the components scattered across her workbench. "What I really want is a way not merely to transmit, but to record and store the sound as a phonograph does. But one can't very well go about with a phonograph strapped to one's head, and there's no use trying to miniaturise the workings; I've tried." She nodded towards what I had taken to be a very small model phonograph with an abnormally large bell. "I shall have to create something entirely new. ...All the same, for the purposes of our job, the transmitter should be sufficient. The battery is somewhat bulky, I know," she added, motioning towards the part of the device hooked over my ear, "but we can work on concealing it in your hair."

Which reminded me that while all this was very interesting, Miss Nijam had omitted certain pertinent details. "Apropos of the job—I don't mean to pry, but just what does it consist of?"

If she noticed my gentle sarcasm, she made no sign. "I was just getting to that." Reaching into her pocket for the same newspaper clippings I had glimpsed yesterday—my advertisement—she pointed to the line drawing of my head. "It was this that drew my attention."

"My face?" I blushed with pleasure, but felt no less in the dark. "I thought I should capitalise upon it. People find a medium more convincing when she's young and fascinating."

"The resemblance was precisely what I wanted." Miss Nijam took out another paper and smoothed the folds out. I found myself looking with amazement at the detailed sketch of a young woman with masses of fair hair, full lips, and a cleft chin. Below it was printed a list of physical attributes—*tall & fair, about five feet and eight inches, blonde hair, blue eyes; last seen in an upstairs room of the Schloss Frohsdorf, Kleinwolkersdorf.*

I stared as though mesmerised. Was it a drawing of myself?—I could put my finger upon no definite point of variation from my own features, and yet the picture seemed undefinably other—perhaps because of the wide-open, ingenuous eyes.

"I don't suppose you happen to be the missing princess, Marie-Caroline d'Artois," Miss Nijam inquired in an off-hand sort of way. "Are you?"

"A princess?" I could not quite stifle my laughter. "Me? If only I was! I can assure you, Miss Nijam, had I such resources at my disposal, I would hardly be *here.* I am Mary Angelica Dark, of the Saltoun Road, Brixton Darks; but most people call me Molly." Still, the sketch was very like me, and a wild suspicion struck me. "Heavens, you don't expect me to impersonate this lady, do you?"

Miss Nijam remained impassive. "Go easy on the sketch. I paid handsomely to have it liberated from the Viennese police department." After a moment, during which I realised an impersonation was precisely what she intended to carry out, she continued. "Marie-Caroline d'Artois was the only child of the late Comte de Chambord, the Legitimist pretender to the French throne. He died a little over three years ago; and shortly thereafter, Marie-Caroline vanished without a trace. The police have long given her up for dead, but last week an advertisement was placed in the *Wiener Tagblatt* and several other newspapers, offering a reward for information leading to the return of the princess. I made some discreet inquiries. It seems that the girl's mother, Countess Maria Theresa, is in failing health. She never really believed her daughter was dead, and awaits only her return to die in peace."

This disconcerting woman spoke with the uttermost composure, as though she proposed nothing more remarkable than a stroll in the Vienna Woods. As for me, I should have been glad to sit down. Instead, I supported myself against one of the benches.

"You expect me to walk into a palace—"

"A castle, as a matter of fact."

"—a castle, present myself as a princess and the long-lost daughter of the family, and collect a royal inheritance."

"Nothing ventured, nothing gained." For the first time, I thought I detected the hint of a smile on Miss Nijam's lips. "It's no more than every other mountebank in the empire is trying to do at present."

"No one will believe *I'm* a French princess."

"They will if your French is half as good as your German. Presumably the old lady *wants* to be deceived; just read the advertisement and tell me you don't think she will welcome you with open arms. All you need do is put on a good enough show."

Had any other person proposed such a thing, I should have been laughing up my sleeve at them. But Miss Nijam spoke with such calm assurance—such devastating logic—that she could have made madness seem like reason. Obediently I scanned the advertisement, and found it a heartfelt plea begging Marie-Caroline to return: all was forgiven.

Had she only wanted her daughter returned in order to gloat, it might have been a different story; but there was sincerity in the small, cramped print. If the old countess *did* want her daughter to live and be happy, then it might very well work to present her with an imposter.

I looked at the words again, imagining how it must feel

to lose husband and only daughter within months of each other—to be left alone and grieving and ill, never to know whether that daughter was dead or alive, happy or miserable. Poor old Countess! If I did this, I would have the chance to really help her, as I had tried to help the guests at my séances.

—No! What was I thinking?

"But wouldn't that be dishonest?" I said, trying not to actually accuse Miss Nijam of thievery to her face. "Besides, you said yourself we'd be competing with practised mountebanks. I've been an honest woman all my life, and—"

I broke off, conscious that she had pinned me with an incredulous look.

"You're a born confidence trickster, Miss Dark," she said flatly. "Anyone can see that. I'll grant, it's mostly people of your own class you've been swindling—"

"Helping," I protested. "They come to my séances hurting, and they go away feeling whole."

Miss Nijam stopped speaking for a moment; she looked me over thoughtfully, and then she continued in quite a different voice: "Helping, then, with a little benign deception. Bad luck aside, you've been doing it extraordinarily well, even without the inventions I've offered you. Anyone would think you a professional; I did. At the Schloss Frohsdorf, you would have me and my inventions to make the imposture convincing. Besides, it needn't drag on any longer than the two of us are safe. The Countess can't have much longer to live; in the worst case, we can strip the castle of its moveables and be gone before anyone suspects. Paintings, jewellery, curios."

I opened my mouth, but all I could utter was a sound of indistinct protest. Miss Nijam did not seem like a normal person: she was utterly cold and calculating, and I thought her mice would agree with me.

"It isn't as though we'll be dispossessing anyone," she added. "Marie-Caroline is dead or quite determined not to return; and otherwise the property would only go to buy some royal cousin another yacht or a Fabergé tiara or some such toy."

I had to take a moment to catch my breath. "But it doesn't *belong* to us," I said. "We don't deserve it—we haven't earned it."

"Neither have the cousins. Why should an accident of birth make them any more deserving than you or I? Wealth," said Miss Nijam, as though this was incontrovertible fact, "should go to those who will employ it for the scientific advancement of humanity."

"That's all very well for you," I said, after a bewildered moment, "but I'm not a scientist, and whatever I can do for the poor Countess is hardly worth a fortune. It wouldn't be a fair exchange—I could never earn so much."

"Surely that's for the Countess to decide," Miss Nijam said. "If she has an ounce of sense she knows that her daughter must be dead. What she really wants is a sense of *dénouement*—of closure; and she's willing to pay a fortune to get it. As for *earning* it, why, anyone will work hard to get a thing they want. It's how they use it afterwards that tells you whether they really deserve it. ...You aren't here because you want a yacht, I gather."

I thought about this a moment. After all, it was no different to what I had already been doing at my séances; only the remuneration was a great deal more than twenty *kronen*. And I was *good* at my chosen profession, even though there was no name for it, even though I had to pretend to be a medium in order to pursue it. Moreover—"My mother has consumption.

She needs treatment at a sanatorium."

A nod. "So you agree."

I winced. What would my mother think if she knew I meant to save her life at the price of my honour? I didn't want to be a cuckoo's child—a *kuckuckskind,* in Herr Kohler's term. But then I remembered how fiercely pleased I had been to know that all his money would go to another man's child. Such a malevolent person didn't deserve to have it himself—or to pass it on at his own whim. And after all the Countess of Chambord was not an ordinary person, like Miss Nijam or—well, let us simply say, like myself. She was royalty; and that meant something more sinister on the Continent than it did at home in England.

So I said diffidently, "Aren't you forgetting one important detail?"

"That would be highly unlikely, but by all means, say what's on your mind."

There was no delicate way of putting this. "Pardon my language, but if these people are royalties, aren't they—well, monsters?"

Times and fashions have changed since those days in Europe before the war, and young people no longer quite recall what it was like to live in a world ruled by monsters. The German royalties were werewolves; the Russians were vampires; the Danes and Greeks, sirens. Only English royalties prided themselves on being ordinary mortals; but the Continent was ruled by dreadful creatures, red in tooth and paw.

Apart from anything else, I was not particularly interested in braving a castle full of them.

"Quite right," said Miss Nijam. "In fact, they're melusines—

serpents from the waist down when wet. That is why we will succeed when all others fail."

"I beg your pardon?"

"That is why the other mountebanks will fail," she repeated patiently, beckoning me towards the long, sheet-covered table. "Observe."

She drew off the dust-cover and disclosed to my startled eyes a long, thick, iridescent serpent's tail, densely covered in shimmering green scales and cinched at the open end with a wide belt. My throat went dry, and I glanced nervously at the mice, suddenly afflicted by visions of Miss Nijam trying to attach the contrivance with pins to my backbone.

"A—a prosthetic *tail?*"

"It's hollow, composed of synthetic flesh grown upon a whalebone structure and powered by batteries, which we'll conceal beneath your petticoats." Miss Nijam ran a loving finger across the scales. "Showy, but effective. Give them one look at this, and not a single one of them will doubt your identity."

"They will if they find a prosthetic tail in my luggage," I murmured. Miss Nijam, rather disconcertingly, heard me quite clearly through her own implant.

"It's collapsible, and besides, I shall be acting as your servant. Rest assured no one will go anywhere near your luggage."

"How...how does it attach?"

"Just with the belt. I did consider a direct connection with the spinal column, but your brain wouldn't know what to do with a tail and we've no time to conduct the necessary modifications. So instead I've designed it for basic naturalistic movement patterns and installed some simple controls in the belt. Well?"

Well—despite my misgivings, I was beginning to believe in Miss Nijam. A simulation of the melusine form, however imperfect, would surely put me some distance ahead of my rivals and buy me the benefit of the doubt.—With that thought I realised, somewhat dizzily, that I was really going to do this. These people were monsters worse than Herr Kohler had been—one did not become a melusine without *someone* dying for it—and I was about to walk into a den of them. I would take all the remuneration I saw fit for incurring such a risk—like a hero of old, Sieglinde plundering the hoard of a marauding dragon—and if I saw the chance I would do the old Countess a solid bit of good while I was about it. I would save my mother, and if she was going to be disappointed in me, well, that was nothing new. She would be quite startled enough to know about the séances—and any number of other things.

"Well," I said slowly, "I have one more question, if I may."

"Of course. It's you who'll be wearing the apparatus, after all."

I blinked at her, surprised that she was still engrossed in her invention. "No, it isn't that sort of question. It's personal. I need to know what's in it for you; why exactly you're taking the job."

Miss Nijam was suddenly perfectly expressionless. "I don't see the relevance of that information."

The relevance was so obvious that I was not quite sure I believed her. It was the sort of thing I was accustomed to explaining to children, not to a grown woman. All the same, I gave her the benefit of the doubt. "If we're to enter a partnership, we need to know we can trust each other. I've done you the courtesy of telling you about my mother, but

I need my own reassurances so that I know how far to trust *you.*"

For a moment she looked away from me; and when she fixed her dark eyes upon me once again, she looked positively fierce. "Someone I loved also vanished. But this person is still alive; I'm sure of it. I will scour all of Europe if I must, but I cannot do that without money and the power it gives. Does that answer your question?"

It did not merely answer the question: it was the first really comprehensible thing she had said to me all day. "Amply." I held out my hand. "In that case I am with you, Miss Nijam."

"Good." She took my earpiece instead of my hand. "And please—don't be formal. Call me Nijam. Now, let's get you into this tail. You'll need practice, if you're to make a convincing melusine."

I went home late that evening, aching a little from my own clumsiness and the tightness of the prosthetic's straps, and wondering whether I was about to make the most colossal fool of myself. At least, I thought rather gloomily, if this venture went south, I was unlikely to survive to be embarrassed about it. Belatedly, I wished I could feel the same certainty Nijam felt, that the real heiress was not likely to turn up and expose us—or worse still, be cheated by us out of her rightful inheritance.

Before I fell asleep, I sat down and dashed off a letter to my mother, telling her to find a sanatorium at once and gain admittance; whatever the cost, I would send the money.

Alea jacta est, I thought. There was no turning back; like Julius Caesar, I had crossed the Milvian.

Chapter IV.

Our destination was the Schloss Frohsdorf, the castle forty miles south of Vienna where the last male-line descendants of the Bourbon kings had retreated to live out their days in tarnished splendour punctuated by infrequent and half-hearted attempts to regain their throne. It was two hours from Vienna by train. Nijam and I employed the journey in rehearsing the story we had concocted upon the previous afternoon as I glided to and from in my false tail, getting accustomed to the disguise.

That is to say, I had suggested a story, and Nijam had disposed of it with a few brusque words.

"Eloped with your *dancing-tutor*? It won't do. Too easy to disprove."

She was so dreadfully matter-of-fact that I couldn't help tweaking her a little. "I should think it's exactly the sort of thing the countess has been hoping to hear all these years—that her daughter was drawn from her side by an irresistible passion for a humble suitor and cut all ties rather than receive a parent's curse. Above all else, she wants her daughter to be happy. I shall tell her that I have been waiting in romantic obscurity for the fuss to die down. Then I shall tell her all about my little house," I added dreamily, "covered in roses. She will *adore* the roses. What a shame we could not also produce a golden-haired child. I feel she will expect a golden-haired child."

To my delight, she had taken me entirely seriously. "What if they ask you something the real Marie-Caroline should know—the name of your first pony or your favourite governess? What if they ask you to produce the husband?"

"Well then, let's kill the husband," I said brightly. "I shall nurse him devotedly through his final illness, and with his expiring breath he will direct me to reconcile with my mother and beg her forgiveness for having parted us. Now I have returned, suitably repentant."

All I received was a flat stare. "We shall have to plead amnesia. Tell them you woke up in a hospital with no memory after having been knocked down by a horse-tram, and have been working as a governess ever since. I shall be a fellow servant, who has come to keep you company. You decided to answer the advertisement when someone noted your resemblance to the missing princess."

"A governess!" I had shaken my head, barely able to conceal my laughter. "Nijam! Where's your sense of poetry?"

"We are not writing a comic opera, but accounting for a three years' absence."

"If you say so." It was probably no good trying to explain that even if I pled amnesia—which I would evidently need to—in my own mind I still needed to establish a certain congruent fiction to link the flight from Schloss Frohsdorf to the waking of the amnesiac. The Countess needed to feel that my story was plausible.

"The simplest explanation is always the best," Nijam had added, before I could put this into words, "and this one sounds like something that might actually occur."

"It does, doesn't it?" Indeed, I could scarcely help wondering whether something like that *had* happened to the real Marie-Caroline. I pictured her sitting in my cold, cheerless room at the top of the von Hügel house, eating cold carp and congealed pudding off a tray, listening to the sound of music and laughter drifting up from below, and all the time with no idea that she was a princess and entitled to as much as she liked in the way of chandeliers and jewels and handsome young officers wearing the most beautiful uniforms in Europe. My heart ached for her. "It makes one wonder what really happened, doesn't it?"

"Oh, it's quite evident what happened. The girl ran away from her friends, fell among scoundrels, and suffered a tragedy, that's all."

Really, Nijam was heartless.

At Weiner Neustadt, we hired a rickety old post-chaise to take us the remaining five miles down the Leitha valley to the Schloss Frohsdorf. The approach of winter had turned the broad river-meadows brown and sere; the trees were grey and ghostly, but the low green hills to the east sheltered us from the cutting winds of the Hungarian steppe. Only the occasional farmstead broke up the lonely serenity of the landscape, and I could not help feeling as though Nijam and I had slipped out of the modern world altogether and into a fairy tale, or a Walter Scott romance. I half expected to run across a mad prophetess, a band of outlaws, or at the very least, a royalty in disguise.

I was far more likely to run across ghosts. I shivered, wondering exactly what it would be like to enter a house where monsters had lived for nearly a hundred years. The sights that awaited me might be horrible; and in any case I must be on my guard. Once, in Paris, where I had my first Continental situation, I had spent three minutes trying to buy a galette from a street vendor who turned out to have died twenty years previously, after a life of such unvarying routine that the street itself did not know how to forget him. What can I say? I had thought the man hard of hearing. My young charge, who was with me at the time, was so disconcerted by this event that I had shortly been obliged to seek a new situation.

Soon, the chaise passed through the small, picturesque village of Kleinwolkersdorf and entered the grounds of the Schloss itself. An elegant cast-iron gate and dark cypresses framed the buff-coloured house, which glowed weirdly beneath the grey, lowering clouds of that chilly November day. The neoclassical façade, with its mock pediment, was pure Baroque country house; but a sunken lane served as a moat and the grounds were overgrown with hedges and tall cypresses. It was exactly the sort of house that, had I come to it in a novel, I should have expected to contain at least five shocking secrets and a housekeeper who was up to no good.

Nijam's thoughts were on more practical matters. "Tell the driver you'll pay him to wait. If they throw us out in the first half-hour, we shan't want to walk all the way back to Wiener Neustadt."

Taking a deep breath and reminding myself once more of the role I had to play, I stepped from the carriage.

Our knock upon the massive double door was answered by an extremely elderly butler in a wig and knee-breeches, such as I doubted had been in vogue, even for servants, for some sixty years. I noted this without, I flatter myself, giving any outward sign; but as for the butler himself—at the sight of me his mouth fell open, and he blinked through his spectacles, entirely startled out of his professional courtesy.

"Madame!" he said, speaking French. "Is it—can it really be—"

I answered with a hopeful smile and a few words in the same language—which, like German, I had learned to speak like a native during my years in France. "Do you know me, then, monsieur?" My happiness did not need counterfeiting: if my resemblance to the missing princess was good enough for this ancient retainer, the first hurdle was cleared.

"I—that is not for me to say, mademoiselle," he said, pulling himself together. "May I take it that you've come in answer to the advertisement?—Wait here, if you please; in the Gold Salon. Cerise!" he added to a housemaid scarcely any younger than himself, who was passing through the entrance-hall. "Run and fetch the Princess; she will want to speak to this candidate."

So saying, he led us through the gleaming, pillared white hall towards a door to the left that gave onto a small and exquisite sitting-room, wallpapered in gold with one window that looked out onto the broad sweep of gravel at the front of the house. I was relieved to find that no imprints were visible.

"A princess?" I asked Nijam, when we were alone. She had omitted to tell me anything about the other denizens of the Schloss; I might have noticed it had we not been so busy yesterday afternoon perfecting my disguise and story. "Another one? I was under the impression we had come to see a Countess."

"Princess Margaret of Bourbon-Parma, I take it," Nijam said. She had gone to the window and now stood there with a brooding air, silently assessing the moat and the driveway beyond where our carriage waited. "Her mother was Marie-Caroline's paternal aunt; her husband is the son of a maternal aunt and pretends to the thrones of both France and Spain."

I had no hope of understanding this. "You'll have to make me a diagram."

"You are not supposed to remember any of these people. The only important thing to know is that she and her family are the people you stand to disinherit."

"Excuse me," I said, somewhat exasperated. "I beg to differ. I had no notion of there being other relatives in the house! How can I deceive people without knowing a little about them?"

Nijam did not answer: she must have heard the approaching footsteps before I did.

A middle-aged lady entered. Her morning-dress must have been tailored professionally to fit her like a glove; I did not care to wonder how much the lace had cost. Otherwise, with her heavy-lidded eyes, receding chin, and towering coiffure of shellacked curls, my first impression was one of sleepy apathy. That altered when she caught sight of me, however. She stilled, just for a moment; and instead of widening with surprise, her eyes narrowed with instant suspicion.

"You've come about the advertisement, Mademoiselle—?"

"Wagner," I said readily. "That is—it's the name I took after I got out of hospital. I don't remember anything from before the accident."

For a moment, Princess Margaret observed me through her spectacles and did not say a word. Under her scrutiny, I could feel myself beginning to perspire; but the story still flowed plausibly from my lips. "It was a horse-tram, they say. I don't really remember. I've been working as a governess

47

since. This young person is my—"

"Am I to understand that you yourself are claiming to be my cousin, Marie-Caroline?" She interrupted in a disparaging way, as though I was barely worth her notice, and Nijam was not at all.

"I really don't know, madame," I said, swallowing my indignation. "That's for you to say. I didn't see the advertisement myself. A stranger approached me to say that I resembled your unfortunate cousin, and would I accompany him to the Schloss Frohsdorf so that he might collect the reward. I didn't much care for his manner, so I refused. But then I thought—well, I've always been alone in the world. I *must* have a family waiting for me somewhere. I know it is presumptuous of me to think that it's you, but one must make a beginning."

I was relieved to see her expression soften. After several years as a governess, I was more than adept in the soothing of ruffled aristocratic feathers, and my humble tone had evidently done its work. The princess rang a bell and was answered instantly by the butler. "Desire the Baron to step in, will you?"

First a princess, and now a baron? I resisted sending Nijam a reproachful look. I could not help finding this a bad omen, for I had read a number of gothic romances, all of them positively bursting with barons, who had all been shocking scoundrels. Hopefully Nijam was correct, and my ignorance would stand me in good stead. I must take things as they came and hope the baron would prove to be as relatively manageable as the Princess Margaret.

Ah! how little I knew.

The princess turned to me again. "My aunt, the Countess

of Chambord, is in failing health, and her advertisement has brought upon her a flood of visitors, very few of whom have had anything of value to impart. It has fallen to me to conduct interviews and determine which, if any, can provide helpful information. Do you understand?"

"Perfectly, madame."

"Excellent. Please recount the whole story. Be specific—names, places, dates. For instance, what was the hospital at which you first recovered your wits?"

She took a pencil and notebook from the table at her elbow, evidently meaning to note down all my fibs and then have them verified. The trick, of course, would be to convince her so thoroughly that it never entered into her mind to carry through.

"Are you familiar with the Sacred Heart hospital?" I began.

"In Vienna?" She looked at me over the top of her spectacles. "Tolerably familiar; yes. Until recently, the Countess was an honorary member of the hospital board and endowed the new maternity wing."

For a moment I faltered. These people were royalty; they existed on quite a different scale than even the von Hügels, with far more powerful connections. Any lie I concocted concerning this hospital could—and would—be exposed with a quick exchange of telegrams.

What, I asked myself, would Lambert Warbeck, or Perkin Simnel, have said under these circumstances?

"It wasn't a hospital in Vienna," I amended. "It was in Bulgaria—the Sacred Heart in Sofia."

This was a gamble: I had never been to Bulgaria in my life, and I had no notion of there being any such hospital in Sofia, but my words produced a remarkable result. Princess Mar-

49

garet's pencil stuttered to a halt, the tip breaking. "Bulgaria!" she exclaimed. For a moment, she simply stared at me with protuberant eyes, as though I had suddenly become far more interesting than I had been a moment ago. "Tell me, does the name 'Dragomir Smilets' mean anything to you?"

For a moment I felt something close to panic. Was Bulgaria a mistake? Was I expected to know this person's name? Perhaps I ought to have mentioned Russia—or Timbuktoo! Nijam would be no help; she stood behind the sofa, motionless and speechless from all I could tell, and possibly in the grip of the same panic.

All I could do was tell the truth; for that is at the core of all the strongest lies. I shook my head with an honest display of wonder. "No, madame. I'm afraid not."

Her lips tightened in something like triumph. It was at this juncture that the door opened and the butler announced, "Baron Smilets, madame."

The Baron himself entered the room.

For me, all coherent thought fled—what was left of it.

Although I remained outwardly calm, within I felt all the sensations of one who has unwittingly introduced a candle flame to a gas leak. By this, I do not mean to give you the impression that I had recognised the Baron. Far from it: he was, in the fortune-teller's cliché, no more than a tall and dark stranger—a lean, pantherish man whose black hair was combed back from a pale, bearded face. Add to this sketch high cheekbones, lips both thin and sensuous, and grey-green eyes of a mesmerically compelling force, and you may comprehend the effect upon my circulatory system. When he paused and fixed those eyes upon me, it was as much as I could do to breathe, much less speak. I was acutely aware of the dry, overheated atmosphere in that tiny room; the gold brocade wallpaper seemed to shrink around me until it was a tunnel which led only to him.

"Baron," I heard Princess Margaret say, as though from a long way off, "this young person has replied to the advertisement."

"I know who she is." His voice was as velvet-dark as the coat he wore, tinged with the smokiness of Slavic consonants. He had not taken his eyes from my face. Now he advanced towards me. "Give me your hands," he said, and even if I had wished to, I could not possibly have refused. He raised me to my feet. I caught a whiff of his scent: the clean, sharp, cold scent of pine layered over the musk of something warm and very much alive. For a moment those hypnotic eyes searched mine; and then, in a voice thick with emotion, he said, "It is she—it is my own Marie-Caroline."

Somehow, despite being comprehensively flustered, I understood intuitively that I had come across one of those rival mountebanks of whom Nijam had spoken.

The next instant, to my complete bewilderment, I was enjoying this singular man's embrace as he devoured me with kisses.

Chapter V.

No, I *don't* mean to enlarge upon the experience; a lady must draw the line somewhere. Suffice it to say that I returned to the present to find myself reposed blissfully in the Baron's arms, trying to remember where I was and why I happened to be there. The Baron, who had left off kissing me, addressed someone in the room. "But where did you find her? I thought her dead and buried in Sofia. It is a miracle!"

I must have made some weak sound, for he looked down at me with tears in his eyes. "Ah! My little wife can tell me that herself. But what is this? You seem unwell?"

In fact, I have to admit that I had rarely felt better. I had not been in the same room with Baron—Dragomir Smilets, if that was really his name—for more than two or three seconds before I had experienced a powerful and, under the circumstances, completely improper curiosity as to what it might be like to kiss him. I was merely a little dizzy at the celerity with which this unspoken wish had been granted. To an even greater extent, I was shocked at myself. What would my sisters think if they saw how I was behaving? It was not the way I had been raised. Why, he wasn't even English—he was merely a rakishly handsome imposter so sure of his own powers of fascination that he would boldly accost a perfect stranger as though she was his wife. In fact, I would wager a great deal that I was not even the first girl he had kissed!

These conflicting emotions held me perfectly motionless and speechless until, after a moment, the Baron released me from his embrace. My knees shook: he was obliged to steady me a moment before I could keep my feet.

"She does not remember you, Baron," Princess Margaret said matter-of-factly. "You have frightened her."

"She doesn't remember me? But how could she have forgotten? The masque at the Opera Redoubte? The *böreks* in the Volksgarten? The little house in Sofia, covered in roses? My little mouse, of course you remember."

I rallied my thoughts. Whatever game this man was playing, my own was very simple: I was the real princess, suffering from amnesia, and remembered nothing. Baron Smilets might be a clever trap concocted by the Princess to unmask me—that, or an imposter who saw in me some opportunity to improve his own standing. The one thing he could not possibly be was the real Marie-Caroline's husband, because if he was, he would hardly be taken in by my imposture.

Besides, he had invented a little house covered in roses, and I found I was not *quite* so foolish as to believe in *that*.

So I said, with a shake in my voice I didn't need to disguise: "No, monsieur. I remember nothing before my accident."

"Then we must help you to remember," he said earnestly. "Madame, will you give me permission to speak to my wife alone? It has been more than two years, and I..." His voice shook with exquisitely counterfeited emotion. "There is so much I wish to ask."

"Perhaps I should call upon the Countess first," I stammered, feeling suddenly unequal to a *tête-á-tête* with this volcano of a man.

Princess Margaret was evidently less than satisfied by the turn this interview had taken. Perhaps it had been her hope that the two of us would unmask each other and enable her to throw both of us out of the house. Instead, we had spontaneously embraced. With a sour expression, she glanced at the clock on the mantelpiece. "The Countess always spends her afternoon resting and will not receive visitors until the evening. You might as well have your luggage brought in, Mademoiselle Wagner. Dinner is at seven; we dress formally, in tails and orders, if you have any."

With that she sailed out, and I dared to send a glance to Nijam, who nodded imperceptibly in approval. We had survived the first half-hour: from now on, the game was ours to lose.

Still, the Baron had complicated matters. So far I had survived him by the sheerest luck, having chanced to corroborate his story; but a reckoning was coming, and I would need to face it without a plan.

The Baron tightened his grasp upon my left hand, which he had not relinquished since our embrace. "Are you warm enough, my dove? Shall we walk in the garden?"

The garden promised privacy—a notion that equally pleased and frightened me. "Er—you might as well see to the luggage, Nijam," I told her as I was whisked away.

The Baron led me through a corridor which skirted the small courtyard-garden at the centre of the castle, and from thence through a vestibule at the rear of the house which opened upon a bridge of white stone leading across the moat to a terrace. Beyond the terrace, a gravelled walk bordered by tall dark hedges led to an icy, glittering fountain.

"Do you remember nothing of all this?" the Baron asked me in a low, rumbling voice, for all the world like the purr of a great cat.

"I'm afraid not," I murmured. If I had to stage the recovery of my memories, I was determined to do so only after I had learned enough of the details of Marie-Caroline's life to make my imposture convincing.

On the terrace, the Baron paused to scrutinise me as though he meant to tear from me my secrets by the sheer magnetic force of his personality. I had nothing to lose by seeming helplessly overwhelmed, so I blushed and murmured, "Please don't look at me like that."

I half expected him to let his mask fall and propose an alliance. Instead he averted his eyes and said, "Forgive me. This must all be very strange to you; but as for me, all I see is the woman I love and believed dead. If I have offended you, I apologise most sincerely."

He spoke warmly, solicitously; his thumb caressed my fingers, and he raised my hand to his lips. I felt a little dizzy, as though I had had a little too much brandy. Oh, it was worse than I had thought at first! This man was evidently a practised seducer, his every word and action calculated to a nicety and employed to trap me. I must not be another in a lengthy line of romantic and financial conquests; yet in the guise of a lost princess, I could neither run away from him, nor send him packing, as all my instincts warned me to do.

"I *may* forgive you," I said, rallying my own weapons—a bashful glance from beneath the eyelashes, a gently impish look, "if you will tell me how you know me."

He smiled as though caught up in pleasant memories. "Take my arm...there. It was during Carnival exactly three years

55

ago, at the Opera Redoubte ball, as I said. You were dressed as a sylphide, all in white. We danced three waltzes and when midnight came, you unmasked and told me your name. I knew then that my passion was hopeless. A princess could never descend to a mere baron."

"Me, I was braver than that?" I ventured. I knew exactly the sort of story he was telling, and was not averse to adding some flourishes of my own.

"Indeed," he said, with a laugh. "Your aunt, the Princess, had taken a house in Vienna for the season. At every ball I looked for my sylphide. In time she visited me by day as well as night. Her aunt thought she was walking with her friends; in fact, she was meeting me in the gardens. At first we spoke of dogs and duchesses and of distant lands. Then we spoke of history and kings and emperors and of the myriad voiceless people who had found their voice. And at last…" A silence. "At last we spoke of a small house in Sofia, covered with roses, where we hoped to make a home."

He was marvellous; he had the knack of making me *want* to believe him.

That made my own play-acting all the more natural—terrified as I was of losing myself completely in the masquerade.

"And did we?" I asked wistfully. We had descended from the terrace and now walked between the tall, looming hedges towards the fountain, which was enclosed in a circle of dark evergreen.

"For a short time, we did." The Baron pressed my arm. "It was all very romantic, let me assure you—our meeting in the village late one night; our flight to Sofia; the battle I had to marry you without too many questions being asked—but one day you will remember those things for yourself, I hope." A silence, heavy with regret. "At length, one day, you went to call upon an acquaintance. You never returned. I feared the worst—searched every hospital in vain. It did not occur to me to think you might have lost your memory, and with it, your name."

"How you must have suffered!" I murmured. In fact, I was thinking that it was considerate of him to share his story; it would give me the chance to ensure that my own tallied with his at every point. Only it left me with a question: what did he mean by making me a gift of this rigmarole? He was going to some trouble to secure my collaboration: why?

In silence, we circled the fountain and paused at the opening of the hedges. Beyond lay the towering pines of the castle's park. Beneath them shadows and pine-needles lay thick upon the ground; I glimpsed the domes of the deadly white mushrooms known as deathcaps. I felt I stood upon the threshold of some trackless wilderness, and one step would take us both into uncharted territory.

Perhaps the Baron felt it too, for he also hesitated.

"Tell me," he said in that soft, intimate voice, "how you came to be here, my love."

"There is not much to tell," I answered modestly, continuing in my role. "I awoke in a hospital with no memory of my past, but in time I was able to find employment as a governess with a family that was travelling to Vienna. I have always known there was something lacking in my life, but..."

"But?" he prompted, when I did not continue.

"I don't know how to say it," I admitted, and it was not entirely play-acting. "How can I know that what you tell me is the truth?"

A long silence. I did not look up at him, although I felt the

57

air thicken with tension as his arm imperceptibly tightened, pinning mine against his side.

"You do not trust me."

"It isn't that," I began with not-entirely-feigned timidity. But this was the only sensible thing I could say. If my story was true, and I *had* lost my memories, I would not readily accept a perfect stranger as my husband. Besides, I was quite sure that the Baron himself was an imposter, and it was time we proceeded from getting our stories straight, to negotiating the terms of our collaboration. Why was he helping me? What did he expect to gain?

I looked out of the garden, into the trees. It was only a park, bounded by fences; and I knew what I was doing here better than he did himself. I stepped forwards, through the gap in the hedge, and he followed.

"I must think of all eventualities. Perhaps you are honestly mistaken, and I am not your wife. How could I hold up my head among decent people if I had taken someone else's husband? Or perhaps one of us is an imposter—intentionally deceiving the other! I make no accusations—it's only that I should hate for you to feel any lack of confidence in *me*. You are offering me your name and protection. If we are to love one another, the best gift each of us can bring the other is that of trust."

He frowned slightly. "But I am your husband. I do trust you; implicitly. What proof will you accept? I have the wedding license with your own name upon it, in your own hand."

A forgery, no doubt. Which raised a new question: Nijam and I had come armed with a prosthetic tail. What did the Baron Smilets have that the crowd of other mountebanks did not? How had he gained his foothold within the family? A title, and the wedding licence?—No, there must be something more; something personal. A sample of the missing princess' handwriting, at the very least. Possibly more: letters? A diary?

Did he know something about Marie-Caroline that we did not? Could he even be—a thrill of horror shot through me at the thought—could he even be responsible for her disappearance? Perhaps the tale of seduction at the Carnival masque was true!

The possibility was a horrible one, but I quelled my fear with an effort. Even so, the Baron might serve my purpose. "I don't know how you could prove you are my husband," I said, still playing the ingenue. "What do you know of me? Do I take my coffee with cream? Do cats make me sneeze?"

"Alas," he said with a rueful laugh. "I never met you in the company of a cat."

We walked a little further in silence. I stole a glance through my downcast lashes and found him watching me with those mesmeric eyes, his mouth drawn down a little at the corners as though he were prey to unhappy thoughts.

"Say, then, that one of us is an imposter," he said at last. "Each of us has something to gain from the other: a stronger claim, to the extent that either of us is recognised by the other; and the assistance that each of us can give the other in carrying out our little charade." He hesitated; lifted my hand to his lips. "I trust you, because my heart tells me you are my own Marie-Caroline, and she would never betray me, with her memories or without them. But you should trust me, because whether or not I am the scoundrel you think me,—no, my sweet, listen—I have been here longer than you have; I can help you navigate the shoals and reefs of this family, who will not give over their inheritance if they can help it."

He would never say such a thing if he thought there was a chance I could be the real princess—would he? I forced myself to look him in the eyes, all lucent gravity. "Are you threatening me, Baron Smilets?"

His reaction took a moment too long, as though an instant's calculation interposed between the instinctive hurt in his eyes, and the moment at which he released my hand. *"Bozhe moi,* no, of course not!"

"Then I am free to refuse you?"

"Little mouse, you are free to wipe your feet on my heart, if you wish."

At the look he gave me, my insides turned to cotton-wool, all soft and fluffy. "I could never do such a thing," I whispered, giving him my hand again; and I tried not to mean it. With whatever veneers of love or alliance we might conceal our true goals, I could not allow myself to forget that it was the inheritance the Baron wanted, not me. He would not hesitate to betray me if he saw the opportunity, and I must be entirely willing to return the favour.

"I will make you a gift of help," he said, squeezing my hand. "Do you know what the princess meant just now, by saying we must wear tails to dinner?"

"Tail-coats, surely?" I stopped myself. "Oh. *Oh.*"

"Indeed," he said gravely, turning to guide me back towards the house.

Chapter VI.

"I know what you mean to say, but I don't quite see how I *could* have got rid of him," I told Nijam that evening, peering into my mirror in an attempt to see that my hair was appropriately neat and tidy. "Of course I promised him nothing."

I had been given a small bedroom on the first floor, over-looking the gardens south of the house. Although I gathered that I had been tucked away into one of the smallest and least consequential of the castle's rooms, this was quite the most luxurious apartment I had occupied in the whole of my life. The marble fireplace alone must be priceless; I could have sworn the cream-and-gilt wallpaper had been manufactured with sinful quantities of real gold leaf, and as for the heavy velvet curtains draping the window, I couldn't help wondering what it might feel like to wrap myself up in them. The effect was overwhelming: looking at it all, I found myself wondering if this was what Mr Carlyle had meant when he referred to Midas-eared Mammonism, the worship of money for its own sake.

While I did my hair and dressed myself in the shabby white gown I had last aired at the failed séance, Nijam herself had opened the chest in which she had transported the melusine tail, and set about checking the batteries to ensure they were sufficiently charged.

"At present, the Baron needs us as much as we need him," she said very softly, her voice transmitted to my ear via the headpiece. I had been somewhat disconcerted to learn that she had listened in quite easily, if silently, to the whole of my conversation with that volatile gentleman. "We have a Marie-Caroline. The princess has a stronger claim than her lowborn widower, naturally. But then, on the other hand, the Baron seems somehow to have ensconced himself here, which means that he must have convinced the Countess he really knew her daughter. He might have caused trouble for us if he had refused to recognise you. Instead, he's bought us the time to show off the tail."

Having assisted me to slide into the prosthetic tail and buckle it around my waist, Nijam connected it with the heavy batteries in each of my pockets.

"You aren't interested in sharing the inheritance with him, then?" I inquired, smoothing my skirts down over the scales. I was glad I would only be wearing the tail to dinner, for in the prosthetic it was much easier to sit than to move about. With my legs trailing backward at a serpentine angle inside the tail, the sinews of my lower back would quickly begin to ache with the effort of remaining upright.

"There's no particular reason to share," Nijam said with a shrug. "We aren't running a charity for Bulgarian adventurers, and we don't need the Baron's assistance. Keep him dangling after you long enough to establish yourself in the role, then announce that you are dissatisfied with his story and cut him loose."

I wished I felt equally confident that our rival could be so easily disposed of. "He's very good," I said doubtfully. "I half suspect him of having seduced the real Marie-Caroline and done away with her."

"Why on earth would you think that?" Nijam frowned. "The only reason he would go to such lengths would be to get his hands on the inheritance, and he clearly believes he stands a better chance of doing so either in alliance with the princess herself, or with a fair approximation of her. If he'd really got his hands on Marie-Caroline, he would never have allowed her to escape him. There's the gong for dinner. Here are your dentures, and remember not to lisp."

She inserted the dentures into my mouth—they were crafted with two needle-sharp incisors to sit over my own, evoking the elongated, snake-like fangs of a melusine. I opened and closed my mouth to get reacquainted with the feel of them. "I wonder if the real melusines are venomous?"

"Highly," Nijam said. "Each melusine kiss drains away a year of your life, but a single melusine bite will kill you in three minutes."

I slewed around to stare at her. "You *knew* this? Very kind of you to tell me!"

"Don't worry. I've worked with monsters before; protocol strongly forbids using fangs on fellow royalties."

"That's another thing," I objected. "You never told me there would be relatives in the house."

"We had more important things to discuss. The main thing is that your tail passes muster. So long as you manage not to embarrass yourself in some other way, you have nothing to fear."

The gong went, forestalling my explanation that in my view, the personal angle was at least as important as whether my tail passed muster. Instead, I muttered, "Nothing's certain but love and war."

"It's death and taxes, actually."

"What?"

"Nothing's certain but death and taxes."

She spoke rather brusquely, and I let out a sigh. "The problem with your soul, Miss Nijam, is that there is no poetry in it."

She replied only by raising her eyebrows.

Pressing a switch beneath my sash, I reared up off my chair to behold myself in the mirror. I had the front of my skirt pinned up a few inches, in artful folds, to allow for the motions of my tail; the effect, as I slithered across the room, was just inhuman enough to make me shudder. I averted my eyes from the mirror, trying not to imagine what it would be like to dine with an entire family of melusines.

"Wish me luck," I said, putting a brave face on it. Nijam did not return my smile.

"Do try not to embarrass yourself," she said; and I realised that she, too was feeling nervous.

With trepidation, I went out into the hallway and found myself face to face with my father's imprint.

"You're late," I murmured, since there was no one passing by to see me converse with thin air. It was some hours after sunset. He smiled sadly, spoke words I could not hear, and bent down to kiss my forehead before disappearing. I sighed. At one time, I had been able to avoid seeing him by refusing to be alone at sunset. Of late, however, he came at the first moment he could catch me alone—which meant that the imprint was getting stronger, not weaker.

Most imprints faded with time. I remembered a street corner in Vienna where a child had been killed after running

64

into traffic. Its imprint remained for weeks, re-enacting the tragedy every time I walked to the post office. The sight I might have been able to bear, if not for the sense of pain and terror that overwhelmed me in the presence of the violently dead. I had changed my journey, walking half a mile further to avoid the corner where the child had died. Six weeks later, the street had forgotten; only a white cross nailed to one of the trees nearby, and some windblown posies, remained to commemorate the tragedy.

I wondered what would happen to me if Daddy's imprint became stronger still—if I could find no way to stop blaming him for what had happened because of his death. What happened when I could no longer distinguish between past and present, real and imaginary? They'd lock me up in an insane asylum.—I shuddered, trying not to dwell on past memories.

I could not afford to end up in one of *those* places. My father's ghost would surely rest once his family was provided for; the part of me that could not forgive him his improvidence would then be satisfied.

The rest of the family was already assembled in one of the downstairs salons when I made my entrance. For a moment I hesitated on the threshold, overwhelmed by all the gleaming parquetry, gilt wallpaper, and glimmering chandeliers—a bead of sweat ran down between my shoulders with the effort of holding myself upright. Within the room, the gas was turned down low, leaving the place partially in shadow save for the reflections that gilded the darkness. I heard the murmurs of conversation cease and had a vague impression of turning heads, stifled gasps, and the swaying, coiling motion of three or four serpent-people twitching in surprise.

"Bozhe moi," a low voice said at my elbow. I turned to find the Baron himself beside me—he must have followed me downstairs. Though the light was dim, I thought he had turned a shade paler, if possible. His gaze fastened on the thick coils of Nijam's tail, which protruded from beneath the folds of my skirt, gleaming a metallic greenish-purple in the dim gaslight.

After a moment he wrenched his staring eyes away from the appendage and offered me a shaky smile. "You look..." he began. Then, recovering himself, he swept a bow and offered his arm. "You look beautiful."

He hadn't known whether to believe me until now. But now—ah! Now he was convinced.

It would be interesting to see how the wicked baron behaved *now.*

Within the salon, the family awaited me in blank silence. There were five of them, two men and three women. As the Baron and I advanced towards them, I caught a whiff of some cloying, musky scent, faint but feral; I found myself clinging a little more tightly to the arm of the comparatively unexceptional man at my side, who despite being a rogue and a rival seemed suddenly a rock of safety in this terrible place.

Princess Margaret recovered first. "Well! I suppose we can go in now. Offer your arm to your aunt, Jaime. Robert will take me in. And I suppose the Baron can spare an arm for Blanca, if that is agreeable to Ma—"

She caught herself.

"To Mademoiselle Wagner," she added after a moment, but her lips tightened in annoyance as they closed. What had she been about to say? *Marie-Caroline,* no doubt.

She too, against her will, was convinced.

With that, we went in to dinner. The youngest of the company, Blanca and Jaime, walked on human feet; but the three older personages wore tails, as I had been instructed to do. Discreetly studying these appendages, I was still more impressed with Nijam's work. My own prosthetic, made of synthetic flesh grown on a whalebone structure, did not move quite so freely or powerfully; but the length, girth, and iridescent sheen of the tail was exactly right.

The Baron handed me to my seat, apparently still rather speechless. With a stifled sigh of relief I stretched the kinks out of my spine and unfolded my napkin. No one was impolite enough to stare at me, save one: the youth, a little older than myself, whom Princess Margaret had addressed as Jaime.

With a smile I didn't like, he said something under his breath in a language I didn't understand: it might have been Italian, or Spanish.

"What's that supposed to mean, Jaime?" The youngest lady—Blanca—spoke in French. A devastatingly pretty girl with masses of dark hair and an imperious little head set on an elegant neck, the diaphanous froth of lace and chiffon with which she was dressed served only to underline an air of strong-minded determination which I am afraid I found instantly attractive. Now she levelled all that imperiousness at Jaime, but he took it without flinching.

"I beg your pardon, mademoiselle," he said, addressing me in the same language. "My cousin detested the tails. I can scarcely bring myself to believe you are she."

"Oh, come!" the young lady protested. "What else could she possibly be?—A *laundry*-maid?"

"That's enough, children," Princess Margaret interposed tonelessly. "It isn't our place to decide such things."

Jaime repeated the unpleasant smile before addressing himself to the soup. The young lady leaned forwards; I caught the scent of lilies, very fresh and clean amidst all that musk.

"I do apologise. Jaime is not my favourite brother…but alas, he is the only one I have." She gave a dazzling smile that made my heart stutter uncomfortably. "I am Infanta Blanca of Bourbon and Bourbon-Parma, but you may call me Blanca."

"Infanta?" The Spanish title puzzled me.

"Of course Infanta…Papa is the Duke of Madrid, you understand, and if he had his rights he'd be the King of Spain as well as France. But there: you've forgotten us all, haven't you? Let me introduce you to the others. The thundercloud there is my brother Jaime. Princess Margaret of Parma is our mother, and the older gentleman is our Uncle Robert, the Duke of Parma. This is his wife, Maria Antonia of Portugal."

I bowed to each of the personages introduced in turn. Jaime scowled; with his vividly dark eyes and small but luxuriant moustache, I could identify him at once as the handsome villain required in every adventure story. Princess Margaret nodded, frigidly civil. Uncle Robert was a coarse-looking middle-aged gentleman with approximately the shape—and the coiffure—of an ostrich egg. His beard had gone grey, but his moustache remained black; and on the whole, I thought I would sooner expect to meet him sticking up unwary travellers in a Mexican desert, than dining at the table of royalty. He ran a tongue around his mouth as though to clean his teeth of errant soup before displaying them in a cheerless grin. As for Maria Antonia, his duchess must have been at least fifteen years his junior, a languidly pretty woman with an elongated oval face and vacant eyes. From her voluminous dress I deduced she was shortly to expect a happy event—her seventh, in fact, as I was later to learn. The Duke had already twelve children by a former marriage, six of whom were inbred to the point of mental incompetence. Maria Antonia, not being so closely related to him by blood as his first duchess, had proven a happier match.

"There's too much olive oil in this *gazpacho*," Uncle Robert said, after a perfunctory nod to me. "When our aunt dies, Margaret, I hope we will be able to find a better chef."

I tasted the soup and narrowly avoided making a face—for besides the olive oil, and the garlic, and the spices, and the odd reddish colour, it was *cold*. I glanced around the table, but no one seemed to find this odd. I took another sip, grateful that at least I knew which spoon to use.

"Well, Smilets," Uncle Robert said, finishing off his soup, "this makes you the odd one out! You've certainly married up. What's it like to have a wife with a tail?"

The Baron's teeth showed within the darkness of his beard. "Let us say that I like to live dangerously."

"It takes all types to make a world. Can't say I'd ever wish to be a male dainty myself."

There was a silence. From my vantage point beside the Baron, I could see his sinewy hand clench on his knee beneath the table until the knuckles whitened. For an instant I felt that the room was about to explode with the force of his unuttered emotion.

In those days, *dainty* was an ugly word for those unfortunate souls who could make no other living beyond selling their bodies for monsters to feed upon. Naturally, those who used such language had no terms of corresponding contempt for those who used dainties. Indeed, as I was to discover, they were often the very same people. The Duke of Parma had just referred to the Baron as a gigolo or something even lower, and for a moment I scarcely knew whether the fury I felt was my own or the Baron's.

"Language!" I said severely, without thinking.

Uncle Robert stared at me, his thick eyebrows crawling like loathsome caterpillars up his face. Beside me, the Baron's fury suddenly abated and he sent me a look of startled amusement. Blanca stifled a laugh behind her glove.

"Careful, Uncle—next she'll be sending you to bed without any pudding. Didn't you say she worked as a governess, Mamma?"

"With whom did you governess, Mademoiselle Wagner?" Princess Margaret inquired.

"It was no one important," I said apologetically. Despite earlier adjustments, my story could remain fundamentally the same. "The name was Erdos; they were Hungarians operating warehouses in Sofia, Vienna, and a host of other cities inside and outside the Empire. They travelled regularly."

It had not escaped my notice that none of the family had apologised for calling the Baron a dainty. The fact that they could do so with impunity was a little staggering. As Marie-Caroline d'Artois, I was now moving in circles elevated nearly as far above the von Hügels and Smilets of the world, as the von Hügels had once been elevated above plain Miss Molly Dark.

"Do you like children?" Blanca asked me, in a manner that suggested she found such a weakness incomprehensible.

"Very much," I said warmly. "I have three—"

I stopped myself in the nick of time. Something inside me very badly wished to please this lovely creature. I had been going to say *sisters*.

70

"That is to say," I added, "I *had* three charges, little girls. I will miss them."

"What changed your mind about the tails, may I ask?" Blanca asked, point-blank on the heels of my answer. I was on my guard against myself by now, and stopped to gather my thoughts.

Nijam had explained to me that royal monsters were not born, but made. The ability lay dormant in their blood until awoken by preying upon another; and from then on, melusines would reveal their serpentine nature when doused with water, so that one could always tell when one of them had been bathing recently.

Still, not every royalty wished to make the change, and Nijam and I had prepared for the possibility that Marie-Caroline had had such idealistic notions about monstrosity. She would not be the first, of course. The late Crown Prince Rudolf, who had shot himself at Mayerling a handful of years previously, had also harboured liberal views on the subject of defanging. All the same, such views were yet firmly in the minority, and it would have been rather odd if Marie-Caroline had shared them.

Still, we had been unable to discount the possibility altogether, for my tail would require one of two explanations, depending on whether Marie-Caroline had been a melusine at the time of her flight from her home; and if I volunteered the wrong explanation, it would quite shipwreck our venture.

Since Marie-Caroline had *not* been in possession of a tail when she left home, therefore, I must employ Explanation B: When the amnesiac princess had seen the advertisement in the newspaper, she had made the change to melusine by way of experimentation, as a means of satisfying herself as to whether

her claim held any substance. Only once the experiment was met with success did she present herself at the Schloss.

I was still reviewing my answer when the Baron stepped in, evidently meaning to assist me. "She doesn't remember, madame. That happened before we lost each other." He regarded me tenderly, almost possessively. "It isn't my story to tell. But it was done for the purest of motives: as she told me herself at the time, *Love comes into being through useful service to others.*"

"Swedenborg," Blanca said, raising her eyebrows. The name meant nothing whatever to me. "Marie-Caroline repeated those words to me once, on one of the few occasions I met her." And she gave me a thoughtful sort of look.

I felt more certain than ever that the Baron must have some connection to the real Marie-Caroline; of what nature I could only guess. But his answer had, of course, only made things harder for me.

It was Jaime who instantly seized upon the thin spot in the Baron's story.

"If that's so, Miss Wagner, how did you account for your transformation to melusine every morning at your bath, or with every shower of rain? Surely that ought to have suggested you were no common governess."

Thankfully, Nijam and I had prepared Explanation A for just such an eventuality. "It didn't, as a matter of fact. I was quite under the impression that I must at some point have been so foolish as to let a melusine kiss me—and that my transformations were due to this indiscretion."

Jaime looked disappointed, but his sister clicked her tongue sympathetically. "It's a common misunderstanding, I believe; but quite unfounded."

"Allowing a melusine to feed upon one no more makes one a melusine than it would make one royalty," Princess Margaret put in with a supercilious laugh. "I'm surprised that rumour persists."

"Turning tails was the right choice, whatever the reason," the Duke harrumphed, holding out his plate for a helping of duck confit. "After what happened at Coburg last year, it's more important than ever to guard the royal privileges."

He added something else in a language I did not know, but which I felt quite sure must be Italian. His wife crossed herself and, after a moment, Princess Margaret followed suit. I observed this with some curiosity. I had heard of nothing out of the ordinary happening in Coburg last year, unless it might have been the scandalous elopement of a German princess with a Russian Grand Duke on the eve of her marriage to someone else. The papers had been full of it for weeks, but surely there was nothing in that to threaten royal prerogatives?

Ah, but that reminded me: at about the same time, the police forces of the Continent had received a sharp setback owing to the sudden dissolution of all their revenants. I recalled Count von Hügel greeting the news with great pessimism, declaring that a revolution would surely follow; the Countess spoke with commendable courage of her fate, to be hanged from a lamp-post by the mob. Personally, I was glad the revenants were gone. Slavishly obedient to the commands of their superiors and prone to responding to any perceived resistance with lethal force—it was impossible to pass the reanimated corpses in the street without fear, even if you were neither a suffragette nor some other form of political dissident, which I certainly was not.

The official explanation for the cessation of revenants—which had left the streets littered with their decomposing, uniformed bodies—was simply that the means of producing the creatures had been found to be defective. It was, of course, a laughably thin explanation: for one thing, if such had been the case, new methods would no doubt have been found and attempted. But no new revenants had appeared for a little more than a year. In the meantime, naturally, the suffragettes and anarchists had breathed a sigh of relief and stopped blowing things up quite so often.

Could the revenants' disappearance be linked somehow to the Coburg wedding? I could well imagine the royal prerogatives being threatened by the sudden disappearance of such a terrifying, unquestioningly obedient body of servants.

My suspicions were confirmed when the Duke of Parma continued. "I've received discreet inquiries from a certain highly-placed personage," he continued in indeterminately-accented French, "asking whether a revenant state could possibly be induced by mesmerism. It is feared that without such a means of regulation, the police and military may not be sufficiently loyal or obedient."

Princess Margaret sent him a withering look. "Someone asks us the same thing every few months. We are *Bourbons*, Robert. We do not *work* for *pay*."

Well, if that didn't take the biscuit! Here they were, a gang of pretenders and exiles, assembled at the deathbed of a dying countess, ready to gobble up whatever they could get in the way of her inheritance, but they were too good to work for pay? I had never heard anything so shocking in my life. I was raised to believe that anyone could get anywhere in life through honest hard work; but these people expected their wealth to be handed to them on a platter, without ever doing anything to justify it.

Only then did I really hear what the Duke of Parma had said. *Mesmerism?*

Did this mean that in addition to life-draining kisses and venomous bites, melusines were also in possession of unnatural mesmeric powers? Would they turn me into a revenant if they caught me, or simply bite me?

"Nijam," I murmured as the dinner party broke up. "Is there something *else* you failed to tell me about the melusines?"

It took a moment before her voice came crackling into my ear over the transmitter. "Don't worry about the mesmerism. It only works on the weak-minded."

"Nijam!"

She did not vouchsafe an answer, and I had no opportunity to inquire further, for as Robert and Jaime settled in to their cigars and cognac, and Maria Antonia and Blanca made their way to the drawing-room, Princess Margaret approached me. "The Countess of Chambord is awaiting us, mademoiselle."

Baron Smilets appeared at my side, offering his arm with a bow. I took it reluctantly, for as helpful as he had been at dinner, I would have preferred to face Maria Theresa alone. Beyond that, I was a little nervous of his hearing the faint whirr of gears and batteries within my tail.—Thankfully, if there was anything to hear, the rustle of Princess Margaret's silk gown and my own quickened breath must have drowned it out as we ascended the stairs. I kept my mind off the coming interview, my last remaining battle, by dint of wishing with all my heart that the evening was over and I could rid myself of the confounded tail.

Maria Theresa's suite awaited us at the head of the great

stairs at the westernmost corner of the house. A maid waited in the small antechamber; in answer to Princess Margaret's nod, she scratched upon the door with a fingernail and entered. I would have followed, but the Baron caught my arm, sending me a slight shake of the head. Indeed, a moment passed before the maid and a white-clad nurse emerged backward through the bedroom door, bowing as they went. They then held the door open with a scarcely less profound bow for the princess, the baron, and myself to enter.

On the enormous four-poster bed within—propped up on pillows, wreathed with the coils of her own serpentine tail, holding a prayer-book folded piously within her hands—the might-have-been Queen of France awaited my coming.

Chapter VII.

Baron Smilets bowed so profoundly, and with such exquisite grace, that I felt sure he must have been a courtier at some time, whatever else he might be now. My own course of action was not so clear. Princess Margaret had executed a peculiar yet graceful manoeuvre in which she sank deeply among her own coils. My own tail was not designed for the same movement, and if I bowed forward from the waist, I might overbalance and bloody my nose upon the priceless Aubusson carpet. Instead, I pressed a hand to my heart and bowed awkwardly from the neck.

"Mademoiselle Wagner," the Countess of Chambord greeted me in French that was still tinged with an Austrian accent. "Approach. Let me see your face."

She held out her hand as I obeyed, and I was faced with another dilemma. Downstairs I might have been visiting any aristocratic country seat; upstairs I had suddenly entered a royal salon, and I had no idea whether I was meant to shake the hand or kiss it. I might have turned to the Baron, who was evidently willing to help; but happily the Countess rendered the question immaterial. Strongly grasping my hand, she drew me into the light of the green-shaded lamp at her bedside, which was arranged in such a way as to throw all its light into my face without illuminating her own.

Her scrutiny lasted only moments before she released a long—almost a hungry—sigh. "The face is hers," she murmured around her elongated, venomous teeth, "but the tail, that is conclusive. My *petit choux* has returned!"

With that, to my alarm, she first pressed her lips to my hand and then held it to her withered cheek; I felt the hot tears run upon it.

"Madame, hush," I murmured. My blood thundered in my ears. It was not merely that I am English, and such a flood of tears would have made me uneasy at the best of times. In fact, I was already half-mesmerised by my proximity to the old melusine, with her needle-sharp incisors, her restless coils, and her suffocating scent. I felt as though one false move would lead to my death. "Please don't cry. I am here now; I am home."

"You were a wicked girl to run away from me like that," she sobbed.

"I'm sorry, madame." My eyes had adjusted to the light, and I saw her more clearly—a thin, shapeless old creature with a strong jaw and a somewhat bulbous nose, her grey hair dressed in soft wings which covered her ears in the style of fifty years ago. "I ought not to have done it, I know."

Her tail writhed around her in the bed, brushing my skirts, so that I instinctively pulled back.

"Don't leave!" she cried, dragging me nearer by main force. "Sit, sit.—Who else is there? Is that you, Margaret? And the little baron? Leave us, both of you. I will speak to my daughter alone."

Princess Margaret dipped into another profound curtsey, but the Baron sent me a questioning look. I wished I could beg him to stay, but that would expose me: surely one melusine need not fear another. Instead, I summoned a smile and nodded. The princess and the baron backed from the room, and the old lady gazed on me as though she meant to mesmerise me on the spot.

"You've grown," she whispered. "You're taller. And older. You've changed."

I reassured myself that it was the sort of small-talk every mother makes when seeing her child again after a period of some years. "For the better, I hope."

"I worried for you so much," Maria Theresa whispered, a slight frown passing across her brow. "But…a *baron?* You are a Bourbon princess, my love! Why did you do it? Why did you go away so suddenly, and without saying a word to anyone?"

"I would tell you, madame, but I don't remember."

"It must have been *something* terrible. Apart from that matter of the singing-tutor, you were always such a happy, biddable girl!"

It was all nonsense, of course. Happy, biddable girls do not flee their homes. The old lady had not known her daughter so very well, after all.

With a faint crackle of warning, Nijam's voice sounded in my ear. "Ask about the singing-tutor."

I had been about to do that in any case. "The singing-tutor, madame?"

"That Jew you insisted on taking lessons from in Wiener Neustadt. Very stubborn about it you were, too. But that was years ago. You were going to marry Jaime instead; it was your father's dearest wish."

If anyone knew the real Marie-Caroline's whereabouts, I

would wager the Jewish singing-master was the man. I had been right, after all. I had *guessed* a romantic elopement. No doubt the young princess had wished to escape that handsome young devil, Jaime!

What would the real Marie-Caroline do, I wondered, if she caught wind of my imposture? What if the melusine Countess discovered I had deceived her? Or for that matter, what if I did as planned and banished the Baron as a fraud once I had secured my own position in the house—would I then be expected to marry Jaime?

By now, the perspiration prickling my skin had nothing to do with physical exertion. It was a dangerous game I was playing.

"We suspected him, naturally," the Countess continued. "We ran him to ground in Vienna. Ottakring, if you can believe it. But there was no sign of you—no sign at all. It was Smilets all along—a baron, not an organ-grinder! Small mercies."

Her voice had gone faint and rambling, and through all my anxiety, I was struck by a pang of pity. I might not be this lady's daughter, but I was here at her bedside; and the least I could do was show her kindness, in the way that Marie-Caroline herself might have done, had she returned.

"I know you only wanted the best for me, madame."

"I wanted you to be safe." The soft old voice cracked again, the hand tightening upon my own. "That is all I ever wanted. Your father had the opportunity to become king, do you realise? He was offered the crown not once, but twice. The second time, you had been born, just when I had given up all hope of holding a child of my own in my arms. I never confessed it to Robert and Margaret, but it was I who begged your father not to accept the crown of France. Too many of the Bourbons have met their end at the hands of the mob. I could not bear to think of the same thing happening to you."

There were tears in my own eyes by the end of this speech. Moving slowly, with the same sort of instinct that prevents one making sudden movements in the presence of a dangerous beast, I took her hand in both my own. "I cannot bring myself to regret it, madame. You did a noble thing, and if I had known, perhaps I might have returned to you sooner."

"I am so tired," she added after a moment. "Ring for the nurse, and stay with me a little longer."

Having done as she asked, I settled into the armchair next to the bed. Her withered hand still clasped my own; I compelled myself to breathe slowly, not to shrink away from the monstrous, pitiful creature. The nurse entered, unpinned the countess' hair, prepared her for bed, and was gone by the time the clock struck ten o'clock. It was then that an imprint appeared through the closed door: a tubby, bald, bearded old gentleman in a comfortably large and rumpled frock-coat. In fact, the only remarkable thing about him was his tail. He approached the bed, looked at the countess with unmistakeable domestic affection, said a few words, and kissed her forehead. As he leaned down, I saw the countess smile and close her eyes to receive the benediction.

The imprint—no doubt the dead Count—faded away, leaving Maria Theresa dreaming happily against her pillows, and myself prey to all manner of bitter thoughts. The Countess was haunted, as I was haunted; but only by happy memories. The Count, exiled pretender as he was, had provided for his wife's comfort and security. My father, a businessman of intelligence and ability, had left his wife and children in poverty, and I was reduced to a particularly dangerous form of thievery in order to do what he left undone.

And yet—so far, Nijam and I had succeeded. The whole family accepted me as the lost Marie-Caroline. I must take care—these people were a whole world beyond anything I had yet experienced. Power and wealth I had expected; but the strange food, the strange languages and manners, the quotations from thinkers I had never heard of—this was a breed of Continental that fell entirely outside my experience: equally Spanish and Italian as they were French and Austrian; educated, polished, clever—and monstrous. I stole a glance at the creature nested amidst her glittering coils in the bed. In England we did not have monsters, of course; but it had somehow never occurred to me that to Continental royalties the tails and fangs might be something as comfortable and as familiar as a favourite pair of carpet-slippers.

I sat with the Countess an hour longer, until her breathing had quietened and lengthened. Her hand relaxed its grip as she drifted into sleep; and her tail disappeared, contracting into the two ordinary human legs with which she had been born. With a sigh of relief, I got up, cautiously withdrawing my hand from hers; but her grip suddenly contracted on mine.

"You'll still be here tomorrow?" she murmured.

"Of course I will," I murmured. "Good-night."

I emerged from the countess' suite shortly before midnight. As I slithered towards the south corner of the house and my own room, the only thing I could think of was ridding myself of the awful tail, for my back ached and my legs chafed within its hot confines. The journey seemed to be taking longer than it should; and then halfway down the corridor the tail gave out entirely and went limp, depositing me upon the carpet.

The batteries must have run out. Thankfully, the corridor

was silent and empty, with no passers-by to see me measuring my length upon the carpet in this ungainly fashion. Windows to the left of the corridor looked down upon the castle's courtyard, while the doors to the right seemed to lead into some large and empty apartment, if the cool draught issuing from beneath the three closely-set doors was any indication. I pulled myself up by the nearest doorknob, pushed it open, and wriggled through with my tail.

I found myself upon a gallery overlooking a huge dark room two or three stories high. Beams of coloured moonlight illuminated the room faintly through its stained windows, glinting from polished stone and precious metals. As my eyes adjusted to the darkness, I recognised a semicircular nave above the shadowy shape of an altar: it was a chapel, small but majestic.

The main thing was that I would have privacy, for there was no one here but me—and God. Piety made me hesitate to do what must be done: it had been some years since I had last attempted to strip down to my knickers in a place of worship, and on that occasion I had only been three. Then I felt uneasily reminded that from a certain point of view this was hardly the worst thing I had done all week; and besides, I was trying to save my own life. With an apologetic prayer, I dove beneath my own skirts, released the belt at my waist, disentangled the batteries from my pockets, and eased myself out of the horrible device.

As I rose to my feet, rubbing the small of my back, a clock somewhere in the castle struck midnight. At the same moment, I saw a movement in the chapel beneath.

I crouched down at once behind the balustrade, gazing between the white marble posts as pale lights began to flicker atop the massive silver candlesticks to either side of the altar, and also in the alcoves behind it. There was no sound as the pale figure below crossed the black-and-white checkered floor, reached the altar, and knelt before it.

My breath caught as I recognised the supple figure of a young girl. The hair beneath her hat glinted like gold in the candlelight. She settled a small valise beside her as she prayed. For only a moment she lingered there; and then she rose, genuflected, retrieved her bag, and hurried out again.

Catching a glimpse of her pinched, anxious face and a sense of her worry as she cast a hurried glance about the chapel, I nearly choked with surprise. Despite the shadows—despite the fact that she was no more than a passing memory, I had no trouble identifying a face so very like the one that met me each morning in the mirror.

I had just seen Marie-Caroline's ghost.

Chapter VIII.

I have not always been able to see ghosts: my childhood was quite unexceptionable. My gift made itself known the same year my father died. I was visiting my grandmother at the time, and we went to the churchyard to pay our respects to my grandfather's grave. I had been startled, to say the least, when he appeared in a puff of domestic affection to put an arm around my grandmother's waist. Somewhat disconcerted, I had averted my eyes, only to be met with the grisly sight of a railway worker's recent death. He and some other men were preparing the ground to lay rocks; there was an explosion, and a tamping-iron with which the unsuspecting man had been tamping the gunpowder preparatory to blasting some rock, was shot clean through his head. You may imagine the horror felt by a young girl at this sight. I bolted back to my grandmother's house in a panic, where (some time later) I succeeded only in making her understand that I had had some sort of waking nightmare.

I returned to St Alphege's that term to find that some of my fellow-students had silent companions with them—memories of dead siblings, parents or grandparents who never strayed far from their side. One of these, a small, solemn girl with great dark eyes, had taken up with my especial tormentor, a baronet's daughter who believed herself quite the most important person in the school. I saw at once that I had been given a powerful—nay, even a devastating—weapon of offence; but I told myself I must not descend to using it. That resolve lasted only three months, until one of my particular friends became the subject of a spiteful rumour. I knew at once who the culprit was; and I had observed the imprint long enough to be fairly certain how to leverage our tormentor's hidden wound.—That was how I came to hold my first séance: as a means of taking revenge. I convinced the baronet's daughter to come, gave her what appeared incontrovertible evidence that I was in communication with her lost sister, and then delivered a "message" so devastating that the girl suffered a nervous breakdown and was sent home to recover. She never returned to St Alphege's, but her parents, who were patrons of the school, insisted upon knowing what had happened; and I was quickly identified as the culprit.

I think it was for this reason that the history mistress, Miss Mackintosh, took me to visit Hanwell Asylum. There, in a miserable little padded cell, I was introduced to a nameless inmate, between whose shrieks and gibbers I was made to understand that she had once been a medium herself. She had always been a little odd, I was told, but went stark raving mad shortly after the death of a family member.

One trifling detail that stood out to me was that the onset of mania had occurred in—a cemetery.

I will never know exactly why Miss Mackintosh took me on that horrible little expedition—whether she thought there was some moral peril associated with becoming a medium and wished to frighten me out of it, or whether she understood something of what I could do, and meant to warn me of the dangers I might face. Nevertheless, I had learned my lesson. My gift gave me a terrible power over the minds of others; it was also a terrible risk to my own freedom and sanity.

I did not even tell my mother—I did not like to confess to having broken the mind of another human being. Instead, I simply made myself a double promise: first, that from now on, I would use my gift to mend and not to destroy; and second, that I would keep my abilities a secret wherever I could.

It was a promise I still meant to keep. But if the Schloss Frohsdorf held memories of a dead princess, there was something far more sinister afoot than the game Nijam and I had been playing; and that altered things entirely.

Chapter IX.

With my tail bundled up in my arms, I let myself back into my room to find Nijam sitting at the dressing-table, which she had covered with an array of mechanical bits and bobs.

"Nijam," I hissed, throwing down my burden and tearing the transmitter from my ear. "I've made a terrible discovery."

"So have I," she said bleakly. It struck me that she had not, as I thought, been working. Her elbows were propped on the table so that her hands covered her mouth; her eyes, large and haunted, stared into their own depths through the mirror.

"Why, what is it?" I asked, venturing closer. A crumpled handkerchief lay before her, spotted with blood. Nijam's beautiful dark eyes lifted to my own, and she let her hands drop from her face to display a red and rather swollen nose.

"Good Lord!" I cried, forgetting Marie-Caroline at once. "Did someone strike you? Are we discovered? How shall we get away?"

"It's not that," she said lifelessly. "Alphonse Schmidt is here."

"Alphonse who?" I asked stupidly. The name had no significance to me.

"The one I was looking for," she said. "He's here."

* * *

Nijam did not tell me the entire story at once; but the way it had happened, as I later heard it, was like this:

Having dined below stairs in the servants' hall, she made her way up to my room, where she intended to do a little private tinkering on an idea she had for her sound-recording device. She emerged through the green baize door at the top of the back stairs to find herself face-to-face with a godlike young man whose striking beauty might have arrested the eye of any mortal woman. Nijam, however, was not just any woman. As it happened, his every feature was impressed as with a hot iron upon her memory: now she beheld in the flesh the same chiselled jaw, blue eyes, and sleek blond hair she saw in all her sleeping and waking dreams.

It was he—Alphonse Schmidt—it was *he,* and yet his eyes fell upon her with complete indifference as he stood aside with a polite bow to let her pass.

Nijam was utterly bereft of speech. It had been more than a year; yet he said nothing, merely stood waiting for her to vacate the doorway. Just as she might have been about to recover her breath, she saw the black sleeve garters he wore and realised the significance of his presence by the servants' stairs. Was Alphonse a valet now? How the blazes had he become a servant? Did he have any idea what a tragic waste that was? Did he know her? How could he not know her? Her hand fluttered up as though to smooth her hair—she arrested it halfway. She must seem like the most perfect idiot. She did not know what to say, what to do. There was no social rulebook for meeting the man you adored and being cut by him—cut dead—but that pain was shrunken to a pinpoint beside the sheer agony of her own embarrassment, for he was now looking at her as she had seen him look, in the past, at a chemical retort gone terribly wrong. The same kindly puzzlement. *Patty, was there by any chance something different about this lot of mercury fulminate?*

With a strangled sound of panic, she dipped her chin and rushed past him into the hallway. All she could think of, in that moment, was finding the appropriate solitude in which to recover from this ghastly shock. Instead, she received a second.

She recoiled, dizzy with pain, from the unyielding surface with which she had just collided. For a moment she thought someone had opened the door of my room and struck her across the face. Then she realised that nothing so dramatic had occurred; she had only tried to rush through the door without first opening it.

"Fraulein!" A well-remembered voice came to her ears like distant music. "Fraulein, are you all right? Can I help you?"

There was a warm, steadying hand upon her shoulder, but she could barely see him through the tears streaming from her eyes. To make matters worse, her nose began to run as well. She dragged in a sniff. "Yes, I'm perfectly well. Thank you."

"Would you like a handkerchief?"

Nijam stared up at him, speechless. She could see him clearly now, as painfully beautiful, as gently solicitous as ever. He grimaced slightly and touched his own nose. "Your nose, it's bleeding. Here."

He offered her a beautifully clean and snowy handkerchief, and she took it mechanically, applying it to the hot trickle on her upper lip. Watching her, Alphonse Schmidt frowned slightly and tilted his head to the side.

"Pardon the question, fraulein, but—do I know you?"

* * *

"—*And?*" I cried, as Nijam halted in her tale. "You can't stop there! What happened after?"

Beneath the brown of her cheeks, a dusky flush had arisen. Nijam appeared to be violently uncomfortable. "Nothing happened," she muttered. "I ran away. I didn't even learn what name he is going by—or whose valet he is."

The poor girl, she evidently needed help. "That shouldn't be too difficult to arrange. If we—"

"*We* will do nothing!" Nijam said forbiddingly. "This is my own private affair, thank you!"

I felt utterly quelled. Though I had scarcely known her three days, the dangerous business upon which we were both engaged had almost led me to think of Nijam as a friend. Now, however, the facts of our position reasserted themselves.

"I suppose your interest in this job is finished, then," I said. "You wanted the inheritance in order to find Alphonse Schmidt; well, you have found him. It might be just as well. I have made a startling—"

Scowling at her reflection, Nijam interrupted me before I could go on.

"No, my interest in this job is very much *not* finished. Something is wrong with Schmidt, and I must get to the bottom of it. He did not respond at *all* in the way I would have expected based on our past acquaintance."

I cleared my throat delicately. "Well, there's a bit of it going around. I mean to say, if you had mistaken some other person for your friend, you would hardly be the only person in this house who had done so."

"Nonsense; it is certainly he," Nijam said irritably. "Do you think I don't know my own—." She halted, then went on with stiff self-consciousness: "He responded with his customary gallantry. I *know* it is he. Only, if he had known me he would certainly have spoken to me."

"Perhaps there is something of which he is ashamed," I suggested, "and he was afraid to acknowledge you."

To that, she responded only with an adamant shake of the head.

"Well, I suppose this means the job is still going forward," I said with resignation. I must think how to break the news to her, then. "Did you learn much in the servants' hall?"

"Not a great deal." Nijam picked up a small wandlike device, lit a hot blue flame at the end of it, and began melting small pieces of metal onto a larger piece of metal.

"Do take care not to burn the furniture," I interposed.

She gave me a blank look that I interpreted, since I was beginning to know her, as annoyance. "I've learned that Marie-Caroline's former apartments are in the northern corner. She had a canary named Astolpho, now dead, and a mare named Bradamante, still in the stables. She was a rather quiet, retiring girl, slow to air her own opinions—or, indeed, anything else. That's all I was able to discover about her."

"She loved Ariosto," I deduced with a smile, for I recognised the names of her pets. "She named her horse after a lady knight in quest for love, and her bird after a boneheaded young knight who travelled to the Moon, where the missing wits of all the lunatics on Earth are found stoppered up in bottles, and so regained his own."

"I'm glad it means something to you."

"It's all out of *Bulfinch's Mythology*. Didn't you read that as a child?"

"I didn't have the time for such diversions," Nijam said loftily, still working at her widget. "I had *Metals in the Service of Man* and *Wood Identification and Use* to read." A pause. "Most of the gossip in the servants' hall had to do with your arrival; the fact that you had a tail caused quite a sensation. The old butler swore he'd known from the first it was the princess."

"And what about the Baron? Did you learn anything about him?"

"According to Princess Margaret's lady's maid, he's been here four days, mostly because of the wedding certificate with his name and Marie-Caroline's on it; but until your appearance this afternoon, it was generally supposed that he was a fraud. In any case, the Bourbon-Parma lot are pretty determined not to let a commoner get his hands on the inheritance."

"I take it Marie-Caroline doesn't stand to inherit the claim to the throne?"

"Salic law forbids women inheriting titles. So, no. The Count of Chambord passed all his pretensions to his nephew Carlos, the duke of Madrid—Princess Margaret's husband. It's the house and fortune we stand to win, if we can hold our position here. You should have asked Maria Theresa about her will."

"My dear Nijam! A prodigal daughter would hardly demand a look at the will on her first evening home."

"I don't see why not. The old lady is dying, after all, and if you shilly-shally the rest of the family certainly will not. Before you appeared in tails, Princess Margaret was heard to express her opinion that you were a fraud working in collaboration with the Baron. The prosthetic has given her a great deal to think about, but these people have become accustomed to looking upon the inheritance as their own. We ought to move quickly if we wish to secure it."

"Right," I said, "and I'm afraid they aren't above foul play, either." I drew a deep breath: there was no help for it. "Nijam, I have reason to believe Marie-Caroline is dead."

"Well, naturally she is dead," Nijam said blankly. "Where's the foul play in that?"

I had vowed to keep my gift a secret; but this was a case of necessity. I laced my fingers together, silently begging her not to disbelieve me a second time.

"When people die, they often leave certain—memories—behind them. Such memories can become linked to a person, or a place. And the stronger or more harrowing the memory, the stronger the imprint." Nijam regarded me in an uncomprehending silence. I let out a gusty breath. "I see ghosts. That's how I conducted my séances. I behold and read memories, not spirits.—Well, for the most part, not *really* spirits."

Nijam's stony expression did not alter. "Tell me what happened."

"Well, to begin with, it went quite the way I expected. When I asked the ladies to think of their dead loved ones, I saw Frau Hofbauer's little boy, and—"

"Tonight, here; with Marie-Caroline," she interrupted, testily.

"Oh." I summarised what I had seen in a very few words. "So I know that she is dead, and probably had a *most* unpleasant time of it."

Nijam returned her attention to her blue torch and continued working. In a voice carefully neutral she said, "Are you sure you didn't nod off?"

"Of course not! I'm telling you, I see the dead! So far in this house I've seen the Count of Chambord, Marie-Caroline, and my own—"

"Look," Nijam said in a voice so reasonable, it made me want to hit her over the chignon with one of her own spanners, "you may believe what you like, but since there's no means whereby ghosts can be empirically proven to exist, I don't mean to join you."

"I'm not going mad, if that's what you think," I said, rather hurt. I ought to have known better than to break my vow.

"I don't think you're mad," said Nijam. "Only superstitious. In any case, it makes no difference to the job. We knew Marie-Caroline had likely died shortly after fleeing the castle."

"Then why does the castle remember her so clearly?" I insisted. Nijam made no answer. "Don't you see how this changes things? If there's any possibility at all that it was one of the family who did this, we must be on our guard."

"One of the family? We don't even know whether the Bourbon-Parma lot were in residence at the time."

"I'll bet you anything they were. Marie-Caroline was about to be married off to her cousin Jaime. Perhaps it was a crime of passion! Perhaps he killed her rather than let her flee to her singing-tutor!"

"The problem with *your* soul, Dark, is that it has a sight too *much* poetry in it," Nijam said drily. "Even if one of the family was responsible for Marie-Caroline's death—which remains *entirely* unproven—what could they do about our little masquerade? They can't very well stand up and say, *I know for a fact that this young lady is an imposter, as I murdered the real Marie-Caroline myself.*"

"What could they do about—? I'll tell you what they could do about it! They could tie up the loose ends by murdering *me."*

"That really would not be a rational course of action. It's difficult enough to get away with one murder; two would be asking for trouble."

"I really think you overestimate the intelligence of these people." Sinking onto the bed, I ran my hands through my hair. "Look, Nijam, perhaps we should call it off. You have what you came for, and as for me, I'm beginning to think the game isn't worth the paper it's printed on."

"The candle," she corrected. "The game isn't worth the candle."

I frowned. "That can't be right. Candles are worth a great deal more than paper."

Nijam took a deep, slow, patient breath. "It's your mother's life you're speaking of, Dark. Surely that's worth any amount of candles, or paper, or what-have-you. And in any case, it's as I said: whatever you may or may not have seen in the chapel just now, there's no hard proof that it was one of the family who killed Marie-Caroline—or even that she is dead at all, for that matter."

When she put it like that, of course I had to agree. "Still, it seems to me that as a matter of self-preservation, we really ought to try to learn more about what happened on the night of Marie-Caroline's disappearance. Apart from anything else, if I'm to recover my memories, I'll need to know. If you will continue to gossip with the servants…"

Nijam looked resigned. "Gossip is not my strong suit, but I'll do what I can. And you must speak to the Countess about her will tomorrow, or as soon as possible. I gather she isn't expected to last the week."

I still felt that one could hardly barge into an old lady's

house as her long-lost daughter and immediately ask to see her will, but I pacified Nijam by saying, "Tomorrow is another leaf. I'll do what I can."

It was just as well she had me, I reflected. Heaven only knew how much trouble she might have run into, alone.

Chapter X.

Nijam had gone upstairs to her bed in the servants' quarters, but despite the lateness of the hour, the day's experiences had left my thoughts too full for sleep. Released from the confines of my false tail and comfortably attired in my dressing gown—of faded blue wool, it had seen better days, but still retained some of the military-style panache it must have had when new, three or four owners previous to myself—I felt a second wind.

Accordingly, just as the clock was striking half-past midnight, I was stealing in at the door to Marie-Caroline's former suite. As with the countess' rooms, one entered through a small sitting-room, which, like the rest of the house, was done in gold-and-cream wallpaper. The sofa and armchairs and even the escritoire before the velvet-curtained window were all gleaming baroque curves and pale upholstery, and the walls were full of mirrors and candelabra, portraits and landscapes. Every surface was free of dust, and there were fresh flowers upon the occasional table. The room, as I had hoped, had been left scrupulously untouched; it must have waited three years in the hope of its mistress' return.

I put my lamp down carefully upon the escritoire and went through the drawers, finding a leather-bound copy of Perrault, watercolours, and a sketch-book containing any number of knights and fairies and ballerinas interspersed occasionally with portraits—the count and countess of Chambord, some people who looked like servants, and even, I was surprised to note, a sketch of the Infante Jaime, recognisable even without his moustache by means of his large dark eyes and haughty bearing.

One of the final pages had been cut away, so carefully that I almost missed the excision. I wondered if this had once contained a portrait of someone Marie-Caroline did not want her family to know about.

The next drawer down contained fresh pens, letterhead, blotting-paper, sealing-wax, and so on, but there was none of what I hoped to find—that is, samples of Marie-Caroline's handwriting; perhaps letters or a journal in her own hand. Closing the drawer, I called to mind the image I had seen in the chapel. "Marie-Caroline," I said softly, holding that memory in my mind. I waited, and after a moment a faded imprint in white appeared, so indistinct that I could not make out her features, seated at the escritoire writing in what might have been a journal. A moment later she rose, closed the shadowy book, and moved through the door into the larger bedroom beyond. Retrieving my lamp, I followed her. This apartment contained a luxurious bed (canopied), a potted palm (flourishing), and a dressing-table, chest of drawers, and wardrobe (all gilt). The faded imprint led me to the last of these and went through the motions of opening the drawer at the bottom of the massive cabinet. I followed suit and here, tucked behind a folded fur cape and smelling strongly of camphor, I found two little leather-bound journals.

The imprint dissolved into shreds; perhaps that was the last anyone would ever see of it. Closing the drawer, I turned up my oil-lamp and began hurriedly turning pages.

The first journal began some five years prior to Marie-Caroline's disappearance and seemed mostly a catalogue of daily habits: how she spent her time, when she had gone out riding, whom she had seen. It struck me at once that she had had a peculiarly solitary and joyless youth: one would scarcely have known there was a military academy at Wiener Neustadt not five miles away, stocked to the eaves with handsome young officers. Her social life had mostly consisted of her parents' visits from French dignitaries and diplomats—hardly the sort of visitor calculated to bring a ray of sunshine into a young girl's life.

The second journal, however, was different. This one began less than two years previous to the disappearance; and as I skimmed through the pages, I noticed that Marie-Caroline began to express herself more freely. At first she did this merely by copying down quotations. Words in English leaped out at me from the muddle of French: *I would that I were worthy to be any man's Friend.* They were attributed to Mr Thoreau, but I thought I heard Marie-Caroline's own voice there. I certainly heard it a few pages further on when another quotation caught my eye: *Love comes into being through useful service to others.*

So! the Baron had also searched these rooms and read these books.

I turned a handful of pages at once. Here, there were still not many useful details about the final months of Marie-Caroline's life (*"Rode Brada to the village; saw a golden eagle very close"*) apart from the fact that the *Singing lesson Wiener N.* trips had abruptly ceased; but the journal had begun to contain thoughts of her own, usually in commentary upon the excerpts from what she was reading.

For instance, she copied down the words of Marcus Aurelius: *Death and life, success and failure, pain and pleasure, wealth and poverty, all these happen to good and bad alike, and they are neither noble nor shameful—and hence neither good nor bad.*

Below this were her own thoughts: *Although wealth may keep one in physical comfort, it can neither make one happy nor good, and what is the good of having wealth if one can neither do good to others nor have the happiness of being with the people one loves?*

I turned the next page to find myself at the end of the journal, where the latest entry was dated some six months before Marie-Caroline's disappearance. That was unfortunate: just as she had begun to express herself, she had begun a new journal, and it had undoubtedly disappeared along with the princess. All the same, I now had a much better idea of the person I was supposed to be impersonating. Marie-Caroline had been a reader, a dreamer, a thinker; wistful for a larger world and lonely within her own, despite the loyalty that held her here, silent and dutiful, in a world that had contracted to little more than the castle walls.

I must revisit these books at my leisure; but for the present, I had learned enough to go on with. I returned both the journals to their hiding-place and closed the drawer as softly as I might. It still made a soft grating sound, however, which must have masked the sound of the opening of the outer door. For this reason, my first indication that I was not alone came when I stepped into the sitting-room to find myself face to face with the Baron Dragomir Smilets.

He did not startle, as I did upon seeing him, for he must

have guessed at the identity of his fellow intruder the instant he entered the room.

"Now this is very interesting," he murmured with an air of tolerant amusement. The lamp he carried made a dramatic chiaroscuro of his strong, pale features. "What are *you* doing here, little mouse?"

I summoned back my wits, which had fluttered off and made fair to depart by the window. If only I had had the sense to bring the transmitter with me, I might have called upon Nijam for help!

"I believe I have a better right to ask that question than you do, Baron. As I understand it, this was *my* room."

"So it was."

I found myself backing away as he advanced: it was very late, and dark, and lonely in this room, and his tread was absolutely soundless, so that once again I was reminded of nothing so much as a great, hungry panther. I fetched up against an occasional table, and he took my lamp from me and set both the lights down on it before gesturing towards the sofa. "Please sit."

I obeyed meekly. There was a great deal of information I needed from the wicked Baron, and I was quite certain it would be best obtained by living up to his expectations, and playing the helpless *little mouse*.

You may say that it was not quite an honest thing to do, but I happen to think that if a person will be dishonest, he has forfeited his right to the honesty of others.

"I'm grateful for your help earlier," I began in a voice appropriately low and tremulous. "You have been as good as your word."

He had made no motion to sit; his dressing-gown, in a black-

and-burgundy paisley, was almost as mesmerising as his eyes, which he now fixed upon me thoughtfully.

"Do not thank me. You may not remember it, but I swore to protect you."

The absolute sincerity with which he spoke knocked me a little off my balance. For a moment I felt dreadfully, disastrously tempted to believe him. Then I rallied. For one thing, he had certainly never met the real Marie-Caroline in his life; for another, this Continental gallantry was nothing more than a weapon, designed—no doubt—for the ruin of girls like me. I would be proof against it—I *must* be proof against it.

Reflexively, I took the offensive.

"Is that why you lied to them about my tail?" I accompanied the words with the wide-eyed, beseeching look that worked so well on train-station porters and street sausage vendors. "You see, that part I *do* remember. It was…very recent, and part of the reason I chose to come here."

The Baron regarded me with an unreadable expression. "I was sorry to see you relinquish a dearly-held belief, but would you have preferred me to tell the truth? The Parma relations need very little reason to doubt you."

"They will doubt my story in any case, the moment they ask themselves how it was that a common governess was able to remain dry and undiscovered every day of the past three years." Wondering if I had revealed too much, I bit my lip and melted into longing. "If you *really* knew me, you would not feel the need to lie for me."

"That is why I followed you tonight," he said, composedly. "There were certain proofs I wished to show you." Reaching into the capacious pockets of his dressing-gown, he took out a thick piece of paper which, when unfolded, proved to be a wedding-certificate bearing Marie-Caroline's name in what had to have been a pretty decent forgery of her signature. It was dated in Sofia.

"There is also—this," he added, producing another small journal. I took it with a sense of foreboding and opened it to find that it was indeed Marie-Caroline's final journal, the last entry of which was dated about the time of her disappearance.

Rising, I carried the book nearer the light. The final entry was only another quotation, this one from Schlegel's translation of Shakespeare:

Farewell! God knows when we shall meet again.
  I have a faint cold fear thrills through my veins,
  That almost freezes up the heat of life.

But unless, like the ill-fated Juliet, Marie-Caroline had feigned her own death in the course of her escape—which I had every reason to doubt—I could not say exactly to what the lines were intended to refer.

"Where did you come upon this?" I asked eagerly.

"Naturally, it was with your things when you came to me."

That *would* be his story, of course. At any rate, if he was in possession of Marie-Caroline's last journal, it explained how he had come to secure a foothold at the castle.

I didn't hear him move: only between one breath and the next I realised he was standing behind me, so close that my back brushed his chest. He reached around me and took my hands, leaving the journal upon the occasional-table beneath the lamps; first his lips brushed the fingers of my right, and then the fingers of my left. His eyes sought mine in the mirror above the side-table, pinning me with an intent gaze. "Well, little mouse? What do you say?"

I could say nothing. With both my hands captured and raised I felt curiously vulnerable and exposed. The next instant I realised what he was doing, and I almost felt angry. It was one thing to play games of deceit, but he was not trying to outwit me any more: he was trying to seduce me.—No, he was trying to seduce *Marie-Caroline* with this coolly-assumed counterfeit passion.

Just like that, I realised what it was he was after. He was actually mercenary enough, if he could not steal the inheritance, to marry it!

"I think *you kiss by the book*," I quoted, twisting to confront him. He released me without protest, and I shoved my hands into the pockets of my gown to put them out of harm's way. "No, please, hear me out. I can't help wondering why you came here at all. Having lost me, what did you have to gain from intruding upon these horrible people, who say such demeaning things to you? What else am I supposed to think, except that you hope to receive part of the inheritance?"

His eyebrows rose, and once again I thought I saw that glimmer of amusement, quickly quashed. "I'm injured, my dear. What is wealth, after all? It can make one neither happy nor good, and what is the use if one cannot be among the people one loves? I came because I knew you had loved your mother, and I knew you would not wish her to be surrounded by monsters at her death."

He might even have been convincing, if not for that unguarded smile, and the fact that he had just repeated the very words I had read in Marie-Caroline's journal within the hour.

The clock on the mantelpiece struck one. Tiredly, I said,

"One would expect you to say something of that sort, wouldn't one?"

This time he did not try to stifle his amusement. "I suppose one would." The journal lay upon the table where I had dropped it, and now he reached out to slide it into his pocket.

"May I have that?" I asked gently. "It belongs to me, I think."

His hand splayed out protectively against his pocket. "It's all I have," he said. "What will you give me for it?"

I bit my lip. I had not been very generous with him, and it might still be dangerous to earn his enmity. "I will give a few more minutes of my time, and the opportunity to tell me the truth about something."

"Ask," he said with a little French shrug.

He was clever and false, and the Marie-Caroline I had come to know through her journals was a romantic child, gentle and sweet. I didn't for a moment think he would answer me truthfully, but I thought that whatever his answer, it might be revealing. "Why me? You're a man of the world, and I was only a sheltered child. Did you really love me, or was this the plan all along?"

"My dear!"

"I know nothing; I remember nothing," I said, letting my voice shake. "Humour my fears. What made you love me?"

He stood in silence for a long moment. At last he lifted one of the lamps so that the light fell on both our faces, revealing the slightest change of expression.

"Here is something that is true," he said. "I was raised as a beast of prey, and for many years I never thought I could be anything else. Weakness for me was an invitation; and until I met you, I never met something I really wanted to protect."

Almost, I believed him. It was the first halfway true thing

he had said to me. A beast of prey? Well: I had known that from the start.

I bit my lip a moment, then whispered, "Who are you, really?"

He looked away, almost as though the question had hit a tender spot, and he could not bear to answer it. I realised, with a heady rush of power, that I had really surprised him.

If so, his surprise lasted only a moment before he met my eyes again. He was smiling faintly now. "Who am I? I am not really Baron Dragomir Smilets, my little mouse. But I already told you that."

"Oh?"

"My real identity is my greatest secret. You must not tell a soul; it's as much as my life is worth."

"On my honour," I assured him, now really curious.

His smile was bittersweet. "I am the equal of any exiled Bourbon princeling, for my true name is Grand Duke Vasily Nikolaevich Romanov."

Such was the spell he wove that for a moment—for just a moment—I really believed him.

Then my heart fell as I realised what a ridiculous fib it was. Weariness overwhelmed me, and I went over to the table to collect my own lamp. "All right; if you say so."

"You don't believe me?"

"Prove it," I said, turning. My back was against the door, the knob in my hand, my escape assured. "The Romanovs are vampires; all the world knows that. Show me your eyes, your fangs."

"That would hardly be gentlemanly," he replied drily.

"Of course not. Good night, Baron. Sleep well"—and although I did not believe him to be the literal variety of monster, I was glad when I was out in the corridor with a closed door between us.

Chapter XI.

I locked my door and, having said my prayers, went to bed still shaking my head. I had the greatest of professional respect for the bad Baron, and had I not known him for a certainty to be a fraud, I might have believed a great many of his lies. But really, one would have to be hopelessly gullible to believe him a Romanov grand duke! I had never *met* a vampire, of course, but all the world knew that after dark they were difficult to mistake for an ordinary person.

The only explanation for such a flimsy deception was that my helpless-fawn performance, combined with my tail, must have taken him in completely. He no longer thought himself dealing with a foe worthy of his steel, but with an innocent child. The reason, at any rate, was evident. By claiming to be a Russian prince, he raised himself to Marie Caroline's exalted rank and made himself eligible for her hand.

As I fell asleep, I wondered idly what forged credentials the Baron would produce to substantiate such a claim. A forged letter of accreditation from Tsar Nicholas himself, no doubt.

Some hours later I awoke with a start, conscious that I was no longer alone in the room. My involuntary shriek was answered by another, and I blinked the sleep from my aching eyes to find that morning had come, and a rather elderly housemaid of perhaps sixty years of age was lighting the fire.

"Lord, mademoiselle, I'm sorry," she panted, putting a hand to her own heart. "I didn't mean to wake you!"

I fell back onto the pillows, limp with relief. "No, it's I should be apologising for frightening *you*."

Perhaps it was not the sort of thing a princess would say, but the maid blinked two or three times before a delighted smile crossed her face. "It's good to have you back, if I may say so, madame."

In France only princesses of the blood were addressed as *madame* regardless of age or marital status, and I gathered that Marie-Caroline, at least, would have spoken in such a manner. "I'm afraid I have forgotten your name," I told her.

"It's Faustine, madame."

"Then please continue with your work, Faustine, and don't mind me." I closed my eyes and thought regretfully about sleep. The bed was big enough to get lost in and soft enough that I would scarcely have minded, but already the blood circulated briskly, stirred up by the momentary conviction that a melusine had slithered into my room and was contemplating whether to mesmerise me or merely to inject me with venom. My mind, in addition, was buzzing with thoughts. It was no use trying to sleep: my day had begun long before I was ready for it.

When Faustine was gone, I drifted from beneath covers as light and warm as clouds, found paper and ink in the small escritoire by the window, and spent some leisurely minutes practising Marie-Caroline's handwriting and signature as I recalled it from my researches into her journals. There was a pencil and several sheets of thick, creamy notepaper in the desk as well; thoughtfully, I began work on a sketch of the

Count of Chambord, as I recalled him from his imprint last night.

As I worked, I considered my next steps. The Baron must be dealt with very carefully. I must not appear to favour him, or the Bourbon-Parmas might catch a fright. On the other hand, I did not think it wise to cut him off altogether. Apart from one misstep, he seemed frightfully well equipped for the imposture he was carrying out; besides which, I had not forgotten his veiled threats yesterday afternoon in the garden. As for the family—although for the moment they were completely demoralised, sooner or later they would rally in an attempt to protect what they viewed as their rightful property. I must move quickly and press my advantage before they found a way to expose or neutralise me. Which meant, as Nijam urged, ensuring that Maria Theresa's will was made in my favour. But my task would be a great deal easier if I could actually win over the family.

An idea occurred to me. I rang for Nijam, and a minute or two later the transmitter crackled into life from its hiding-place beneath my pillow. I snatched it out and fumbled it into my ear halfway through an acidly spoken reproof.

"…beautifully designed device that will render all such primitive measures obsolete. What is it, anyway?"

"Good morning, Nijam! I need a riding-habit, if you can find one. Blanca has invited me to join her and Jaime this morning, and it occurred to me…"

"*Can* you ride?"

I hesitated and smiled. "Oh, come, it can't be *too* difficult."

A beleaguered sigh. "Horsemanship is a *skill*, which must be learned over time, and you are supposed to be accomplished in it. Did you learn nothing from that debacle at the séance?

If you can't ride, you mustn't go anywhere near the stables."

I bit my lip to contain my laughter. "Nijam, Nijam! I had a pony when I was a child at my grandfather's rectory in Oxfordshire. There isn't much the two of us didn't get up to on the summer holidays. I'll be quite all right."

I might have been laughing, but on Nijam's end there was only a silence that seethed with unspoken things. At last she said, "I'll find you a riding-habit."

* * *

Marie-Caroline's old riding-habit was a little short on me, which was just credible; I might have been in real trouble had it been too large. I was still fidgeting with the cuffs as I found my way to the stable, which I found to my left as I exited the house by its front door.

I once again summoned up the mental image of Marie-Caroline as I approached the building, and was rewarded by a vision of the girl on a large grey horse, which curvetted daintily as it edged across the gravel in the direction of the park. This imprint was a little clearer; if Nijam was correct and the horse was still alive, no doubt it had helped to keep this memory of its mistress fresh. I had no time for more than a quick glance, however, for the morning calm was broken by an angry voice upraised in a language I did not recognise, except for a curse. Within the stable, in a liquid flow of Spanish or Italian, Jaime was consigning something to the devil.

I stopped just outside the stable door, straining my ears for the equable feminine reply, which was made in French. "Well, what do you propose to do? She looks like Marie-Caroline; she has the tail; she's even convinced the servants, and they knew her far better than we ever did. If that's not enough for you, what is?"

There was a silence before Jaime said in a lower but still furious voice, "We ought to mesmerise her. Force her to give up the truth under questioning."

"Jaime, no."

"Why not?"

"Well, for one thing, she would be immune to it, and for another thing, it would be a monstrous thing to do to a fellow Bourbon, even if she *is* no more than a distant cousin, which I don't believe for a moment! Don't you think the poor creature has been through enough already?"

The possibility of the Bourbon-Parmas choosing to mesmerise me had certainly occurred to me more than once during the course of the previous evening, and if Jaime was already saying it, time was certainly short before his elders, at least, agreed.—Which meant that it was high time I stepped in to nip that thought in the bud.

I trod briskly in at the door and called out breathlessly. "Here I am! I *do* apologise for being late."

Jaime turned to greet me with smouldering hostility, but Blanca's smile lit up her face, nearly striking me speechless. "Not late at all; it's only that Jaime and I are early."

My riding-habit was demure grey, but Blanca's was a rich berry-red, which only accentuated her dark and striking colouring. I thought, with some discomfort, that I had never seen a more beautiful woman; and I considered how unfair it was to be attempting a delicate impersonation in the presence of two such overwhelmingly attractive people as Blanca and the Baron.

"We had your horse saddled," she said kindly, when I did

not speak. Jaime wordlessly offered me the reins of a chestnut gelding; but in his other hand he led the same flea-bitten grey I had observed a moment before, in the courtyard.

I hesitated. "Are you sure it was this one?"

Smiling thinly, he relinquished the grey. "So," he said, "you *do* remember something?"

I slipped the grey—Bradamante—a lump of sugar, which she accepted phlegmatically. "It feels more like a dream than a memory," I confessed. "I'm not sure I even know how to ride, but..." Remembering Marie-Caroline's sketchbook, I gazed at him with big, unfocused eyes. "Did we perhaps go riding once before, you and I? Before you grew the moustache?"

The mocking half-smile faded from his lips and he sent an uncertain glance towards Bradamante, who was nosing my jacket for more sugar and already inclined to be affectionate.

Perhaps I was only imagining it, but I felt a little of the hostility ebb from the air. "I suppose it's possible," Jaime said; and I could not help feeling that he meant more by the words than a simple answer to my question.

"Shall we?" Blanca mounted, settling her knees and skirts around the horns of her side-saddle. More carefully, using a mounting-block, I followed suit. Then, with Jaime bringing up the rear, we left the stable and started towards the park.

"We'll take it easy at first," Blanca told me, all cordiality. "You and Brada must both be out of practice."

"How long has it been?" I asked, keeping my seat rather nervously. Bradamante had a light, springy step quite unlike the pony I had ridden as a girl, and I hoped I was not cutting too ungainly a figure on her back.

"We last went riding together the week you disappeared." There was something wistful in Blanca's voice as she guided

114

us onto the path leading among the trees. Pines and naked, leafless oaks filled the park, wrapped with wisps of early-morning mist. "Mama had brought all of us to visit: Jaime, Beatriz, Elvira, Alicia, and me. It was all a set-up, of course."

"A set-up?"

"Well, *you* know." She sent a glance behind us and leaned closer, lowering her voice. "You and Jaime were meant to take a fancy to each other."

I, too, glanced back, allowing my gaze to linger until Jaime met my eyes.

"And did I?" I asked softly.

"You ran away," Blanca said with an amused smile.

"Did I? How cruel of me! Were you much disappointed, Jaime?"

"Not particularly," he said.

His frankness cut straight through the spell I had attempted to weave, yet I could not help but laugh. "You are a great deal less gallant than you look, cousin."

"A deficiency I shall endeavour to mend, since it displeases you."

There was a note of dry humour in his voice, and Blanca laughed. "Don't thank him," she told me. "It isn't his manners he means to mend; it's his looks. He intends to gain a little weight and a few more chins, and become more elderly and eccentric by the day."

"How else? At last, I would be free to go about my own business without this constant persecution."

"Persecution? Some men would enjoy the attention of pretty women, Jaime!"

"It isn't the pretty women who bother me. It's their mamas. At any rate, I'm not ready to be married and I have other things on my mind."

I could not help laughing, but with it I sent him a melting look and added, "Won't you be content with the number of chins you have, Jaime?—for me?"

Jaime smiled mirthlessly. I could see that any flirtation between us must be uphill work.

Nijam's voice crackled warily in my ear. "What are you doing, Dark?"

She may not have understood, being composed entirely of cold steel; but naturally the gentle reader will already have divined my purpose. The Bourbon-Parmas saw me as their enemy because I threatened their hold on the inheritance. Even before Marie-Caroline's disappearance, they had attempted to gain control of it, consolidating both the fortune and the claim to the throne by means of a marriage between the princess and Jaime. Now, it was clear that if they were to accept me I must offer them something they wanted: namely, the hope of completing the match.

"You should listen to her, Jaime, even if you won't listen to me. But, my dear!"—Blanca tutted. "Don't let your Baron hear you admiring Jaime's chin!"

Of course, the Baron *was* the greatest obstacle to this plan. "Oh," I said helplessly, "the Baron."

Blanca lowered her voice. "Between the three of us, cousin, do you entirely trust our friend Dragomir?"

"I suppose he may be truthful; but I don't recall him at all. Not the way I recall Brada." I smoothed the mare's neck fondly. "Or for that matter, Jaime." I sent him a shy, confiding look. "It all seems quite strange to me. As I told him myself, I can hardly accept a man as my husband simply because he tells me so. There must be some—some recognition of the soul."

"Such as you felt for my brother?" Blanca conjectured, gratifyingly quick on the uptake.

Nijam muttered in my ear. "I don't like it, Dark. If you mean to pit the two of them against each other, it's a dangerous game and completely unnecessary."

On the contrary: if I might convince the family that there was a real likelihood of my forsaking the Baron for Jaime, I felt certain they would rally around me.

"If only there was some way to be *sure*." I sighed. "If only I knew for a fact that what the Baron says about the two of us is true!—What do you think?" I asked Jaime.

Reader, he *ought* to have suggested mesmerising the man, which would have rid us at a stroke of the Baron, set the Bourbon-Parma hearts at rest, and brought me into the bosom of the family. Instead, he changed the subject abruptly.

"Have you ever been in England, Miss Wagner?"

He was trying to trip me up, of course. I opened my eyes very wide and said, "No; I can't say I ever have." Then a flood of horror overwhelmed me as I realised that I had replied, as he had spoken, in perfectly enunciated English.

I had become too comfortable with them, these beautiful, charming, monstrous strangers.

A flash of triumph showed in Jaime's cold dark eyes. "Then allow me to congratulate you upon how well you speak the language. It took me some years of school in the country before I became proficient."

Something must have tipped him off—some trick of accent or manner had reminded him of the girls he had known in England! Just my luck!

Nijam's voice crackled urgently in my ear. "Don't panic. Tell them it was me. I am half English. Tell them we—"

Pretending to smooth my hair, I switched off the transmitter just long enough to get a word in edgewise. "I find I have a knack for languages. Before taking a position with the Erdos family, I worked for the family of the English ambassador to Sofia, and they insisted upon my learning the language to use with their children."

If he disbelieved that, there was nothing I could do about it. It was true enough in its own way; it was simply the way I had learned to speak French like a native, not English.

To my relief, Blanca came to my rescue. "For shame, Jaime! This is a ride, not an interrogation. Time for a gallop! Race you to the back fence!" She touched her riding-crop to the horse and shot off. With another triumphant flash of his dark eyes, Jaime followed her. Bradamante quickened to a gallop on their heels without needing the encouragement of the crop: she was keen not to be left behind, and, perhaps foolishly, so was I.

It was ages since I had been riding; and now I remembered that the exhilaration of riding a horse at breakneck speed through the woods is one produced at least partly by the terror it evokes. Whether it was the unfamiliar height and speed of the horse, or the slightly off-balance feeling of the side-saddle, or the false step I had just made, that morning I felt more terror than exhilaration. Perhaps I ought to have reined in and allowed the siblings to have their race without me, but to do so would be to admit the inferiority of my horsemanship, and I felt I must repair the blunder I had made by speaking to Jaime in English.

Instead, I gave the mare her head and curled my fingers tightly around the uppermost saddle-horn. In a trice Bradamante and I had pulled level with the other two. Blanca was out in front, bending forward a little. The berry-red wool of her riding-dress rippled with her speed and there was a look of pure joy on her face—supremely confident and unafraid, a child of fortune, beautiful and blissful.

She sent me a flashing smile as Bradamante outstripped her. I did my best to return it—to look as though I knew what I was doing and could live up to Blanca's years of lessons and practice and the best of everything money could buy. But it was a mistake to take my eyes off the path for a moment.

A whirr of wings erupted from the undergrowth to my left; I glimpsed the coppery feathers of a pheasant as it launched from the covert. Bradamante shied to the right, throwing me violently to the left. Despite the ungainly lurch I made, my foot in the stirrup, my knees locked about the horns, and my grip on the saddle should all have saved me. But then there was a soft *snap* as the girth broke. Bradamante and the saddle parted ways, and with a despairing cry I toppled into a ring of mushrooms, ploughed through the dirt, and fetched up against an exposed root. At almost the same moment, the ground shook and dirt sprayed into my face as Jaime's horse cut the ground within inches of my body. Had my momentum carried me a very little less far, I would have been trampled.

"Marie-Caroline!" Blanca shrieked; she turned her horse and almost collided with her brother. I gasped in vain for breath as she and Jaime slid from their saddles and bent over me, Blanca's hand clasped over her mouth. "Marie-Caroline! My dear, are you hurt?"

"I—don't know," I wheezed. "What happened?"

"No, don't get up," Blanca told me, but I pushed to my elbows and began to feel myself all over. The agony was intense, but I was only winded and bruised: by some miracle I had avoided any worse injury.

"I'm all right," I gasped. But then I thought of how narrow my escape had been—I imagined the way my ribs would have cracked and caved in had Jaime's horse put a foot wrong—and I sank down again into the dry leaves and the shredded mushrooms. From far away I heard Nijam calling me; I felt Blanca fanning my face with her hat. I thought, stupidly, that the Bourbon-Parmas were supposed to be my family, and I was failing comprehensively at living up to them. A real princess would not embarrass herself with a slip of the tongue; would scarcely fall from her horse; and certainly would not faint like a ninny once she had done so.

At length things stopped going around and around and I said, to Nijam as much as to Blanca, "I'm all right, I promise."

Blanca helped me sit up and prop my back against a tree, and Jaime, who had knelt at my side doing and saying nothing, disentangled the remains of the side-saddle from my legs.

"The girth burst," he said shortly, lifting a broken belly-strap.

Blanca's eyes were wide and horrified. "Good God, see how terribly worn it is! Do you think…"

Her voice trailed off, and it occurred to me uncomfortably, as it must have occurred to Blanca, that a riding-accident was pretty much the easiest way possible to dispose of an unwanted heiress.

"Do I think what?" Jaime said irritably. "Steiner should have known better than to use an old girth that's good for nothing. I'll have a word with him when we get home. I'll stay here with her, Blanca. You ride to the house and get a dog-cart or something. She's in no condition to walk."

I almost shot to my feet. "No, no, no, I couldn't possibly ask—" I caught my breath, for an ache went through my hip as I regained my feet: I must have bruised it as I landed. Still, I limped gamely to Blanca's side and clutched her arm. "Walk home with me, Blanca. I'm perfectly all right. Really, the exercise will do me good."

"My dear, of course." Blanca put a comforting arm around my waist. "Let's bring you home."

Jaime followed, leading the horses, and I could have fainted again with relief that he did not insist upon waiting with me, alone in the wood.

I did not know for certain that he had just attempted to kill me; but the thought of conducting a flirtation with Marie-Caroline's handsome cousin was no longer half so appealing as it had seemed a bare few minutes before.

Chapter XII.

I felt terribly shaken. Of course I suspected Marie-Caroline's having been done away with by one of her own family; of course I had half expected them to do the same to me. But they had attempted to do so in the course of a genteel morning's exercise, before I had been twenty-four hours in their company. One felt there ought, at least, to have been some warning.

Jaime had announced that the broken belly-strap showed signs of natural wear, and the stable hand who saddled the horse had likely made a careless choice, for none of the side-saddles could have been in regular use of late. I wished I could afford to believe him. None of this added up, I thought as Blanca helped me upstairs. Why should Jaime assassinate his cousin, when he might very easily have married her? I revolved the possible answers to this question in my mind, but none of them made me feel particularly safe.

I had told myself the risk was my means of earning the inheritance, but now I only wanted to eliminate the risk altogether. But how?

Blanca and I reached the top of the stairs to find Nijam superintending two footmen in the removal of the large chest in which she had stored my false tail and its appurtenances.

"Nijam!" I said, for a moment fearing the worst. "What's going on?"

"You're being moved into your old suite, madame. Countess' orders."

That took my breath away. I might be in danger of my life, but I was also so *very* close to my goal.

"Oh," was all I could say.

Blanca squeezed my arm. "What fun! You'll be in the room next to mine but one. This way."

I did not much feel like fun, but I followed Blanca dutifully to the end of the northwest passage and allowed her to conduct me by daylight through the apartments I had inspected by lantern-light the evening before. "This door leads directly into Mama's room," she said, indicating a door in the bedroom's far corner, evidently disused, since a small occasional-table stood before it. "Mine is the next along, down a little corridor; don't be shy to knock if you need anything during the night."

"Thanks," I said faintly. "As a matter of fact, I require solitude. I thought I might lie down for a bit."

"Of course. I'll see you at dinner, if not sooner. And don't worry—Jaime will get to the bottom of that business with the burst girth."

She disappeared, leaving me alone with Nijam and the luggage. In the guise of my lady's maid, Nijam had begun dutifully to unpack my clothing and put it away in the wardrobe alongside Marie-Caroline's things. Now, with Blanca gone, she threw aside her clothes-brush and unlocked her chest.

"Thank goodness there's a bit more room here to work," she observed. "Now, if only I had my forge with me—"

"It's nice to see you alive and well, too, Nijam." My lack of sleep was getting the better of my ordinarily sunny temper. "I was really worried about you, you know!"

Through her mechanical goggles, Nijam blinked at me with comically enormous eyes. "Is something wrong?"

"Oh, nothing whatsoever! Only I was very nearly killed."

"In the park earlier, you did say you were all right." She tapped her implanted transmitter as though to remind me that she had heard everything I said. "Was that incorrect?"

I opened my mouth and then shut it again. There hardly seemed any point. "No. Only, I'm bruised all over, and my nerves are shot to pieces; so if it's all the same to you, I mean to rest."

"Go ahead," she said equably, tying on an apron and filling its pockets with tools. "I'll be working at the escritoire in the sitting-room. Don't forget to finish your unpacking, or people will wonder what I've been doing with my time."

So saying, she vanished into the sitting-room, dragging the chest behind her.

"Heaven forbid any indisposition of mine should inconvenience you in the least," I muttered.

"Your transmitter is on," she replied in my ear. "Do turn it off if you mean to converse with yourself."

I restrained myself from tearing the thing off, opening the door, and flinging it at her. Instead, I buried it beneath one of the fat pillows on the bed and crawled under the covers to sleep.

I awoke some time later to a soft knocking at the door. "One moment," I called fuzzily. My whole body ached and Marie-Caroline's riding-habit had become uncomfortably snug. I smoothed my skirts and hair, splashed a little water on my tired eyes, and opened the door to find the sitting-room beyond empty—empty, that is, except for the Romanov vampire prince who wasn't.

"Baron," I said, surprised. Nijam had cleared her tools from the escritoire, I was glad to see, and the chest, closed and locked, stood innocently beside it. She must have finished her task and departed. Conscious of my half-unpacked bags, I closed the bedroom door firmly behind me. "To what do I owe this pleasure?"

"Forgive the intrusion." He made three steps of it and caught me by the shoulders, looking me up and down with an offensively proprietary air. I felt uncomfortably conscious of my sleep-flushed cheeks, rumpled clothing, and disintegrating coiffure; but although the Baron's piercing green eyes missed none of this, all he said was, "I came the moment I heard of your accident. You were not seriously hurt, I hope?"

Nijam, I thought feelingly, really ought to take lessons.

"Only bruised—and shaken," I said, putting on a show of bravery. "It was the girth that broke; it must have been terribly worn."

His eyes darkened. "Sit down, my dear. Did you see the girth yourself? I was too late; it had been disposed of by the time I reached the stables."

I allowed him to lead me to the sofa and put me into it, almost as though I was a little china doll. "I did, but..."

"I spoke to the stable hand." Beside me on the sofa, the Baron braced his arm against the back of it so that he could study me at close range. His attention was nearly overpowering. "Steiner, his name was. He swore it was only ordinary wear and tear; he didn't look closely at the belly strap before using

125

it. I never saw such a guilty look."

That he took the matter so seriously did nothing for my nerves. I stared up at him with big, haunted eyes and fluttering hands. "Oh, Baron. Surely you can't think he did it on purpose?"

"I think it's likely someone left him no choice."

I touched the tip of my tongue to my lips, wondering what he would make of my suspicions if I confessed them.

"Jaime," I breathed.

His eyes narrowed. "What makes you say that?"

"He seems rather hostile."

"He would have reason to be," the Baron said. "You may not recall it, but there were serious attempts afoot to force you into a marriage to him. That is why you fled to me."

"*Force,* Baron? That is a strong word."

"Ask your mother if you doubt me. The papal dispensation necessary to marry first cousins in this country had already been requested and granted."

No one had told me the matter had gone so far. I was speechless. Poor Marie-Caroline!

"You are shocked," he observed. His eyes darkened a little more. "Do not be afraid, little mouse. The carelessness of this Steiner will not go unpunished, I swear it. I will compel him to tell me the entire truth; and then, when I know who has dared to harm you, I will peel the scoundrel's flesh from his bones."

Not relinquishing his gaze, he bent to kiss my hand before rising to take his leave. I felt nearly as overwhelmed as I pretended to be. It wasn't merely the revelations that had been made—if the Baron's word was to be trusted, of course. Rather, I was unaccustomed to being the target of such a man's attention, and it left me rather dry in the mouth and palpitating at the heart. It was not every day that the handsomest man of my acquaintance bent over my hand, pledging—

I felt suddenly very nervous. All this talk about punishing the poor stable hand and peeling Jaime's flesh from his bones had been very dramatic, but only now did it strike me—flustered as I was by the bad Baron's proximity—that the habitual mocking amusement in his voice was, for once, entirely absent.

"You won't really do it, will you?" I asked nervously. "Punish the stable hand, I mean."

"What, my dear! do you think I am the sort of man to make jokes about my wife's safety? That would look very bad. Worse, even, than refusing to do anything about it at all."

I almost told him in my most governessing tones that he was too old to be acting like a complete barbarian. Instead, I swallowed my indignation and affected a tremulous, pleading voice. "Baron, if you have any regard at all for my feelings, you will leave the poor man in peace. What could a stable hand have to gain from killing me, after all? He did it only for fear of those monsters, I'd stake my life on it."

"Yes; and your life is precisely what you *would* be staking."

"Please."

He looked mutinous, but bowed. "Your wish is my command. I will not lay a finger upon him."

The Baron departed, leaving me vaguely worried about the specificity of his promise. There was, as I had reason to know, a great deal a determined nobleman might do to a nervous servant, without ever laying a finger upon him.

With a sigh, I rose from the sofa and went to change my

clothes preparatory to doing the work of my own lady's maid.

* * *

Where was Miss Nijam, you might ask, whilst I was attempting to dissuade the Baron from his purpose?—In a word: having spent a quiet half-hour at the escritoire, she had tidied away her work and gone in search of Alphonse Schmidt.

She chose her time carefully, knowing that at this particular hour of the morning, with the ladies and gentlemen downstairs going about their day's business or leisure, their lady's maids and gentlemen's gentlemen would be hard at work straightening their apartments. In addition to this, she thought it would be a good idea to familiarise herself with the layout of the first floor.

The house, as I have mentioned, was a hollow rectangle surrounding a small garden-courtyard; it bothered Nijam's sense of geographical proprieties that the four corners, rather than the walls, were oriented towards the cardinal directions. A wide corridor circled the first floor on three sides, well-lit by windows that overlooked the courtyard. Marie-Caroline's suite was situated at one of the terminal ends of this corridor, as was Princess Margaret's room immediately to the southeast of it.

A short, narrow passage skirted Margaret's room to give access to the room beyond. Knocking upon this door, Nijam was met by a rather dour-looking older maid, whom she had met the previous evening at dinner.

"Fraulein, you're just who I hoped to meet," Nijam said, making a mental note that this must be Infanta Blanca's apartment, since it was certainly her maid. "Have you any rectified spirit? I want to make up some curling fluid."

"No, and I'm not a dispensary," the maid said, closing the door in her face.

Nijam understood that by the brevity of her response, the other woman intended to register an offence of some nature. Yet the precise origin of her bruised feelings was opaque, and on the whole, Nijam was grateful for the pithy and direct reply. The last thing she wanted was to be waylaid by a gossip. Relieved, she retraced her steps, passing Princess Margaret's room and my own. Maria Theresa's suite lay at the western corner of the house, near the great staircase which led to the ground floor. Instead of taking this, Nijam turned down the southwest passage and peered through the first doors she came across, which led to the gallery of the chapel from which I had glimpsed Marie-Caroline's imprint on the previous evening. She noted the number and positioning of the windows and judged it highly unlikely that any occupant of the chapel should be clearly seen from the gallery at night. It was, therefore, all the more likely that I had been imagining things.

She proceeded to the door of the next room, which was empty. The one beyond was the one I had occupied the night before. Beyond it, at the southernmost corner of all, her knock was rewarded by a cheerful "Come in!" in accents she recognised all too well.

Nijam drew in a fortifying breath and did as she was bid.

"Good day, Herr Schmidt," she said. For a corner room it was a smallish apartment, and apart from the canopied bed there was barely room for herself and Alphonse Schmidt, who turned to her with a jacket over his arm, a brush in his hand, and an expression that was disarmingly obliging.

"Fraulein! Can I be of assistance?"

"Rectified spirit." It was not what she had intended to say, but it was the first thing that came to mind. "Do you have any? I want it for curling fluid."

"Come in and let me see what I can find," he answered at once. Nijam waited as he put down the coat and brush and began to look through drawers and valises. She ought to begin asking the necessary questions, but was waylaid by an existential despair. It was not, as she had momentarily feared on the previous evening, that he had taken offence and cut her off. He was still very much his old self: obliging, generous, kind to a fault.

Only he did not remember her.

Was she losing her reason? Had she dreamed the whole affair? And what did it matter, anyway? One had seventy or eighty short years to live, and then one perished. In the grand scheme of things, what were the odds that she, a miserable parasite on the skin of an vastly uncaring planet, should have the blind good fortune to stumble across the one man in all the world who had the power to make her happy?—And, having been careless enough to lose him once found, what odds were there that this particular miracle should be repeated?

His voice broke into her thoughts. "Is everything all right?"

"Beg pardon?"

He had stopped halfway through disembowelling a valise, and now beheld her with an expression of concern. "I don't mean to pry. Only you seem upset."

Upset? thought Nijam. Only at the vast indifference of the cosmos. If she said it aloud, he would certainly think her mad. "It's nothing."

He didn't believe her; she could tell that. But he smiled.

"That puts my mind at ease. I will confess, I was a little worried. The last time I saw you, you bloodied your nose."

She felt the flush creeping across her cheeks. "Why should I blame you? It was my own silly fault."

"Well, you ought to be particularly nice to it from now on, because it's a particularly nice sort of nose."

He was making no effort to find the rectified spirit, and Nijam felt a wholly irrational wish that he would just get on with it. As a matter of fact, she did not want the spirit. She did not want to make curling fluid. She only wished that if he meant to treat her as a stranger, he would not stand there, leaning over the valise with his shirt-sleeves rolled up, smiling at her in the most distracting way.

Besides, how *dare* her own Alphonse compliment a strange woman's nose?

Somehow, her conflicting thoughts made it easier to ask the questions she dreaded. "Have you ever been at Heidelberg?"

"Not to my memory. Perhaps we met there, in a former life?"

That touched her in a sore spot. "Reincarnation is empirically unproveable. Whatever my origins may be, I don't believe in things that can't be scientifically verified."

Chastened, he dove back into the valise. "I do beg your pardon, Fraulein—?"

"Nijam." She shouldn't have bitten his head off. "You don't remember Heidelberg at all, then?"

He shook his head, still chastened. "Ought I to?"

Certainly he ought to: it was where he had spent the happiest year of Nijam's short life. The truth trembled on her lips, but she choked it back. If he had forgotten her, she could scarcely blurt out the truth like this. "Apparently not."

He found the bottle of rectified spirit and handed it over without quite looking her in the eye.

"Tell me, Fraulein Nijam," he added softly, "how does one scientifically verify the existence of love?"

"One doesn't," she said, and fled before he could ask if that meant she didn't believe in it. At that moment she could neither confirm nor deny the existence of love, and certainly not to Alphonse Schmidt.

* * *

"All that, and you didn't even ask him whose valet he is?" Through the looking-glass before me, I levelled an incredulous look at Nijam. "You *are* in a sorry state!"

She scowled horribly. "I know whose valet he is. He's with Baron Smilets, although how or why, I cannot imagine."

Nor could I. It was a conjunction too fortuitous to be chance, but I was not quite sure what to make of it.

I would have plenty of time for idle thought, at any rate. The day had been terribly long. I had taken my pencil sketch of the Count's imprint downstairs to make some finishing touches in a public place; and Duke Robert had seen it and nearly choked on his own moustache. After lunch, I had spent an hour with Maria Theresa before going into the village with Blanca to buy the material for a new dress—which, since my lady's maid was not in fact a lady's maid, had been deposited with a local seamstress to be made up. Now, as I dressed myself for dinner, was my first opportunity to hear Nijam's story.

"What happened in Heidelberg, anyway?"

"We attended the university there."

132

"Good Lord! They're allowing women at the university?"

"I was an auditrix, not a student."

Stifling a smile, I imagined the effect a young woman of Nijam's outlandish beauty and crushing unsentimentality must have had upon an institution stocked to the eaves with red-blooded German masculinity. Half of them must have been in love with her, and the other half must have loathed her. "You and Schmidt were an item, I take it?"

Beneath her tawny complexion, Nijam flushed and changed the subject. "I went through the rest of the floor," she announced. "The Baron was in the south corner; then there's a corridor to a suite in the east corner where the Duke of Parma is staying, and Jaime's room comes next, beside Blanca's. But there's no access to her room from the east corner, unless you go through the doors communicating between one room and the next. The corridor only runs three sides of the house."

Still, if what Nijam reported was true, it would be possible for a person to navigate the entire house unobserved, without ever setting foot in the corridor, if the doors between the rooms remained open. To one already rattled by the events of the day, this was a rather fearful thought.

"I received a visit from the Baron this morning. He doesn't believe it was an accident, this morning. He believes someone—Jaime, most likely—tried to kill me."

Nijam frowned. "Then he's wrong. A rational person would kill the Baron and marry *you*."

"A rational person wouldn't be trying to kill *anyone!*" I protested. "Rational or irrational, Jaime is the most likely culprit. If he is the one who murdered the real Marie-Caroline because she refused to marry him, that would explain why he is so convinced, in the teeth of all the evidence, that I'm an imposter."

"If that was so, why should he go to the risk and trouble of killing you?" Nijam shook her head. "You're only an imposter, after all. It wouldn't be difficult to reveal your true identity. Trust me, Dark, it was an accident."

All the same, I couldn't seem to help worrying.

Chapter XIII.

I left the false tail in Nijam's chest that evening and went down to dinner on my own two legs as Jaime and Blanca had done the night before. Nijam agreed with me that the fewer opportunities the real melusines had of inspecting my tail, the smaller their chances of detecting the imposture; and apart from anything else, I was still feeling terribly stiff and sore from my accident this morning. I was glad not to be encumbered with the monstrous thing.

My father's imprint was waiting for me when I left Marie-Caroline's room. I stopped out of habit to let it kiss me—some sense of filial duty prevented me from walking rudely through it—yet deep down, I was a knot of desperation and resentment. Had my mother found a likely sanatorium yet? Would they admit her without requiring money up-front?

In one sense Nijam was right: each day I delayed here was killing my mother. Tonight, I promised myself, I must broach the topic of the will with Maria Theresa.

On the stairs, I met an astonishingly handsome young man with fair hair and blue eyes. He stood still and bowed as I began to descend, and a thought struck me.

"You must be Alphonse Schmidt," I remarked, "the Baron's valet."—He murmured his assent, but I did not move on at once. I said in the friendliest manner possible, "Tell me, who is your master? He can't *really* be a Bulgarian baron, can he?"

That made him open his eyes in genuine astonishment. "Madame!" he protested. "Do you really believe that sir would lie to you? Sir is the soul of honour."

"Forgive me," I replied, trying not to laugh, "then there is no truth in the rumour that he is, in fact, a Russian Grand Duke?"

"None whatever."

"And you have been in his employment—?"

"Three months only, madame, but long enough to know him to be quite as human as you or I. Whoever told you otherwise has been spreading quite irresponsible falsehoods."

Taking pity on the boy, I did not inform him that his master was the irresponsible fabulist in question. Still, it seemed most likely to me that the Baron was precisely whom he appeared to be: a noble adventurer, accustomed to royal courts but far from being royalty himself. Had he been anything else—anything royally monstrous—surely his valet would have discovered it, and in my experience most servants were incapable of boasting about their employers' rank. Why, I myself, on occasion, had referred meaningfully to my employer, the Countess, or my little charges, the von Hügel heiresses.

Dinner was as much of an ordeal as it had been on the previous evening: Princess Margaret was icy, the Duke unbearable, and Jaime mostly silent. The atmosphere would have been positively funereal without the Baron and Blanca to enliven us. The Baron told the charming story he had concocted of his meeting with Marie-Caroline at the Carnival masque. A discussion of dancing turned to music; it was asserted that the lost princess' favourite opera had been *Lakmé*, and by chance it was opening at the Opera in Vienna the following evening.

"We should attend," the Baron announced. "Perhaps the music will refresh lost memories."

Blanca clapped her hands. "What an excellent notion! It will be the perfect opportunity to reintroduce our dear Marie-Caroline to society."

Princess Margaret put down her fork with a clatter. "Surely there's no hurry for *that.*"

"*Please,* mama! The Prince of Tuscany is sure to call on me when I am in town again, and it would be too heartless of me to go without Marie-Caroline. We needn't be away for long; we can spend the night in town and return by the morning train."

The Prince of Tuscany, evidently, was a great inducement: the Princess relented, and the journey was fixed for the morrow. Blanca sent me a conspiratorial wink, but I felt rather shaken. It was one thing to pose as a princess here in the seclusion of Schloss Frohsdorf; it was another to parade myself around the imperial capital under a false name.

"Do you really think this is a good idea?" I murmured to the Baron as he ushered me upstairs at the end of the meal. "You see that the Princess was wary of making my return publicly known. If anyone wishes me harm—"

"That is precisely why you ought to move quickly and consolidate your position," he said in reply. "Once all Vienna has seen you, it will be impossible to do away with you quietly."

No, I thought: once Vienna had seen me, if I was discovered I should be publicly crucified. I felt uneasy about that, but I had set myself a task and my only hope was to steer a bold course. Fortune never favoured faint heart.

I found the Countess lying, as she had lain on the previous night, among the heavy coils and the gamey stench of her own serpentine tail. It moved as I approached, agitated and fretful. Outside, wind and rain beat against the windows, making the panes rattle as though in sympathy with her mood.

I paused on the threshold, repressing a shudder. At least tonight I was on my own two feet, not cocooned awkwardly in a false tail.

"Come in, come in." The old lady extended a trembling hand; her tail writhed. "My dear. You did not tell me you had had an accident today."

Princess Margaret had forbidden me to mention the mishap; she feared that any shock might carry the Countess off.

"It was nothing," I said, venturing closer to the bed until the coiled tail was sliding around and past me, all kinked and knotted like that of a boa constrictor. "I—I didn't want to alarm you."

Her hand found mine and fastened with surprising strength; she spoke in jerky sentences, as though the words were being choked out of her. "You are alive. That is the main thing. It would kill me to lose you again."

"You won't lose me, madame; not by any purpose of my own, I promise you."

The Countess trembled a little. Her tail found me and began by slow cold inches to mould itself around me. "I was to blame," she whispered. "I drove you from me. I would have compelled you to marry your cousin when your heart was set against it."

I touched the tip of my tongue to my lips, acutely aware of

the smooth, scaly pressure against my knees. If I had tried to take a step I would have fallen.

"*Compelled,* madame? Surely not."

"I...I changed my will," she confessed. "I left the whole inheritance to Robert and Jaime. You were disinherited if you refused to marry him."

"Good heavens," I said, frankly appalled. I couldn't help feeling rather proud of Marie-Caroline, whatever had become of the poor girl, for having the spine to run away sooner than yield to such intimidation.

I do not think the Countess quite understood what she was doing, but her coils tightened, drawing me closer. Her face was white, and there were tears on her cheeks. "It was wrong of me, I know... Can you ever forgive me?"

The events of the day might nearly have killed me, but I had not forgotten my purpose in this house—to earn my keep by healing old wounds. All the same, this made me hesitate. I was sure that Marie-Caroline would wish me to speak words of comfort to her dying mother; but to offer forgiveness in the princess' name was surely beyond my right.

I could say nothing but what I thought Marie-Caroline might have said in my place, for all that I was acutely aware of those gleaming fangs, the lithe strength of that encroaching tail. "I think in time I will be able to forgive you, madame. But you've surprised me considerably, and I must consider it."

"I'll change my will. I'll send for my lawyer tomorrow. You shall be reinstated in your inheritance."

"You are very kind." I had had the chance to begin reading Marie-Caroline's journals more closely that afternoon, and I was coming to feel that I really knew her; that she might have been a friend, and that she had deserved much better than this. Whatever forgiving words I might say to Maria Theresa, it was Marie-Caroline who had been wronged, and she was dead. The damage was done. There was nothing Maria Theresa could do or say to set things right.

That knowledge was a terrible burden, filling me with doubt. I had now come to think of the inheritance as Marie-Caroline's rightful property, not my own. Previously, I had soothed old hurts at the modest rate of twenty *kronen* an hour; but how could I justify taking so much in exchange for so little? The rest of the family might be monstrous, but Marie-Caroline had done no wrong: *she* was no melusine. For the first time, I wondered if I was truly being a little dishonest.

I suddenly felt I could scarcely breathe beneath the weight of these questions, beneath the weight of the huge, stifling coils that surrounded me. "May I sit?" I gasped.

With a murmured apology, the Countess loosened her coils and I sank into the chair by the bed, burying my face in my hands. It was a little late to be having second thoughts now, I reminded myself. Perhaps I could not earn this fortune, but I must continue the deception; to save my life if for no other reason.

Perhaps it was just as well the subject of the will had come up tonight, with Maria Theresa dying, and Marie-Caroline cut out of the inheritance altogether. I imagined the bad Baron prevailing upon me to marry him, only to discover that the money had gone to the Bourbon-Parmas after all. It would serve him right, too! I had half a mind to accept him, just to see the look on his face when he learned how he had been duped!

I caught myself before I could burst into overwrought

laughter. I must remain calm and cool-headed if I was to secure my own life, and that of my mother. "Must we wait for the solicitor, madame? If, God forbid, anything was to happen to you in the next day or two, I should be left destitute."

"Nothing will happen to me; I won't allow it." Her breathing was heavy and tired, like a bellows that needs mending lest it give out altogether; yet in her voice was all the self-assurance of an autocrat. No doubt it was difficult for her to imagine a summons she would be unable to refuse. At length she said, "There is an older will in Vienna with my solicitor, leaving all my property to my daughter. I can reinstate it by destroying the new one. Look in the bottom drawer of that chest. There's—there ought to be a wallet in there with certain documents inside."

I obeyed her, pulling open the drawer and unearthing the leather wallet. Inside were certain letters, title deeds, and so on; but of the will there was no sign, even after I had searched it twice.

I felt a moment's involuntary relief. There was a part of me that had begun to doubt what I was doing.

"It isn't here, madame."

"Oh." The Countess blinked wearily. "Now I remember: Margaret took it away for safekeeping. No matter. I will contrive to live until the lawyer comes."

"If you'd prefer, I can ask Aunt Margaret to return the will…"

But the Countess was no longer listening to me. Her husband's imprint appeared, shuffling across the room in comfortably worn slippers, and bending down to kiss her on the forehead with that gesture so like that of my own father.

When the Count faded away, I found the Countess watching

me. "He appears to you, too," she whispered happily.

"Yes," I said, forcing myself to smile. "Why wouldn't I see my own father's ghost?"

The Countess smiled, too drowsy to notice the bitterness I could not quite conceal. Having said good-night, I backed into the corridor and softly closed the door..

When I looked up, Marie-Caroline was coming down the passage towards me.

I could not have moved to save myself. As the imprint came nearer, I saw that she wore a riding-habit and carried a valise in one hand. Outside Maria Theresa's door she hesitated for a moment, the tears trembling in her luminous eyes. A dizzying wash of feeling swept over me: anger, grief, desperation, hope.

Then she went on, down the stairs. For a moment I stood blinking in the turbulence of the runaway princess' thoughts, and then I turned to follow her. I do not think I had any particular plan; only I felt that I must follow and learn what I could.

Making as little sound as possible, I followed the imprint until the stairs deposited us both in the downstairs passage, a mirror of the one above. Marie-Caroline turned to the right and disappeared within the chapel. I followed. As she had done last night, Marie-Caroline knelt before the altar in prayer before proceeding around the inner courtyard and out by the rear vestibule.

I was about to follow Marie-Caroline out of the house altogether when a soft sound startled me almost into an early grave. I turned to find myself facing Blanca—Blanca emerging from the library in the guise of a melusine, carrying a book in one hand and a lamp in the other. Her hair was damp and clinging as though she had been outside in the rain.

"Marie-Caroline!" she said. "How you ssstartled me!"

"Oh, Blanca, it's you—I nearly died of fright myself." I put a hand to my heart, glad it was she and not one of the other melusines I had met with. I had never seen her in this form before, and drew nearer in fascination. Her tail, green and iridescent in the lamplight, was mesmerisingly beautiful by comparison to that of the old Countess. For a moment—let the reader forgive me, for I mean to be perfectly honest—I wondered what a real melusine looked like beneath all those layers of lace and dressing-gown. Then I shook myself, putting the thought resolutely aside. I must have been staring quite shamelessly.

"I'm sssorry," Blanca was saying, hissing between long, curving fangs. "I don't like to be ssseen this way, but one must bathe sssometime. What are you doing downsssstairs?"

I glanced into the vestibule. Of course, the imprint was gone, leaving me none the wiser as to the events of that night three years ago. When I turned again, Blanca was very close to me.

"Is sssomething there?"

She smelled fresh and sweet, like lilies. Beneath that scent was something a little darker, a little muskier, serpentine and just a little thrilling.

"No," I said. And then, because at that moment it was the only thing I could think of to say, I added, "Please don't apologise. I've never seen a lovelier tail."

"Truly?" In the glow of her lantern, her eyes were luminous with pleasure. For a moment she said nothing, as though waiting for me to continue. Then she said, "You ought to have worn yours tonight. It makes you look…powerful."

Oh, I thought. Oh *dear.*

For a moment I felt the way I had standing at the edge of the garden with the Baron: as though one step further would take me beyond the hedges and into the wilderness. But I did not mean to run into the wilderness with the Baron, and I would not run into the wilderness with Blanca, either.

The thought quelled the urge I had felt, just now, to confide in her. Blanca had been here, after all, upon the fateful evening when Marie-Caroline had disappeared, and it had struck me that she might be able to shed some light upon the events of that night. But I could not admit to anyone, least of all the Bourbon-Parmas, what I had seen; for that would mean admitting myself to be an imposter, and I did not think that even Blanca would find that easy to forgive.

I drew back a step, feeling suddenly very cold and lonely in this great, dark, echoing house.

"I don't feel powerful when I wear the tail," I said frankly. "I feel trapped. As for why I came downstairs, I felt like reading a while before bed. I must have lost my way to the library."

"It's jussst through there," Blanca told me; and there was now nothing in her manner but cool politeness. "I was choosing sssomething myssself. Good-night," and to my great relief, she slithered away upstairs.

I went into the library and to my great delight found the English edition of *Can You Forgive Her?* in three volumes with uncut pages. As I tiptoed upstairs again, I resolved to take the next opportunity that presented itself to see everything Marie-Caroline's imprint could show me.—Then I wondered what Blanca had made of our exchange, and whether my excuse for wandering abroad at night had deceived her.

Despite all her charm, I was learning to be cautious of these people, for even the ones who seemed to be my friends concealed an awful savagery beneath their outwardly civilised appearance.

* * *

Once again, I startled awake from troubled dreams with a muffled cry of alarm.

"Lord, madame!" said a voice from the direction of the fireplace. "There I go waking you again. I do beg your pardon."

"Don't give it a moment's thought, Faustine," I muttered, rubbing my bleary eyes to reassure myself that the maid kneeling at the hearth, half lit by the grey light straggling in around the curtains, was really she. "It's my fault. I'm unaccustomed to having someone in to light my fire; I suppose I shall learn to sleep through it in time."

I put it down to a trick of the light that Faustine seemed rather older than she had yesterday. Come to think of it, all the servants in this house seemed to have one foot in the grave. Except for Nijam and that golden-haired young Adonis of a valet, Alphonse, the staff of the castle were all well into their twilight years: rather unusual, that. Most of them had French names, so perhaps they were old retainers who had followed their masters into exile.

"I'll be more careful in future, madame," the maid promised, bending over her kindling again. But as she worked, I heard first one sniff, and then another. I pushed back the coverlet to look at her; then stiffened at the sight of a third person in the room.

A man—clothed as a labourer—stood beside Faustine, staring directly into my eyes with an expression of the most

145

ghastly terror!

"Faustine," I said, when I was able to find my breath—"Faustine, *what has happened?*"

There was a moment's silence. Then Faustine made an inarticulate sound and burst into tears.

"Oh! I beg your pardon," she said, and rushed out of the room, leaving the fire behind, unlit.

The imprint vanished along with her. I put a hand to my heart, which was going like a steam-hammer. Someone had died—but whom? and why?

Chances were it was only some connection of Faustine's—I of all people had reason to know how dangerous a labourer's life could be. All the same—having collected my wits, I dug under my pillows to unearth the transmitter. "Nijam? Are you awake?"

A crackle sounded in the earpiece. "I am now," Nijam said in a quietly murderous voice. "What is it?"

"You realise, don't you," I said shakily, "that if you were a real maid you would already have been up and dressed for hours?"

"Indeed. It is one of the many excellent reasons why nothing could possibly induce me ever to become a real maid."

No doubt that was why she was able to converse with me so freely: the maids with whom she shared a room must have been up for ages. "I'm sorry I woke you, but something is wrong with Faustine. She was terribly upset just now."

There was one of those long, irritated silences, with which I was beginning to be familiar. "You woke me up to tell me one of the housemaids is upset? What do you think I am, Dark? An agony aunt?"

This time the irritated silence was on my end. If she had

not been so stubbornly sceptical, I might have told her the truth of what I had seen. "No, only I thought there might be some news afoot in the servants' hall. I'm afraid it might be a death."

"A death—you mean the Countess?" The voice on the other end was taut, alert. I heard the *ping* of mattress-springs as Nijam arose from her bed. "That would be just our luck, now that you've finally spoken to her about the will. Stay where you are. I'll reconnoitre."

Ten minutes later, the transmitter crackled again. "Dark?" Nijam's voice was hushed, barely audible beneath the clatter of dishes and murmur of voices—she must be in the kitchen or the servants' hall. The commotion was cut off by the sound of a door closing, and Nijam's footsteps began pattering on the back stairs. "Someone died, to be sure, but it wasn't the Countess. It was one of the stable hands."

My heart dropped into my boots. "Not Steiner?"

"That was the name."

My mouth went dry as I recalled the man's staring terror. Could one of the melusines have attacked him, or—? The Baron's promise yesterday to punish those responsible for my accident came to mind, making me shudder. "How did he die?"

"The doctor just looked in to say heart failure. No word as to what caused it." There came a silence broken only by her quickened breath. "Certain varieties of snake venom will do that. This is no coincidence, Dark. If the stable hand needed to be silenced...then you are undoubtedly correct. Someone is trying to kill Marie-Caroline and make it look like an accident."

I had been buttoning up my blouse, but now I sat all in a

heap on the occasional-chair by my bed. If even *Nijam* was convinced of foul games afoot...

"Dark? Are you there?"

"I heard," I said numbly. The next instant the door of my sitting-room burst open and I uttered a ladylike squawk. But it was only Nijam, pale with worry.

"Hush, you'll wake Princess Margaret," she said, gesturing towards the communicating door that led into the next apartment. "We must think. Whoever it is, there must be a way to outmanoeuvre them—to hold them in check."

"Hold them in check?" I said faintly. "Shouldn't we be leaving?"

Nijam looked stubborn. "But this is a sign of success. Our imposture is working. If someone is trying to kill you, it can only be because they truly believe you are the real Marie-Caroline. The question is, who would be so desperate to secure the inheritance? It has to be one of the Bourbon-Parmas, most likely Jaime—or the Duke." Producing a notebook and pencil-stub, she made a note. "I'll ask downstairs. If one of the family is in some financial difficulty, we have our suspect."

"And what then? I don't like exposing either of us to such risk."

"We always knew there would be a risk; why should we give up now? Forewarned is forearmed, after all." She shrugged. "Remember, whoever it is, they're handicapped because they think you are a princess and cannot be killed, like a stable hand, with impunity. What a shame we have this trip to Vienna, just when a little investigation might expose our killer and secure the inheritance!"

"A *shame?*" Vienna seemed to promise security—people—an

outcry, should I disappear. "I can scarcely wait to get out of this awful house."

"The notion of wasting my time in such a way doesn't appeal to *me* at all."

"Oh, come. At least you'll have the chance to spend more time with Alphonse Schmidt."

"That's precisely what I'm afraid of," she muttered.

Reader, I couldn't understand it at all. She evidently *loved* the man, yet as far as I could tell she was avoiding him as she might a leper. Unable to elicit any sense from her, I finished dressing and went nervously downstairs to breakfast.

As I took the passage to the dining-room, I saw Blanca and Jaime in the garden-courtyard locked in some animated discussion. Suddenly Jaime threw his arms wide, and his voice lifted so that I could hear it through the glass of the window: "Stop trying to protect her! I never wanted your help in this."

Blanca caught his arm in warning; her eyes went beyond Jaime and settled upon me, where I stood watching by the window. She smiled, but I thought the look on her face rather strained.

In the dining-room, the atmosphere was no less strained. The Duke, glaring over his newspaper at his sister, seemed to have received some unwelcome item of news. As for Princess Margaret, she only buttered a croissant in a long-suffering sort of way.

"Make a new will?" snapped the Duke. "Whatever for?"

"Robert," Margaret warned him with a look in my direction.

He turned to look at me. "Oh! Marie-Caroline understands, I'm sure. Don't you, cousin? Property has always descended through the male line in our family. What would you do with a castle, anyway? Doesn't your little Baron have a comfortable palace to put you in?"

"I haven't asked him," I said, searching in vain for a kippered herring or a bit of fried bacon among the pastries, fruit, and toast that decorated the breakfast buffet. In truth, I believed in a palace even less than I believed in the existence of a Baron Smilets.

The Baron smiled. "In fact, I have three. A townhouse in Sofia; another in Saint Petersburg; and an estate in Moldavia. This castle is beautiful, but small for my tastes, and inconveniently distant from the city. I would recommend my Marie-Caroline to sell it. At a fair market price, of course. Perhaps you would be interested in purchasing?"

The Duke gaped, no doubt at the thought that he should have to pay good money for a property he looked upon as practically his own. As for Princess Margaret, I thought she might actually stab the Baron with her butter-knife.

"You must reason with our aunt, Margaret!" the Duke said at last, turning to his sister.

"I have already sent for the lawyer," the Princess replied icily. "If you have anything to say to her, you may say it yourself."

The door opened as I took my seat, and Blanca strode in, followed by her brother. Except for the glowering look on Jaime's face, there was no sign of the disagreement in the courtyard. "Good morning, coz," she said, dropping a kiss on my cheek. "Are you ready to visit the opera?"

Chapter XIV.

"Does this bring back any memories?" the Baron asked, leaning close enough that I breathed in the clean, severe scent of his cologne. He smelled like a pine-forest in winter—cold and spicy and faintly alien—but for once, even the bad Baron's proximity was barely enough to tear my attention from the spectacle before me as Delibes' music welled and ebbed, full of lush melodies.

I nibbled my lower lip, considering my answer. I had been occupying Marie-Caroline's shoes—and, tonight, her simple pearls and outmoded evening gown—too short a time to pretend to have recovered all her memories. "I—I don't think I remember anything. Not yet."

"There is time. What do you think of the opera?"

The opera was my first, and I was electrified. The bass, a stern Indian priest in trailing robes and grey false whiskers, was a lissom youth of perhaps twenty. His daughter, a delicate maiden of eighteen, was played by the *prima-donna*—seven feet tall, three wide, and rapidly exiting middle age. Even now the hero, a nondescript tenor who barely reached her shoulder, gestured at the stage, warbling something in the most exquisitely lilting tones about the very spot where the maiden's little foot, as he described it, had trod.

I couldn't help wishing Nijam was here; I had a feeling her comments upon the performance would have been most illuminating. Alas, upon our arrival in the metropolis by train we had deposited the servants with our luggage at the hotel before sallying out to dinner and the great opera-house. The transmitter was in my pocket in case of emergency, but it was switched off, Nijam having begged me not to transmit the entire performance.

"The music is *glorious*," I murmured. "I could almost believe every word of it."

The Baron chuckled appreciatively. "Ah, then you have the secret of opera safe and sound. The trick is to believe, even though you know it is all false. Watching an opera, the audience plays its role as much as do the singers."

I believed him, for he was a man adept at playing roles.—Wonderfully adept, I thought, recalling with a ladylike shudder how he had kissed me with such a practised counterfeit of passion. I did not want to be practised upon.

I have recorded my sensations upon travelling to the Schloss Frohsdorf, of having slipped into the world of a romantic melodrama. Now, returning to Vienna in the guise of a long-lost princess, I felt as though I had sunk even further into the phantasy. The Vienna that welcomed me was a looking-glass city entirely different in disposition to the daylit world in which I had strolled with Ada and Steffi to feed ducks in the Volksgarten: it was a night-time place of shadows and flashing jewels, where the beautiful uniforms and dashing moustaches which never deigned to acknowledge the governess, bowed and twirled before the princess. Not quite knowing what to say, I found myself grateful for Blanca's social effervescence—and even, in a way, for Jaime looming silent and brooding behind me. It was their presence that verified my pretensions. With them, I was Marie-Caroline d'Artois, princess of the exiled Bourbons. Without them I should have sunk like a stone, and I wanted to cling to them like life-preservers.

The curtain fell on the first act and the lights flared, illuminating the jewel-box interior of the great opera-house. It was all done up in red-velvet and gilt, from the petit bourgeois crammed with their wives and mothers-in-law into the stalls, to the upper crust in their boxes, or the hungry-looking students and artists in the high galleries at the back. The audience applauded, stretched and got up; and Blanca, who had drooped beside me yawning at intervals into her glove, now picked up her opera-glasses and leaned forward to make a systematic survey of the assembled dignitaries. As she did so, she made discontented sounds under her breath: I gathered that her prince of Tuscany was proving to be elusive. The rest of us, however, were not left to languish. Jaime and the Baron were kept busy greeting the steady stream of visitors who filed in and out of our box—most of them intent upon an introduction to Marie-Caroline—until at length, to Blanca's delight, the Prince of Tuscany *did* turn up.

"Now that you are here the fun can begin," she declared, linking her arm through his and sending me a conspiratorial wink. "Do take me visiting, Leopold. They've kept me locked up in a castle for weeks. I'm dying for some company."

Gallantly, he consented; and Jaime, frowning, followed.

Amused, the Baron watched them go. "Dear me—we appear to have been left unchaperoned! Quickly, think of something very wicked to do before someone else spoils our tête-à-tête."

I know I ought to have frozen him with a look of ineffable

disgust; or better yet, shrunk from him in maidenly fear. As it was, all I could do was dive behind my fan to conceal my laughter. "I know just the thing. Only it is so terribly wicked, I am not sure you will care to be associated with me afterward."

"Try me," he said.

We had been supplied with programme notes: now I took one and with a few deft folds transformed it into a paper dart. I had, of course, a whole repertoire of paper darts, learned in the course of my employment. The particular make I now employed was one of which I was quite proud, as I had developed it myself by mistake. There are paper darts that fly straight and true; and there are paper darts that twist madly in the air and can be counted upon to hit anything *but* their target. I folded one of the latter and handed it to the Baron with a flourish.

"Little mouse,"—he spoke gravely, but his eyes danced with laughter—"little mouse, the angels will weep for you."

And with a flick of his wrist he launched the dart upon its journey.

I had folded the thing with care and it performed beautifully, shooting upward in a straight line for about fifteen feet before making a sharp left turn, describing a demented arabesque upon an updraft, and curving directly back the way it had come to land in a box a little nearer the stage, where it was greeted with a gentlemanly gasp of surprise and a little gale of laughter.

"Oh, Baron! You hit a very official-looking gentleman."

"So I did!" he murmured, astonished. "Be warned, when they come to arrest me I shall give you up at once. They won't even need to use thumb-screws."

"So ungallant!" I was about to take my seat again, lest we be identified as the source of the disturbance; but then Blanca appeared beside our ribboned-and-medalled victim, holding the dart. "Oh, and there's Blanca!"

Seeing me, Blanca made a droll face and hurled the dart back in our direction. It veered away and plummeted to the stalls; but she had already taken the arm of the official-looking gentleman and was pointing, laughing, in our direction.

"The traitor!" I said ruefully. The official gentleman had raised his opera-glasses. He was not laughing; instead, his lips tightened until they nearly disappeared. Then he lowered the opera-glasses and looked at us with blazing eyes—red eyes—red as blood.

My heart stood still. Beside me, the Baron seemed to have turned to stone.

"Oh dear," I stammered. "I don't suppose we would actually get in trouble, would we?"

"I have made a terrible mistake," the Baron said in a voice so different to his customary tones that I glanced at him to be sure it was really he who had spoken. "We must leave at once."

His dread infected me: my blood ran cold as he steered me to the door. Outside the box, in the blaze of gold that served as a corridor, the crowd had thinned as people returned to their seats for the second act. The Baron's hand fastened like a steel band around my arm as he cut through them, his stride lengthening until I had almost to run to keep up.

"What is wrong, Baron? Do you know that gentleman?"

"I do."

"Who is he?"

"Someone who knows I am not whom I pretend to be."

"And who *are* you, honestly?" As we swept down the grand

staircase towards the two great doors opening onto the street, I caught hold of the banister. "Unhand me! I insist on knowing what is wrong!"

The Baron turned upon me with a flash of bared white teeth. *"Honestly,* it is as I told you: I am Vasily Nikolaevich Romanov." His gaze slipped past me, alighting on something at the top of the stairs; he muttered words under his breath in his own language. *"Come."*

I followed his gaze to see two men running after us to the head of the stairs. Dressed in bowler hats and plain dark suits, they were quite evidently policemen of some sort. One of them shouted something in an incomprehensible language; and then the Baron—*Vasily*—had dragged me into the vestibule and thence out, into the cold and the wet and the haloed gaslight of the Ringstrasse.

"What became of giving me up?" I panted, as we crossed the road to where the ranks of carriages and shivering coachmen awaited the termination of the performance. Behind us, a whistle sounded and was answered with running footsteps.

"I cannot leave you; they have seen you in my company.—Schmidt! *A moi!"*

There was a distant shout of answer from somewhere among the carriages.

"I'm afraid," Vasily murmured under his breath, "that my poor Schmidt is about to receive a very severe shock."

I did not doubt it; Nijam's Alphonse had been quite offended by my suggestion that his master was something other than he seemed to be.

We came upon our carriage and found the horses waiting patiently with steaming breath that floated, gilded by lantern-light, in the wintry air. The conveyance had been hired for the evening—an extravagance justified by the fact that it had been raining an hour or two since, and the melusines among the party preferred not to get wet. Nijam's Alphonse was, for reasons that would shortly become clear to me, acting as our coachman that evening, and ought to have been waiting on or beside the box. But of the young valet himself there was no sign. Seeing this, the man at my side came to a halt with a sharp intake of breath that might have been alarm, or might have been relief.

"Into the carriage with you, my dear."

As he threw the carriage door open, he sent a glance over his shoulder and I followed suit. The sight made my blood run cold. Within the Opera there had been two men on our trail; now there were six. As they closed in, they produced short, sturdy truncheons. One carried a revolver.

The sight made me feel rather faint. I grasped at Vasily's arm. "Who are they?"

He didn't answer, but I felt the tension in his body: his arm was like quivering steel. Just as they were about to reach us, a shadow darted out from between two carriages and set upon our assailants in a terrifyingly rapid flurry of blows. Fists, elbows, and knees came into play: taken by surprise, first one and then another of the strangers dropped to the ground.

There were glints of gold as the lamplight struck sparks off the warrior's head: my lips parted in astonishment. "Is—is that Herr Schmidt?"

Vasily turned to me. "Into the carriage," he said without ceremony. I was by no means certain I wished to obey. Prince or baron, thief or traitor, he was evidently a thoroughly bad lot. His manservant had already demolished at least three policemen. I was supposed to be a princess, and had more need than most princesses to behave in a manner that was above reproach.

It was the purest survival instinct that impelled me into the carriage. Revenants might be a thing of the past, but the police were still expected to be unquestioningly, unhesitatingly obedient to their masters, and I was now well on the wrong side of the law. I scrambled into the box and Vasily followed on my heels, slamming the door just as one of our pursuers reached it and seized the knob. Before he could get it open, he was plucked away and sent sprawling across the cobbles, out of our path. Having thus cleared the way, Nijam's Alphonse reached towards the bench for the reins and whip. He cracked the whip, started the horses moving, and vaulted onto the box almost in one movement.

"Good heavens!" I cried, greatly impressed, "where did you find him?—at the circus?"

"As a matter of fact, I retrieved him from an English reformatory." This piece of information caused me to open my eyes very widely indeed. Alphonse Schmidt had hitherto struck me as being the very last person likely to require the custody of the law.

Shouts rang out from behind us as the carriage accelerated into the Ringstrasse. Behind, I caught a glimpse of our pursuers picking themselves off the street, running after us with waving arms. Then the carriage turned sharply onto the Karntner Strasse, throwing Vasily against me. At the same moment came the loud report of a pistol, repeated twice more. One of the carriage-lamps shattered, and Nijam's Alphonse uttered a cry of pain.

A panel of glass separated us from the coachman's bench—Vasily threw it open. "Schmidt! Are you hurt?"

There was no answer but the thunder of the horses' hooves. Seeing that the valet was listing to one side, I threw myself forward, latching both hands into his coat. "He's fainting!"

"Schmidt!" Vasily cried. "Hold him, madame!"

"What are you going to do?" I gasped—but it was too late; he had thrown open the carriage door and leaned out, swaying wildly, to catch hold of the bench arm-rest.

Hoofbeats echoed from behind us. I turned in my seat. We were being followed—indeed, our assailants were practically upon us: I saw their faces as pale ovals through the windows of a plain brougham that crept inch by inch level with our own.

Through the opening before me, I felt Alphonse slipping. His arms moved through the sleeves of his unbuttoned coat; in another moment I would lose purchase on him altogether and he would plunge forward, beneath the wheels. Impeded by the reckless speed of the vehicle, Vasily was still trying to manoeuvre himself onto the bench. There was a jolt that broke his handhold on one of the lanterns, and the sound of our headlong career changed as the carriage ran onto the Elisabeth Bridge that crossed the River Wien.

It was here that our pursuers pulled level with us at last.

I did not see what happened next. There was a loud splintering sound; the whole carriage shook; the wheels locked; the box fell. I fell from my seat, losing my grip on Nijam's Alphonse. After what seemed a noisy, bumpy, nightmarish eternity, the horses plunged to a squealing halt.

Shakily, I pulled myself from the slanted floor of the carriage and looked about me. Vasily was nowhere to be seen. The plain brougham had come to a halt athwart the bridge ahead of us, and already men spilled out of it. Another drew up behind, positioned to cut off any retreat towards the Ringstrasse. Serious, stocky men converged upon the wrecked carriage—catching the horses, pulling open the door to the box and shouting at me in a language that I was pretty sure must be Russian.

"I do beg your pardon," I said meekly in French, "but I don't take your meaning."

My interlocutor—a short, broad ruffian with instinctively untrustworthy side-whiskers—made his meaning clear with a gesture: I must come out or be fetched by main force. Choosing to preserve what little remained of my dignity, I gathered up the white satin skirts that encumbered me and climbed shivering into the street. From here, I saw what had done the damage to our carriage. One of the Russians must have thrust a folded umbrella through the spokes of the rear wheel and into the springs, splintering the wheel and making the steel struts of the umbrella into an egg-whisk.

I had feared that one of the bumps I had felt during the crash had been the wheels running over Nijam's Alphonse, but now one of the Russians dragged the valet's groaning body from the wreckage of the bench, depositing him upon the cobblestones of the road. Alphonse must have regained consciousness at some point, for he now struggled to his knees, pressing a bloody hand to his ribs.

I wished I could do something for him, but what? The six policemen, despite looking rather the worse for wear after Schmidt's attack outside the Opera, had us surrounded—and even if our carriage had been in anything like working order, the two broughams in which the Russians had arrived blocked the bridge to either end.

The one holding the revolver spoke in French to both

Alphonse and myself. "Where is he? Where is the Grand Duke?"

I opened my eyes very wide. "A Grand Duke? I can't imagine who you mean." Oh heavens, a Grand Duke! thought I. So it was true! But—that was a title granted only to the sons and grandsons of emperors. What on earth had I gotten myself into?

"The man who was with you at the Opera—we know he got into the carriage with you. Where is he?"

"My friends, you're quite mistaken," Alphonse replied, very earnestly. "Contrary to rumour, the gentleman you mean is Baron Dragomir Smilets, a Bulgarian nobleman of impeccable antecedents—"

One of his captors pulled back a fist to strike him, and I interposed quickly, thinking that it would be a great pity to let Nijam's beautiful Alphonse be in any way defaced.

"Oh, you mean *Vasily?* I don't know precisely where he is at present. He must have fallen from the carriage!"

Alphonse sent me a reproachful look, evidently not the least bit grateful. I shook my head at him. I owed Vasily nothing—not as myself, who had excellent reason not to trust him, and still less as Marie-Caroline. And I *did* want to do Nijam a good turn, if possible.

The Russian with the revolver spoke to his men, and three of them split off from the group, first circling the broken-down carriage and then hurrying back in the direction from which we had come. Fog, rising from the stream, had shrouded the bridge in soft clouds, so that between this and the darkness of night, they were quickly out of our sight. While two of the policemen remained to watch Alphonse and myself, the man with the revolver put his weapon away and went to the second carriage, which stood waiting a few metres off: the window was up, and a sinewy hand, adorned with a signet ring, was visible rapping impatient fingers against the door. As the Russians conferred, their hushed voices drifted towards me through the fog: and then stopped dead, because a sound came out of the darkness.

It was not a very loud sound, just a few scuffling footsteps and a grunt. Then—silence.

The revolver appeared again, and its owner stepped away from the carriage, his shoulders tense and alert. "Ilyich?" he called in the direction of the men he had sent away.

Still there was no answer. Beside me, Alphonse's breathing quickened, and he seemed to gather himself into a tighter coil.

The man with the revolver said something sharply to his remaining two men, beckoning them over to join him. With that, things happened with bewildering swiftness. Alphonse's minder seized him by the collar. At the same moment, the side-whiskered man who had been breathing down my own neck reached towards me—but his gesture was arrested with a grunt and a flurry of movement which I barely glimpsed from the corner of my eye. Flinching, I turned to find—nothing. The man with side-whiskers had disappeared.

From the far side of the carriage came a fading yell, cut off by a splash in the water below.

All the hairs on my head prickled. One moment the man had been standing beside me; the next he was plucked from my side and tossed from the bridge—but by what, or whom? Now there were only two of the Russians left, and they exchanged brief terrified glances.

The man with the revolver advanced towards me and settled his weapon, cold and heavy, against my breastbone. He was so close that I saw the sweat beading thickly on his pale skin as he lifted his head to stare into the gathered shadows behind the broken carriage.

"Vasily Nikolaevich!" he called, and added something in his own language.

With his thumb, he pulled back the hammer on the revolver.

I dared not move, but the breath I took was too loud, too quick—too much like a sob.

Vasily darted from the shadows and collided bodily with the Russian. The revolver went off. The bullet struck the carriage beside my shoulder with a sharp *crack,* and a splinter lashed out, striking my bare arm.

To my left, the last of the policemen stood motionless with shock. Nijam's Alphonse moved without rising from the ground: his hand shot up to grasp the other man's arm at the same moment that his legs locked around the Russian's feet. The man fell heavily: I heard the dull thud as his head struck the pavement.

A brief gargling scream drew my attention back to the man with the revolver. Vasily had his face buried in the Russian's neck and now wrenched away with a curiously animalistic gesture that was accompanied by an even more horrifying sound. I saw a bloom of raw flesh and seeping blood across the Russian's throat; and then the Grand Duke hurled his convulsing victim away from him and spat a mouthful of something dark and wet.

"*Sir!*" Alphonse said, shocked; but as for me, I screamed, and it was no pretence at all.

Vasily wiped his mouth on his sleeve. Yet as he turned I saw the smear of red across his cheek—the dark wetness on his coat.

163

"Madame," he said, reaching out for me, "are you hurt?"

With one final squeak, I collapsed onto the doorstep of the broken carriage. "You—you tore out his throat! You *monster!*"

He gave me a bitter and bloody smile. "You dared me to show you my fangs, did you not?"

There came the sound of hands slowly clapping. Behind Vasily, the waiting carriage creaked as the man with the signet ring descended.

"Bravo, Vasya! Very well fought." The voice spoke in heavily-accented French. "Still, what a shame to be so weak, so slow. And the blood—it doesn't taste so good as it once did, hmm?"

Vasily turned and went still, still as a hunted animal caught in the glare of torches. I instantly recognised the man who approached us, puffing meditatively on a cigar. It was the medalled gentleman from the Opera, and at this closer range I saw quite clearly that in addition to the blood-red irises of his eyes, his teeth were elongated, the canines white and sharp.

I was in the presence of a vampire—a real one.

Alphonse got to his feet, putting himself squarely between the monster and his master. "There's been some misunder-standing," he said, rather desperately. "Sir, tell this gentleman who you are!"

The erstwhile Baron paid his servant no heed. "Nikolasha," he murmured. His hands knotted into two white fists. For a moment, I thought Vasily was about to spring bodily upon the newcomer. Instead, he turned and plucked me from the carriage like a rag doll. I am ashamed to admit that in this moment, the blood of the Brixton Darks was not, in any sense, up: I felt as though I was drowning in the cold, sterile scent of pine, mingled as it now was with the hot metallic stench of blood.

"Forgive me, my dear," Vasily whispered, "but it is the monster I need now."

I could neither fathom what he meant, nor protest at his awful proximity as he whisked me to the parapet of the bridge and hurled both of us over the brink.

We fell for a terrifying moment that seemed to go on forever. Then we struck the water with a blow that would have taken my breath away even if the cold had not. Moments later there came the muffled sound of another splash as Nijam's Alphonse followed us. Down, down, we sank, until my feet found the soft silt of the river-bed. Then, our trajectory reversed, we rushed upwards until with a heave and a splutter we emerged into the raw open air of the November night.

I was neither a swimmer nor a diver, and had struck the water with an ungraceful slap that left me sore, terrified, and utterly helpless. For a moment I could only cling to Vasily with weak choking sounds.

"What's this?" he demanded roughly. Beneath the trailing weight of my evening gown, his hands fastened irreverently upon my legs. "Why haven't you changed? Where's the melusine?"

Transferring his grasp to my shoulders, he thrust me ruthlessly beneath the surface. I came back up spluttering; a good deal of the river had gone down my unprepared throat.

"Change," he growled, "why don't you *change!*" and down I went again, my thrashing hands clawing helplessly at his coat.

When I came up again I was almost weeping—I really thought he was about to hold my head under until I drowned. "Stop," I sobbed, "for the love of God, stop it! I'm not—I'm not—"

"*Bozhe moi,*" he said blankly, "you *aren't* the princess?"

A glowing cinder floated from the bridge overhead and plopped into the water beside us. Vasily stilled and looked up; I saw the shape of a head and shoulders leaning over the parapet. As lazy as the smoke from the cigar that glowed between his lips, that pleasant voice drifted down from above:

"I only want to talk to you, Vasya! The others can go, for all I care."

Something smashed against the parapet where the vampire stood—what appeared to be a glass bulb, which shattered when it struck the stones and showered Nikolasha in droplets of the liquid contained within. He recoiled, cursing. Alphonse's voice drifted out of the darkness from the direction of the far shore. "Sir! Sir, we must go!"

Vasily knew my secret—he knew I was useless to him—and for a moment I was sure the Grand Duke would abandon me to my fate, unable to swim in a filthy canal on a late autumn evening in Vienna. Instead, with a low string of words in villainous-sounding Russian, he slipped an arm around me and towed me towards the shore.

Chapter XV.

The silence in the lift was deafening until, at last, Alphonse spoke.

"Do you think they were much hurt, sir?"

"For pity's sake, Schmidt, what does it matter?"

A shuffle of feet. "Well, sir, they were only doing their job."

Vasily raised his eyes to the heavens. "Those gentlemen, Schmidt, were from the Okhrana—the Tsar's secret police. Their *job* is to trespass where they're not wanted. Besides, Vienna is the capital of a rival empire! They're supposed to be protecting Nikolasha, not rampaging in the streets. Whatever we did to them, believe me, it's nothing compared to what would have happened if the Austrians had picked them up. It may yet mean war."

I listened without comment. Since it was, against all odds, true that the bad Baron was indeed a disgraced Russian prince, it was no great surprise to learn that he was also wanted by his Emperor—although what had brought this to pass was beyond my guess.

Hunched over the bloody gash in his side, Nijam's Alphonse nodded meekly. "Of course, sir. Only I don't like hurting people if it isn't necessary."

The Grand Duke shrugged. After that, there was an

uncomfortable silence that went on and on until I cleared my throat diffidently. "Well? Aren't either of you going to *talk* about it?"

"Talk about what?" Vasily asked, coldly.

"The fact that you've been lying to poor Herr Schmidt here!"

Alphonse looked defensive. "In what way has sir been lying to me, madame?"

It wasn't *my* place to enlighten him. I looked expectantly at Vasily, who heaved a sigh.

"Come, Schmidt, you ought to have arrived at the truth by now. I'm not really Baron Dragomir Smilets."

Alphonse's mouth dropped open; but anything he might have said in reply was forestalled as the bell went. We stepped out of the lift and stood, shivering and dripping, in a hallway glimmering with mirrors and marble.

Following our impromptu swim, we had taken a nightmarish rush through the streets to a little tenement on the Rilkeplatz, outwardly dingy but comfortable within. In the fourth-floor hallway where we had now arrived, the fugitive Grand Duke rapped upon one of the doors and cried, "Mimi! Mimi! Open up!"

The door inched open and Vasily attempted to push through it—to no avail, for the chain held it fast. Through the crack thus opened, I glimpsed ash-brown hair and a gamine little face with large hazel-green eyes and a stubborn, pointed chin.

"You!" she said in bad French. *"Voi kauhistuksen kanahäkki,* Vasya! You look terrible."

"Never mind my looks—my friends and I need a place to lie low."

"Oh, no! I'm not in your employment anymore."

"Please, it's a matter of life and death."

"It will do you good to be down and out for once. I don't run a hotel, you know."

"There's money in it. Is someone with you? We'll go away if you're expecting company."

"No one tonight." Her mouth twisted. After a moment, the chain rattled and the door opened again, wider. "Might as well come in, then. Who's with you? They'll cost extra."

"Mimi, you're an angel." Vasily dropped a kiss on her cheek. "Now, if you have a chair for the lady…"

His voice trailed off as he took in the state of the apartment. It must have been a lovely place once—not as extravagant as the Schloss Frohsdorf, but very prettily papered in cream and pale green. I would describe the rest of the furnishings, but there were none. The place was perfectly bare except for a large mirror that reached from ceiling to parqueted floor, and an armchair in teal velvet and polished mahogany that was far too nice for someone as wet and muddy as myself.

The little woman pulled a threadbare shawl more tightly around her thin shoulders and dipped her pointed chin with a look that challenged Vasily to say anything, if he dared.

He did not dare. Instead, he followed me to the tiny fire, where I knelt in the waterlogged ruins of my gown, rubbing my goosefleshed upper arms.

"I have to apologise, mademoiselle. It was far from my intention to expose you to such regrettable scenes."

Although the river had washed most of the blood from his face, his teeth were still glossed a nightmarish red. I would almost have found it more comforting had he possessed the red eyes and elongated teeth of a vampire. Worse, in his manner was a distinct alteration: at the Opera he had been all gallantry and charm, and now he seemed cold, almost wary by comparison.

Of one thing I was glad. There was an unruly part of myself that must be persuaded to remain impervious to this man's charm, and I hoped that it might now be totally convinced.

Still, I did not know what to do, what to say. I was in the possession of a secret which could cost this terrible man his life—and now, being an imposter and no princess at all, I was worthless to him. One incautious word, and might I be the next to have my throat torn out?

If any moment called for the judicious application of feminine wiles, this was it. I burst into tears.

"Here," he said more gently, pulling a flask from his coat pocket. "You're in shock. Drink this."

He held the flask to my lips and I tasted a rather nice cognac. It is one of my small vices that I am fond of brandy, even neat. It reminds me of having a sore throat as a child, and being allowed a nip out of one of Daddy's big cut-glass bottles; a remedy which young Molly *may* have requested somewhat oftener than was strictly necessary. Sadly, the role I had set myself to play did not permit a taste for strong liquor. I turned away with a delicate shudder.

"Oh! it is so nasty!" I cried piteously. "I cannot! Please do not make me!"

To my great annoyance, he responded more like a rational being than the hero of a romantic melodrama. "Be at ease, I don't mean to force it down your throat. You've already swallowed half the River Wien at my behest…Cognac, Schmidt?"

Nijam's Alphonse had folded to the floor near the door, putting his back to the wallpaper. As he accepted the flask, Mimi caught sight of the bloodstain on his hands and waistcoat, and her finely arched eyebrows rose.

"Your man is bleeding."

"So he is. I have an excellent explanation—"

"You always have an excellent explanation, Vasya. It is one of the few things you are really good at."

"You injure me, Mimi. It's such a pretty excuse; I've been rehearsing it all the way here."

"Really, it's a matter of no importance to me, so long as you don't lead trouble to my door."

While Vasily assured Mimi that he had taken care not to be followed, I managed to extract Nijam's transmitter from its hiding-place in the damp, clinging folds of my pocket. I had encased it within a little tin snuff-box in case of accidents, and found to my great relief that not only had it come through the night's adventures intact, but it had survived its drowning.

I switched it on and said in a rather shaky voice, "Nijam? Can you hear me?"

Her voice was fuzzy with distance. "Barely. Where are you speaking from? If it's the Opera, the range on this thing is much less than I thought. I shall have to recalibrate—"

"I'm at 5, Rilkeplatz, on the fourth floor," I told her. "Do you have that? There's been an accident. The Baron and his valet are with me, but Herr Schmidt's been hurt. We'll need changes of clothing; and a first-aid kit, if you can lay your hands on one."

There was a moment's silence, during which I looked up and found Vasily watching me. Beneath his hawk-like gaze, I felt exactly like the little mouse he had named me.

Nijam wasted no time on anxious questions. "I'll be there within fifteen minutes."

"Please." I clicked the transmitter off and faced the Grand

Duke, who might not be a vampire, but was quite as frightening.

All along, of course, I had been doing my best to charm him with my performance of feminine delicacy. He must be terribly angry with me for duping him, and now it would be as much as I could do to save my life, to say nothing of the job I had undertaken.

Vasily's eyes became very cold and bleak. "Get me a glass of water, Mimi. I bit out a man's throat tonight and found it much less enjoyable than it used to be. While you're at it, my poor Schmidt is bleeding somewhat freely, if you have anything with which to stanch the flow... Now, mademoiselle," he went on, addressing me, "let us be honest with each other. Whom have I the honour of addressing, and to whom were you speaking just now?"

I opened my eyes very wide. "I only wished to be helpful. I was calling my maid. She will be along in a few minutes with everything we need to patch up Herr Schmidt and return to the hotel without making a stir. You mustn't worry: Nijam can be trusted, I promise."

"She may come, and welcome. Two necks are as easy to wring as one." The very gentleness of his tone made the words all the more terrifying. "Listen to me very closely, mademoiselle. If you tell a soul of the things you have seen tonight, or my true name, I will make it my first business to hunt you down."

Somewhere in the depths of my own terror, I found the wit to see that he, too, was afraid—afraid like a wild animal, backed into a corner, ready to bite and tear. I did not for a moment feel any pity for him: he was willing to use me as ruthlessly as I was willing to use him.

"Please don't feel obliged to do anything of the sort," I squeaked. "Don't you remember the fable? Even a little mouse may be of assistance to a tiger."

"You have something to propose, little mouse?"

If he was afraid, then he was as vulnerable to me as I was to him. "Dark," I confessed. "My name is Molly Dark. I'm not a princess."

"Molly Dark," he repeated silkily. "I ought to have known from the moment I lost myself in those blue eyes. I've never been even slightly interested in princesses."

"I shall take that as a compliment."

"It isn't. All it means is that you are not vain and spoiled, and have just enough decency to be taken advantage of."

My injured pride got the better of me. "I may not a princess, but with Nijam's help I've been quite able to pass as one. I take it both you and I are in need of a little money. Perhaps we can help each other."

He laughed softly. "Perhaps! I must confess that it would be a great relief to have the money without being compelled to marry for it."

"Really, you were willing to marry me, purely for the sake of Marie-Caroline's inheritance?"

"Why not? I had everything I wanted once—money, power, *teeth*. All those things are gone now, some of them for good. But the money—the money I can have back, and with it some small measure of power."

"May I ask why?" It was, of course, the same question I had put to Nijam, that afternoon in the warehouse when she told me about Alphonse Schmidt. "What would you do with such an inheritance?"

He smiled thinly at me, then turned to where Mimi stood in

the doorway that led to the kitchen. With her patched shawl, bare feet, and upright posture, she looked like a princess reduced to penury.

"Mimi Laine," Vasily said, taking from her the glass of water she held, "tell Miss Dark what you would do with a king's ransom, if you had it."

"What would I do?" Mimi tossed her little head, throwing the thick, ashen hair back from her face. She was not precisely a beautiful woman, but what is mere facial symmetry beside such goblin-like fascination? "I'd stop dangling around Europe, begging for roles at every opera-house. I'd go to complete my training at the Royal Ballet School in Copenhagen. I would become the greatest dancer in the world. After my death they would boil and eat my shoes as they did Taglioni's. And I would only take lovers if I wanted them."

"Only if you wanted them?" Vasily's eyes laughed. "Mimi, I'm hurt! All those sweet things you said to me, last summer in Paris—were they lies?"

"I deny it, Vasily Nikolaevich. I never said a sweet thing to you."

"No more you did. I would never have looked at you twice if you had. At that time I had a terrible appetite for punishment."

"And I had a terrible appetite for money, since I had been thrown out of the Imperial Ballet School in Petersburg for the crime of saying that Finland should be free." She shrugged. "No one wants a *failed* ballerina as a mistress. I knew myself lucky to secure you."

I felt slightly faint. Oh, what would my mother say if she could see me now, sheltering under the roof of a perfectly brazen demimondaine! I scarcely knew what to feel. I did not quite understand why a Grand Duke should find it necessary to punish himself by conducting a joyless affair with a woman whom he paid to be cruel to him, but that it had been a punishment for both of them, I could well believe. On that account I could not help feeling sorry for them. Yet, although one expected men to sow some wild oats—and Vasily, after all, was a Grand Duke—I could not help feeling scandalised to the marrow of my bones by the practicality with which the fallen ballerina spoke.

Then again, Mimi did not *seem* like the sort of shiftless person who would sell herself for money; she evidently had ambitions, and was willing to work hard to achieve them.

"Are you performing at the Grand Opera at present, Miss Laine?" I inquired.

"I don't know, does it *look* like I'm performing at the Opera?" she retorted. "There are six dances in *Lakmé*—six!—and I wasn't able to find a part in any of them. And of course I had secured this flat on the understanding that I was to be a member of the *corps*. It's as I said: no one wants a failed ballerina. I suppose I shall sell the last armchair and that mirror and go to Copenhagen next."

"And if I had a king's ransom, Mimi, I should be your patron and sponsor, rather than a beggar at your door." Vasily glanced towards Alphonse, who was bleeding silently in the corner. "Perhaps, also, I should no longer require my valet to risk his life in my defence."

Mimi followed his gaze. "Don't get that on the wallpaper," she said sharply. "Aren't you going to see to him, Vasya?"

"I don't know if he would consent to having his wounds tended by a Grand Duke," Vasily said; and he actually had the cheek to sound hurt. "Well, Schmidt?"

"Oh, for heaven's sake!" Mimi ran into the kitchen to

retrieve a jug of water and a clean tea-towel. The valet and the Grand Duke, meanwhile, watched each other in wary silence.

"You deceived me." When he spoke at last, Alphonse's voice shook. "Did sir not trust me?"

"Well, I knew you would take it badly, Schmidt, or I might have told you the truth sooner."

Alphonse was immediately cowed. "I don't mean to be ungrateful—"

"Ungrateful? Nonsense!" Re-emerging from the kitchen, Mimi glared at Vasily. "Don't let him pull your strings! If he knew you'd take it so badly, he ought to have told you the truth at the beginning, as he did me."

"He told you?—and not me?"

"I really do think you owe him an explanation, your grace," I put in.

"*And* an apology!" Mimi said, "or out on the street you go, Vasily Nikolaevich!"—Really, she was perfectly fearless.

Vasily sighed. "This never used to happen in Petersburg," he muttered. "Recall, Mimi, that I never told you who I was or wasn't—had we not already made each other's acquaintance in Russia, I might have kept it from you, too. I kept it from you, Schmidt, because servants talk, and in my precarious state I thought it best to surround myself with people who trusted me implicitly."

"You doubted my loyalty, sir."

Vasily's voice hardened. "There have been occasions when I've attempted honesty in the past, Schmidt, and I've generally found it a pretty thankless effort. No one really wants to know the truth about a monster."

"Try me." Alphonse's voice was thick with emotion. "I know what I owe you, even if you do not."

"Try you? I suppose I must, since I don't much like the notion of bleeding you dry. As Nikolasha observed, it's lost its appeal as a pastime." Vasily turned to me. "Well, Miss Dark? Did you receive a satisfactory answer to your question, earlier?"

"I think I did," I said, thoughtfully. "We each want the power to protect ourselves and the people who depend upon us." Moreover, my courage had revived somewhat. Despite all the threats and cajoling, I found, with gratitude to Mimi, that it was difficult to really be afraid of someone whom a five-foot-four ballerina had threatened to throw into the street. Perhaps, after all, Vasily was all bark and no cattle!

"You have dependents, too?" He raised an eyebrow. "Children, perhaps, or a husband?"

"Nothing like that," I assured him, laughing. "My mother must go to a sanatorium before it's too late to treat her consumption. My younger sisters need support in their vocations. And for myself..." I sighed, thinking that perhaps I was not quite as different to Miss Laine as I had thought. "For myself, I wish only to take a husband if I want him."

"Then, Miss Dark, I think we might be able to reach an agreement."

I bowed my head in acquiescence. Of course, any agreement we made would require Nijam's consent; but I didn't think she would be unreasonable about it. If there was one thing of which Nijam had an excess, it was reason. Any more of it, and she would be obliged to commence an export trade in the commodity.

Mimi, meanwhile, had stripped Alphonse to the waist, revealing a nobly sculpted torso which I felt slightly guilty for noticing, particularly as it was bleeding from a long but shallow gash in the side.

"It's only a flesh wound," Vasily observed with evident relief.

"I told you it wasn't serious, sir."

"It still needs a clean. Hold still," said Mimi, bending close to apply a steaming cloth. It was while she was thus employed, of course, that Nijam arrived.

Chapter XVI.

"I'm in the fourth floor hallway," Nijam told me, her transmitted voice now quite crisp and clear.

"Oh, thank goodness. Half a moment." I threw open Mimi's door. Nijam stepped within, saw the tableau ("The Dying Slave, Or, When Rome Was Grand") and turned to stone.

"This is my collaborator, Miss P. Nijam," I announced. Nijam remained in a state of perfect congealment: only her eyes kept flickering from Alphonse, to Mimi, to the ceiling, and back again. She was evidently in shock. Trying to be helpful, I added, "You never told me what the *P* stands for, Nijam."

"It's Padma," she said in a thin, strangled sort of voice. She blinked and looked at me as though realising that she had been startled into an admission she would never have made of her own free will. "But if you use it I shall never speak to you again."

"Believe me, of all the threats I have received this evening, that is by far the nicest."

Too late, it occurred to me that this was not very flattering to Nijam; but she had not even heard me speak. Setting her valise down beside Alphonse, she said very fiercely, "What happened? Who is responsible for this? Was it Jaime?"

Vasily had been watching her laughingly, with eyes that missed nothing. "I believe the responsibility lies with Miss Dark. It was she who folded the paper dart—very badly, I might add!"

On the contrary, the dart had been folded—as it had performed—*beautifully*. But just then it seemed unwise to enlighten him. "May I remind you who threw it straight at the one man in Vienna who knew your face?"

"You were throwing paper darts?" Nijam was bewildered. "Wait: you told the Baron your *name?*"

"Not a Baron," I said.

"Well, of course not. *That* was always clear—"

"Allow me to present the Grand Duke Vasily Nikolaevich Romanov," I continued. "Wanted by the Okhrana—whose attention we attracted by throwing paper darts."

Nijam gave me an incredulous look. "Even you could not be so gullible, Dark! This man isn't a grand duke: if he was one of that cursed brood, he'd be a vampire!—Will someone *please* tell me what is going on, in a rational manner, from beginning to end? And for the love of God, will that man *please* put on a shirt?"

In the end, while Mimi finished bandaging Alphonse using the contents of Nijam's valise, Vasily and I took it in turns to relate the events of the night.

"So," I finished brightly, "what do you say to taking the Grand Duke into our confidence?"

"It appears we have no choice," Nijam said, exchanging a mistrustful glare for Vasily's faint, mocking smile. "What's the proposed split?"

"Half and half," Vasily said at once.

"There are, excuse me, *three* parties to this agreement. You cannot be proposing we should give you half the inheritance merely for not exposing Miss Dark."

"Why not? I did more than that, anyway: I secured your admission to the house. Without that, you would scarcely have had the opportunity to display your tail.—How the deuce did you manage *that,* by the way?"

"Trade secret," I said automatically, but Nijam said, "It's a prosthetic. I make them."

"You make them! Miss Nijam, allow me to congratulate you on your handiwork. You took me in completely. Why aren't you in America? They say prosthetics have caught on there to a far greater extent than in Europe; with your talent, you could be making a fortune."

A flush, just barely detectable. "Not in any way I'd care for. In America they've begun fitting prosthetics to their labourers to enable them to work longer and harder, and the slaves particularly have no choice in the matter."

I didn't understand that last bit. "Slaves? I thought all that traffic was abolished."

"Did I say *slaves?* A slip of the tongue. I ought to have said *working prisoners.* The penal codes, you see, were used to fill the post-war labour shortage."

She spoke with rather more warmth than I had yet detected from her. "Nijam! I had no idea you were such an idealist."

"I'm not," she said more coolly. "I simply know what it is to be suspected as a degenerate merely for the colour of one's skin. I would have nothing to do with such work. Anyway, that's beside the point. The point is that Miss Dark and I have successfully impersonated Marie-Caroline, and while I am willing to acknowledge your past assistance, sir, it remains clear that the Bourbon-Parma family are adamantly opposed to your inheriting. As matters stand, you are more a liability than an asset to our task. I think a recognition in the amount of ten per cent. would be more than ample."

The offer seemed suicidally low to me, but then, I had been present for the confrontation on the bridge, and Nijam had not.

To my relief, Vasily only laughed. "You cannot be fool enough to expect me to take so little, Miss Nijam. I presume you were thinking of presenting me with perhaps as much as a quarter. But I am becoming industrious in the course of my afterlife. I would be willing to earn my keep, and besides, I must think of Schmidt's future as well as my own. I will accept no less than even thirds."

"That seems fair," I said hastily.

Nijam sent me a look of daggers. "Not to me, it doesn't. You and I will speak about this, Dark. In the meantime, we should return to the hotel before our disappearance is remarked."

The following half-hour was taken up with hastily patching up Alphonse and changing our garments. As we bade Mimi farewell, Vasily said to her:

"Come to Wiener Neustadt when you have sold your mirror. There is a *danseuse* living in retirement there, a pupil of Taglioni's. I will put in a good word for you."

Mimi's narrow face lit up like a lantern. "Give me her name and I will take tomorrow's train," she promised.

Outside, on the Karntnerstrasse, Vasily hailed a cab for Nijam and myself. "Time is fleeting, ladies," he told us. "Have your talk, and when we reach the Opera I will hear your verdict."

Our conveyance whisked us away, leaving Vasily and Nijam's Alphonse waiting in the street for a second cab.

Meanwhile, within the dimness of the box, Nijam pinned me with one of her most irritable glares.

Perceiving that she was building up a fine head of steam, I forestalled her by saying, "I don't understand you, Nijam! There was poor Herr Schmidt half dead on the floor, and you scolded him like a midwife. I thought you loved the poor fellow."

"I should be greatly obliged, Dark, if you would confine your remarks to the topic at hand. What can you mean by offering that adventurer a third of the inheritance?"

"I watched him kill a man tonight—one of those that attacked us." I could not bring myself to say how. My voice had gone a little squeaky with fear.

Nijam's eyebrows shot up. "That is hardly an argument in favour of an alliance."

"It *is* an argument in favour of not antagonising him. Don't forget that we are in possession of his secret. I shudder to think what he might do if we let the fat out of the bag."

"The cat," Nijam said wearily.

"What do cats have to do with it?"

"Cats come out of bags. Fat goes in fires. Paper darts do *not* belong at the Opera. What were you *thinking*, Dark?"

"I wasn't thinking."

"Evidently."

"How was I to *know* there was a Russian potentate in attendance?"

"You weren't to know that—you were to think twice before making a public exhibition of yourselves!" There was an uncomfortable silence. "Do you really believe the Baron—the Grand Duke, that is—poses a risk to this endeavour?"

I considered this for a moment in silence. "I don't think he would kill us."

"What makes you so certain?"

"I'm not certain," I said frankly. "I'd bet on it, all the same. Men like that pride themselves on a code of conduct which forbids them offering overt violence to a lady. I seem to have convinced this Vasily Nikolaevich that that is what I am."

"You will appeal to his sense of *chivalry?*"

"He evidently has one. He's never offered *me* violence—and at no point did he abandon me to his enemies, even when it might have made his own escape more certain. No; if he did anything, he would try to outwit us, not to wring our necks. He might seize control of the inheritance, for instance, based upon his supposed relation to the heiress. Offering him equal thirds is our best guarantee to keep him happy, while salvaging what we can for ourselves—and keeping an eye on him should he decide to betray us."

There was a lengthy silence as Nijam considered this. At last she said, "Thus far, your assessment of human nature has been more accurate than mine. Very well: since we have no other choice, I will agree to the division in even thirds. But the Baron must relinquish all claim to Marie-Caroline's hand."

I agreed, relieved to find that she had at last come to my way of thinking. In any case there was little time to discuss it further, for we soon arrived at the Hotel Imperial, that palatial edifice of white neoclassical marble. Since the night had left its mark upon me in the form of damp and disarranged hair, we lost no time in retreating to my rooms on the second floor. Here, Blanca and I shared a suite consisting of two bedrooms opening onto a luxurious cream-green-and-gold sitting-room—an arrangement echoed more sparsely upstairs, where Nijam and Blanca's lady's maid shared a smaller room in the servants' accommodation.

Just as I had finished combing my hair, a knock at the sitting-room door heralded Vasily's arrival. "Come further in," I said, beckoning him into my own chamber. "The sitting room isn't private, and Blanca or her maid will be arriving any minute. Are you alone? Where is Herr Schmidt?"

I asked that question for Nijam's sake, since she evidently did not mean to ask it herself. Vasily assured me he had seen the injured hero safely upstairs to bed, and added that he had come to receive our answer.

His brows rose as we told him that we would agree to a three-way division so long as he gave up his claim to Marie-Caroline's hand.

"You can scarcely expect me to agree to *that*," he said, rather disdainfully. "The moment you and I call it off, the Bourbon-Parmas will throw me out of the house altogether, and we will be quite unable to assist each other."

"We will contrive to manage without you," said Nijam, with fortitude.

"It would be better to keep me around," he argued. "I know how people like the Bourbon-Parmas think, and what they expect."

"He's right, you know," I told Nijam. "So far, all my experience has been with bourgeois ladies. His grace's assistance has been invaluable."

Nijam's eyes narrowed. "We need to know you will not press your claim to the princess' hand," she said, addressing Vasily.

"Oh!—in *that* case—" and, reaching into his breast pocket, he extracted the false marriage certificate and handed it to me with a flourish. "An earnest of my good faith. You may destroy it at once, if you like."

As a guarantee of his good faith, it was hardly worth much. Surely, if he had fabricated one marriage certificate, a second would scarcely present any trouble—but there was little Nijam or I could do about that.

"And Marie-Caroline's final journal," I wheedled him. "We are partners now; do let me see it."

"I don't have it with me, but you shall see it when we have returned to Schloss Frohsdorf."

There seemed little else we might be able to extract from him, so I turned to Nijam. "Are you content?"

"For now," she said, echoing my own thoughts.

"Then we have an agreement. Shake hands on it?" Vasily grasped hands with each of us in turn, and then Nijam went into the hallway to make sure that the coast was clear for his departure.

It had been a refreshingly businesslike meeting. As we waited for Nijam's return, I ventured to say, "I'm glad for this arrangement."

"Oh?"

"From now on we will be able to work on a purely professional basis, without all that exhausting business of pretending to court each other."

There was something altogether too mocking in the smile with which he answered mine. "Did you find it exhausting? I was quite refreshed by it, myself."

What was *that* supposed to mean? I was still trying to parse his comment when his smile chilled to ice and he said, "Are you afraid of me, Miss Dark?"

"Afraid of you! Not particularly." It was true. If a woman

like Mimi Laine was not afraid of him—but then it occurred to me to wonder whether Mimi was quite sane herself.

"You ought to be," he said, all gleaming teeth and bitterness. "You may not be a princess, Miss Dark, but you are very much a lady, and so I ask you to promise me something."

I opened my eyes, very wide and innocent.

"Promise," he went on, seizing my hand, "that when all this is done and you have what you need for your family, you will leave this game behind you. The world is full of monsters, my dear, both with tails and without them."

"Monsters!" I said, drawing a fortifying breath. "And do you include yourself among their number, your grace?"

"Myself most of all."

Well, of course he could scarcely deny it, after what I had seen with my own eyes. Although I had argued for an alliance with the man, I beg the reader not to believe that I gave him my trust. Vasily's chivalry only went so far: he cared only about the money, and while I was willing to share with him if I had no other choice, I did not mean to let him swindle me.

All these thoughts flashed through my mind as I stood looking up into his grim face, with its cold eyes and thinly-drawn lips. Now, suddenly, a commotion intruded upon our respective thoughts. The sitting-room beyond the bedroom door was flooded with voices. I heard Nijam's voice lifted in protest, Blanca saying something about the police, and the tramp of a great many feet. Startled, Vasily and I turned towards the door just as it opened and a great crowd of people spilled in.

Chapter XVII.

The silence that descended was as sudden and positive a thing as the former uproar. At the head of the procession that had invaded my room was a pair of short, beefy men in bowler hats and side-whiskers. Behind them stood Blanca, and a Nijam whose cheeks had gone, if not precisely pale, a rather unhealthy-looking grey. Beyond, craning their necks to see, were Jaime and the Prince of Tuscany; there were also a couple of journalistic-looking men with pens and notebooks at the ready, and a prosperous-looking citizen whom I recognised as the hotel's manager.

"What is the meaning of this?" I gasped, so overwhelmed that I forgot to withdraw my hand from Vasily's grasp.

"Why, you disappeared from the Opera, cousin!" Blanca cried, putting a hand over her heart. "Your carriage was dis-covered broken to shivers on the Elisabeth Bridge! What was I to think, but that some terrible misfortune had overtaken you?"

The bowler-hatted men—detectives, no doubt—snatched off their hats in some consternation, and now apologised for their intrusion. Releasing my hand, Vasily smiled upon them and shook their hands; I saw a glint of gold as he did so.

"I'm terribly sorry for the trouble," he said winningly. "It happened that the princess felt unwell in the overheated Opera, and begged me to conduct her home. As for the carriage, I really cannot explain its condition. We chose to walk, since the rain had cleared."

The policemen bowed and said that they quite understood, but it fell to one of the journalists, pencil poised, to ask the question I had been dreading.

"And you, sir—I take it that the rumours are true, then? You are the princess' husband?"

Everyone was looking at us. Everyone was silent, waiting for an answer.

No one said what was going through everyone's mind. Vasily had been discovered ensconced tête-à-tête within the princess' private chamber. Times—and morals—had become easier than they were in my mother's day, but even so, I was supposed to be a princess, and quite above reproach.

Had I had my wits about me, I might have fobbed them off with an explanation—a betrothal, for instance, might have explained our intimacy in a way that preserved my reputation without binding me to the Grand Duke for good—but for one decisive moment, all I could think of was my mother's face when she saw my portrait in the newspapers associated with such a scandal.

It was ridiculous, of course—even if such a thing happened, the name linked with it would have been Marie-Caroline's, not my own. But the thought held me speechless a moment too long: and in that moment, my opportunity was lost.

Vasily turned back to me and tucked my hand within the crook of his arm. "This lady," he affirmed, "is my wife. She has just recovered her memories of that fact. Isn't that so, my dear?"

Nijam was shaking her head at me. I knew what she meant to convey, but it was too late—Vasily had seized the advantage.

"It is," I whispered, hiding my face in his waistcoat, as though overcome with emotion. "My own Dragomir!"

* * *

Nijam, in a few pithy words delivered via transmitter in a moment of privacy, told me that I was being a middle-class English prude, and that on the Continent they were more forgiving. But the longer I brooded over the evening's events, the more certain I felt that under the circumstances, it was the only thing I could possibly have said. The Bourbon-Parmas might not approve of Vasily, but for the present it was safer to present a united front: to contradict each other in public would call into question the veracity of both. In any case, the thing was done, and might ultimately prove to my advantage: all of Vienna would now hear of Marie-Caroline's romantic elopement and return. There was a certain kind of security in that.

There was little time to discuss the matter the following morning, taken up as it was by our return to Schloss Frohsdorf. The whole journey home, Vasily danced attendance on me with gallant assiduity until I could cheerfully have throttled him. Deep down, I scarcely knew who I was angrier with—Vasily for his betrayal, or myself for having allowed him the opportunity to speak. For the sake of appearances, however, I played my part to the hilt: giggling like a schoolgirl, holding the traitor's hand, and fatuously explaining the way in which the opera was supposed to have jogged my memory. Blanca watched us with every appearance of real pleasure, and only Nijam and Jaime, for very different reasons, spoiled the mood with their scowls.

Arriving back at the Schloss around midday, we found the house in a sleepy mood, which enabled Blanca to corner me in the courtyard as I was coming away from lunch.

"I was *so* pleased to hear you'd recovered your memories," she said, putting an affectionate arm around my waist, "but I wanted to ask you something first. Please don't take it amiss, but are you sure you *did* remember marrying the Baron? You aren't simply—accepting him to stave off scandal? I wouldn't ask," she added, as my face warmed with embarrassment, "only we did come upon the pair of you rather suddenly, by surprise as it were. You may confide in me, you know. I don't want the Baron or anyone taking advantage of you."

She was terribly perceptive, and it bothered me that the only thing I could do was lie to her. "I did remember him, truly," I assured her in a meek whisper, wondering how I could extricate myself from her arm without causing remark. "And I am happier than I can say."

Blanca sighed, deep and satisfied, and squeezed my waist. "Dear cousin! I'm truly glad to hear it, you cannot imagine. But what about the rest of the family? You ought to tell them; right away, at dinner tonight. Between you and me, I wonder if you might not face a good deal of trouble because of this. Some of the family would sooner die than see the Schloss given to a mere Baron."

Or even kill, thought I with an involuntary shudder, recalling the burst girth and the dead stable hand. The journey to Vienna, though not without incident, had relieved me of the burden of wondering when next there would be an attempt upon my life. Now I must be once more upon my guard—I could not afford to relax my vigilance for a moment.

Thanking Blanca for her advice, I escaped to my room, where Nijam awaited me with grimly folded arms and, unusually for her, not a screwdriver or a soldering-torch in sight.

"You promised me you would handle Vasily," she began by way of preamble. "You were ready to head him off if he took the opportunity to betray us."

"I really am sorry," I said humbly. "I was so flustered in the moment that he was able to say what he liked."

"And now you are tied to the 'Baron' and liable to get all of us thrown out of the Schloss together. There's no help for it now, of course. You will need to make it work as best you may."

"At least Blanca is on our side," I pointed out hopefully, but Nijam, who had listened via the transmitter to the exchange in the courtyard, snorted.

"I shouldn't trust her overmuch if I were you. I overheard the Infante shouting in her room a little while since. I don't know what he said; it was in Spanish." Nijam pressed her hands to her temples, looking—for a moment—curiously lost. "There are too many factors at play. This game has become horribly complicated. I wish it could be simplified somehow."

"Sometimes one can only weather the storm," I told her, trying to be encouraging.

"I don't want storms. How can anyone function in circumstances of total unpredictability?"

I blinked at her, struck by a thought. "Is that why you won't tell Alphonse Schmidt you love him—because you don't know how he'll respond?"

She stared at me for a moment with parted lips. "No, that

isn't it," she snapped. "It's because I know *precisely* how he'll respond. How can I tell Schmidt what once lay between us? He would feel obliged to return my feelings. I abhor all such forms of manipulation."

"How is it manipulation to tell someone the truth?" Nijam did not reply to this, either by word or by expression. "Is that it, then? Is driving him away the only possible alternative?"

"I cannot conceive what business you think it is of yours." A bundle of letters lay beside her on an occasional-table, and now she picked them up and thrust them towards me. "Speaking of *your business,* while we were in Vienna I collected the mail you asked me for. Don't forget to burn it all thoroughly when you're done with it; the last thing we need is one of the housemaids coming upon a letter addressed to Molly Dark."

This said, she threw back the lid of the chest and dove into her collection of tools, wires, and tiny cogs. Since she evidently wished to be alone, I retreated to my bedroom and looked through my correspondence. There were one or two bills, which I tossed into the fireplace without reading. But there was also a letter from home, and I tore it open with eager fingers.

My mother wrote that after some inquiry, she had discovered a small sanatorium which had recently been opened in Norfolk, where she might undergo a cure for a lower price than in Switzerland or Scotland; and for that matter there would be a great deal of money saved on the journey. She had inquired as to the cost of two months' stay, a figure which made me open my eyes and whistle. It was not a *very* great sum, but it was just enough to be beyond our reach, unless we should sell our house. And that, my mother seemed to think, would be ruinous.

I spent the afternoon composing my reply, telling her to go to the sanatorium at once, whether it meant taking a loan from Sir Humphrey or some other of Daddy's former associates, or mortgaging the house if this could not be arranged—for Sir Humphrey's business took him often out of the country. Having blotted and directed the letter, I slipped it into my pocket, ready to be posted. My mother's letter, also, I kept. The reply was as incriminating as the original, and I might as well keep the latter until I had posted the former.

This done, I sat down to finish reading Marie-Caroline's old journals. By now they had become full of new and somewhat uncomfortable thoughts. *A good man leaveth an inheritance to his children's children: and the wealth of the sinner is laid up for the just,* Marie-Caroline had copied down, and then in her round schoolgirlish hand had added the thought, *Wealth is not given us to be used as we like. It is given on trust, to be used for the good of our neighbours, and will depart from us if we use it wrongly.* That made me wonder whether Marie-Caroline herself had felt entitled to inherit her parents' money; and I found myself thoughtfully contemplating the well-stocked jewel-box upon the dressing-table. She had not even taken the traditional course of lining her unmentionables with diamonds.

Shortly after this, the gong sounded for dinner. I called Nijam in and had her affix my false tail, for if I meant to foist an unwanted baron upon the family, it was incumbent upon me to put on the best show I could.

Nijam was still fussing over the tail, asking whether she should fasten it more tightly, when my father's imprint appeared, walking into the room with the same familiar, shuffling gait as ever. As ever, he spoke voicelessly and pressed a kiss to my forehead. He had never intruded upon me in the presence of a third person, and for a moment I went quite stiff with dread. Was I going mad?

Nijam recalled me to present matters by snapping her fingers under my nose. "Dark? Did you hear me?"

"Yes," I said automatically. She repeated herself anyway, saying something about being sure to return to my apartments by midnight, lest the batteries that powered my tail should give out as they had upon my former excursion as a melusine. I assured her that I would: apart from anything else, I meant to make another attempt at following Marie-Caroline's imprint, which I knew from my previous two evenings at the Schloss to appear promptly on the stroke of twelve.

I repressed a shiver. If the imprints were encroaching upon my life in such a manner, was it really wise to seek out more of them? As I left the room and slithered towards the stairs, I felt the cold air of the asylum breathing down my neck.

It was Vasily who banished my goose-pimples by meeting me at the top of the stairs and leaning forward to take my hands and kiss my cheek. "You look splendid," he told me with an unbidden half-smile. I knew he was referring to the tail as a matter of purely professional courtesy, but could not help feeling warm and pleasantly flustered all the same.

"Between you and me," I told him, shaking off my foreboding, "I think we are about to light a fire beneath the Duke Robert's chair."

"Most appealing—but is this to be a literal or a figurative fire?"

"I'm shocked you must ask. Figurative, of course! I imagine the shock of learning that the last heiress of the Bourbons has ratified her marriage to a mere Baron will be far more distressing than genuine flames."

His eyes lingered upon me just a little too long for comfort. "Sometimes, you remind me of someone I once knew."

"Really? Whom?"

His eyes crinkled at the corners. "Someone who would have kindled a very literal fire. Shall we?"

We descended the stairs and crossed the courtyard towards the drawing-room where the family habitually gathered before dinner. It had been my intention to follow Blanca's advice and confess at once to the family; but the opportunity was not afforded us. Instead, we entered by the French windows to find the decrepit butler in the act of ushering in a sombrely-clad gentleman by another door.

"Herr Brunner," the butler announced, his voice shedding a damper upon what there was of the party's spirits. Hearing the name, the Duke of Parma let loose a snort of something that certainly did not resemble a welcome.

"Ah! The lawyer! This is the final straw!"

Clutching a briefcase beneath one elbow, Herr Brunner bowed. "Her Grace has requested my attendance to draft her a new will." With that, he caught a glimpse of me and Vasily. "So it's true then! Madame, allow me to proffer my hearty good wishes and congratulations upon your return. A happy day, a very happy day indeed.—I read about it in the papers. And your husband, too!" He fixed the Grand Duke with a somewhat less enthusiastic gaze. "Sir, my felicitations upon your advantageous marriage."

"What's this?" Princess Margaret said sharply. "The papers? A marriage? I've heard of no such thing."

"I learned of it just now," said Duke Robert, breathing stertoriously, and tossing a newspaper down beside his sister.

"How do you like this, eh? Our cousin has abandoned her high station in life! She was born a royal countess; she has made herself a mere parvenu baroness! Disgraceful!"

Princess Margaret snatched up the paper with a gasp. Over her shoulder, I glimpsed pen-and-ink portraits of Vasily and myself, romanticised almost beyond recognition. *"Royal Fairytale,"* Princess Margaret read under her breath. *"Runaway Princess Regains Memories—And Love. Romantic Scene at the Opera.* Marie-Caroline! Did you mean at any point to inform your family of this development?"

"I meant to tell you this very evening," said I, chastened. It was bad enough to be caught backfooted in such a way, but the worst thing was the lawyer's presence.

Duke Robert scowled at Vasily. "Well, there we have it! The last remnant of the great Bourbon patrimony, handed over to some Bulgarian no one has ever heard of!"

"Obscure I may be," Vasily said with a glint of teeth, "but at least *I* was not sent into exile because I was too weak to hold *my* patrimony."

"What are you saying? You dare? Damn your eyes, sir, if you were in any way my equal in rank, I should call you out!"

"And if you were in any way my equal in skill, I should accept," Vasily said above the general outcry. At that, the Duke almost turned purple.

"I'll thrash him!" he cried. "To be so insulted in my own house!" His wife got up in a languid sort of way to assist the lawyer in holding him back.

"An error of fact," panted Herr Brunner. "The house is not yours, my lord, and certainly not during the lifetime of the present incumbent. Pray calm yourself. Such wild talk will not assist you at all."

"Sit down, Robert, and show some dignity," Princess Margaret said, and such was the force of her personality that her brother did as he was told. "You presume upon your welcome, Baron.—Herr Brunner."

"Madame?" puffed the little lawyer, straightening his coat jacket.

"The Countess of Chambord is old and in failing health. I do not know whether she is of sound mind and competent to be altering her dispositions."

"Have no fear, madame. I will speak to the Countess and form my own opinion of her mental faculties before making the will."

Princess Margaret bowed her head, but I detected in her manner a grim dissatisfaction. Unless he was hopelessly corrupt, Herr Brunner must conclude that Maria Theresa was quite clear in her wits and perfectly entitled to restore the inheritance to her daughter.

I exchanged glances with Vasily and saw that he had come to the same conclusion as myself. The family would not give up their inheritance easily. They meant to fight.

But even at that late hour I could not have imagined the lengths to which they would go in order to secure what they already looked upon as their own property.

Chapter XVIII.

"I don't think my cousins are willing to let a mere baroness inherit," I confided to Maria Theresa that evening. "Princess Margaret made a point of telling the lawyer you were not sufficiently of sound mind to be re-making your will."

"What a nerve the girl has!" said the Countess wrathfully. "Am I to be bullied out of leaving my property to my only child?"

"Then you don't mind that I've married a baron, madame?"

"Well, at least he isn't a singing-tutor." There was a moment's silence. "In any case," she added in more subdued tones, "even if he *was* a singing-tutor I have forfeited my right to object. Don't be afraid, my dear—Herr Brunner is an honest man, and won't let Margaret frighten him. Tomorrow you shall be returned to your rightful place."

Such an admission could not have been easy for the autocratic old lady to make, and for a moment I could scarcely speak for genuine emotion. Marie-Caroline was dead and gone and would never be able to say it herself; but I was so bold as to kiss the countess good night and tell her that all was forgiven.

I felt somewhat unsettled in my mind as I watched Maria Theresa drift into sleep. Not because I was about to deprive the Bourbon-Parmas of their share of the inheritance: they were, except possibly Blanca, a pack of bullies who despised anyone a step lower than themselves. But how I wished that Marie-Caroline was still alive, that I might reinstate her in the place to which she belonged!

Marie-Caroline had undoubtedly departed the castle for good reasons. What disaster had befallen her? She had deserved happiness, and I could believe that if anyone was capable of finding that elusive blue bird, it was she. Kind hearts, if that's the expression I'm looking for, are thicker than water. For a moment I imagined the life Marie-Caroline wished for, a life of simple comforts and no great wealth; happy, contented, and virtuous, among friends who loved her undemandingly. I saw in my mind's eye, not the rose-covered house I had at first imagined, but something rather like our own plain little house in Brixton, with its privet hedge out the front, and myself leaning against the gate, waiting in the gilded evening for the return of a handsome man with enthralling green eyes... It was that preposterous image which shook me from my daydream, and I recoiled at my own fatuity. I might as well imagine Blanca in *that* role. The duplicitous Grand Duke was not for the likes of me—a pleasant domesticity was not for the likes of Vasily—and apart from all that, if I was to marry at all it must be to one who could help to assure my family's financial security.

When I returned to my own suite, I found the chest locked and Nijam gone, doubtless to bed. It was still an hour short of midnight, when Marie-Caroline's imprint could be expected, so I decided to employ the spare time in tidying the bedroom. Morning-dresses and cologne-bottles and travelling-cases were all strewn about where I had dropped them during the course of the day, and anyone who entered would be able to tell at a glance that my maid was not doing her job.

As I wriggled from the hot confines of my tail, I switched on my transmitter and made a brief report on the evening's events and complications.

"Forget about opposition from the family," Nijam directed in a whisper. "Let's keep our sights on the will. That's the main battle now."

She sounded a little more confident now than she had this afternoon; reflection must have shown her some way forward. Swathing myself in my dressing-gown, I switched off the transmitter and quickly straightened the room. Later, I was to remember that when I picked up my day-dress, I wondered whether I had really left it straggling over the floor like that: I was quite certain I remembered tossing it across the occasional-chair. My mother's letter, however, together with the reply, was still safely tucked into the pocket. Using the key she had left with me, I stowed them both in Nijam's chest along with the equally incriminating tail.

With my room tidied, it occurred to me that the evening's business was not yet over. There was now a third member of our alliance, and I still had time to pay him a visit before Marie-Caroline's imprint appeared. Sighing, I started along the corridor towards Vasily's room.

I had just rounded the western corner above the great staircase when a faint rustle and the almost inaudible creak of a floorboard warned me of someone approaching from the south. Preferring not to be seen abroad at this hour, certainly not without my tail, I hid behind the heavy velvet curtains in one of the window-alcoves to my left.

The person in the passage proceeded with a soft, rustling

slither that told me it was a melusine. As it approached my
hiding-place it stopped, and I heard the sound of *sniffing.* I was
reminded rather forcibly of a time when I had been hiding in
a tree from a large and unfriendly dog which seemed to think
that apples grown on its master's land belonged exclusively
to its master: it was an ominous, predatory sort of sound, and
after a moment it rustled nearer. I pressed my back against
the window. The catch prodded against me, and I found
myself wildly calculating my chances of survival should I hurl
myself from the heights as opposed to allowing the melusine
to discover me.

Just as I had given myself up for dead, a door opened
somewhere further down the passage. "Good evening, sir," a
voice said. "Does sir require some assistance?"

The voice belonged to Nijam's Alphonse, and I could have
called down blessings upon his golden head. The melusine
beyond the curtain snapped, "Mind your own business" and
resumed its slithering. I tweaked back the fringe of the curtain
and saw Robert of Parma, clad in a luxurious dressing-gown
of brocade and velvet, retreating in the direction of the stairs.

Shaken, I emerged from my hiding-place. "I'm much
obliged to you, Herr Schmidt," I whispered with feeling
gratitude. "Is Vasily in?"

"He is, fraulein; do you wish me to accompany you?"

It took me a moment to realise he was offering to chaperone
us. It would, however, look pretty odd for a man's valet to be
present at a *rendez-vous* with his own wife. "That depends,"
I said. "Is your master the sort of man to offer a woman an
insult?"

To that he responded with genuine horror. "Fraulein! Sir
would never. Sir is a perfect gentleman."

"And I," I said with some amusement, "am a perfect lady. Thank you, Schmidt; that discharges your duty, and now you might as well get some rest."

I entered Vasily's room to find him also dressing-gowned. "Ah, Miss Dark," he greeted me. "I was about to come in search of you myself."

"My mother would be shocked to hear of such goings-on," I said lightly, going over to warm myself at the banked-down fire. "For that matter, dear little Schmidt was pretty shocked when I passed him in the corridor just now."

"I flatter myself that it's rather convenient, this new arrangement of ours. We may collude all we like, and if we are caught, we are only indulging in a little conjugal familiarity."

I sent him my most disapproving look, but he pretended not to see it. "Yes, and I'm sure the same thought will occur as forcibly to the Bourbon-Parmas. You've made this whole affair vastly more difficult. Maria Theresa has promised me nothing shall dissuade her from reinstating her daughter in her will, but you heard what Princess Margaret said to the lawyer. I'm afraid the melusines are about to revolt—and that's without your offending the Duke."

"I must apologise for that," Vasily said, frowning. "It was ill-judged. If I was truly a baron I would know my place and the obsequiousness due to it."

That nearly made me laugh. "Well, I've known barons, and obsequiousness is not the precise word I should employ to describe any of them."

"Had you been born a princess, you would have seen a different side to the species," Vasily said with a glimmer of humour. It passed, and his brows contracted to a scowl. "And had I still my fangs, I should have accepted Robert's duel and taught him a lesson he should not quickly forget."

"Heaven forbid!" I shuddered delicately. "It's a great mercy that in England we have a royal family who are *not* monsters."

He sent me the oddest look. "Do you really believe that?"

"You may see it differently, your grace, but yes; I think it *is* a mercy to have *one* kingdom in Europe where the people are safe from the depredations of their rulers, and I believe I am not alone in the opinion. But as regards our predicament, a solution has occurred to me. If it's a prince of royal blood the Bourbon-Parmas want, why can't we give them one? Surely a Russian Grand Duke would be sufficiently royal for the last Bourbon princess."

"It would never do—they would expect a vampire, and I am clearly not one of *them.*"

"One day," I said coaxingly, "you really must tell me how that came about."

"Must I?" he replied with soft laughter. "It wouldn't do, little mouse. To tell them I am a Russian prince, in my defanged state, would be as good as sending a telegram to Petersburg to say *Vasily Nikolaevich Is Here.* And if that was known...it would not only be the Okhrana on my trail then. And you would not wish to be within a hundred miles of me when *that* happens."

"All this, and you won't tell me what you did? Was it assassination? Did you kill the late tsar? Or run away with an actress? Or were you rude to someone's grandmother? Come, your grace, if you don't tell me *something* I shall die of curiosity, like the proverbial rat."

"It's a cat," he said, now laughing in earnest.

There I could correct him. "On the contrary, I'm reliably informed those come in bags."

"You shall go into a bag if you won't behave," he began, but before the conversation—or whatever it had degenerated into—could proceed, the electric lights flickered and went out, leaving only a small oil-lamp burning on the table beside Vasily's bed. The transmitter in my ear shrieked, forcing me to tear it from my head. The next moment, impelled by an icy wind, the door of the room burst open.

I looked up to behold—Maria Theresa.

The old Countess stalked into the room in a blast of awful cold. She wore no tail, and was clad in her nightgown, with the fine paisley shawl about her shoulders which she had worn when I bade her goodnight. Most old ladies would have appeared rather comical in such a get-up, but there was nothing funny about Maria Theresa at that moment. Her face—or what could be seen of it beneath the grey hair that whipped about in the chill wind—was pale and drawn, the eyes flashing with anger; and even had she not been angry, there would have been the fact that she was dead; those phenomena of wind, chill, and darkness could only be caused by the passion of a suddenly unseated spirit.

The shade pushed back her wild grey hair with a gnarled hand, and pointed the other at me.

"Marie-Caroline!" she cried in a shrill voice. "Avenge me, my daughter!"

She looked perfectly solid, but I knew that if I touched her I would feel only a sensation of icy cold. All the same, I could not forbear reaching out to comfort her.

"Who did this to you?" I asked.

"To think I should be bitten in my own bed!"

"A melusine?—Quickly, madame, which of them?"

"It was dark—I was asleep—I did not see. Swear you will

see justice done! Swear they shall not profit from this—"

But at that moment her own words seemed to choke her. She recoiled from me with staring eyes.

"You are not she," the Countess gasped, her face suddenly transfigured with an expression of horror that struck me to my heart. "Your face, your voice, are not hers! *Kukuckskind!* You are not my daughter!"

The next instant she vanished, like the light of a candle winking out.

Chapter XIX.

The lights came back up with a flicker. Vasily stood with his back against the door, which at some point he had closed. For a moment I could only stare at him without really seeing his pale face and wind-ruffled hair.

One of her own family had murdered the Countess rather than let her alter her will to recognise Marie-Caroline, yet for the moment, one word only rang in my ears.

Kukuckskind—the cuckoo's child! Maria Theresa had at last penetrated my disguise and seen the imposter beneath the princess. I suspect, from this and other encounters, that the departure from the body frees the mind of its mortal imperfections, rendering the memory sharp and clear: she must have seen at once that I was not the Marie-Caroline of years before.

I felt myself gripped by doubt. I had wished to earn Marie-Caroline's inheritance as honestly as I could—by mending the old Countess' heart, at considerable personal risk. Now I stood among the wreckage of all my good intentions. She knew now, wherever she was, that I was a fraud, and that the forgiveness I had offered her was a lie. All my pretensions to deserve such a fortune seemed, now, entirely hollow.

"To whom were you speaking just now?" Vasily's wary voice

intruded upon my thoughts.

"Maria Theresa is dead," I whispered. "Murdered in her sleep by one of the melusines."

He uttered a disbelieving laugh. The look I sent him dashed the smile from his lips. For a moment he only stared. Then he muttered something under his breath, tore open the door, and departed.

I did not accompany him; *I* did not need convincing. I wrapped my arms about myself and walked to and fro, trying to summon my scattered thoughts. The motive for Maria Theresa's death was clear: the family had no intention of allowing her to make a new will. Any of them might have done it—Robert, whom I had passed in the corridor, or Jaime, who might have stolen by while Vasily and I spoke, or Princess Margaret, who would not have needed to tiptoe past Vasily's door at all.

If these people were willing to kill one of their own—if they had murdered Maria Theresa—then it seemed even more certain that they had killed Marie-Caroline, too. I swallowed a bitter sense of shame. Maria Theresa had begged me, as her daughter, to avenge her. It seemed the smallest way in which I might make amends. Yet how? I could neither bring the monsters to justice, nor reinstate Marie-Caroline in her rightful place. All I could do—if I lived long enough—was deprive them of the inheritance.

It would be something, at least. I recalled what Marie-Caroline had written in her journal: that the wealth of the wicked was laid up for the just. I did not know if I was just; but I knew the Bourbon-Parmas were wicked.

Vasily returned, closed the door, and leaned his forehead against it. When he turned to me again, his face was pale and

I knew he had viewed the body.

"How did you know? Explain."

I felt a little numb, as though the blood fled my cheeks. Things had gone badly enough when I had confided in Nijam—when I had let my secret slip at St Alphege's. I could not bear to reveal my one vulnerability to this man. "I cannot. Please do not ask me."

"The wind, the darkness, the words you spoke: *Who did this?* You refuse to explain these things?"

"You would never believe me. You would think I am mad."

"I think you might be clairvoyant," he said, watching me narrowly. "You *knew* she was dead."

There was no help for it; I had to say something. "We were visited just now by the shade of the Countess—by her ghost, as you might say—who told me a melusine had bitten her as she slept. No doubt to prevent the making of a new will. She begged me to avenge her."

For a moment Vasily watched me without changing expression. At last he made a sound of assent.

"We would both be glad to do so; the only question is how."

His words were so much the opposite of what I had expected that for a moment I could form no words. "You believe me, then? About the ghosts?"

"My dear, I'm a former vampire. A pretty hypocrite I should be, not to believe in ghosts." I thought I saw a tell-tale flicker of something in his eyes—fear, or guilt. "Perhaps even now there are some following me about."

Mutely, I shook my head. In fact, the imprint of a girl had suddenly appeared beside him, leaning her head against his shoulder. The image was blurred with time, but had dark hair and black eyes and red lips, and wore the sturdy, colourful dress of a peasant. Something about the look in Vasily's eyes made me feel that I should be committing a violation merely by seeing her, so I did not like to admit that I could.

But I stored away every detail in my memory. Vasily was no mere spiteful schoolgirl, and a day might come when I needed a weapon to use against him.

"Thank you for believing me," I added, and my voice trembled with real gratitude.

"Why shouldn't I? I beheld the corpse with my own eyes; I saw the fang-marks upon her breast."

"Her breast?" I echoed faintly.

"A bite on the torso envenomates the victim more quickly and effectively than one on the limbs. I suppose that answers the question of whether melusine venom is deadly to their own kind." He tapped a forefinger against pursed lips. "If there's no will, our best game is to turn detective, and prove who did this. The law will allow no murderer to profit from the crime."

"Prove a melusine a murderer?" I objected. "And on whose word—that of a ghost? You aren't a Grand Duke anymore, your grace. They don't prosecute royalty on the word of people like us."

"What other choice is there?"

"Maria Theresa was of the opinion that she could rescind her present will by destroying it." I began once again to pace the room. "That would reinstate the former will, which is in Herr Brunner's vault in Vienna, and leaves the entirety of the property to Marie-Caroline."

Vasily grasped the direction of my thoughts at once. "We might destroy the will and make it appear that the Countess herself had done so. But in that case, we must move quickly.

The thing must be done tonight, before the body is officially discovered. Where's the present will?"

"That's the difficulty," I confessed. "Princess Margaret has taken it; otherwise, the Countess might have destroyed it sooner."

"I presume it will be kept in her room."

"Which she is at present occupying," I reminded him.

He was so minutely focused upon the matter at hand that all other considerations, of politeness or gallantry, had faded away. "That's no great obstacle. We must fetch her out long enough to search the place. *The Turkish Diplomat* might work."

"I beg your pardon? Who is that?"

Vasily laughed at me. *"The Turkish Diplomat* is the name of a confidence-trick—nothing a lady like yourself would have heard of, naturally."

"Oh, dear!" I said faintly. "I don't like the sound of that!"

"Precisely," he said with a sharp-edged smile. "I expect it to be very uncomfortable for everyone involved—which is why it will be a resounding success. What an excellent thing that Mimi has come to Wiener Neustadt! We shall need her help. Do you fetch your prickly friend, and I'll send Schmidt for Mimi."

It was then half-an-hour before midnight. Two hours later, after much tiptoeing, whispering, shushing, and complaints that no one could be expected to operate at full mental capacity on such disturbed sleep (this was Nijam), the five of us were at last reassembled within Vasily's quarters. Outside, the night was a stormy one. Wind and rain lashed the house, providing a constant susurrus to disguise our stealthy preparations.

"We'll run a variation on *The Turkish Diplomat*," Vasily

announced, smoothing out a hastily-sketched map of the first floor which Nijam had produced while Alphonse was away on his errand. "Mimi's task, once the coast is clear, is to creep into Princess Margaret's room and find the will. How long," he added to the ballerina, "do you think you'll need to search a room a little larger than this one?"

Mimi, who was clad in dark red knickers and tights rather like a circus acrobat, glanced around her. "I think not above a quarter of an hour. Less, if she has hidden the will in one of the customary places. The underwear-drawer, for instance."

"Perfect!" Vasily rubbed his hands. "And to ensure you're not surprised in the midst of sifting the Princess' knickers—Miss Dark?"

"Nijam will remain in communication with you using this transmitter," I told Mimi, passing her the aforementioned gadget. "She and Alphonse will be stationed in the passageway to keep watch; between them they ought to give you ample warning of any interruption. You'll be perfectly safe."

Mimi looked at the transmitter with distaste. "Where is the fun in that?"

"Where's the *inheritance* if you get caught?" Nijam said testily. She was in a bad mood, not just from the lack of sleep but also from the fact that the plan required her to work alongside Alphonse. "For heaven's sake, please wear the transmitter."

Alphonse, who had begun to look apprehensive from the moment he had been told that he would work with Nijam, said, "What will sir and Miss Dark be doing?"

"We'll be distracting the princess with the scandal of a lifetime." Vasily's lips peeled from his white teeth in something that was not quite a smile. "Do you object,

Schmidt?"

"Not at all, sir; only will Miss Dark's presence be sufficient to protect you? The princess is a melusine, after all, and they don't take kindly to you. The opportunity to do you some harm might be tempting."

"Oh, believe me, my boy, I'm counting on it."

"Don't be a fool, Schmidt," Nijam added, not entirely unkindly. "If one of the melusines took it into their head to do away with the Baron, what could *you* do about it? Throw yourself in front of him, and get bitten for your pains?"

"Well, it would be my duty," Schmidt said bravely, "and I hope to meet it with fortitude."

Nijam had no reply for that, save some muttered words about *a crying waste* and *the brightest mind in bionic chemistry.* No one but myself heard her, because Vasily had glanced around the assembly and said, "Before we begin, does anyone else have questions?"

"Yes, I do." Frowning, Mimi raised a hand. "This confuses me, Vasya. Where is the Turkish official?"

Vasily smiled. "Tonight, my dear, that role will be played by *me.*"

* * *

My heart beat loudly in my ears as I stood outside the door communicating between Princess Margaret's room and my own. Terrible premonitions fleeted through my mind. Surely the princess would see straight through our feeble deception and respond with whatever monstrous urge took her fancy. Surely she would mesmerise us, or bite us, or strangle us in the great coils of her tail!—Still, it must be risked: or I must lose the inheritance and altogether fail my mother and the girls.

Summoning up all my courage, I beat a soft little tattoo against the door, then turned the knob—there was no reason for the Princess to lock her door, what did *she* have to fear?—and rushed in, raising my lamp to fill the room with light.

"Cousin Margaret!" I sobbed, glad to see that her lower half, at any rate, had reverted to human form. Nijam had been unsure how long the transformation would last, but I had observed that the tail generally disappeared with the onset of sleep. "Cousin Margaret, come quickly. I think he's having some sort of fit."

She must have been a light sleeper, or otherwise had been lying awake, for she sat up at once and said, "What on earth do you mean? Has someone been taken ill?"

"It's Dragomir," I said, using the name by which she had introduced the Baron to me.

"Is it!" she said, almost cheerfully. "A fit, you said? How on earth did it happen?"

"I—we were—I can't explain! Only he is having fits! I can't think what could have brought it on, unless…"

"Show me," she said, climbing out of bed. Vasily had been correct: the thought of the despised Baron being taken suddenly ill was all too tempting for the princess. A pitcher of water stood on one of the small tables next her bed, and she picked it up and brought it with her. I led her into my own room, being careful to close the door tightly behind us.

The sight that met our eyes within was, as Vasily had promised, extremely discomfiting. He lay sprawled across the disarranged bed in his dressing-gown, clutching with a trembling hand at a naked bosom which, being as nobly sculpted as a Grecian marble, had become the primary origin of my own discomposure. To create the impression of a cold sweat, I had sprayed him with a little flask of water clearly intended for the potted palm in the window; and he completed the illusion by breathing in a quick, panicked rhythm.—Oh, my poor mother, if she had seen me then! I promised myself I could never, *never* confess.

On the other side of the sitting-room door, which had been tightly closed before the commencement of our little comedy, Alphonse waited with one eye pressed to the keyhole. The instant I had closed the communicating door between my own bedroom and Princess Margaret's, he waved to Mimi. In a trice she slipped out into the hallway and darted into Margaret's chamber.

Meanwhile, I fluttered over the purported Baron, straightening his dressing-gown with an idea that it might render the events of the evening a little less deplorable if he was more decently clad. "Please! Can't you help him? Where does it hurt, Drago?"

"My—my chest," he gasped. *"Sacre bleu!* it hurts!"

The performance would have been a great deal easier had we had in any way a receptive audience, but we did not. Princess Margaret neither gasped, not tutted, nor rent her garments; possibly she had not the imagination for any of it. "Chest pain," she remarked, in a rather censorious tone, which brought the guilty blood to my cheeks. "I shudder to think what sort of acrobatics must have provoked such an attack. Give him some aspirin."

"Aspirin!" I cried. "Aspirin! A pain-killer! Can't you see he's dying? We must send for a doctor!"

215

Vasily let out an encouraging groan, perhaps to help conceal the sound of Mimi's soft movements within the Princess' room.

"There's no doctor closer than Wiener Neustadt, and by the time he was fetched it would already be too late. Aspirin thins the blood and may prevent damage. There is some in my room."

She reached for the communicating door.

"No!" I started up with an involuntary shriek of real alarm. "No, don't leave us! I—I have some aspirin right here—in my valise." I flung open the wardrobe, dived into the carpet-bag, and came out with a small tin that rattled quite promisingly. Margaret grimly poured a glass of water as I slipped an arm beneath Vasily's head. "Here, swallow this," I told him, dropping one of the little pills between his lips.

His mouth contracted, and he blinked at me with real apprehension. "What *is* it?"

"It'll make you feel ever so much better," I assured him, taking the glass from Princess Margaret, and putting it to his lips.

Meanwhile, in the sitting-room, Nijam listened anxiously via her transmitter to the soft sounds of Mimi's search.

"Have you found it yet?"

"I'm working on it," Mimi replied shortly.

"Have you looked under the mattress?"

"Yes."

"See if there are any locked drawers or cabinets." Nijam bit her lip. "And pockets. Go through the pockets of the clothing in her wardrobe."

"*Perkele,*" Mimi muttered under her breath. "How does one turn this thing off? It is more trouble than it is worth."

Nijam bit her lip. The next moment a hand dropped quietly upon her shoulder, and Nijam almost leaped out of her own skin. The fact that it was Alphonse Schmidt did little to reassure her.

"It's all right, Fraulein Nijam. Mimi knows what she's doing."

The fact he felt sufficiently familiar with the ballerina to address her by her Christian name may have caused another small part of Nijam's heart to wither and die, but all she said was, "You're supposed to be watching the keyhole!"

"I was," he said humbly, "and I came over to tell you—"

He caught his breath as, within the bedroom, our voices became a little clearer, together with the sound of heavy, uneven footsteps.

"—that," he finished.

"Quickly," Nijam hissed, seizing him by the waistcoat at the same moment that he caught her by the elbows. In this manner, with a wonderful economy of movement, they dragged each other into the corridor and ensconced themselves within the nearest curtained alcove.

"Stop breathing so fast," Nijam hissed, finding, to her annoyance, that they were now most uncomfortably tête-à-tête. "You'll give us away."

"Do you mind?" Mimi put in via the transmitter. "The two of you are worse than people who cough at the theatre!"

The occasion for Nijam and Alphonse's headlong flight was that, Vasily having taken his pill, Princess Margaret had announced that she had done all she could and would be retiring.

"No, don't go," Vasily gasped, playing our trump card. "You must help me get back to my own room. I'm dying, I can feel

217

it. I can't possibly die here. Think of the scandal!"

"What scandal? I thought the two of you were married," Princess Margaret said drily.

"You don't understand!" I cried, in a fine panic.

"It would ruin you all," Vasily said. "I'm—I'm—tell her, my love."

Now came the ticklish bit: the story we had concocted, which walked I knew not what delicate border between truth and falsehood. "There's something we've been keeping from you, madame," I said, wringing my hands in not-entirely-feigned anxiety. "Drago is in the pay of the Russian Emperor. If he dies here, the tsar will certainly make a fuss about it!"

Princess Margaret, not entirely credulous, narrowed her eyes. "Marie-Caroline! Do you mean to tell me you have gone and attached yourself, of all people, to a *Russian agent?* That you have brought into this house a traitor to our good friend the Emperor Franz Josef?"

"I'm not a traitor!" Vasily protested thickly. "I'm loyal to the Slavic people!"

"It makes no difference," the princess said. By now she had been induced to believe us, if only because it provided the perfect pretext upon which to get rid of the Baron. "You must not spend another night under this roof. We are no longer in France, Marie-Caroline! We occupy this estate, this rank at court, only at the goodwill of the Austrian emperor. If it was known we were in bed—absolutely in bed!—with the Russian emperor, it would be the end of all the privileges and protections we enjoy!"

"Not if you help me keep it a secret!" I protested.

"Ah!" Vasily groaned, clutching at his bosom. "Quickly! I feel another fit coming on!"

After that, Princess Margaret had no choice but to help us. Supporting Vasily on either side, the two of us dragged him through the hastily-vacated sitting-room and thence out into the corridor. It was a long journey, which Vasily enlivened by having another fit just outside the chapel.

Meanwhile, in the alcove, as soon as we had turned the west corner, Alphonse gave an explosive gasp which made Nijam's heart leap up her throat for the second time that morning.

"Confound it, Alphonse!"

"You told me not to breathe!"

"I wish you *would* stop breathing," Mimi observed fretfully.

"Go out and keep watch, Schmidt," Nijam said, ejecting him through the curtains. "Signal me the instant Princess Margaret returns. Miss Laine, they've gone towards the Baron's rooms. You have—" she checked her pocket-watch—"another eight minutes."

For the time being, there was nothing she could do but wait. While I helped Princess Margaret to manoeuvre a fainting Vasily into his room, Nijam sat with her eyes fixed to the dial of her watch until presently Mimi spoke in a hissing whisper.

"Miss Nijam? I hear footsteps. Someone is awake in the room next to this one."

Marie-Caroline's apartments were now empty—which meant the footsteps must belong to Blanca, whose room adjoined Princess Margaret's on the far side. "Hold still a moment and don't move. Likely she'll go back to bed." Nijam swept the curtains aside, looking into the corridor. "Schmidt," she hissed, for it had been determined that if all else failed, Alphonse should form our last means of defence against the melusines, allowing those of us who were able to escape.

She observed Alphonse at his post in the west corner,

staring like a dog at point in the direction in which Vasily, Princess Margaret, and I had gone. "Schmidt," Nijam repeated, but he never glanced in her direction. Instead, he suddenly dashed from her sight.

What had happened was this. It was, if you recall, a rainy night; the wind lashed the house, rattling the shutters and providing a cloak for our deeds. Just as Princess Margaret and I had wrestled Vasily onto his bed, a terrible banging began at the window.

"It's those confounded shutters," Princess Margaret said. She unlatched the rattling pane, and it blew open; with it came a torrent of wind and rain, which soaked her in a moment to the bone. At once—oh, it was a dreadful sight—her legs twined together beneath her skirts, and elongated into the glittering, metallic tail of a melusine.

She reached out and wrestled the shutters closed before latching the casement again. The whole room seemed full of the glistering coils of her tail and the musky, sulphurous stench of snake; and in that narrow space, at that unearthly hour, it struck me how entirely helpless we were before this inhuman creature.

The look upon both our faces must have pleased her, for she slithered nearer and bent over Vasily as he lay, wrapped in his dressing-gown, upon the coverlet.

"How do you feel *now?*" she hissed.

He managed a weak smile. "Entirely overwhelmed, madame—by your kindness."

The clock on the mantelpiece told that twelve of the fifteen minutes we had promised Mimi were past. Somehow, we must fill another three. I said effusively, "You've saved us both a great deal of embarrassment, madame. How can we ever repay you?"

Her face tightened with a curious blend of wrath and avarice. "You might leave this house, and put an end to this foolishness about the will. I have five daughters to find husbands for, and a son to establish in the situation to which his blood entitles him. I cannot afford to be implicated in your downfall."

"Your maternal feelings are a credit to you, madame." Vasily managed in a tolerably steady voice. "Still, you ought not to forget that my wife is also entitled by her blood to a royal situation, and I should be an improvident husband if I overlooked her interests."

"You! You upstart, you traitor—I will drain you myself rather than see you inherit the Bourbon patrimony."

With that, she seized Vasily's face in a crushing grip, and imprinted a kiss upon his lips!

"Stop it at once!" I cried, seizing her by the shoulders and trying to drag her away from him. She thrust out an arm and sent me reeling through the door of the room. It was this that caught Alphonse Schmidt's attention and brought him pelting down the corridor towards me. By the time he arrived, he had withdrawn from his coat pocket a delicate globe of thin glass, which he hurled at the feeding melusine. His aim was wild, and the globe merely shattered against one of the bedposts; glass and water droplets went everywhere save for where they were intended. All the same, one small drop must have fallen upon the princess' arm. Releasing him, she reared back with a hiss of pain.

Vasily dropped limply upon the bed. The next instant Alphonse threw himself between the melusine and her prey, for all the world as though he meant to carry out his duty and offer himself up to perish in his master's stead.

"Salt-water!" Princess Margaret said, terribly offended. "How dare you? You might seriously have injured me! As for the Baron," she added, turning to me, "let this be a warning to him. He has lost a single year of his life; he must pray he loses no more. Tell him he must quit this house in the morning. As for you, either you must go with him or never see him again."

She swept past me and out of the room. For a moment I was barely capable of believing that the melusine had gone, and was not about to poison or drain or strangle us all where we stood; and then it struck me that Princess Margaret had gone too soon, with two minutes yet to run, and would catch Mimi in this murderous temper!

"*Nijam*," I whispered, putting a hand to my ear—but of course Mimi had my transmitter!

Within her alcove, Nijam was weathering a crisis of her own. Blanca's door opened, and the Infanta ventured from her room yawning. Arrested by the thin line of light shining from beneath her mother's door, she rapped on it, saying "Mama? What's going on?"

Nijam did not dare to call a warning: besides which, Mimi must have heard Blanca knocking at the door. Nevertheless, she rapped a pattern of short and long beats against her temple—a code in Morse, which had been arranged beforehand as the signal to abandon the mission.

"I haven't finished," Mimi whispered from within the room. "Make me a distraction, will you?"

"Miss Laine, *withdraw!*" Nijam hissed in desperation; but the soft crackle of the open transmission went dead. Mimi must have located the off switch.

Cursing Alphonse beneath her breath, Nijam was about to

hurl herself through the curtains when Blanca spoke again.

"Oh, there you are, Mama! What on earth are you doing up at this hour—and in tails?"

Peering from her alcove, Nijam experienced another mental upheaval at the sight of the approaching Princess Margaret, a melusine in full glory. "Miss Laine, you must *get out*," she whispered, beneath the cover of the storm; but the connection was quite dead, and the only reply came from Princess Margaret.

"Go to bed, Blanca; I was only dealing with a little rat that had got into the house, and was annoying me."

Nijam clasped a hand over her mouth, fearing heaven only knew what.—Blanca kissed her mother good-night, and then both the ladies disappeared into their respective rooms.

Nijam stood listening with her heart in her mouth. But there was no sudden movement within the princess' chambers—no shriek of terror, no plea for mercy, no sound but for the banging of a shutter, which must have worked itself loose, against the outer wall of the house. "Miss Laine," she whispered once more. "Answer me, I beg you!"—There was no answer. Nijam dashed across the hallway and through Marie-Caroline's sitting-room to the bedroom beyond. Here, by the door that communicated between that room and that of the princess, Mimi might possibly have effected her escape; but there was no sign of the ballerina here, either. That left only one possibility—that Mimi had been trapped in Princess Margaret's room—and that did not bear thinking about.

Worse—what could have induced Alphonse to flee, and Princess Margaret to change her shape, and then to speak of little rats invading the house? Since there was nothing she could do to aid Mimi, Nijam hurried towards Vasily's room, fearful of what she might find.

At the melusine's departure, I had picked myself up off the floor and flown to Vasily's side, where Alphonse was already crouched shaking his unconscious form and calling his name. I pressed my hands to my mouth, thinking that although Vasily was a complicating factor which it would have been a pleasure to do without, I could not wish him to die betimes at the hands of such a monster. Happily I had little time to contemplate such a possibility, for he gave a gasp and opened great staring eyes.

"Good Lord," he said. "I feel like a corpse. How do I look?"

"About the same as ever, sir."

"She stole away a year of your life—and you worry about your complexion!" I cried, feeling myself on the brink of hysterics.

"Don't laugh, my dear; my face is my only fortune. A year of my life—it feels like ten. I suppose there's justice in the world after all! At one time I rather doubted it... Fetch me a mirror, Schmidt. I want to inspect the wreckage. And a glass of water... and, if you can manage it at all, a pork pie, a mug of beer, three apples and a hunk of cheese. After an ordeal like that I could do with some solid, English-style nourishment."

The door opened and Nijam appeared in a state of tightly-condensed panic which manifested itself in a few terse sentences. "What happened here? Princess Margaret has returned to her room *a lá* melusine, and I've lost all communication with Miss Laine. And where were you, Schmidt? We had a *plan.* You were meant to be guarding the passage!"

It took a few minutes to get the story straight. Alphonse explained that he had caught a whiff of that distinctive serpentine scent, and then had seen me expelled bodily from the room. "I'm sorry to have abandoned you, Miss Nijam, but my first duty is to my master."

"And his duty was to the *job*," Nijam said icily, but she did not dwell upon her injured feelings. Instead, she turned to Vasily. "You say she threatened you? *Put an end to this foolishness about the will*—why then, she must believe her aunt yet to be alive. Evidently, Princess Margaret was not the one who killed Maria Theresa."

We digested this information in silence. Princess Margaret had attacked Vasily. Some unknown person had killed Maria Theresa. Could it have been a third melusine who had arranged my accident in the wood, and then murdered the stable hand to cover it up?—Or a fourth who had killed Marie-Caroline? The way things were going, I shouldn't be surprised to find that the whole pack of them were killers.

In the meantime, we were not out of danger by any stretch of the imagination.

"And you have no idea what happened to Mimi—or the will?" I asked. "She did not escape by the door to my own room?"

"I looked," said Nijam. "She wasn't there. There was no commotion—it's possible she found a place to hide. It's more likely that she was found and put under mesmerism. We must prepare ourselves for the possibility that she is even now telling the princess everything. Exactly how far do you trust Miss Laine, your grace?"

Vasily, who was propped upon the pillows looking as pathetic as an invalid in a play, spread his hands. "Mimi has never been able to afford loyalty."

"Then if she's caught, it will be carpets," I gasped.

Alphonse sent me a look of some confusion.

"I believe she means *curtains*," Nijam told him drily. "The question is, what ought we to do about it? If Miss Laine was caught, we would be best advised to escape at once. On the other hand, if we vacate the premises and she is still at large, she might run into trouble looking for us. We cannot afford to act precipitately."

Demimondaine she might be, but we could not possibly abandon Mimi to the mercy of these monsters. "There must be *something* we can do to help her."

"Oh? Will *you* start having fits? That trick isn't likely to work twice, and if Miss Laine has betrayed us—"

"Ladies, ladies!" Vasily interjected. "Have a little faith in Mimi! We didn't merely trade endearments, you know, that summer in Paris. As a ballerina, she may be indifferent; as a mistress, abrasive; but as an acrobat—"

There came from the window a tapping sound against the shutters. At first, I thought the shutter was merely working its way open again, but Vasily smiled.

"Ah, what did I tell you? Open the window, Schmidt, and be quick about it!"

Alphonse threw open the casement and then, more carefully, unlatched the shutters. In came a quantity of wind and rain; and, clad in a light harness of the sort which I could have sworn had its origins in the raising of Wagner's valkyries, or the lowering of Handel's angels, Mimi Laine swung through the window and alighted upon the sodden carpet. A quick jerk of her gloved hand, and the thin line by which she had been suspended from above slithered in at the window and landed in neat coils upon the floor. She was thoroughly wet from the rain, which had plastered her ash-brown hair against her face and neck; but her cheeks were flushed, and her eyes sparkled with excitement.

"Ah!" she said, *"now* the spruce is on fire!"

Chapter XX.

For a moment, bereft of speech, none of us uttered a word. Then Vasily said, "Do I take it you have the will?"

"You'll never guess where I found it—tacked to the back of the dressing-table mirror!" Her eyes opened wide. "Oh, chicken-cage of horror! Did you want it?"

A profound silence fell upon the room. I touched the tip of my tongue to my lips and said, very carefully, "We wanted it very much, Mimi! Do you mean to say you don't have it?"

"I thought you wanted it burned!" Mimi said. "I stopped by the dead old woman's room and made a little bonfire on a tea-tray. I left a few scraps behind, of course, to identify it. Did I do wrong?"

"No," I said thickly, passing from the depths of despair to the extremes of relief; and Nijam added heartily,

"Excellent work—I could not have done it better myself!"

Mimi's eyes narrowed. "Oh? You think you could have done it as well? In that case, next time you shall come scaling roofs with me."

"Not on your life," Nijam said readily. "I was wrong to doubt you, Miss Laine. In the future—*if* I ever take leave of my senses to the point of repeating this evening's antics—I shall trust you implicitly. And now, since the job is done, I don't know about you, but I mean to sleep."

With that, she nodded jovially to us all, and strolled out by the door without so much as a "good-night", and certainly without bothering herself to engage in any such common-place, mortal ceremonies as relating the evening's events, toasting our success, or even seeing to our guest's comfort for the evening. How very like Nijam!

In her wake, Alphonse dashed for the door, muttering something about escorting her upstairs—which I thought was uncommonly brave of him, and not because of the melusines. Mimi yawned and asked whether it was true that the room next door was empty, and when assured that it was, she ambled off to ensconce herself within. I looked at Vasily, and Vasily looked at me.

"I *meant* to propose a celebratory cognac," he said, with a shrug. "But since everyone else has gone, and *you* detest the stuff—" I felt more annoyed with myself than ever, but did not think I could risk shattering his illusions of delicate femininity—"I shall content myself with asking one question before I bid you good-night."

His question seemed somewhat ominous. We had argued vigorously over the wisdom of telling Princess Margaret the Baron was a spy for the Russians; as I had warned him, she had now ordered him to leave the house. Lord knew how *that* was to be repaired, but I had a feeling that he was about to manoeuvre me into another corner.

"Cognac?" I said with a dainty shudder, to put off the evil day. "I thought in Russia you were all very keen on vodka."

"Which is why those of us with any taste go abroad to Paris as soon as possible," he replied. "Speaking of taste, Miss Dark, I insist upon an answer: *what* was the vile lozenge you forced down my throat half an hour ago? What will it do to me? Have I time to put my affairs in order?"

"Oh, is that all?" Somewhat relieved, I produced the tin. "Why, it was only a cough drop. Eucalyptus-flavoured. It's from Australia. Extremely salubrious, I'm told."

"It tasted like petroleum," he said. "Perhaps I should thank you. If the fair princess *had* taken it into her head to bite me, doubtless her venom would have been powerless before the malevolent force of this—eupepsia, or whatever you call it."

"Oh, don't be such a baby. At your age!"

"Those are harsh words, but I will forgive them. I love it when you play the governess, Miss Dark. Do you think you'll make a better man of me?"

"Not at all," I said, alarmed. I did not want Vasily thinking I had any particular concern for him at all.

"Oh, it's quite flattering to be thought capable of reform. I warn you, though: I'm a hopeless case, and I mean to remain so."

He was laughing at me for being, as he thought, a naïve little governess and smitten with him. I felt my cheeks turning pink with mortification. Perhaps I was a *little* smitten, but I was not half so naïve as I seemed, and I meant to have the last laugh in the end.

"I'm far more worried about the Bourbon-Parmas," I said, as cuttingly as I knew how. "Do you think Nijam is correct, that Princess Margaret cannot have killed the old Countess? It must have been Robert or Jaime, then. If we were able to prove the thing in court, it would secure us the inheritance at once, besides doing something to set things right."

"Don't allow your ideals to mislead you, my dear. You and I cannot afford to set foot in a court of law." He fell silent for a moment, watching me in a calculating sort of way that made me want to squirm. "Earlier tonight, you warned me that the family was utterly opposed to my receiving the inheritance. I did not quite believe the situation to be so dire, but you have carried your point. To foil us, someone in this house was both willing and able to commit murder."

We were not to avoid the topic, after all. "Still, I asked you to reveal your true name and rank," I pointed out. "Of course that is out of the question now. If it would be so disastrous for you to be in the tsar's pay, you could not possibly confess to being his cousin."

I was startled, in that moment, by my own feeling of relief. If the Bourbons had accepted Vasily and myself, how could I have found the courage to do my duty by Marie-Caroline? I could not help but recoil from the thought of accepting her estate before I had, at the very least, brought her killer to justice.

"On the contrary," Vasily said. "A spy is nobody, but a Romanov cousin? The Bourbon-Parmas would welcome a grand duke with open arms. They might lose their friends at the Austrian court, it's true, but they would gain even more powerful friends in Petersburg—and at the same stroke win back the affections of the French. The Third Republic may be finished with the *ancien regime,* but they still covet an alliance between Russia and France. Why, if my cousin Nicky—the new tsar, that is—had not been so infatuated with Alix of Hesse, he would have been married off to that Orléanist princess, Hélène." The expression of his face was terrifyingly hopeful. "More than that, a brilliant match with a supposed Bourbon princess might be the one thing able to restore me to my family's good graces. They *must* take me back, then—and under the Tsar's aegis I should be amply protected from the rest of my enemies. What about it, Miss Dark? Shall you and I pull off the diplomatic coup of a lifetime?"

"But then I should have to impersonate a melusine for the rest of my life," I objected. "Which, under the circumstances, is likely to be brief and much too eventful!"

"Not in the least," he urged. "Your mother and sisters need never want for anything again. Isn't that what you want? You would gain far more than the Bourbon inheritance. My estates, my palaces, my income should all be at your service, once they are returned to me!"

More than the Bourbon inheritance! I felt almost dizzy. I knew already that I could not possibly earn the Bourbon inheritance; I did not want to burden myself with anything more.

"I couldn't," I said faintly.

"You don't understand. A Romanov fortune is enough to make this place look like a hovel. More than enough to keep a thousand families secure from anything short of an anarchist's bomb. Really, there's not the slightest flaw to the plan."

I was not entirely immune to his words. As he spoke, I saw myself surrounded by glittering luxuries of gold and crystal, jewels and silks—and by my side, his noble figure adorned with stars and ribbons, would be Vasily himself.

My mouth felt suddenly parched.

"What can you be saying?" I whispered. "Our success should be entirely dependent upon our willingness to live as man and wife!"

"Not in the least! We might go about our separate lives, on opposite sides of the world, if we liked." He shrugged carelessly, but there was nothing careless in the shrewd eyes that fixed upon my own. "You wished, once, not to take a husband unless you wanted him. Perhaps I might be to your taste, since I should never dream of imposing upon you."

He *was*—he was proposing marriage to me; and just such a marriage as I had always resigned myself to, a marriage for money. But on what unprincipled terms! What—did he really expect me to believe that, having once inveigled me into such a marriage, he would treat me like a sibling, with strictest propriety? That itself would be intolerable: for while I had long accepted the necessity of marrying wealth, I had had some notion of marrying at least as much for love as for money; and at that moment, I confess, the thought flashed into my head that if I was to commit the awful indiscretion of marrying Vasily Nikolaevich, I wished at least to get some enjoyment out of him!—But no, he could not *really* mean that, for he was too keenly aware of his own power. Even if he did not at present mean to impose upon me, I did not for a moment doubt that it would happen eventually; and then whatever brief passion I succumbed to would be repented for with a lifetime of tears; loveless, friendless, perhaps childless; without even the comfort of my own religion, for I should be obliged, of course, to betray it and convert to Orthodoxy in order to marry him. Then, in due course he would throw me aside and go on to other conquests—peasants or ballerinas, dainties or governesses, as his fancy took him. He might disguise his offer as liberty for myself, but what it truly meant was libertinage for *him,* and that was a state of affairs I would never accept.

I would *not* allow myself to feel anything for a creature who saw me only as a means to wealth; a monster who was still a monster, even with his fangs drawn.

Naturally I could not say this to his face, because he was loyal to me only insofar as I promised him a return to the manner of life to which he was accustomed. Trapped between Vasily and the Bourbon-Parmas, needing to pacify both of them, I could not afford altogether to wash my bridges of the idea.

"You're asking a great deal of me," I said at last, timidly. "I—I should need time to think it over."

"Then do so," he said, very agreeably, "but don't leave it so long that I turn up drained of my youth from melusine kisses, or am thrown out of the house altogether. And—one more thing. One with the power to see the dead and learn their secrets should be more circumspect about whom she entrusts with such information. In your place, Miss Dark, I should not have told a duplicitous adventurer about it at all."

It took me a moment to realise that the duplicitous adventurer he referred to was himself: I had not expected such honesty. I sent him a look of apprehension melting into trust. "But *you* won't impose upon me, will you, Vasily? You promised just now you would not."

"I—," he began, and broke off. After a moment, more savagely, he said, "Go away, child. I have betrayed every woman who has ever trusted in me, except those who expected to be paid. I have proposed nothing different to you, do you understand me?"

"I understand," I whispered, casting my eyes demurely to the carpet.

I returned to my own room with a mind that swarmed and buzzed like a hive of bees. There was, of course, no hope of sleep. I was caught in a dilemma—marry a fugitive prince, or lose the inheritance, and my mother along with it.—And if

I married Vasily, I should lose my mother just the same, for I would never, never be permitted to see her or my sisters again, for fear of giving myself away; my life should cease to be worth a penny the moment it was suspected I was not the last Bourbon princess. No—I was not yet so desperate. I must find a way to secure the inheritance without Vasily; and he himself had shown me the chink in his armour. He knew himself to be by nature treacherous, and had gone to some pains to tell me so. A man so obsessed with his own propensities for betrayal would scarcely be on his guard against the wiles of a diffident little mouse; and in this, the Bourbon-Parmas would doubtless stand my allies.

It did not occur to me to wonder whether I was being treacherous with one who was, after all, my ally. Vasily would have done the same by me—had indeed done so, to some extent, at the hotel in Vienna. All the same, I felt a moment's gratitude—and not for the first time—that my mother and sisters were not here to witness my duplicity.

Since sleep was hopeless, I lit my lamp and buried myself once again in Marie-Caroline's old journals. At this point in the princess' journal, the *Singing lessons Wiener N.* had come to an end, but there had been no explanation as to why; only I thought the tone of the entries had become a little more hopeless, as Marie-Caroline's world had contracted to a dreary set of quotations from a list of improving books, and occasionally a ride within the park. And then, quite suddenly, in a flood of words, she spoke:

I climbed the wall this afternoon and walked all the way to Wiener Neustadt to lay bare my heart.—And had it broken for my pains, for F. says that I am only a young girl and his student, and that it would be wrong to take me away from my family, and heaven knows what else! I ought to hate him for saying such things, as though I can't be trusted to know my own mind—as though I ought to like being kept a prisoner in this gilded cage—but I can't, for I know that when he looks at me he sees a real person and not just a little Bourbon doll, valuable mainly by virtue of having been manufactured in a palace.

After that the journal went back to its dreary relating of events, and I put the leather-bound volume down to think over what I had read. F., whoever he was, seemed a decent sort; a great many men would see nothing wrong with taking advantage of a smitten young girl, especially if there was an inheritance to be won—and once again I thought sadly of Vasily.

I was still mired in thought when, shortly after the clock had struck six, the housemaid entered to kindle the fire. It was a dark morning; the rain had stopped, but the wind still lashed the house, and the sparks flared with a ghastly yellow light around Faustine's hunched figure as she worked. I closed my eyes, wishing for a little sleep, but something in her figure had caught my attention and teased at my thoughts.—I blinked until she came into better focus. The firelight outlined the housemaid in a harsh light that concealed as much as it revealed; yet as she turned her head aside to gather her newspaper, her matches and her coal-scuttle, I saw very clearly the glint of the flames in her white hair, and the deep lines etching her face. It was not so that she had looked when I had first come to the castle, scarcely five days previously!

I must have made some startled sound, for Faustine cast a furtive glance towards me where I lay in the shadow of the canopy, watching her with eyes that started out of my head in horror.

"I beg your pardon, madame," she said in some chagrin. "I have woken you again.—Is something wrong?"

"No, Faustine, thank you," I whispered, forcing the words through stiff lips. She dropped a curtsey and went away, moving carefully, like a wooden puppet—or, perhaps closer to the mark, like a rheumatic. Sinking back upon my pillows, I ground the heels of both hands into my eyes, wanting to burst into tears of sheer despair. Poor Faustine! It became suddenly, horribly clear to me why the servants of the Schloss Frohsdorf were one and all ancient and withered. Who could tell their true ages now? The butler, who tried to ascend the stairs with the quick grace of a younger man, only to pause halfway to gasp for breath; Faustine herself, whose lined face and white hair seemed incongruous when compared to her modish dress and trim, almost girlish figure… Someone, or perhaps several persons, among the family had steadily drained the life from them, treating them no better than dainties.

The Schloss felt suddenly like a great tomb, suffocating and oppressive. Despite my weariness, I could not bear to stay idle another moment. Besides, there were errands to run. I rose and dressed.

I found Mimi in the room next to Vasily's, still clad in the wine-red tights and knickers of a circus performer, and to all appearances dead to the world. Her dreams must have been pleasant ones, for there was a faint and almost childish smile upon the face that, when waking, was so hard and sharp and goblinish. As I bent over her, the light of my oil-lamp fell upon a pattern of livid, purple marks clustered upon the left side of her throat. I knew at once what they meant. Mimi was, or once had been, a dainty herself—had sold her blood

237

for money.

I moved incautiously, throwing a beam of light into her eyes. Mimi woke with a gasp and lashed out with a hand that had been tucked beneath her pillow. I felt something thin, cold, and horribly sharp press beneath the angle of my jaw. All the stories I had ever heard, of the monster-bitten transforming inexorably into the very sort of creature that had preyed upon them, rose up in my mind; I wondered if I was looking my death in the eye, or whether I was doomed to something worse—transformation into the same sort of monster!

Then Mimi puffed a fair strand of hair out of her eyes and fell back upon the pillows, withdrawing a small, wicked-looking pocket-knife from its place beneath my chin. In almost the same moment I recalled Princess Margaret's certainty that monstrosity, like royalty, was incommunicable.

"Don't *ever* do that again," Mimi snarled. "I don't like being crept up on in my sleep!"

"I beg your pardon," I said, quite cowed. "But you can't stay here; it will be light soon, and the house will be astir. Here: I brought your dress."

This was a sensible day-gown in pale blue calico, which she pulled on over the fetching circus-outfit until the only sign that remained of it was an occasional flash of red-stockinged ankle. "I couldn't help noticing your scars," I added apologetically, fixing my eyes upon the ceiling as she dressed. "Did...did you have them from the Grand Duke?"

"It wasn't Vasily." She stomped upon an ottoman to do up the laces of her boots. "He was already toothless when I took up with him."

Really, Mimi was not at all a respectable young person.

What sort of company was I keeping? Whom had I be-come—the companion of demimondaines and thieves? Still, it almost frightened me that I did not despise her. Poverty and desperation had driven me to keep such company; I could scarcely blame Mimi if far greater poverty had driven her to far greater extremities.

"But he's had dainties before," I conjectured.

"Oh, all the Romanov princes have; if they don't make a selection by the time they're eighteen or nineteen, their fathers take them to the Opera and make them choose from among the *corps de ballet*." She straightened, sending me a grim little smile. "We aren't just performers, Miss Dark; we're a menu."

"Horrible!" I said, with a shudder.

"It makes us better dancers. We become stronger, faster, more graceful."

"For their entertainment?" I could not help remarking.

"It's a living," she said with a shrug. "And that's all it is. So don't worry about me, Miss Dark: I'm no rival of yours."

What had she seen between Vasily and myself?—and if she had seen, how much more must *he* have seen? I must have been horribly unguarded.

"Worry about you!" I said, turning away to hide my blushes. "I'm sure there's no reason I should concern myself with Vasily's amusements." So saying, to forestall further discussion, I led the way out into the corridor.

The morning was wet and grey, and no one but the servants was yet astir. Mimi followed me with perfectly soundless footsteps all the way down the stairs, past the chapel and library, and out at the back door. Together we stole into the park, wending our way through thick, wind-tossed shadows and between deep, wind-ruffled puddles towards the gate of the estate. As we walked, I congratulated myself upon escaping an uncomfortable subject. Mimi, however, was not to be escaped.

"Perhaps you *should* concern yourself with Vasily," she said as we neared the shelter of the park wall. "He's changed since I knew him in Petersburg. That is partly because he is hunted now wherever he goes, and can no longer afford to laugh at life. But I have never seen him so serious as he is with you."

"Serious!" I exclaimed, thinking how often I had caught him laughing at me. "That's a funny word for it, Miss Laine. How do you mean, he's hunted wherever he goes?"

She gave a shrug. "You saw for yourself what happened in Vienna."

"Yes, of course. But there are others—he said it wasn't only the Okhrana after him."

"The Okhrana!" she repeated with a shiver. "If they are the ones hunting him, it must be a matter of imperial security, at the very least!"

It seemed my inquisitiveness was doomed to frustration—Mimi plainly knew less than I did myself. "Then you don't know either, what it is he's supposed to have done?"

"The copybook's blank," she said. "No, perhaps that is not true. I think it has something to do with Vasya's lost teeth. If he found a way for the royalties to be defanged—or even if he had only done it himself—then they might call him a traitor to his people, and try to put him down. Although I do not understand it. Vasya is not the sort to put himself willingly at any disadvantage."

"My thoughts precisely," I observed. "Hullo! Here's a wicket gate."

I had meant to conduct Mimi to the village by means of the front gate, but this one, being hidden from view of the house by the trees, was evidently better suited to a stealthy departure. It was unlocked: all Mimi needed to do was lift the latch and pull it open.

When she did so, I recoiled. On the far side of the wall stood a little white church with a cheerful, red-tiled roof; in place of a steeple, there was a little onion dome atop the bell-tower. Even in the dripping morning air it was a charming sight; but between me and the church, shadowed by dripping pines, stretched a modest little graveyard.

Already halfway through the gate, Mimi observed me thoughtfully. But all she said was, "Aren't you coming?"

"I'd better not," I said regaining my breath. I hoped she did not notice how I had recoiled into the shadow of the wall, where I could see neither the graveyard nor any unquiet memories it might contain. "I'm grateful for your help, Mimi. Here: I can give you the money to hire a cart to take you to Wiener Neustadt; and I'll send more when I have it."

A swift smile flashed across her little goblin face, quite transforming it; and she pulled a hand from her pocket to display something that swung heavily from her fingers, glittering and flashing even in the wind-lashed semi-darkness.

"Thanks, but don't bother," Mimi said. "I've already paid myself."

—And by an audacious theft! For a moment I struggled to find my voice. "Good heavens! Are those diamonds? Where did you find them?"

"In the old lady's room," she said with a shrug. "She won't miss them; she's dead now. These will get me to Copenhagen, at any rate."

"Copenhagen," I repeated. I might object to Mimi's morals, but I felt somehow loath to say goodbye. Miss Laine had gone to great lengths to help us tonight; I felt a sense of camaraderie, and a wish to see her settled in some secure and honourable employment. "I thought you had found a teacher in Wiener Neustadt?"

Mimi scowled, a look that made her resemble a goblin more fiercely than ever. "It seems I am *not worth coming out of retirement to teach.*"

"Mimi! How dare she!"

"I don't care," she said, stuffing the jewels into her pocket. "I'll show them I'm more than just a royal dainty. I can work hard; all I need is the right teacher. *Au revoir,* Miss Dark. If you need me again, send to Vienna; my lease doesn't run out for another few days, and I have a few matters of business to attend to before I go."

"There *is* something you can do for me, as a matter of fact," I added, withdrawing my letter from the pocket of my skirt. "Once you reach Vienna, will you post this? I'd do it myself, but it's rather urgent; and I don't like to send it from the Schloss in case anyone should find me out."

Upon receiving a few *kronen* to cover the cost of the post, Mimi agreed; and I returned to the castle. By the time I left myself in again at the back door, the household had been alerted, not just to Maria Theresa's death, but also to the destruction of her will.

Chapter XXI.

For Maria Theresa's sake, I hoped her shade had indeed gone on in a timely fashion to a different and better world, for her deathbed had become the scene of some very unseemly wrangling.

"What can you mean?" Princess Margaret nearly shrieked as I climbed to the head of the stairs. The passage outside the Countess' apartments was full of quietly weeping servants. "You can't be telling me the will has been revoked?"

A deferential murmur informed me that the unfortunate Herr Brunner was the recipient of her wrath.

"She cannot simply have *burned* the will—it was in *my* possession!" Margaret rejoined. Another remark by the lawyer was cut short: "It was stolen! And even if she *did* somehow retrieve it, she cannot have been in her right mind to burn it!"

Herr Brunner remained persistent. This time, as I entered the sitting-room, his words were quite clearly audible.

"The Countess was entitled to the possession of her own will, surely," he observed. "As to her state of mind—in the absence of any contrary evidence, we must assume she was in the possession of all her faculties, and that her decision to burn the will was consistent with her intention of having me

243

travel from Vienna to make her a new one. Don't be angry with me, madame. Legally, the fact remains that the will now in force is the one in possession of my firm, leaving the house and fortune to Marie-Caroline."

"This is insupportable," Princess Margaret hissed. *"You* are the executor. It's *your* decision which will to send for probate. I demand you use a copy of the burned will!"

I found Vasily and Jaime studiously ignoring each other at opposite ends of the small, narrow sitting room, while Blanca sat midway between them looking primly amused. Evidently, the unexpected death of the Countess had distracted Princess Margaret from the business of ridding the house of the Russian agent. Of the Duke and Duchess of Parma, there was no sign.

"Under the circumstances, I can do no such thing," Herr Brunner answered. "At this point I think you would be best advised to consult your own lawyers, madame. This is a matter for the courts, if you intend to take it so far."

Crossing the sitting room towards me, Vasily gravely extended a hand to usher me to the bedroom door.

After the visitation of Maria Theresa's shade the night before, I had little stomach for the role I must play; but play it I must, or abandon the inheritance to these monsters. At the door, I let out a sharp little gasp and put a hand to my mouth. Herr Brunner turned to me and, after a moment—during which Princess Margaret only sent us a look as venomous as her bite—said: "Madame, please accept my very sincere condolences."

Retrieving my hand from Vasily's grasp, I moved in reverent silence to the foot of the bed. Maria Theresa's corpse had been decently composed, her nightgown and shawl arranged in such a way as to conceal the fang-marks in her breast; but there was something indecent all the same in her utter stillness, in the skin waxen and grey from this untimely surcease of life. It took me no effort at all to utter another stricken gasp and fill my eyes with angry tears.

I *must* find a way to put this right, thought I. But I could not imagine how.

Herr Brunner cleared his throat softly and turned to go, but Princess Margaret arrested him with a single sharp word.

"Wait! I tell you, that will was stolen from my room." Her basilisk glare moved from me to Vasily, who had sunk into a chair by the door; and I saw her eyes narrow, as though something was for the first time becoming painfully clear to her. "Why, it must have been taken from my room, for it was in my hands only yesterday afternoon. Herr Brunner, I believe that it was some other person who burned the will, and not Maria Theresa herself!" She turned upon Vasily. "You're looking very well, Baron, for someone who was suffering a heart attack in the small hours!"

I let out a reproachful gasp. "Aunt Margaret! Can't you see how weak he is? Why, he can barely stand!"

"There, there, my sweet," Vasily said soothingly. "Madame, I wonder if I might have a word in private?"

Princess Margaret flushed with triumph. "I knew it! But no—if you are ready to confess, you must do it here before everyone!"

"I don't know that I would call it a confession, precisely." Vasily bestowed a charming smile upon the princess, the lawyer, and even Jaime, who stood beside his sister watching us in silence. "Only it sounded to me as though madame might be about to commit herself to some very injudicious accusations, and I thought it might be advisable to present her with some accreditation, that she might know I am telling the truth.—Madame," he finished, arising from his seat and with a profound bow presenting the princess with a folded document.

Princess Margaret sent him a suspicious look, but opened the envelope all the same. The document within bore a heavy seal and a short message in a bold, spiky hand. The Princess looked—paled—and gasped.

"What is this? It's preposterous," she insisted.

Vasily seemed to be enjoying himself hugely. "Not in the least. Marie-Caroline will vouch for me."

I tried to get a look at the document over the princess' shoulder, but was forestalled when Jaime took the letter from his mother. He cast a dispassionate glance over it, raised an eyebrow, and let out a low whistle of surprise.

"Vasily Nikolaevich Romanov? A Grand Duke, no less, with a letter of accreditation from the Tsar!"

I *knew* it! I sent Vasily a reproachful look. How dare he force my hand a second time!—He returned me a faint shrug, as though to say *I warned you not to delay too long.*

"It's true," I said stoutly, knowing that it would be no use denying him. "To tell the truth, we were recognised at the Opera by a relative of his."

The faint disbelieving smile vanished from Jaime's face as though by a parlour maid had wiped it away with a duster. "I daresay it is true," he said. "Blanca and I were with Grand Duke Nicholas at the time. He excused himself immediately he laid eyes on the Ba—on this gentleman."

"But this gentleman is no vampire," Blanca pointed out with an arch look.

"Alas, no!" Vasily said. "Not any more: I was caught up in that unfortunate business in Coburg."

"Then it's true, the rumours we've heard?" Princess Margaret paled. "It will be the end, absolutely the end.—But, you must forgive us—and especially my brother Robert. How could we have known you were a Grand Duke? Of course you will not object to our asking the Grand Duke Nicholas to verify your claim."

"I'll consider it," Vasily replied warily, "although I ought to warn you that I'm not on the best of terms with my brother."

"Your brother!" Princess Margaret said faintly. There was a humming silence in the room, and I could tell that all of them believed us. The thing was too audacious, too easily disproved, to be a lie. "Why didn't you tell us before?"

"As I explained last night, I'm an agent of my Emperor, and can scarcely disperse his secrets abroad."

I narrowly restrained an unladylike snort: if Vasily *had* at one time been an agent of the tsar, that time must surely be past.

Vasily retrieved the letter from Blanca, who had taken it from her brother and was reading it with one of her quiet smiles. "Forgive me, mesdames, monsieur, for interrupting your mourning. Unless there are other questions—?"

He paused expectantly, but Princess Margaret only said, very distractedly, "No, no, please don't trouble, your grace."

"Very well; I shall see you at breakfast." Vasily withdrew, leaving the Bourbon-Parmas and their lawyer looking uniformly flabbergasted.

"I must go and speak to Robert at once," Princess Margaret said after a moment. The lawyer excused himself likewise, and they hurried away leaving Blanca and Jaime exchanging thoughtful looks.

Tossing her head, Blanca addressed her brother in Spanish. I did not speak the language; but I did catch a couple of phrases that were perfectly intelligible to a French-speaker: *Grand Duke,* and *he is suspicious.*

I turned back to the corpse, bending my head as though in silent prayer, hoping to glean something more from the conversation.

Jaime growled something that sounded like, *Not in front of her,* and then, very clearly indeed: *Why would he lie about such a thing? What would he hope to gain?* "I," he finished in proper French, "am going down to breakfast."

"So will I, as soon as I've dressed," Blanca replied, stifling a yawn. As her brother left the room, she approached me and touched my arm. "You must forgive our rudeness; we have had more than one terrible shock this morning. Are you hungry, my dear?"

"Thank you, but no." I slipped away from her touch and retreated to the armchair by the bed, where the corpse of Maria Theresa lay a mute witness to these events. "I should like to sit here a while, if I may."

Alone, I sank into thought. I had told Blanca the truth: my appetite had fled. Poor Maria Theresa! Here she lay, cold and lifeless; and it was at least partly my fault. If the Bourbon-Parmas had not been frightened into fits by my impersonation of Marie-Caroline, or if I had denied Vasily the chance to declare the fictitious Baron to be my husband, Maria Theresa would doubtless still be living this morning. She would have died in time; perhaps at no very distant date, but peacefully and naturally—not bitten by a member of her own family!

Nonetheless I *had* interfered, and now she was dead; and

her heirs—her murderers—had nothing better to do with their time than to shout and wrangle over her body. Taking her hand gently between my own, I whispered, "I know I have deceived you, but I can promise you..."

And there I stopped. I had begun to wonder whether I should simply give up the inheritance and report Maria Theresa's murder to the authorities; for there was, after all, the evidence of the melusine bite upon the body. Yet now that Vasily had revealed his identity, I could scarcely abandon the game lest he be left exposed and helpless before his enemies. He was not a good man, and I did not mean to go along tamely with whatever he had planned; but I did not want him dead or imprisoned, either.

I could promise nothing save that the murderers would not profit by their crimes; and it seemed insultingly little to offer.

Half an hour passed in total solitude. Nijam, if the soft and steady breathing at the other end of my transmitter when I switched it on was any indication, was still plunged into a luxurious slumber. Vasily made no appearance, denying me the minor satisfaction of accidentally dropping a daddy-long-legs down the back of his neck (there was a fat one in the corner behind the dressing-table, and it badly wanted to be dropped down *somebody's* neck). This outlet was closed to me, however; and with every minute that passed, I felt more wretched about the whole affair. I wished devoutly that I had had the good sense to do as Mimi had done, and make my escape with whatever I could find in the jewel-boxes. It was too late now, of course, for I could not leave Vasily in the lurch.

It was no use sitting here cudgelling my weary brains for nothing. Tonight I would follow yesterday's interrupted plans:

this time I really would follow Marie-Caroline's imprint, and learn all it had to teach me. In the meanwhile, I should go in search of breakfast—but first, I must change my clothes before I caught my death of cold. The bottom six inches of my skirts, as well as my boots, were still drenched from the morning's walk.

I returned to my suite—was about to enter the sitting-room—when a distant voice called out to me. "Marie-Caroline? Come in; I want to talk to you."

It was Blanca's voice; I turned and saw her door standing ajar at the end of the short, dark corridor that led to her room. Unsuspecting, I did as bidden—went down the corridor, pushed open her door, stepped in—and found myself in the presence of the monster.

The Schloss was old-fashioned and had not yet installed running water in its bedrooms. A bathtub had been set down before the fireplace, and Blanca sat within it amidst the sleek and shining coils of her tail. She was not wearing a stitch of clothing; one glance satisfied all my curiosity upon the topic of melusine anatomy, and then, following the habits of a lifetime, I raised my eyes and set them upon the ceiling.

"I—I beg your pardon!" I stammered, thoroughly mortified and not a little afraid. No doubt this was merely the deplorable laxness of Continental manners, of which I had had some experience—but I could not help thinking of poor Maria Theresa, dead with fang-marks in her breast.

"Oh, shut the door and don't be sssuch a prude! Anyone would think you had never ssseen a melusine before!"

Hearing the souse of water and the whisper of her scales against the tub as she reared up from the water, I fixed my eyes upon her again with a stifled gasp of alarm.

Blanca transferred herself to a chair positioned beside the tub, allowing her tail to slip from the water, scattering puddles upon the priceless Aubusson carpet. From the waist downwards she was all metallic, gleaming scales; something like a mermaid in a picture book, but more serpentine and with sharp, elongated teeth.

I ought to have been repulsed by her monstrosity; I was not. She was beautiful—terrifying—powerful. I ought to have looked away—it is no good, if one means to deny oneself a thing, to tantalise oneself with it—but I hesitated, and was lost. I felt myself captured by her dark eyes, and before I knew what I was doing, I had closed the door behind me.

"Hand me my dresssing-gown, will you?" She pointed to the wrapper flung across the bed. When I hesitated, she laughed. "I'm not going to bite you. I only want to talk."

After all, Blanca was the only one of these people I liked, and there was surely no harm in a little talk. The thought merely drifted across my mind as I handed her the wrapper, a luxurious thing in colourful Chinese silk, which she belted loosely around her waist.

For some reason, I could not look away from her eyes—eyes that seemed to pierce directly through me, to subdue my will beneath her own.

"I meant to asssk you about lassst night," she said conspiratorially, rising from her chair and slithering nearer. "There was a great deal happening, wasn't there? A death—and nearly two?"

My throat was oddly dry; I swallowed to moisten it. "The Baron—Vasily, I mean—took a turn."

"Old people take turns," Blanca said, laughing. She reminded me of him, a little. She was terrifying, and beautiful, and knew it. "He was in your room, wasn't he? What's it like, cousin, when a man loves a woman?"

"I haven't the faintest idea," I said, shocked. If I had been thinking straight, I would have remembered that my story had been different last night. Then I remembered the previous occasions upon which I had felt the same impulse, to tell her the truth and keep nothing back.

Why, I wondered, did I feel so urgently disposed to trust this girl?

"No, I didn't think ssso." Blanca's eyes were still intent upon me, and difficult to escape. "Did you know, I've never so much as kisssed a man. I've kisssed girls, though; at the convent, we practiced on each other." Her fingers brushed mine. "I could show you, if you want. You'd like that, wouldn't you?"

For a moment I could say nothing at all. I confess that I felt a desperate curiosity. There had been similar experiments at St Alphege's, of course, but I had never partaken. At that time I was learning that there were certain things about myself I must keep hidden—my father's disgrace, my visions of the dead—and I had been in no mood to incur further disapproval. That was long ago, however; and a part of me would have been as glad to kiss Blanca in this moment, as I had been to kiss Vasily in the little drawing-room some days ago.

But I had chosen my path long ago. I would not violate the laws of religion and society; it would be a bad bargain indeed to give up the security of marriage and children for the loneliness and disgrace of—running into the wilderness with Blanca.

I would not do it for Vasily; and I would not do it for her sake, either. In that moment it was the habit of a lifetime that ruled me: I replied with tolerable politeness, "No, I wouldn't;

but thank you all the same."

She replied with a horribly attractive pout. "Come, don't be coy! I've seen the way you look at me. It doesn't bother *me,* you know, if you like girls the sssame way you like men. Plenty of people do."

There she misjudged me. You see, until I went to school, it had never entered my mind that there was anything peculiar about me at all, and even now I did not quite believe it. I found women as desirable as I found men; and I still found it difficult to conceive that I was unusual in my inclinations—that the rest of the world's population did not feel the same.

I could not help laughing. "Yes," I said, "plenty of people like all sorts of things, but that can have no bearing upon *my* behaviour, if I choose differently."

With that, at last I turned away from her—broke the spell of her eyes, and drew in a breath unburdened by her dominant will. In the same moment it was as though a cold hand fastened about my heart. Why, what had I been thinking—why had I not seen it sooner? Blanca was a melusine—her kiss would drain me of life, proving once and for all that I was not whom I claimed to be.

It was a trap—and under the influence of her mesmerism I had nearly fallen into it.

"Why not—where are you going?" Blanca hissed, interrupting herself in quite a different voice as I backed away from her. "Look me in the eye when I ssspeak to you!"

"I think not." I reached blindly for the doorknob, not quite meeting her eyes, but not quite turning my back on her, either. "What is it that you *really* want from me, Blanca?"

"Very well," she said, putting her hands on her hips. "I *know* the Baron, or the Grand Duke, or whoever he pretends to be, is wanted by the Russian sssecret police. Leopold of Tussscany had it from the Grand Duke Nicholas, and told me. *And* I know that you are no cousin of mine. I've known it ever sssince the Opera. Your name is Molly Dark, and you're an *Englishwoman* from *Brixton*."

I felt the blood rush to my heart; my fingers became icy cold, and my head buzzed. What I felt for Blanca—*that* was no terrible secret, enough to frighten me into submission. But this—this was.

"I *beg* your pardon?" I whispered.

"Number 45, Saltoun Road," Blanca recited with a triumphant smile. "What were your sisters' names again? Emily, Katherine, and Lilias? They sounded like clever girls. Your mother must be proud of them. I wonder what they'll think when you turn up dead in a Vienna canal?"

My mother's letter—she must have read the letter. Blanca must have searched my room last night while I sat with Maria Theresa; my morning-dress *had* been moved from its place, and its pockets rifled! Ah! Nijam, how right you were to warn me!

"You," I said numbly. "Were you the one who killed Maria Theresa?"

"How dare you?" She dealt me a hard, stinging slap. "That's the Countess of Chambord to *you*. Now, listen to me very carefully. I am giving you a little friendly advice: *run away*. Go now, before the rest of the family finds out." She was much too close; her smell was like lilies and death, and her sharp white teeth glistened with poison. "I like you, Molly Dark, but I don't like you well enough to hand over my inheritance. If you are still here tomorrow morning, you and your Grand Duke will rue it."

Chapter XXII.

I fled to my own room momentarily expecting either to hear the soft, slithering approach of the melusine, or to feel her needle-sharp teeth in my unguarded skin. It was all up with us—I was discovered—we must move quickly to save what we could from the wreckage.

"Nijam! Nijam!" I panted, switching on the transmitter once I was safe within my own suite. "Something dreadful has happened!"

"Already?" she mumbled, as though my frantic summons had dragged her from sleep. "Confound it, Dark! Can't you keep out of trouble for a *few* short hours?"

Ten minutes later, having come downstairs to hear my story in person, she was no happier. "All right: what is it now?"

"Blanca knows I'm an imposter." I wrung my hands together. My mind had been busy in the minutes since I last spoke to Nijam, and the words came out in a rush. "She said she has known it ever since the Opera. How? The only thing I can think of is that when I accepted Vasily as my husband...oh! What if Blanca knew where Marie-Caroline had really run away to? She and Jaime were both here when Marie-Caroline disappeared; if the princess had confided in her..."

I stopped, partly to catch my breath and partly to see

whether Nijam had followed my wildly careening train of thought. She knitted her dark brows and said, "If Blanca knew you were not Marie-Caroline, why is she just now revealing it?—and why to you, rather than the whole family?"

The blood rushed to my face. *I like you, Molly Dark—I've seen the way you look at me.* Could it be genuine regard for me?—No, I didn't believe it; there had been no real liking in her manner; only something hard and bright and utterly self-absorbed.

"I don't know, but she gave me one day's grace in which to remove myself. Nijam! You don't suppose *she* might have murdered Marie-Caroline?"

Nijam frowned. "Unlikely. If Blanca had killed her cousin, then she would surely have known *you* to be an imposter from the start. If it was one of the Bourbon-Parmas—which doesn't seem such a wild notion now that the old Countess is dead—Jaime is more likely. He was suspicious of you even on the first evening you wore the tail. And he's not such a pleasant fellow himself. I'm given to understand that *he's* the reason some of the maids are aging so quickly."

I shuddered. "Do you know, I overheard Jaime in the garden the other day telling Blanca to stop trying to help him. Perhaps *he* killed Marie-Caroline—and Blanca suspects it, and is trying to protect him." I let out a sigh of frustration. "It all comes back to that night, and who killed Marie-Caroline!"

"I disagree; it doesn't matter in the least who killed Marie-Caroline," Nijam said testily. "Or Maria Theresa, for that matter. It might have been any or all of them. We aren't here to stop these people murdering each other; we're here to steal a fortune! What does Blanca have, besides conjecture? She may try to make trouble, but it's only her word against yours;

and with an honest-to-goodness Grand Duke in our pockets, we *may* be in a strong enough position to weather it."

The look on my face must have given me away.

"Dark," Nijam said balefully, "she *does* have only conjecture, doesn't she?"

"She knows my name," I muttered. "She searched my room."

There was a short and withering silence. "What was it? The letters? The letters I *told you* to destroy?—How could you be so careless? What were you thinking?—No, don't say it; you weren't thinking at all; that much is clear. Could you not keep your mind on the job for even *one day*? Throwing paper darts at the Opera—letting Vasily tell all and sundry you are married when you knew full well it would provoke a crisis—and now leaving your proper name lying about where anyone could find it! What if she calls upon the von Hügels to identify you?"

"I locked the letter in the chest," I objected, "as soon as I had sent my reply. It's my mother; she needed to hear from me."

"She *needs* you to provide *medical care*," Nijam said in a muted fury, "and without the inheritance you can do no such thing. Now not only is your mother's life in danger because of your incompetence, but so is yours—and mine, and Vasily's, and Alphonse's, and even Miss Laine's. Good Lord!—Maria Theresa is *dead,* and Alphonse has already been shot once, because of you! Now you have brought *all* of us down. What if she hands the lot of us over to the Russians? There's no salvaging this."

I felt as though I had been flayed, dissected, and pinned out like a specimen. But Nijam's final words were almost liberating. If there really was no hope of getting the inheritance, then I was free—free to do what I had come to see as my duty.

"We have one day before Blanca speaks," I began slowly.

"Yes; and if we leave now, we might possibly get across the border to Germany, or to Switzerland, before she sets the police on us."

"As a matter of fact," I said, "I thought that we had one day in which to do some table-turning. Why did Blanca give us a day's grace? Why didn't she speak to her family at once? Something is keeping her quiet—something makes her hope we run away of our own accord, rather than forcing a confrontation. She is trying to frighten us.—But why? What is Blanca afraid of? If it doesn't have something to do with Marie-Caroline, I'll eat my shoes."

"Your hat," Nijam said automatically, but I could tell I had intrigued her. "You think we might be able to make her hold her peace?"

"Blanca tried to frighten me just now, Nijam. She used all her powers—even the mesmerism—but she did not actually use violence. Why not? *Why is she afraid to confront me?* I sorely doubt it's out of any regard for me."

"You mean, she might honestly wish to spare your life? No. She might warn you in that case, but she would not threaten you."

"Exactly," I said, drumming nervous fingers upon the back of the chair in front of me. I was too full of pent-up energy to sit. "We have until tomorrow morning to find what Blanca is afraid of—and use it."

Nijam sighed. "It's dangerous, Dark, but I'll stick with you for now. Still, I want you to know one thing." Her brows contracted until they were a single black bar across her scowling face. "If you do anything—anything at all—that results in Alphonse Schmidt being harmed again, I will

258

personally ensure that you suffer for it."

I had already been threatened by a melusine this morning; I was in no mood to be threatened by a mere prosthete. "I'll do my best," said I, "but you know very well that your precious Alphonse is wrapped around Vasily's little finger, and I can't protect him if he takes it into his head to throw himself into danger to protect his master. You had best speak to him yourself."

"*Me?* Why? Aren't you going to warn Vasily about Blanca?"

I thought about this a moment. "No," I said at last. "Better for us if Vasily thinks everything is going well. Heaven knows what he will do if he thinks we might hurt his prospects. All he cares about is the money, after all; he might repudiate me and propose to Blanca, and then we should certainly be for it."

"Then what *is* the plan?"

The plan was simple, but getting her to agree to it would be ticklish. Nijam did not believe in ghosts.

"I have a couple of leads on Marie-Caroline," I said evasively. "I simply mean to follow them."

* * *

Marie-Caroline's imprint appeared at the usual time, around midnight. Having dressed warmly, in a sturdy dark riding-habit, I had taken the precaution of going downstairs to the rear vestibule, where I waited silently in the darkness for her coming.

The imprint passed me quite close, shining with a faint and ghostly light that amply illuminated her figure and face. Marie-Caroline, on that night three years ago, had carried a small valise and worn a pretty white blouse over her riding-skirt; her feelings were a heady mixture of despair and hope. Apart from that, she seemed to be in perfectly sound health. How had she died? I opened the back door and followed her into the cold, wet night half dreading whatever it was I was about to witness.

It was not quite so wet and inhospitable a night as the one previous had been, but the wind was brisk and the moonlight fitful, smothered as it was with flying clouds. To my eyes, however, the imprint was sufficiently visible to lead me unerringly to the stables.

Marie-Caroline busied herself in saddling a ghostly horse. Watching her, I followed suit with the tangible Bradamante, having bribed her first with a lump of sugar. Getting the horse out of the stable and down the gravelled drive past the house might have been a ticklish business, except that Marie-Caroline had left me an excellent example: she opened the door at the rear of the stable, and led us by a roundabout path, not entirely dissimilar to the one Mimi and I had taken that morning, to the schloss gate. From there, we took to the saddle and went stealthily through the village before turning north towards Wiener Neustadt.

The ride—up a small path by the side of a stream—might have been pleasant in warmer weather: on a spring afternoon, say, with birdsong and profusions of spring flowers to enjoy. As it was, the night was fitfully lighted by the fugitive moon; the wind lashed my hair and skirts; and the countryside, during the brief moments when it became visible, seemed a lonely, desperate place and ripe for mischievous deeds. I was glad to walk my mount demurely in Marie-Caroline's shadowy wake, hoping to avoid any slippery edges or rabbit-holes that might bring Brada and myself to grief. Despite having indulged myself in a couple of hours' sleep that afternoon, I was very tired. My eyes itched, and I felt myself sinking into a waking dream, half staring vigilance, half shivering trance: again and again I startled at the sound of a fox screaming in the distance, or at the imagined fall of some stealthy foot behind me.

Vasily had spent much of the day with Princess Margaret and the lawyer, beginning to arrange the legal matters in the winding-up of the estate. While he was busy, I had sent a reluctant Nijam to distract Alphonse while I made an unsuccessful search of the Grand Duke's room, looking for Marie-Caroline's final journal. The reader will recall that he had promised me a look at it in Vienna; but subsequent requests had been put off: there was more pressing business to attend to, or he did not have the book readily to hand. I knew then that he would never willingly relinquish it.

Blanca I had seen only at dinner, where she had greeted me with her customary good humour: a performance which I now found to be almost sinister, following the threats she had made against my sisters.

Now, keeping a sharp watch on Marie-Caroline's ghostly imprint, I wondered whether I had misjudged. I had expected some grisly ambush on the road, yet already the lights of Wiener Neustadt had come into view ahead of us. Had the killer also followed Marie-Caroline so far from the Schloss? That seemed unlikely; yet how else could he possibly have harmed her?—But it was too late now to turn back, and I had no other lead. I must go on.

We entered the town—to all eyes I must have been a rather ghostly figure myself, a black shadow upon a grey horse—and within a very few minutes arrived, as I had already guessed we would, at the train station. Marie-Caroline tethered her horse to one of the posts there and lingered for a moment with her face buried in its flank; I felt a wrenching sense of loss, and then she kissed Brada's nose and ran in at the station-gate. I followed. A guard was sleeping behind the desk. I stole past just in time to see Marie-Caroline throw herself into the arms of a phantasmagorical young man who waited expectantly upon the station platform. For some time neither of them looked up. Their bittersweet joy was like a rocket going off, bright enough to paint weeping colours across the sky. I reeled a little and perhaps uttered a sound of astonishment at the sensation. Then a distant whistle sounded in my ear; and some moments later the pair parted, as though they had heard it themselves, or its three-years-gone counterpart. The young man picked up Marie-Caroline's valise, put an arm around her shoulders, and stepped into the light of a gas-lamp which illuminated the platform.

That was when I caught a glimpse of his face—and uttered a second exclamation of sheer surprise. By some miracle, I knew him. Marie-Caroline's beloved was the very young man who had attended my séance only a week ago in Vienna.

I recalled now the wife he had lost and wished to speak to—his speechlessness at the sight of me, as well he might be upon his meeting one who bore so striking a resemblance to his own dead love!

My brain was still reeling from the revelation when the distant train arrived in a rush. The platform was deserted, except for a single passenger who waited in the shadows nearer the gate. No one alighted from the train. It was late, and the cargo was mostly composed of freighted goods. There was one carriage, however, illuminated by lamps which shone upon a mass of sleeping third-class passengers. The lovers moved towards it and then faded away like the ghosts they were.

Marie-Caroline's imprint had told its story; and now I had only to act upon it.—Easier said than done. I had seen the young man's face, but whom could it be? He was poor, he lived in Vienna; that was all I had learned at the séance. There were other clues: *that matter of the singing-tutor,* as Maria Theresa had put it. They had tracked him down in Ottakring, the industrial quarter where so many of the poor lived; but there had been no sign of the princess. In any case, how could there have been? By then, Marie-Caroline herself was dead, I knew not how—but that young man did; and *he* had been alive within the week.

I don't think I ever really doubted that the despised Jewish singing-tutor and Marie-Caroline's handsome young lover were one and the same; no more than I despaired of finding him somehow in the metropolis. No—what held me motionless as the train steamed and sighed at the platform, was the thought of all the people who were relying upon me: not only my mother and sisters, but Nijam, and Vasily and Alphonse and Mimi. For if I set foot on that train, it was all over as far as getting the inheritance went. All the same, Maria Theresa had been murdered, and Marie-Caroline had died betimes, and if there was a chance there was anyone in the world who had loved either of them, they deserved to have justice. The Bourbon-Parmas did not deserve the inheritance, and I had failed to earn it; but perhaps, I thought, there were some things too valuable to be earned or deserved. Perhaps they were simply bestowed as a gift upon the sort of person who would conduct himself honestly even when a lovesick young heiress begged him to run off with her.

The train whistled again, and I threw myself across the platform and in at the door.

Chapter XXIII.

The carriage was not particularly full. As I settled myself on one of the hard seats facing the engine, I felt that I had cast myself into the unknown and could not guess what might follow. There came a jolt, and the train moved off, slowly at first, but quickly gathering speed; my heart went pit-a-pat in time with the clacking wheels. One thing at least, I thought, was well: I could not possibly return to the Schloss by morning, and so Blanca would be pleased to think that her plan of intimidation had worked. Nijam, I hoped, would make a swift departure with Alphonse; and Vasily, if he insisted on staying, must rely on his own wits to save him. It was cowardly of me, of course, but I did not particularly relish the thought of confessing to their faces that I was throwing up the whole affair on a whim. That would create a scene, and I hated scenes. This way, I might never be able to show my face in Vienna again, but at least it would do away with any need for explanations.

I was still entertaining these guilty thoughts when a shadow fell over me, and I looked up to see—Vasily Nikolaevich.

For a moment I had no power of speech: he might have been summoned, like the fiend, merely by thinking. Or—was he dead? Had the monsters already discovered my flight and killed him?

Vasily sat opposite me, smiling gently; he had a way of smiling that bared all his teeth, which were very white within the shadow of his beard. "Good evening, little mouse," he said softly. "You look pale. What happened? Have you seen a ghost?"

"Don't laugh," I said feebly, "but in fact, yes."

"That's very interesting!" he said. "No, don't say anything more at present. There will be time for explanations when we get to—wherever it is you are going."

"Vienna," I said, almost soundlessly.

He studied me a while in leisurely silence. "I'll humour you," he said at length. "Vienna it is."—and so saying, he stretched out his legs, folded his arms, and fixed unblinking eyes upon me.

I surveyed his lazy posture, and saw that his shoes were muddy, and the hems of his trousers spattered with more of the same. "You *did* follow me all the way from the Schloss," I said indignantly. "I *thought* I heard something!"

I had an appreciative gleam from his half-lidded eyes. "You took me by surprise, Miss Dark. I had not the slightest notion of your setting out to Vienna on such short notice, or I might have worn stouter boots." After that, we did not speak again, except when the conductor came through to demand our tickets. I professed to have no money, so that Vasily was obliged to pay for both of us. Then I tried to rest; but Vasily's eyes never left me, nor did they relax from their expression of calculating vigilance. We reached Vienna when the clocks were striking three. Vasily haled me from the carriage, tucked my arm rather tightly beneath his own, and called a cab.

"Where to?" he asked, with a polite ferocity that told me he had not yet forgiven me.

"To the Rilkeplatz," I told him.

"Nonsense! You didn't come all this way to speak to Mimi."

"I came to get away from the Schloss, and Mimi is the only person I know who might help me. I suppose I shall travel to Copenhagen with her. An English governess might be able to find a decent position there."

"To Copenhagen!" He raised an eyebrow. "Out with it, Miss Dark. What haven't you told me? Why this headlong flight? I suppose you couldn't face the prospect of marriage to me; is that it?"

"It may shock you to hear it," said I severely, "but not all my decisions are made with reference to you, your grace! I am leaving because Blanca knows who I am. She has known since the night at the Opera."

Vasily said something impolite in French. "She knew! What could have tipped her off, I wonder? It wasn't meeting my brother; it's *your* imposture that failed. Ah: your acceptance of myself as your husband. I take it she must have known that Marie-Caroline really ran off with—"

He stopped.

"With whom?" I asked.—He smiled ferociously. "You *do* know," I conjectured, opening my eyes very wide at him. "You must have learned it from the final journal!"

He touched his breast pocket, and I thought I saw a faint, book-shaped outline there against his heart.

"Aren't you going to let me see it?"

"If we are no longer allies, why should I?" He regarded me with a very cold sort of amusement. "I don't believe you've been quite honest with me, my dear. Why so interested in Marie-Caroline, if you'll be on the train to Copenhagen in the morning?"

"Well, *I* don't believe you ever meant to let me see the journal at all," I said with a girlish pout. "All this time you've been telling me it was not to hand, when you've had it your pocket all along! Of course you'd never be stupid enough to leave it in your room, if it had the name of Marie-Caroline's real lover in it. Good heavens," I went on, becoming genuinely agitated, "to think that whoever that poor man is, you have always known precisely how to find him! Don't you care for *anyone* but yourself?"

"No," he replied instantly. "Why should I? and what does it matter to you, in any case?"

"Well, it occurred to me," I said recklessly, "that if *we* can't have the inheritance, perhaps Marie-Caroline's real husband should!"

There was a cold, black silence; so cold and so black that I shivered, becoming aware how little the flaring gas-light that intermittently streamed through the windows of the cab really illuminated it. I wondered if I had misjudged in tipping my hand; I had intended to provoke him into revealing his own—

Suddenly enough to make me gasp, Vasily's hand fastened upon my wrist.

"This is enough, my dear," he said. "I can't allow you to run away, and I certainly can't allow you to throw away my best chance of rehabilitation on some poor devil of an outcast organ-grinder. I won't make you play my wife for long, but I'm exposed; I've committed myself now, and it's finish the job or finish myself."

I made no reply to that: his words were terribly final, and I did not think he would listen to any argument. In any case I had satisfied myself that Vasily could not be depended upon.

"Mimi will put us up for the night, and then we'll return to the Schloss," he went on, as the silence lengthened. "Blanca will not trouble us. We'll buy or blackmail her if we must. Agreed?"

"I don't want to put you in any danger," said I meekly. "Whatever you think best, I'm sure."

"There's a good girl," he said, releasing me.

I rubbed my bruised wrist and thought mutinous thoughts. If Vasily was exposed to danger, it had been his own choice, not mine; and if I had been loath to accept the inheritance when I knew of no more deserving heir, I surely could not stomach the thought of taking it now. There was right and wrong beyond riches and poverty; and of course I could not afford even to save my mother's life at the expense of my own conscience. Vasily might think the money fair game if we could get it, but I would never be able to forget that Marie-Caroline had a living husband, who had loved her, and for whom she had fled her home and family.

In a few short minutes our conveyance deposited us upon the steps of Mimi's lodging. Upstairs, she answered at once to our knock. *"You* again," she muttered, beckoning us into her bare apartment. "Something told me it wouldn't be long. Don't you know what time it is? When I said to call on me, I didn't mean at half-past two in the morning."

Seeing that she wore a dress of rather yellowed white tulle and a pair of ballet shoes in which she had evidently been practising before the mirror, I said with disingenuous meekness: "I'm terribly sorry to rouse you from your sleep."

Vasily, despite himself, released a snort of laughter.

"It's Mimi," he said, "she has moved beyond the need for

269

sleep, unlike us lesser mortals."

"If it's a bed you want, she can have mine and you can have the armchair," she said briskly, "and it'll be five *kronen* apiece; unless you want breakfast—"

"Take it all," Vasily said impatiently, dropping a handful of silver into her palm. "No; wait, I must have enough to pay for the fare back to Wiener Neustadt. No doubt you are wondering what brings us here—"

"Not particularly," said Mimi, tucking the coins into a shabby, beaded pouch. "Make yourselves comfortable."

Vasily looked at the armchair in a resigned way. "I'll do my best, though I can't promise unqualified success."

"I'll find you a blanket," I told him, still feigning meekness. At Mimi's gesture of invitation, I went into the bedroom, which was nearly as bare as the main room: the bedstead which must once have stood here was gone, and in its place a thin mattress lay on the floor beneath rumpled covers. There was only a threadbare blanket to cover it, and a woolly rug crocheted by hand, which I took up and bore back to Vasily.

"Are you sure you'll be all right out here?" I asked solicitously, for I couldn't help noticing that the armchair stood in lonely splendour near the door, and I should be obliged to slip past it in order to get out. "You'd sleep better in the bed, and I..."

"Won't do; there's not room enough for the three of us," Mimi said, breathing hard. She had returned to her exercises before the mirror, repeating the same steps time and again—a quick, darting, diagonal movement, and then a sustained spinning motion upon one toe.

"That wasn't what I meant," I said, blushing violently.

Vasily's eyes laughed at me. "Don't worry; I'll be quite

comfortable here. I couldn't possibly call on you to give up your bed and sleep in an armchair."

"There's nothing else I can get you? A pillow? Some warm milk? I can't help but feel that this is all my fault. I was so frightened when Blanca told me what she knew—"

"Little mouse, little mouse," he said, almost caressingly, "you should have come to me."

"How could I, when you told me not to trust you?"

"You can always trust me to safeguard my own interests. Go and get some sleep. Our train home leaves before nine."

"You're not angry with me anymore?"

"How could I be?" With a quick, gallant gesture he kissed the knuckles of my hand. "Go."

Really, he *did* look tired. "Mimi had some laudanum, if you wanted help sleeping."

After a moment's hesitation, he uttered a hard laugh. "What am I worried about? Thank you; I'll have some."

In fact, the collection in Mimi's kitchenette incorporated not only laudanum but chloral hydrate. I did not think either of them were for her personal use; Mimi was far more likely to be following the example of that larcenous American gentleman, Michael Finn. Not knowing the correct dosage, however, I left the stronger drug on the shelf and brought Vasily the laudanum, with a spoon to pour it out with.

"Thank you, Nanny," he said wryly. "Go to bed, you two."

Mimi threw a knot of wood onto the fireplace and followed me into her room, closing the door behind us.

"We aren't really going to share the bed, are we?" I asked nervously.

She looked up from unwrapping the ribbons of her satin shoes. "What, do you think I'll bite you?"

271

I couldn't help glancing at the livid bite-marks across her neck and shoulders. No, I did not think she would bite me. In no sense was Mimi a beast of prey, like Blanca; and I *knew* that I was not.

"No," I said, "I don't."

"Good, because the night will be cold and uncomfortable anywhere else."

Having added our outer garments to the covers, we crawled beneath them. The mattress was every bit as thin and narrow as it had first appeared, and I lay rigidly still, trying not to move or breathe too loudly so as not to keep Mimi awake. What would my mother say if she could see me now, obliged to seek my rest beneath the same moth-eaten blanket as a scarred dainty?—Then I considered what Blanca had said this morning, about not minding if I wanted to kiss her—as though an inclination towards one's own sex was not something everyone felt as a matter of course. Perhaps, after all, this was true! People did not usually speak of such things in the hearing of a young lady, but the more I thought of it, the more little things made sense that had once confused me—like the disdain with which some of the St Alphege's girls had responded to the experiments of the others.

But then, if I was *different*, what would Mimi say if I confessed to her? Unconventional as she was, she might put me out of her bed if I made her uncomfortable—or her house. She might draw her knife on me again!—Perhaps I was a coward, but I decided not to risk it.

After the previous night's adventures, not even these discomfiting thoughts could keep me awake. Soon sleep crept upon me like a thief, and I sank into oblivion.

I awoke at first light, having twitched the curtains open

far enough to permit the first faint rays of dawn to shine upon my face. Mimi was still fast asleep. I felt half dead with exhaustion, but if I allowed myself more sleep, I would not wake until Vasily dragged me from my pillow; and that was no part of my plan.

I slithered out from under the covers and climbed into my skirt and jacket before slipping into the main room of the apartment. Here, the curtains were drawn, but a little light struggled in around the curtains and reflected in the great mirror, faintly illuminating the chamber. Opposite me, Vasily reclined in the armchair with his head thrown back against one of the wings. For a moment I wondered how I could ever have mistaken this man for a mere baron, for his body was one long, imperious sprawl of wealth and hauteur.

I tiptoed nearer. Vasily's eyes—for once—were closed, the long dark lashes fanning across his cheekbones. Apart from the mulberry silk four-in-hand which he had pulled from his neck and tossed over the back of the armchair, he was fully dressed; and he had eschewed the use of the rug I had given him last night, leaving it folded on the floor. I picked it up, moving very quietly, and draped it over his arms and legs.

With the same movement, I slipped my hand into his jacket, found the journal, and drew it out.

Vasily moved sleepily. His breath hitched—and his eyes opened.

"Miss Dark," he murmured.

In another moment he would look down—he would see the book in my hands. Repressing a shudder, I slipped the volume between the folds of my skirts, smoothed back his hair, and kissed his forehead.

"Go back to sleep," I told him in a comforting murmur. "I'm

only letting the cat out."

Mimi had no cat—but Vasily was tired, half asleep, and softened by my earlier ministrations. With a sigh, he shifted slightly and closed his eyes again. I closed my own for a moment in turn, trembling a little with the intensity of my reaction.

When I opened them again, I found Mimi observing me sleepily from the open door leading to her own room.

Her eyes fixed upon the purloined journal, and a brow rose.

She must have seen the theft. I quickly put the book into my pocket, signing for her to be silent, and following it with a gesture of supplication. Smiling wryly, Mimi rubbed a thumb against a forefinger: she wanted money. I patted my pockets, certain that I had nothing of a significant enough denomination to purchase her silence; but then, at the bottom of one, I found the twenty-*kronen* piece given me at the séance by Marie-Caroline's husband. I could think of no better use for it: I handed it over, and Mimi, who had tiptoed to my side, opened the door to let me out.

I flew downstairs, hailed a cab to take me to the Ringstrasse, and rifled Marie-Caroline's final journal for clues until it divulged a name: *Franz* dotted a page many times, and in the margins, in an idle scribble: *Mr and Mrs Haber.* That was all I had time for: the carriage crossed the bridge upon which our memorable confrontation with Vasily's brother had taken place, and shortly thereafter we had arrived at the Opera.

The hour was still early and the Opera was nearly deserted; yet, to my relief, I was able to find a class of young ballerinas repeating their steps to the music of a put-upon-looking pianist. I was able to get his attention when the ballet babies took a short break for bread-and-butter and coffee.

274

"Yes, Countess?" he asked hopefully.

I had, of course, introduced myself under a false name. "I was looking for one Franz Haber, a singing teacher. He was recommended to me some time ago, and as I've newly returned from Budapest, I thought I'd inquire about lessons."

"Haber!" the accompanist said, "now that's a name I've not heard in some months! You mustn't have heard about it in Budapest, but he's no longer taking students—that is, there are none who will take him. There was a scandal, you understand, with a young student. I'm sure a lady like yourself would prefer not to be mixed up in something like *that*."

I tutted. "What a foolish thing to do, to be sure! What do you suppose he's doing now—factory labour?"

"Oh, no," the accompanist said. "He's been working the Ringstrasse with a barrel-organ, singing Mozart, poor devil, to keep body and soul together. If you've a mind to see him, he's usually installed at the Volksgarten on a Saturday morning, near Uncle Hamit's *börek* stand."

At the Volksgarten, Uncle Hamit was already putting out his first trays of hot, crisp cheese *böreks*. I bought one, returning an uncomfortably non-committal reply to his inquiries after Ada and Steffi, whom I doubted I should ever see again. There was no sign among the early street performers of Franz Haber, the poetic-looking young man from the séance. Still, when I asked Uncle Hamit if he knew the organ-grinder, a broad smile broke over his face.

"Franz!" he said. "He usually doesn't come until ten o'clock. I can give you his address, though, if you like. 10 Wurlitzergasse, Ottakring."

This was better than I had dared to hope, for it had been my dread that Vasily would know where to find Herr Haber, and might ambush him before I could speak to him. Spending my last two *kronen* recklessly on another cab, I hastened to the address and within a very few minutes was knocking upon a door in a poor and dingy tenement. When it opened I found myself in the presence of the young man from the séance, with his dark poetic eyes, his curling hair, his threadbare coat and ragged gloves. He looked terribly thin, cold, and weary; and within the house there echoed a racking cough horribly like my mother's.

"I beg your pardon," I said diffidently, "but are you Franz Haber, by any chance?"

"That depends who's asking," he said, evidently trying to pass the words off as a joke. Then he caught a good look of my face under the brim of my hat, and his fists clenched.

"You!" he hissed. "You're the medium—the one who's been pretending—"

He caught himself before speaking the name, and for a moment he struggled with his feelings in silence. Evidently he had *seen* the papers.

"I knew you'd be angry with me," I said meekly. "But it was Marie-Caroline who brought me here, you know."

He glanced up and down the stairwell as though he expected to find it infested by policemen or bodyguards. It was, thankfully, empty. "Maria is dead," he said flatly. "You can have her old name and her old life if you want it; she didn't care for those things."

"Please don't be angry," I protested, throwing myself against the door as he attempted to close it. "I didn't come here to threaten you; I came to find out who killed her."

There was a silence. Franz Haber fixed a bright, almost feverish eye upon me and spoke hoarsely:

"If you think—for one moment—that *I* am responsible for her death—"

"No, no," I said, distressed. "It never crossed my mind. Only since I came to the Schloss Frohsdorf there have been two more murders, and I thought..."

"No one killed my wife," he said in a voice still hoarse with emotion. "She sickened and died before we had been married a week. There was no reason for it; she had never been weak or delicate. God wished her in heaven. That is all."

"That can't possibly be all," I insisted. "Forgive me, but you can't really believe that!"

"What else am I to believe—that I killed her? That she could not survive my poor hovel, or such coarse fare as I was able to provide?"

"You misunderstand me! All I know is that Maria's is not the only death connected with those monsters—and I can't let them get away with it."

"Of course not," he said, after a moment's bitter reflection. "If you can prove foul play in Maria's death, you can prevent their inheriting."

"All right," I said, throwing up my hands. "Herr Haber, you may not want Marie-Caroline's fortune yourself, but you have the power to say *who* shall have it. Speak now, and the fortune goes to me, a stranger. Or hold your tongue, and it goes to a pack of monstrous killers. It's your choice entirely."

For a moment I was afraid he would simply wash me out to dry. Instead, his mouth twisted indecisively. Another fit of coughing emanated from the apartment behind him, and a female voice inquired as to whether he meant to stand letting the cold draughts roam in and out at will, or invite the guest in.

"Come in, then," he said, relenting, "and I'll tell you what I know.—Sorry, Mother! I didn't mean to give you a chill."

He ushered me into a miserable little single-roomed apartment. The windows were cracked and grimy, stuffed with rags to keep the winter wind out; yet despite this, the place was as cold as charity. A little pot-bellied stove in the corner did little to warm the air, all its efforts being obstructed by a middle-aged lady in a dress which must once have been fine, but was now faded and burned from crouching too close to the fire. Rubbing her thin hands together, she blinked at me through her thick glasses and said, uncertainly, "Why, Franz!—is that—?"

"No, Mother; it's not even her ghost," he said wryly. "Sit down, *fraulein,* and I'll make you coffee."

"Thank you, I never drink it," I said. His generous nature had evidently triumphed over the defences of his grief. "Frau Haber, I apologise for intruding upon you."

"Oh, it's no intrusion," she said, picking up her knitting needles. "Now, sit down and tell me everything from the beginning. And speak up, this time; I didn't catch more than a few words before."

I glanced at Franz, whose wry look told me that he was quite aware that he had been outmanoeuvred, and then again at his mother, whose high colour and racking cough told me that she, quite likely, was stricken by the same disease that promised to carry off my own mother. As I told my story, my conscience struck me sorely: there I had been, dithering over the wrongs and rights of my situation, not knowing that the true heir—for so I must regard Marie-Caroline's husband—was still more desperately needy than myself.

"You see why I felt obliged to seek out the real heir,"

I finished. "Why should the Bourbon-Parmas have the inheritance, after they have schemed and killed to get it?—and why should I and my confederates have it either, when we've done nothing to earn it? You loved Marie-Caroline, and I think she would prefer you to have it above anyone else."

"Maria Charlotte," Franz corrected me, his eyes full of soft and agonising memories. "That was the name she took when she married me... You already know the main points of the story. I gave her singing-lessons when we lived in Wiener Neustadt. She took a liking to me, and I to her. At that time I said nothing to her—not because she was a princess, but because she was my student, and very young. I knew little of the way she felt, until I was informed that the lessons would no longer take place. Then she came to Wiener Neustadt in defiance of her mother's instructions, and told me of her feelings, and that she wished me to take her away. I refused, of course; but then life suddenly became very hard for me in Wiener Neustadt. People turned their backs on me in the street and stopped coming to me for lessons. Threatening signs were scrawled on the wall of our house, until the landlord informed us that we must leave. With no livelihood, I returned to Vienna; but I had begun to understand just what Maria had begged me to take her away from—and so for some time I wrote to her, and she to me. When two years passed with no alteration in her purpose, I agreed to help her escape. She met me at the train station in Wiener Neustadt, and we fled to Vienna together. It had been our purpose to flee further still, but within two days Maria took ill. I spent everything I had saved on doctors, but there was nothing they could do. Within a fortnight she was dead. They...they said it was food poisoning, but..." He gave a helpless shrug.

"You did not quite believe it, either," I observed. Was that why he had attended my séance?

"I believe it," put in Frau Haber, who had listened in attentive silence. "Depend upon it, that cousin of hers, that Infante Jaime, killed her with a slow-acting poison sooner than see her marry another!"

"Don't be foolish, Mother—I'm not sure *any* poisons are that slow, and she always spoke highly of Jaime. Still, it hardly matters now. Maria was buried under my name. It was her final wish to be beside me in death. I knew that if her family were able to recover her corpse, they would take even that away from us, and so I buried the marriage license and all other evidence in her coffin. "

"Except her journal," I surmised, retrieving it from my pocket and handing it over to him.

"Her journal!" he exclaimed, holding the book reverently. "She *said* something about having left it by mistake on the train…"

"That's the problem with bringing something sensational to read," I observed, "you're always losing it. How it came into my hands, I really cannot say. But of one thing I'm absolutely certain: that your Maria's death was no accident."

He set the book against his forehead, as though over-whelmed with his own grief and wishing to be private with it. At length he lowered the book; his face was pale, but stamped with resolution.

"Are you really able to commune with the dead?" he asked me.

Abashed, I shook my head. "I'm afraid not, Herr Haber. Unless the dead choose to visit me very shortly after their death—as Maria Theresa did—I can sometimes see the echoes of past actions and emotions; that's all."

Franz looked crestfallen, but I remained silent a moment longer. I saw at once what I must do, but I did not know whether I could find the courage.

I *must* find the courage. I had come too far to turn back now.

"What I *can* do," I said slowly, "is get at the truth of these murders and see you settled in your wife's inheritance. You evidently need it far more than I do."

He glanced at his mother, and I could tell that he, like me, would have done almost anything to save her. "Tell me how," he said in a low voice.

"Well, for one thing, we will need the contents of that coffin."

"You're thinking of exhuming the body?" He paled. "But that's a crime."

It was worse than that: for me, it was raving madness. Nevertheless, I compelled myself to smile.

"Which," I said, "is why I'll need thieves to help me."

Chapter XXIV.

Having laid my plans, to the best of my ability, with Franz Haber, I ventured out onto the street and hailed the first cab I saw, which was waiting on the opposite side of the Wurlitzerstrasse. Its blinds were drawn, but when the cabbie pulled up before me and curtly agreed to take me as far as the Ringstrasse, I presumed that it must be empty after all.

With the blinds drawn, the light within the carriage was dim. It took a moment for my eyes to adjust, and then I uttered a gasp of surprise as I found that I was not alone. A man was seated opposite me. The carriage took off with a sudden jolt; the man seized my wrists with one hand and pulled the door shut with the other; and I fell back upon the seat, breathing hard, and looking up in terror at—the Infante Jaime.

"Not whom you expected?" said he, with a hard smile. "No—don't scream—you'll be sorry if you do."

"What do you want from me?" I gasped, praying that his presence in this dingy street did not betoken what I thought. His reply dashed my hopes at once.

"I want to know why you're meeting with Franz Haber," he said.

For a moment all I could hear was Frau Haber's voice accusing Jaime of having murdered the lost princess out of spite, because she meant to marry another rather than himself.

"I haven't the faintest idea what you mean," I said, rallying. "Your sister told me to leave the Schloss; so I went." A terrible thought struck me as I remembered the friends I had left at Schloss Frohsdorf—Nijam and her Alphonse, who had no notion of my whereabouts. "How did you find me, anyway?"

Jaime's lips tightened. "That," he said, "is immaterial."

* * *

It is not, however, immaterial to my story; and so I crave my reader's indulgence for as long as it may take to summarise the events of the morning as Nijam experienced it.

Her first notion of anything out of the ordinary having occurred, came in the form of a rude awakening an hour or two before dawn. One moment she was asleep, dreaming unhappily that Alphonse had been bitten by a melusine and was incapable of directing her how to formulate the antivenom. The next moment, the door to the cramped little room burst open and Nijam startled awake amidst shrieks from the other occupants, only to be seized bodily and dragged from her bed.

Wellnigh overwhelmed by the stench of melusine and the slithering coils of a horribly strong tail, there was little resistance she might make—that is, apart from a cogently-outlined argument dwelling upon the imperfections of her attire and the desirability of her being permitted to put on her shoes and perhaps to wrap herself in a shawl before being expected to appear in company. All to no avail: she was dragged downstairs, ushered into one of the bedrooms, and permitted no more than a few moments to blink and clear the sleep from her eyes, before the door opened and another melusine entered—Jaime this time, with Alphonse Schmidt.

"Well?" demanded Nijam's captor—none other than Blanca herself.

"The Baron is gone, too," Jaime said. "His bed hasn't been slept in."

Both of them looked at the sleepy and distracted servants, and Blanca slithered a little nearer Nijam, baring her sharp teeth.

"Tell me at once, and lie to me at your peril: *Where is Molly Dark?*"

Despite her discomfiture, Nijam know better than to admit to knowing that name. "How should I know?" she said wearily. "Whatever you're angry about, I was blamelessly asleep. May I go?"

"Stay where you are!" Blanca turned to Jaime. "Don't you understand? This is precisely what happened three years ago."

Jaime stifled a yawn. "What do you mean—that someone brings the horse home from Wiener Neustadt, saying they found her tethered outside the station? How the devil else is a young woman to flee the house? I thought you *wanted* the imposter gone."

"I *did*." Angrily, Blanca bit her lip. "It's Marie-Caroline all over again. Don't you see?"

"I really don't. If that's all you have to say, you might as well let us all go back to sleep."

"We can't. You don't understand, Jaime—no, listen—"

"No, *you* listen to *me*, Blanca." The Infante's voice hardened. "You must stop this. It's getting beyond a joke."

"No! I'll mesmerise her; then you shall see." She slithered nearer and seized Nijam's jaw with a terribly strong grasp, forcing her to look into Blanca's eyes. Alphonse uttered an indignant cry and started forward, perhaps with some idea of protecting her—but this morning he was not equipped with his customary salt-water globes, and Blanca shrugged him off.

Yet her voice, when she addressed Nijam, was low and gentle.

"I don't want to hurt your mistress, my dear. Only she may be in the power of a very unscrupulous man; and you'd like to help her, wouldn't you?"

Later, Nijam insisted that the melusine's power was something beyond simple hypnotism: the voice and eyes got inside her head, filling it until there was nothing but that voice left to think about. (You will recall that *I* was quite capable of resisting the melusine's charm.)

"Well, yes," Nijam said, "but…"

"Such a beautiful, hapless, helpless child, isn't she?" Blanca murmured; and Nijam was compelled to agree, as much by her own judgement as by the melusine's influence. "It would be no great surprise if you were fond of her."

"But I'm not," Nijam said, seeing the opportunity to set Blanca straight. "She's so horribly incompetent."

"What she really needs is someone to take care of her."

"That she does."

"Someone like you or me."

"Oh, no." Nijam laughed: she thought she saw quite distinctly where Blanca's thoughts were tending, and had no intentions of being entrapped into nursemaiding an engaging child. "Someone like you, perhaps; but I'm only here for the duration of the job, and I have no intention of suffering for her folly."

"She needs *help*." There was nothing in the world now but the voice. "From me, then, if not from you. She isn't clever enough to survive on her own. Why, she might be hurt—or dead—or married to that unscrupulous Baron, who only wants her for her money. If you won't help her, then at least help me, so that I can prevent her making some terrible mistake. Tell me, my dear: where *has* she gone?"

"She's run off on some foolhardy errand."—I had confided this part of the plan to her under some duress the previous evening. Nijam had been broad-minded enough to allow it; although, afterwards, I was hardly surprised to learn that she had adopted some contingencies of her own. "She thinks she can see ghosts. Ghosts! She meant to run out of the house at midnight to find one."

"The ghost of whom, precisely?"

"Who else?—Of Marie-Caroline."

Blanca hissed and released her: whereupon, freed of the eyes and the voice, Nijam realised with a rush of absolute mortification what she had done.

"She knows," Blanca murmured. She turned to her brother, who was restraining Alphonse. "Dark knows everything. I must go to Vienna at once. Tell Mama—"

"Tell her yourself," Jaime said with a scowl. "I'm not your errand-boy. Why are you going to Vienna, anyway?"

The melusine stared at her brother for a breathless moment. "What else can I do, Jaime? I'm going to kill Molly Dark before all of us are ruined."

"This is my fault," Nijam breathed, appalled.—"No, it isn't," said Alphonse stoutly, before addressing Blanca with some indignation. "You lied to us, madame! You said you didn't mean to hurt Fraulein Dark!"

286

Neither the Infante nor the Infanta took any notice of him. Jaime gesticulated despairingly. "Do that and we *will* be ruined. For heaven's sake, Blanca—"

"Don't preach at me," she said furiously. "You haven't the right! Don't think I don't know who's been feeding on the maids! We're exiles, Jaime. We've always known we must be ruthless in order to survive."

Jaime pressed his own lips together; then turned away and paced the room to the window. When he turned, Nijam saw from his face that he had made his decision.

"Very well," he said. "We'll do it your way. But I am coming with you."

There was nothing Nijam could do to persuade them against it. The siblings held a whispered consultation which ended in Alphonse and Nijam being marched to the nethermost regions of the Schloss, where the servants inhabited the lowest floor. The two of them were thrust into a storeroom with thick, raw stone walls; the key turned in the lock; and they were alone.

"I don't believe it," Nijam muttered, burying her face in her hands. She had presumed, of course, that my own midnight excursion would yield nothing with which to blackmail Blanca into leaving us alone. Her plan, therefore, was to wake me before dawn and flee the house together. Instead, I had levanted off to who-knew-where, condemning Nijam—and worse yet, Alphonse—to a dungeon in the Schloss.

After a rather strained silence, Alphonse said, "I certainly *hope* they haven't gone to Vienna."

"Of course they've gone to Vienna," Nijam said cuttingly. "There's only one train that leaves Weiner Neustadt between midnight and four, and that's where it goes." A small window

287

at the end of the room let in a little faint dawn light, and Nijam began to feel her way around the room. Judging from the great sacks and drums, and the husks underfoot, and the homely scent of dusty grain, they had been locked into the room where the horse's feed was kept.

"It's not like sir to rush off without me," Alphonse said in a tone of worry. "Anything might happen to him."

"Such as?" Nijam said. "Vasily doesn't strike me as being a particularly helpless individual.—Thank goodness," she added, since she suspected he must have found his way, as indeed he had, to my side.

"But I'm his bodyguard," Alphonse said, "and it's my duty—"

"Your duty!" On another occasion, Nijam might have restrained herself; but she knew that if the Bourbon-Parma siblings succeeded in murdering me, she and Alphonse would scarcely be long in following them. The rapidly approaching termination of her mortal career may possibly have made her reckless. "For the last time, Schmidt: you are a human being with a life of your own to live, beyond whatever master you've found. You've already been shot in his service; you've been lied to; and now you've been abandoned to the tender mercies of these monsters. For pity's sake, you *must* quit his service. Stop martyring yourself on the altar of duty, and for once in your life, choose to do something for *yourself*."

"I have chosen," Alphonse said with a spark of his own temper. "I chose *this*. You don't know what sir has done for me."

"Oh? And what, precisely, was that?"

"Well, I don't know *precisely*," Alphonse said, "because I have no memory of my past beyond twelve months ago; but I do know that I must have done something sufficiently dreadful to condemn me to an English prison hulk—a reformatory, in fact, where I was trained to become the custodian of order, rather than its destroyer. Sir, being in need of a valet-bodyguard, was gracious enough to engage me—to stand guarantor for my future good behaviour, and to assume all the risks of my reoffending, despite my sentence not having run its course. I am a felon, Miss Nijam, but I hope to mend my ways. Perhaps I can never hope to be readmitted to good society; but if I cannot render appropriate thanks to my employer, then I should be unable even to look myself in the face of a morning."

Nijam stared speechlessly at his indistinct outline. At first she was horrified beyond words—and then, increasingly angry. Alphonse, a criminal? Impossible—laughable—blasphemy against the articles of such faith as she had, that Alphonse Schmidt was as perspicacious as Galileo and as pure as Sir Galahad. The true criminal was whoever had made him believe such a pack of lies.

"That's the most arrant nonsense I've heard in the whole of my life," she managed at last, "and you're deluded if you believe it."

Another strained silence followed. At last, Alphonse spoke. "I've answered your question, Fraulein Nijam, and now I have one for you: What have I done to merit your hatred?"

"Nothing!"

"Nothing?" He gave a short, angry laugh. "Then I suppose it's no use my attempting to apologise."

"None whatever," Nijam said hopelessly. A black cloud of melancholy settled over her. There was no point in trying to explain: not unless she was able to restore his memory in full. Meanwhile, the light had strengthened to the point that she was able to find a metal drum rather smaller and lighter than the rest; the smell suggested it held molasses. "Here, use this to ram the bars off the window, will you? The next train to Vienna leaves at seven from Wiener Neustadt, and we ought to be on it."

"We," Alphonse repeated tonelessly.

Nijam sighed. "Look, Schmidt, it was a mistake, what I said before. Forget you heard it. But I don't hate you; you've misconstrued my meaning entirely. Now: *are* we going to warn Miss Dark and the Grand Duke that they're about to be murdered; or aren't we?"

* * *

I resume my story at the point at which I had endured a rather uncomfortable five minutes in the company of the Infante Jaime.

"One moment," I protested, hardly able to believe my ears. "You are asking me to *help* you—"

"To prevent my sister ruining the whole family, yes," the Infante said. There was a thump, and the carriage rocked sharply. I pulled up the blind to see what had happened, but Jaime reached past me and yanked it down again without pausing to draw breath. "Blanca's behaviour has been increasingly erratic. Something has frightened her, something to do with *you.*"

"And if I refuse?" I inquired. An erratic melusine seemed like the sort of person I should prefer, if at all possible, to avoid.

"It would hardly be in your best interests to refuse, would it? Blanca knows your true name; even if you escape her assassins, it's only a matter of time before your imposture becomes public knowledge. Either way, if you try to secure the inheritance, you *will* die. We Bourbons do not trifle."

The coldness in his voice nearly took my breath away: for a moment I could neither move nor speak. The carriage picked up speed as the horses broke into a trot; and the motion reassured me, for I had learned one thing, at least, in my single glimpse of the street outside.

"One more question," I said demurely. "Were you aware, your highness, that this conveyance is now being driven by my collaborators?"

The Infante looked at me for a moment in confusion; then he, too, seemed to interpret the thump, and the alteration in the cab's speed. He threw open the hatch to the fore of the box where the former cabman had been replaced by two others. I glimpsed the golden head of Alphonse Schmidt, and beside him, peering at us through the hatch, was Nijam herself.

Upon seeing our faces, she produced a remarkably large revolver and levelled it at Jaime.

The Infante swore explosively and yanked the hatch shut again. I said, "You might as well come quietly, you know," but Jaime evidently had no intention of doing any such thing. Instead, he opened the door and threw himself bodily from the carriage. I poked my head out after him and was rewarded by the sight of the last of the Bourbons measuring his length upon the cobblestones of the Ringstrasse—for it was along this thoroughfare that we were now hastening. The fall could not have hurt him, for in a trice he picked himself up and removed himself from the path of traffic.

"Couldn't you have held onto him?" Nijam complained as I withdrew into the carriage. Having opened the hatch again at once, she must have witnessed Jaime's disappearance; though she had not, of course, been foolish enough to let off a shot.

"Nijam!" I said with feeling. "I cannot say how happy I am to see you again."

"Pray do not attempt it."

"Can't you put the revolver away now? Jaime's gone."

"I know," she said icily. "But just because one prisoner has slipped through my hands, I don't see why I should lose the other."

"Prisoner?" I protested. "I know you're angry with me for running off like this—and believe me, I *perfectly* understand—but isn't this going a little too far?"

"I really don't know," Nijam rejoined. "I have tried every other method of getting you to behave, with no result!"

"Is sir there?" Alphonse put in, too busy with the reins to afford me a glance.

"No," I said, chastened from Nijam's scolding. "What, are you here on his behalf?"

"No," Nijam said, at the same moment that Alphonse said, "Yes."

I sighed. "I last saw him at Mimi's, and I think you had better take me there at once. I have something to propose."

Nijam made no reply to this; and the rest of the journey, as we abandoned the stolen cab outside the Opera and completed the journey to the Rilkeplatz on foot, was conducted in an uncomfortable and gelid silence.

"That was a remarkably large firearm just now," I observed in the lift, by way of breaking the ice. "Very difficult to overlook."

"Oh, this isn't mine." Nijam reached into her pocket and handed the weapon gingerly to Alphonse, who accepted it without speaking. "Larger ones are better, anyway. Less kick; more accuracy. If I could find a way to solve the recoil problem, I'd install one into my forearm."

I exchanged startled glances with Alphonse Schmidt and saw that the same thought had occurred to him: Nijam, surely, was quite deadly enough as she was. Within a few minutes we had arrived at Mimi's door. This time the last of her furnishings were gone, and what remained of her belongings were strapped into a valise by the door.

"Back again, are you?" she observed. "I won't be here forever, you know."

"I hope you'll stay a *little* longer," I wheedled. "Where is Vasily, by the way?"

"Oh! he ran off after you the minute he woke."

Alphonse let out an exasperated sound. "Did he say where he meant to go?"

Mimi shook her head, and I clicked my tongue. "If he'd had any luck following me, you would have spotted him in Ottakring. As it is, he's evidently gotten lost, and we might as well stay here to await his return. What brings you to Vienna, anyway?

"What brings us to Vienna is *you*," Nijam said acidly, "and for that, I think you owe us an explanation of your own."

Recognising the justice of this demand, I obliged by relating the events of the previous evening and the present morning. I wondered whether Nijam would baulk at the role played in my story by Marie-Caroline's imprint, but she listened to the whole tale stony-faced before saying, "You left your horse at the station."

"I beg your pardon?"

"That was how Alphonse and I came to be interrogated by the younger Bourbon-Parmas and then locked into the cellars at the Schloss Forhsdorf. Really, Dark, couldn't you have lodged the horse at a stable?"

"No, because then I should have missed the train."

"—Which would have been a tragedy, I take it. After that the game was up, for Blanca stormed into my room to mesmerise me." Nijam flushed and spoke more quickly. "I didn't tell her much, but she knew at once where you had gone; she and Jaime took the next train to Vienna. Alphonse and I escaped and came up on the same train with them. Jaime sent Blanca to the hotel, and went directly to Ottakring. We followed him, of course, and found you at his destination. Now—"

"You let Blanca mesmerise you? Nijam! I would have thought you far more strong-minded than that!"

"I gave you away, so I felt obliged to warn you," she said, in a prim sort of way that suggested she thought that she had done better by me than I had done by her—and I suppose she was correct. "But that's done now, and I'm calling it quits. I found what I wanted—" she glanced at Alphonse, who, having taken up his position by the window, was watching the street in silence—"and now that you've decided to throw away the inheritance, you're on your own. So long."

"So long?—You're *leaving?*" I inquired blankly. "But what am I to do? Blanca wishes to kill me, and Jaime spoke of assassins."

Alphonse had turned sharply from the window when Nijam made her announcement; but she answered stubbornly, without wasting a single look on him. "Buy a train fare to Munich, Dark; even you should be capable of that."

Running away was out of the question: I had made Franz Haber a promise. If I stayed to carry out that promise, then Blanca would try to kill me; and I meant to give her the chance.

Better by far to know when the attempt was coming, so that I might be prepared to meet it.

I could not meet it without Nijam. "I thought I was a prisoner," I objected.

"That was when I thought you might still be of use to me."

"But I need your help!"

"Oh! you *need* my help now! Well, Dark, I'm not in the business of charity."

"It's not a matter of charity, it's a matter of right and wrong. We simply can't let the Bourbon-Parmas get their horrible, scaly little hands on that inheritance."

"Can't we?" Nijam said grimly; and she opened the door to leave.

Her way was blocked by Vasily, who stood upon the threshold about to knock. His gaze sharpened when he laid his eyes upon me.

"Molly Dark, you little Delilah!" he exclaimed, sweeping Nijam before him as he advanced into the room. "A lot of nerve *you* have coming back here!"

"I thought you'd be pleased to see me," I told him, determined to brazen it out. There was a little twist at the corner of his mouth which told me he was amused despite himself. I did not, however, place too great a reliance upon that half-smile. Vasily was not in the business of charity any more than Nijam was.

"Ha!" he replied, folding his arms as though to forbid my leaving again. "I would be *very* pleased to wring your treacherous little neck. I suppose I have *you* to thank for the Habers having abandoned their flat in such a hurry as to take with them only what they could carry."

"Oh! then you *did* follow me to Ottakring."

"Too late by half." He shook his head. "What is it your poet has written? *When pain and anguish wring the brow, a ministering angel thou*—may I be painted as a fool if I ever fall into such a trap again. What have you done? What mess will I have to untangle now?—that is, if it *can* be untangled."

"It's useless," Nijam declared gloomily, as though sensing a sympathetic soul. "She has already made a gift of the inheritance to Franz Haber—and had the face to ask my help in making it over to him."

"I'll need your help, too, your grace," I said in my most bewitching tones. "And that of Alphonse and Mimi, of course."

"To give away the inheritance?" Vasily shook his head. "Uncivil as it may be to ask, Miss Dark, have you taken leave of your senses? I might have made you a grand duchess. You need never have worried about money again!"

Mimi stared at me in disbelief. "You are giving away the inheritance and refusing to marry Vasya? All this time you have tried to swindle others... I think perhaps you have swindled yourself most of all."

"But I *would* have worried about the money. I would have felt *dreadful* about it," I pleaded. "If you had seen Franz Haber, as I did, I'm sure you would wish to help me! He has family who depend upon him, as I have. He's fallen from his former position in the world, your grace, as you have. He has lost someone he dearly loved, Nijam, as you have. Didn't you tell me at the beginning of this venture that there were no better heirs, whom we would be dispossessing? But you were wrong—there *is* an heir. And surely it's right for the property to go to that heir—to the man who really *loved* Marie-Caroline—and not to the melusines who have lied and stolen and killed for it. There are more important things in this world than money."

Nijam's mouth twisted. "I don't mean to say I don't see your point, Dark. If there's a rightful heir at all it's Franz Haber, but I don't see why *we* should—"

"I agree with Miss Dark," Alphonse interrupted, surprising everyone. He reddened beneath our collective scrutiny, but went on with a deferential nod towards Vasily. "That is, if sir will give me a day's holiday or so, I would be pleased to help in any way I can."

Nijam's lips parted; two dark spots of colour burned on her cheeks. For a moment I wondered whether she was about to throw something at Alphonse or embrace him. Instead, she restrained herself and said curtly, "You'll need at least one level head on this committee. Very well. I am with you, but only because I don't want you running into trouble without me. I think it's madness. Didn't you say Blanca had *assassins?*"

"That's why we'll need Herr Schmidt's help," I put in quickly. I did not want Vasily paying too much attention to Blanca's collaborators, lest he arrive at the same conclusion I had: that Blanca's most likely allies would be Grand Duke Nikolasha and the Okhrana policemen who had nearly brought us to grief on the Elisabeth Bridge. "I'm sure Alphonse can take care of anything Blanca can find in the way of hired help. What about you, Mimi? We may not be able to pay you for this one, I'm afraid; but it would be in aid of a good cause."

Mimi shrugged. "At present I'm doing rather well. Perhaps I can afford to have a conscience for a day or two."

"Et tu, Mimi!" Vasily murmured, so that I nearly choked with laughter.

"Well, your grace?" I asked him. "Don't pretend you wouldn't like to know what it's like—caring for someone other than yourself for a change?"

"Oh, no," he said, laughing. "I have been unselfish in my day, Miss Dark; some might even say heroic." (Himself, no doubt.) "I have loved women, my brothers, and Holy Russia with true devotion: and all of them turned on me in the end. No. My days of playing at virtue are long behind me."

"Russians!" Mimi said in disgust. "You're all the same! One little thing goes wrong and suddenly you're writing modern plays about it. In Finland we have been ruled by foreigners for eight hundred years. For centuries our home has served as your battlefield in wars we have nothing to do with—but you don't see us complaining."

Vasily raised his eyes to heaven. "Where did I find the one Finn without any manners at all?"

I felt that the conversation was in danger of derailing into insults. "Do you mean to say that you'll let me run into trouble on my own, without rendering me any of the assistance that lies within your power? Is this gentlemanly, your grace? Is this gallant?"

"It'll be no more than you deserve, you baggage." I suppose I must have looked as crestfallen as I felt, for he said sharply, "No! I'm not falling for that again! You have cost me dearly, Miss Dark, and I don't forgive such things."

Vasily, like Nijam, was of great importance to my plans. For one thing, I must not only secure his assistance but forestall his treachery, and for another, I thought he might come in handy if the Okhrana *did* make another appearance.

"All right," I said. "If you're going to hold grudges against me, I suppose I must call on your brother and turn you over to him. How else am I to know you won't sabotage me?"

"And she seemed like such a lady! Schmidt, are you going

to let her speak to me like this?"

To this, Alphonse returned a look of complete panic. I suppose Vasily read in his manservant's countenance his unwillingness to choose between his employer and his conscience, and found it inexpedient to put the man to the test. In that moment I learned precisely how desperate and friendless Vasily was, for he closed his mouth into a thin white line before turning to me with a rueful laugh.

"I shall help you then, since Schmidt wishes it. But only under protest, and because I have been blackmailed."

"You're a gentleman, your grace," I said, dropping a kiss on his cheek.

"And you are not," he answered feelingly.

I outlined my plan, which was simplicity itself. Marie-Caroline's grave contained sufficient evidence to prove Franz Haber her husband; and since he was her husband, he would also be her heir under Maria Theresa's existing will. The grave must be exhumed and the evidence retrieved, and the whole thing must be done under conditions of the highest risk. Blanca meant to kill us; and even if she failed, there was still the rest of the family to reckon with. Jaime—like his mother—was not above indulging his basest appetites, and we still did not truly know which of the melusines had murdered Maria Theresa or the unfortunate stable hand.

I adopted some changes proposed by Nijam and Vasily, and then, since the evening would be a busy one, retired to Mimi's bedroom for some rest. For a while I lay awake, wondering if perhaps I had misjudged in blackmailing Vasily into joining us. How much of his apparent urbanity was a lie, designed to hide treachery?—Or how much of his vaunted egoism was a front, designed to conceal whatever remained of genuine goodness in the scarred and shrivelled heart he loved to talk about?—I would never know, unless I took the risk of trusting him. But should I expose myself to that risk? My own motives confused me: did I kiss his cheek because I was grateful to him and believed that he meant well?—or because it was part of the role I meant to play with him—the beautiful, engaging child in whom he still so desperately wished to believe?

I must have fallen asleep before I had settled on anything like an answer. The next thing of which I was aware was my father's imprint leaning over me and kissing my brow, as he had that night when he had left us. I was perhaps half or wholly asleep: in any case, when his lips moved, for the first time I was able to comprehend the words.

"Be good," he had said. *"I love you."*

"If you really cared for us," I mumbled, "why did you run the business into the ground before dying of the plague?"

He vanished, and I woke to find that the light was fading and the room had become cold. Nijam lay on the other side of the room, disposed primly on her back with a small cushion under her head and a folded handkerchief across her eyes. My watch told me that it was nearly six o'clock: we must soon prepare for the evening's work.

Now that the time was upon us, doubt assailed me, and I shivered, pulling Mimi's thin blanket more closely around my shoulders. I, too, was about to throw away money my family desperately needed. In doing so, my father had lost his life; in doing so, I would risk my reason and my liberty—and perhaps the lives of my friends.

"Nijam," I said huskily.

She did not remove the handkerchief from her eyes. "What is it?"

There was no point in trying to warn her: Nijam did not even believe in ghosts. "It's time to leave, that's all."

There were more important things than money—or liberty. Yet I could not help feeling horribly guilty, all the same, knowing that I was walking in my father's footsteps and condemning my family to a terrible burden of debt and poverty.

Chapter XXV.

I have always avoided cemeteries, especially large ones. They are at all times thick with sorrowful memories of the dead, which remain longer here than anywhere else. Grieving visitors keep their memory alive; but so do gravestones, wilting flowers, and lonely pinwheels; and most of all, the slowly withering flesh recalls its rarer part, and holds tenacious memories of life. For the body goes into the ground unwillingly, and lies there in an agony of expectation that never quite entirely fades—nor will fade, until the blast of the final trumpet resounds, and our two halves, of clay and air, are reunited as one.

It was in a cemetery, as you may recall, that I had first discovered my gift; and it was in a cemetery that the madwoman to whom Miss Mackintosh had introduced me in the Hanwell Asylum had lost her reason. I was now breaking one of my cardinal rules: for it was in a cemetery, of course, that Marie-Caroline had been interred.

Part of me thought it foolish to worry: the unfortunate woman at Hanwell had been of infirm mind to begin with, and by now I was surely well accustomed to the sight of imprints. Still, as Alphonse picked the locks to the gate of the great Simmering necropolis—a veritable suburb of the dead laid out on sweeping green lawns some two miles to the south-east of the old city—my apprehension must have been evident in my expression. When Vasily opened his dark-lantern to throw a beam of light upon Alphonse's work, his gaze was arrested at the sight of my face.

"What's the matter, Miss Dark? Are you having cold feet?"

I did not bother trying to deny it. I inched a little closer to him with a shiver. "I didn't want to tell Nijam, but I—I'm afraid, your grace."

"Oh?" He seemed amused. Perhaps, at last, he was learning not to trust me.

"I haven't set foot in a cemetery since the day I saw a labourer's head impaled with an iron spike," I said simply. "Graveyards are full of ghosts. Who knows what I will find beyond those gates? If I—if I begin to behave erratically, or to speak to empty air—"

Vasily's amusement faded. "You ought not to have come."

For pressing reasons of my own, that was not to be considered for a moment. "This is why I needed your help," I coaxed him. "Nijam doesn't believe me about the imprints. You do."

The lock clicked. With a sound of triumph, Alphonse pushed the gate open; and Vasily closed the dark-lantern shutter, obscuring my view of his face. "Stay close to me," he said, and I knew that I had carried my point.

I wondered uneasily whether Vasily perhaps needed someone to take care of him. He really did not seem capable of resisting a pretty face and big, pleading eyes.

Within the cemetery the night was dark. Clouds thickly covered the sky and mist wound amidst the leafless trees, so that even wide-open, the lanterns shed only a small and haloed light. To me, however, the whole place was alive with the wispy lights of half-remembered spirits, which glowed and then vanished again like fireflies.

Most of the memories were of an everyday sort, either bitter or sweet. A little boy rushed along the gravel, laughing wildly, and then disappeared. An old lady loomed up out of the fog that cloaked a gravestone, her brows knitted in displeasure; she gave a fretful and soundless speech. A man delivered a slap; a mother a kiss; an old woman sat dozing with her cat; a little girl took a bite of an apple. Yet the feelings that accompanied each imprint were nearly overwhelming: anger and peacefulness, love and resentment jostled against me in quick, poignant succession. I began to understand how such a place might send a person mad.

As we ventured deeper into the cemetery, more terrifying memories assailed me. I watched as a young man with trembling lips raised a duelling pistol and then recoiled with him at the silent impact of an unseen bullet. Black despair drizzled from the limp figures who had hanged themselves from trees and lamp-posts; others floated suspended in the air, their hair and clothing moving ceaselessly in the slow currents of the water in which they had drowned. A few steps further on, and quite suddenly a body plummeted from above with a sensation of utter flailing terror. I could not help watching as it burst like a ripe fruit across the ground. Turning away with a shudder, I beheld a runaway carriage bearing down on me behind four wildly terrified horses—I uttered a shriek and threw myself to one side. For an instant I felt the blinding agony of those hoofs trampling me underfoot.

It was over in a moment; and I felt warm arms about me. "Miss Dark," Vasily said through the darkness of my closed eyes. "They're not real."

304

"They were, once," I said. That was the really horrible thing about it, of course: everything I saw, every dying sensation I felt, had really happened once to a living and breathing person. His arms tightened, and I could not help myself: I spread my hands against the warmth of his shirt-front just to feel the quick, ragged beat of his heart beneath my fingers—just to remind myself of what was and was not real.

After a moment the bombardment of remembered horror faded a little, and I realised how improperly close we had become.

"Keep your eyes closed; I'll hold your hand," Vasily said as I drew back. I did as he suggested, but it was not much use: I might not be able to see the imprints, but I could still *feel* them. Buffeted by conflicting emotions—passing in moments from the heights of joy to the depths of despair and the extremities of agony—I followed him and Alphonse blindly through the cemetery until we reached our destination.

"This is the place," Alphonse whispered.

Shuddering, I opened my eyes. We stood in the Jewish section of the graveyard—walled, dark, and shadowed with cypress trees. It was worse here than it had been outside. Jews, I had already found, suffered more than most people from outbursts of prejudiced violence, and in Austria and Germany they were singled out for particular detestation. My first sight, upon opening my eyes, was an angry crowd which converged upon a frightened boy and began to hurl brickbats. I felt every blow.

I think I must have fallen to my knees—weeping from the boy's pain and my own outrage—when a light shone around me. The horror retreated, leaving in its place a calm and cleansing grief. I looked up.

A gravestone stood before me: upon it was carved, very simply, *Maria Charlotte Haber,* followed by a date three years in the past. Marie-Caroline herself sat at the foot of the grave with one arm crooked about her stomach as though it pained her. She smiled at me through her tears—no, it was not me she smiled at; it was Franz, for I saw her lips shape his name.

Although she resembled me, Marie-Caroline seemed far younger than myself, and on her face was a look of wistful sadness. She lifted from her lap the sketch-book in which she had been drawing and turned it towards me: I saw the face of the young singing-tutor beside her own.

I drew a breath like a sob. "It *is* the place," I told the others. Vasily and Alphonse had stood before the grave in silence; I think all of us felt the melancholy of the young life cut so horribly short—of the lost Bourbon princess, the heiress to the Schloss Frohsdorf, taking refuge in this secret grave among a despised people.

Vasily bent over me. "Are you well?"

I kept my eyes fixed upon Marie-Caroline—or Maria Charlotte, as she had chosen to be known in death—as a drowning man keeps hold of the shattered wreckage of his ship. It was she who held at bay the other horrors of the cemetery, and I did not want her to fade for want of attention.

"Well enough for now," I said, wiping my tear-stained face.

"In that case—" Vasily accepted one of the shovels Alphonse carried— "we might as well begin."

He and Alphonse took off their jackets and bent to their work. I balanced the lantern on my knee and watched Maria Charlotte assiduously as she sketched. There was no one to stand lookout, of course; which may help to explain subsequent events.

It took an hour's assiduous digging, during which I somewhat recovered myself under the imprint's calming influence, before Alphonse's shovel struck something that gave a hollow sound. "We have it," Vasily whispered, and with a deal more grunting and whispering, the remainder of the coffin was cleared, the simple pine box was raised from its resting-place, and Alphonse forced the lock with as little noise as possible. In all that time we had not been disturbed by a night-watchman; but doubtless there were custodians abroad in the cemetery, and we must be careful.

The lid came off. Steeling myself against whatever I might see or experience should the imprint depart, I raised the lantern to look within. Marie-Caroline—or Maria Charlotte, as she had chosen to be known in death—had mummified rather than putrefied: her flesh, although shrivelled, still clung to her bones, and a quantity of pale golden hair remained upon her head. I felt as though I was looking into my own face, sixty years hence, when I should be an old woman. Otherwise, except for her stillness and the faint odour of decay, she might have been peacefully asleep.

"Brr!" said Vasily, with a shiver. "To think we shall all come to *that!*"

"We might fare worse." After the sights that had haunted me since I entered the cemetery, this peaceful corpse bore little terror for me. "By your leave, Frau Haber." The corpse's gaunt hands were folded together over a faded, mildewed envelope, which I extracted gently from her stiff grasp. I handed the lantern to Vasily, freeing my hands to ease open the gummed flap. Within was the marriage license—the real one—and the paper upon which Maria Charlotte had sketched both herself and her husband, together with a sheaf of their letters.

"Evidence," I murmured. It was quite enough to verify the marriage. With these documents, Franz Haber's claim on the inheritance was assured.

Maria Charlotte's imprint still sat at the foot of her grave, working on the very sketch I held in my hands. Vasily, above me, was a dark and inscrutable shadow behind the glare of the shuttered lantern he held.

"All the evidence in one place!" he said, soft and half-laughing. "What a shame if someone was to have an accident with the lantern. We should have no choice but to take the inheritance for ourselves."

Alphonse laughed uneasily, as though he thought the joke in poor taste. But I did not have the valet's faith in his master, and my blood ran cold. "You wouldn't dare!"

"Wouldn't I?" he asked, even more softly.

I will never know what Vasily might have done next, had we not been interrupted. Alphonse reached over suddenly and closed the lantern shutter. "Someone is coming," he hissed. "Listen!"

It was the soft creak of the gate—the stealthy crunch of many footsteps upon the gravel. Almost, I felt relieved. "It's Blanca's assassins," I breathed, tucking the documents safely into a pocket.

Just like that, we were allies again. Vasily caught my hand and Alphonse went ahead of us, silently leading us between the ghostly gravestones towards the wall dividing the Jewish section from the larger cemetery. We had not gone far before lights—warm yellow lantern-light—could be observed flickering hastily through the trees behind us, and there was a tramp of running feet on gravel. Nearer—a pale and beacon-like glow—Maria Charlotte's imprint continued her slow, painstaking work at the foot of her own grave.

I hated to leave the refuge she had provided me; I hated also to leave her body behind, exposed to the probing of official eyes. There was no help for it. If we were caught we would be charged with grave robbery, and I did not think that our being there on the authority of the deceased's husband would make much difference. At least, for the moment, there was very little activity from other imprints. Within a short time we had reached the wall, which was built of rough mossy stone. Alphonse clambered up it without any trouble at all and reached down for my hands. Vasily, with a murmured apology, caught me around the waist and hoisted me into his arms; a moment later the three of us were perched there like oversized pigeons on a roof.

The top of the wall was narrow and rather uncomfortable, being surmounted by a carved ridge designed, like that of a house, to shed rain and snow. We would all have vacated it in an instant, had it not been for the sudden ferocious barking of a dog from the outside of the wall. The beast rushed towards us and congregated at the foot of the wall, leaping up and snapping for our ankles. Meanwhile, more lanterns came rushing towards us from the direction of the gate.

"Back," Alphonse gasped, but when we turned, we saw that the commotion had also drawn the attention of the searchers within the wall. In moments we had been surrounded on either side by a dozen men with lanterns and dogs, and I was looking down the barrel of a revolver for the second time that day.

Their leader addressed some sinister-sounding remarks to us in what I took to be Russian.

"They don't *look* like night-watchmen, do they?" I remarked, and Vasily swore softly in French.

"They aren't—these are Okhrana men." He gave me a very hard stare; I hoped my blush was not too visible in the lantern-light. "I would be greatly tempted to lay the blame for this at *your* door, my dear, except that you would scarcely be foolish enough to spring your own trap before you had got well out of it."

"Well, that's extremely kind of you. They're *your* people; can't you talk your way out?"

"No more comedy!" The Okhrana man now spoke in German. "Come down before we drag you down, Vasily Nikolaevich!"

"Ah, the deuce," said Vasily lightly, although I could tell he was greatly vexed. We were obliged to descend the wall and fall into the arms of the Russian policemen, one or two of whom I recognised from the confrontation upon the bridge. They descended upon Vasily and cuffed his wrists none too gently behind his back. The operation was repeated with Alphonse; but either they had not expected to find me among the gathering, or else they judged that, as a woman, I posed but a negligible danger to them. If so, I was compelled to admit that they were—alas—probably quite correct.

"Where are you taking us?" Vasily demanded as we were marched through the cemetery. He received in reply only an injunction to hold his tongue. I went quite meekly, with my eyes closed, for the imprints gathered in number and strength the further we went from Maria Charlotte's grave. For a little while, the apprehension of what our captors might do to us was swallowed up by the horrors already experienced by the cemetery's occupants.

Mercifully, our journey was a short one. At the centre of

the cemetery was built the octagonal church of St Charles Borromeo, a graceful structure in white stone, surmounted with a green dome. Our captors propelled us up the front steps and through the wide vestibule into the interior. Here, peace received me. I opened my eyes with a long, sobbing breath.

Despite its white-painted walls and gilded frescoes, the church was dark and full of shadows. Lingering imprints dotted the pews, or prayed before the altar beneath the painted images of Christ and his angels. They filled the air with grief and weariness, but also hope. Here at last were no images of sudden violence, no experiences of terror and despair to haunt the mind. Few people have died in churches.

The electric lamps hanging from three of the four arches to the north, west, and south of the church were burning with a cheerful yellow glow, but they did little to chase away the shadows. It was not until we were dragged to the nave's gloomy centre that I saw we were far from being the only living presence in the building. Here beneath the starry blue expanse of the dome, upon the round glass pavement that had been built to let light into the crypt beneath the church, Blanca awaited us in melusine form. She was attended only by two servants: the Schloss Frohsdorf coachman and one of the footmen. Both of them were as ancient, as drained of life as the other servants; and their faces were perfectly blank. Blanca, I realised with a shiver, had mesmerised them.

She seemed taken aback at our entrance.

"What does thisss mean?" she greeted the Russians. "I wanted the ssswindlers dead!"

"Blanca!" I said reproachfully. "I thought we had an agreement! Didn't I leave Schloss Frohsdorf when you told me to?"

"The more fool you," she said with a laugh; and even in that terrible moment I felt how close I had come to falling under her spell. "Why are they ssstill alive?" she demanded of the Russians.

"We are the emperor's servants, not yours," their leader said. "We have what we came for. Do the rest of your dirty work yourself."

With that he delivered a shove between my shoulders, sending me reeling forward. "Hold them!" Blanca commanded, and the footman caught hold of me, and the coachman of Alphonse.

"Stop!" Vasily cried, wrenching around to face the Okhrana leader. His voice was so commanding that for an instant he seemed completely master of the situation: "These people belong to me. I insist that they accompany me. Do you think that because I am an exile, I have no influence in high places? If you abandon my people here, I will know how to make you suffer—injury for injury, death for death."

"I don't *belong* to you," I said indignantly; but my objection was quite useless. The policemen dragged him off, turning a deaf ear to Vasily's protests as they had to Blanca's and my own. The doors slammed behind them, leaving myself and Alphonse alone with a gravely perplexed Blanca.

When Alphonse tensed to spring, she turned upon him with bared teeth. "Don't be foolish," she snarled. "I can kill you with one bite."

"Isn't that what you planned, in any case?" I said in my politest voice.

"I hate the tassste," she said pettishly. "Why couldn't those Russians follow instructions?"

Had we discovered Marie-Caroline's murderer, or was Blanca merely following in her family's bloody footsteps? In either case, I must play for time. Left to her own devices, either she would require one of the servants to dispatch us, or she would overcome her aversions and do the thing herself. Still, all hope was not lost for us. With Nijam, Mimi, and Franz still at large, I would not concede defeat.

"What about your brother?" I inquired. "Surely Jaime would be glad to take us off your hands."

"Jaime!" she said scornfully. "Jaime hasn't the ssstomach for this—he's never had the ssstomach. No: if it's to be done, I'll need to do it myssself."

I tried in vain to disentangle myself from the footman, whose grip was a great deal stronger than I would have guessed from his white hair and lined visage.

"You can't," I panted, "not here! It's holy ground!"

"Then I'll do it outssside. Wait; you had other confederates, didn't you? There was the half-cassste maid—and the little Jew organ-grinder. I take it they will be along presently to find you, at which point I'll make a clean sssweep of the lot of you."

"Franz *did* want to be buried next to Marie-Caroline," I said weakly.

"I can grant a part of that wish, to be sssure," she said. "Reiter, Zamloch—sssearch the prisoners, will you? Yes, both of them!"

The envelope we had gone to so much trouble to collect weighed in my pocket like a guilty conscience: if we were searched, it would be found. I saw, moreover, that Alphonse had gone pale with determination. In another moment he would certainly try something foolish.

"What you want is here in my pocket," I said hastily, to forestall him. "No, Schmidt; it's no use trying to escape."

"Don't do it, fraulein," he said wildly. "Sir gave himself up for those."

Blanca thrust a hand into the indicated pocket and, with a sound of triumph, withdrew the faded envelope. "What have we here?"

I did not answer; it would be difficult enough to explain what Blanca would find within. Before she could open the packet, however, the church door was flung open.

"Blanca!" cried Jaime, "For God's sake, what are you doing?"

His appearance had the effect of throwing us all into a stupefied stillness. Two others followed him into the church—Princess Margaret and the Duke of Parma.

"Mother," Blanca faltered. "Uncle Robert! What are you doing here?"

"We are intervening," Jaime replied, when the elder Bourbon-Parmas did not—for indeed, they seemed at a loss for words at the sight of Blanca's tail and mesmerised henchmen. "Come to your senses, Blanca! What is the meaning of this behaviour? A stable hand dead, a flight to Vienna, fraternising with the Russians, and now this—whatever *this* is!"

"Do you want the Prince of Tuscany to begin asking questions?" inquired Princess Margaret in her colourless voice. "I have five daughters, Blanca, and no way to establish you in the situation to which you are entitled if you squander this opportunity! Is there any truth in this?—Marie-Caroline, is this *your* doing?"

The injustice of this charge quite took my breath away. Before I could find it again, Blanca pointed at me with all the dramatic malevolence of a sorceress casting a spell in a pantomime. *"Thisss* is not Marie-Caroline! It's an imposssster who's been trying to sssteal the inheritance!"

"Don't be ridiculous," Duke Robert boomed. "Of course she's one of us! Haven't you *seen* her tail?"

"I don't know how she managed it, but she *isn't* one of usss! Her name is Molly Dark, and she's nothing but an adventuresss from *Brixton,* wherever that is! Jaime knows about it. Tell them, Jaime!"

"I know that you were speaking wildly about doing away with her," Jaime said, in a censorious tone that reminded me of Nijam. "Come, Blanca! If she's an imposter she should be arrested and tried—not murdered!"

I still did not know for certain what had happened to Marie-Caroline, nor who had drained the last of Maria Theresa's life. But if it had not been Jaime—and if he and his sister had been at odds all this time—

"Blanca won't turn me over to the law," I said. "Nor will she say why she believes me to be an imposter. To do so would be to expose her own actions."

I spoke softly, but my words seemed to echo in that great space as though I had shouted them.

"What actions?" Jaime asked. "What have you done, Blanca?"

"Come, Blanca," said Princess Margaret with a sniff, "clear this up and let us put it behind us."

Blanca turned on me with flashing eyes. "Do you really believe I will sssuffer for the crime of sssafeguarding my own family's inheritance? I am not some little nobody from a place no one has ever heard of—I am a Bourbon. I have a birthright to defend; against the world, if I musssst."

"Blanca!" Princess Margaret's face slackened with doubt. "Explain!"

"Gladly." Blanca turned a flushed, angry face to her mother. "I know that thisss is not Marie-Caroline, because Marie-Caroline is dead. I was not sure of it at first, but I'm cssertain now. She is dead—*I* killed her. I knew she meant to run away with her sssinging-tutor—that she meant to throw herssself and her fortunes away on some miserable little organ-grinder, when it was her duty to marry Jaime. The little fool confided in me. Ssso I brought her coffee that evening before she ran away. I made it ssstrong and dark, and I boiled it with all the deathcaps I could find in the park."

Her mother went perfectly white. "You *poisoned* her?"

"Hear her out," Jaime said, raising a warning hand. He looked almost sick. "Go on, Blanca."

"It's a ssslow-acting poison," Blanca said defensively, "and there was always a chance she'd sssurvive it. I left it to Heaven to decide her fate. But then this imposssster came to the Schlosss, and I—I didn't *know*. I tried to frighten her off—"

"The worn girth," I murmured.

"You sssurvived it, didn't you? As with Marie-Caroline, I left your fate to Heaven. When you lived, I was nearly persssuaded you were genuine."

"Very obliging of you," I said. All the pieces that had puzzled me were fitting together now. "The stable hand you compelled to do the dirty work, though—you did not extend the same courtesy to him. You went out into the rain and finished him the night you found me outside the library."

Blanca shrugged. "It was only when you accepted the Russian as your husband that I knew for certain you were an imposssster. The real Marie-Caroline would never have had the sssense to run off with a Grand Duke."

With the conclusion of this tale there was a long, awful silence. Princess Margaret's hand fluttered against her breast. Jaime had gone white and pale. Even Alphonse looked too scandalised to attempt an escape. The Duke of Parma, too, was greatly affected; he wiped a tear from his eye.

"You killed our cousin," Jaime said in a choked voice. "Is this what you meant by *helping* me?"

"Marie-Caroline betrayed all of usss," Blanca hissed. "Her family, her blood, her classs!"

Jaime's reply was forestalled by his uncle. "My dear girl!" he boomed. "I could scarcely agree with you more! In fact, I put Maria Theresa to sleep for much the same reason, God rest her soul! She would have left the Bourbon fortune to a mere baron!"

Princess Margaret was freshly stricken. "Robert!" she cried. "You *killed* Aunt Maria Theresa?—your *queen?*"

"It only took a single bite," he assured her. "She was dying in any case!"

Beside me, Alphonse looked dizzy. "These people are *depraved.*"

I could not find it in my heart to disagree, even as I devoutly hoped that the *denouement* would reveal at least one family member who was not a cold-blooded killer.

Princess Margaret, perhaps?—But no: she had begun to recover from her dismay, and now said:

"I am shocked, Robert—shocked, and more grieved than I can say; yet, perhaps, it has all turned out for the best. Indeed, I begin to see Blanca's point." Her pale, cold eyes fastened upon me. "The main thing is to secure the inheritance; which, unfortunately, will require finishing the imposters."

Jaime stepped between his family and ourselves. "Mother," he expostulated, somewhat to my relief. "I scarcely believe this. What are you saying?"

"I am trying to secure your inheritance, Jaime."

"That's all any of usss have been trying to do, you ungrateful boy!" Blanca put in.

"By forcing my cousin to marry me, and then murdering her when she refused?" Jaime cried. "I loved my cousin like one of my own sisters, but I would have shot myself sooner than marry her!"

"Jaime! How can you say such a thing?"

"For one thing, she was against it; she loved another. For another thing, it would have been monstrous. We are cousins on both sides! What would become of the offspring of such a union? They would be like Uncle Robert's children—pure of blood; feeble of mind to the point of idiocy!"

"How dare you!" the Duke cried.

"Stand aside, Jaime," said Princess Margaret in her customary colourless voice. "The family requires it of you."

"I'll bite you if I mussst," Blanca added recklessly. "We don't like traitors in *thisss* family."

The whole knot of them was arrayed against us now, with the exception of Jaime; and he, not having taken his melusine form, could not be relied upon to protect us for long. As for Alphonse, his hands were shackled. He stepped in front of me all the same, as though to shield me with his body.

As for me, I had been keeping a sharp watch on the shadows beneath the arches, where doors led into the church's vestibules. Because of this, I knew that the play was done.

I struck my hands together so sharply that the echoes rolled around the church.

"Bravo," I announced. "Very prettily said, everyone.—Herr Haber! Did you catch those confessions?"

"I think so," Franz replied from the shadows of the entrance-way. A moment later he strolled into the light, raising one hand to display a small gadget—in fact, the very device Nijam had spent so much of the previous week at work upon. Franz tripped the switch, and a tinny voice echoed from within:

"I know that this is not Marie-Caroline, because Marie-Caroline is dead. I was not sure of it at first, but I'm cssertain now. She is dead—I killed her."

Princess Margaret gasped. "The Jew! What trickery is this? Quick, Blanca—bite him!"

"Anyone who moves will be shot!" A new voice boomed from above us. With an unpleasant sensation at the pit of my stomach, I glanced up to see the high galleries surrounding the church thick with armed men in the distinctive blue jackets and red trousers of the imperial gendarmerie. "Come along quietly: you are all under arrest!"

Genuinely panicked, I touched the transmitter in my ear. "Nijam? Is this your doing? Did *you* call the police?"

"No," Jaime said from his position in front of me, "it's mine. I mean all this to be thoroughly and lawfully investigated."

"I should never have agreed to help you," I complained. It was during our little tête-à-tète in the cab that I had reluctantly agreed to join Jaime in eliciting a confession from Blanca. It had at no point been certain, of course, that he would keep his promise to let me go at the end of it. I had not even been completely sure he himself was not the killer. Still, the possibility of an alliance—however precarious—had been too good to pass up; and on the whole, I was pleased with the outcome.

The police now flocked in at each of the doors, in a trice surrounding the startled Bourbon-Parmas. Jaime cast a quick glance around the nave, but it was no good, of course. Each of the three entrances was now barred by the police, and other exit there was none.

"Don't do anything rash," he said hurriedly. "You helped the cause of justice today and I'll speak for you; they won't hold you long."

"On the whole, I think I'd rather not risk it," I told him. "Come here, Schmidt—" and before the astonished Alphonse could stop me, I fished the marriage certificate, the love letters, and the sketch in a bundle from his coat-pocket, where I had stowed them as we fled the grave. I had, of course, kept the empty envelope in my own pocket, all the better to distract and mystify Blanca. Now I pressed the documents into Jaime's hands. "Give those to Franz Haber; and oh, you might tell the police to test whatever contents remain of Marie-Caroline's stomach. You'll find her conveniently exhumed in the Jewish cemetery. Good-bye."

I shoved him smartly across the glass pavement and into the arms of the encroaching policemen before throwing my own around Alphonse.

"Now, Nijam!" I cried, stamping upon the clear bricks underfoot.

No sooner was Nijam called upon, than she answered: there came a quick series of sharp reports like the firing of a pistol. Spurts of dust and shards of glass erupted from the pavement beneath our feet, making a neat division around the edge, before the floor opened up and swallowed Alphonse and myself together. We landed uncomfortably in a rain of glass bricks atop a thin and by no means sufficient mattress. Having measured our length inelegantly upon the stones of the crypt floor, we picked ourselves up again. A dark shape loomed up amidst the clouds of dust that now filled the whitewashed crypt—a nightmarish figure with enormous glassy eyes and a grey featureless face ending in a round canister beneath the chin. I believe that Alphonse actually screamed. Then the figure wrenched off the respirator mask to reveal Nijam's flushed countenance.

"Quickly," she said. "This way."

"Where's Mimi?" I asked, coughing.

"She was here half an hour ago to pick the locks," Nijam said, puzzled. "Mimi!"

No answer greeted her call, except the shouts of the gendarmerie above, who now clustered around the broken pavement shouting at us to stand and wait in the name of the emperor.

"She'll be in the carriage." Nijam hastened towards the rear entrance. "We must go."

A dark flight of stairs led out of the crypt. Our path led us directly through the imprint of a rather important-looking gentleman in tails and a monocle, who afflicted me with nothing worse than a sudden and disconcerting sense of *ennui*. Awaiting us at the door was a more formidable opponent. As we rushed up the stairs a startled policeman appeared, throwing up his arms as though to bar our way. Shackled as he was, Alphonse did not hesitate: he caught hold of the dashing blue jacket and cracked his forehead hard against that of the gendarme. The policeman folded to the ground, letting us past into the cold, foggy night air.

A sweep of gravel road surrounded the church. It was empty.

"Confound it, where is Mimi?" I repeated, glancing wildly about. An imprint wandered by, playing the violin; I brushed aside a lingering sense of stage-fright. "And where is our getaway carriage?—*She was meant to steal us a carriage!*"

At the same moment there came a flash of light from the direction of the city, followed by a distant *boom,* shorter and deadlier than thunder. A brief red light illuminated a rising black cloud; the ground trembled.

"What was *that?*" I gasped.

Nijam clapped a hand to her pockets. "Heavens above! I *knew* some of my explosives were missing!"

I had no time to ask what she meant. From within the church, feet trampled; whistles blew; dogs barked. The hue and cry was up.

"Don't talk," Alphonse gasped, gesticulating with both his bound hands. *"Run."*

Together, we dashed for the darkness of the tree-lined avenue leading towards the cemetery gate. The effort was clearly useless, but none of us were prepared to surrender just yet. I flinched as imprints surrounded me yet again. This time I was obliged to keep my eyes open, but at least our headlong speed left me little time to see or feel.

Behind us, I was dizzily aware of lanterns jogging nearer, of the pound of running feet across the gravel. An imprint—a ragged urchin—appeared running beside me. Was the terror I felt my own, or his?—were the figures behind me as plentiful as they appeared, or were they simply the unhappy pickpocket's memory of a hunt to the death, evoked by the predicament in which I found myself?

We were still far too distant from the cemetery gate. A carriage bore down on us, its four horses a storm of pounding hooves and tossing manes. My feet faltered and I braced myself for the moment of remembered impact at which it would crush the fleeing boy.

"Dark!" It was Nijam's scream in my ear. A body collided with my own; moments later the two of us rolled in the dust. A very real spray of gravel stung my face as the carriage—no imprint—drew to a halt beside us.

"Dark," Nijam gasped, relieving me of her weight and pulling me to my feet. "Confound it, woman, you nearly got both of us killed!"

"Get in," called an urgent voice—Mimi's voice. I blinked up to see her on the box, wrestling with the reins in an attempt to get the carriage turned. Alphonse was already yanking at the door: it was locked. He stepped back, drew a revolver—he had confiscated it from the gendarme during our escape—and let off a shot. Mimi screamed something I didn't quite understand. Alphonse yanked open the shattered latch and helped Nijam and myself within before joining Mimi upon the box.

Between them they must have got the horses turned, for in another moment we had rushed away, out of the very jaws of our pursuers. Nijam and I righted ourselves upon the bench-seat and found ourselves facing a pale and startled Vasily.

"I suppose this is a rescue!" he said, raising his eyebrows. "Next time, my dears, would you mind very much *not* firing blindly into a closed carriage?"

Chapter XXVI.

I returned to the Schloss Frohsdorf two weeks later in a carriage sent by the new master to greet the Vienna train. The coachman was my old friend Reiter, whom you will remember from the confrontation in the cemetery church. He touched his cap rather sheepishly when he saw me.

"I have to apologise, fraulein," he began, but I shook my head.

"Oh, you needn't; really. I take it the Infanta had you pretty well mesmerised."

No charges had been pressed against the Bourbon-Parmas in the intervening weeks. As Blanca had boasted, the sufficiently royal could indeed get away with murder. Nonetheless, the melusines had very hurriedly departed the empire; and Herr Brunner's application for probate of Maria Theresa's will on behalf of her son-in-law, Franz Haber, seemed likely to proceed with the utmost expedition. It was not precisely the justice I had hoped for, but it was better than nothing.

I stepped into the carriage to find Nijam already seated in a corner of it.

"Hullo," I said in surprise, for our paths had not crossed since that eventful night at the cemetery. "I didn't know you were still in Vienna! Did you come down by the same train? I wish I'd known; we might have travelled together."

"Or we might have attracted attention and been picked up by the police," she retorted, by way of greeting. "Don't you remember? We agreed our paths must never cross again."

I recalled no such agreement: Nijam had stated it as fact, that night, on her way out of Mimi's flat. There was no point in saying so, however, and our conversation flagged. As the carriage whisked us through freshly snow-covered fields towards the Schloss, I occupied myself by unfolding my mother's latest letter. She categorically refused to apply for a loan to Sir Humphrey—whom, you recall, was my late father's more successful business partner. Instead, she had put up the house for sale and now anxiously reminded me of my promise to provide whatever was necessary to repair the sacrifice. Sighing, I folded the letter again. I had spent the past two weeks working quietly at an expensive hat-shop on the Graben, keeping my head down and hoping that the hue-and-cry would soon blow over. If I had had any sense, I would have fled the city; but Franz had sent to beg me not to leave before he had had the chance to see me again. Since he now represented my one last hope of coming honestly by the money I needed, I had thought it best to oblige him.

The carriage deposited us before the great double doors of the Schloss. As Nijam and I walked into the white entrance-hall together for the second time, I could not help remarking, "At least this time we don't have a false tail in our luggage!"

"This time I brought an arm-cannon," was Nijam's unsettling rejoinder.

"I can't imagine we'll need it," I said. The butler appeared and asked us to wait in the same little gilt receiving-room where Nijam and I had first met with Princess Margaret. We entered to find Vasily, Mimi, and Alphonse already occupying the room.

Seeing us, Vasily rose from his seat. His smile was unsettlingly full of white teeth.

"Perhaps we *will* need it," I murmured to Nijam. She returned me one of her level, expressionless looks, which spoke as clearly as in words: "Don't be foolish—what could he possibly have against us?"

I was *not* being foolish. It is true that, as the reader knows, I had not been *entirely* taken by surprise by Blanca's alliance with the Okhrana. It is also true that I thought it tremendously convenient for the Russians to remove Vasily from the equation once he and Alphonse had done the heavy work of unearthing the coffin. Since Nikolasha was not in the least interested in Alphonse and myself, I had predicted that the rest of us would be left to face Blanca without worrying about a possible betrayal by a self-interested third party. Given all this, it was at least *possible* that Vasily had guessed as much; and once the suspicion crossed his mind, it would not have taken him long to realise that I had laid no firm plans for retrieving him from his brother's clutches. Mimi's impulsive actions in taking the carriage and going to retrieve him from the Okhrana had so evidently caught me by surprise.

In my own defence, I had thought it entirely possible that Vasily would successfully rescue himself long before Alphonse and I could get around to it. What actually happened was this: Mimi, having helped herself to some of Nijam's explosives, had waylaid the Okhrana carriages as they returned to the Russian embassy. She created an incendiary diversion, and in the resulting confusion had substituted our original getaway carriage for the one in which Vasily was being transported.

She had driven back to the cemetery post-haste, and the rest you know.

All the same, it was a nasty moment when I looked into the Grand Duke's face and wondered whether he *knew*.

"Miss Dark," he began in a silky voice—but then, Vasily's voice was always silky. "I'm so glad to see you well. But then, you have a habit of coming out on top."

For a moment I was thoroughly cowed. Then I recalled how little reason I really had to trust him. "Be very nice to me," I said impudently, "and perhaps one day I shall allow *you* to come out on top.—Hullo, Schmidt. Hullo, Mimi! I thought you were in Copenhagen?"

She scowled. "I was, and I even had a place in the academy!"

"What happened?"

"Someone got himself stabbed in the eye with a hairpin."

"I'm sure he deserved it," said I, with feeble politeness. After that, the conversation, which had been lagging, was extinguished altogether. Nijam stared out the window, Mimi rapped her fingertips monotonously against the arm of the chair in which she sat, Vasily pinned me with a half-lidded, smouldering gaze, and Alphonse fastened an apprehensive gaze upon each of us in turn.

"What brings us all here?" I asked after a moment. "Herr Haber asked me to come; I didn't know it would be a reunion."

"Nor," Nijam said frostily, "did I."—She had not exchanged a single word, a single glance with Alphonse.

It was at this moment—mercifully—that the door opened and Franz Haber himself entered. He looked tired, and I had no doubt that he found his new position came with all manner of tiresome new duties; but when he saw us, his face lit up in a perfectly sincere smile.

"Ladies and gentlemen! Thank you for coming—some of you a very long way. I have," he added, once the first greetings were over, "a proposal to lay before you. Do you know what a *dybbuk* is?"

I looked blankly at Nijam, but it was Vasily who spoke. "It's a Jewish legend. A dead spirit that clings to life, haunting the living, often for purposes of retribution or revenge. Something like Miss Dark's shades and imprints, in fact."

"Precisely," said Franz. I think I was the only one sufficiently near the window to hear Nijam's soft snort of contempt. "Let me explain: In the past fortnight, I've done a great deal of thinking. I find myself with more money than I could ever need, and wish to do some good with it. Forgive me for putting it so plainly, but I gather that each of you suffers from a certain amount of financial embarrassment. Miss Dark's family depend on her for their support. Miss Nijam and Miss Laine both lack the funding to pursue their studies. And if the rumours are true, I believe the Grand Duke and Herr Schmidt have been getting by on jewel theft."

Alphonse looked startled. "Those were coincidences! We only happened to be staying at the same hotels—Sir would *never—*"

"Schmidt," Vasily said with a wry look.

Alphonse looked for a moment very confused, and then, as the truth dawned upon him, utterly disillusioned. Poor boy! I feared that in Vasily's service, he had a number of similar shocks to come.

"You were about to say, Haber?" Vasily prompted.

"I meant to say, look at the five of you," Franz went on eagerly. "A medium; an inventor; an acrobat; a confidence-trickster; a bodyguard. Together, the five of you were able to uncover the mystery of a lost princess—to solve a crime committed by people so rich and monstrous, they were able to silence all witnesses but the wronged dead." He paused, taking a deep, hopeful breath. "I received a letter last week from my cousin in Jerusalem. My cousin said that an Orthodox pilgrim killed a Jewish woman, and now her spirit is a *dybbuk* haunting the abbot who has given refuge to the murderer and is protecting him from the authorities. I thought at once of you, my friends. No one else will see justice done, and there must be hundreds of other such cases to address. You would require financial backing, of course; and that's where I come in. I thought an annual salary of—" and he named a figure that would have made me purse my lips and whistle, had I been a thought less carefully brought-up.

"I'll do it," Mimi said promptly. "I don't know anything about ghosts—or abbots—but I'll do it."

"Miss Dark?" Franz asked, turning to me. "It won't work without you; I am asking you specifically to investigate crimes committed against the dead, crimes the police—and the courts—will do nothing to remedy."

"You are too generous," I said in a shaken voice, trying not to think of my sisters' needs, my mother's illness. "How could I earn such a sum?"

"You are more than worth it, fraulein," he said warmly. "What is wealth for, if not to be employed for the good of one's neighbour?"

"My family would be taken care of," I said, thinking out loud in my agitation. "I would even be able to afford a sanatorium for my mother…"

"My mother needs treatment also," Franz interrupted eagerly. "I can afford the best in the world for her; but she will want a companion—someone of her own class, with whom she can converse on equal terms. Perhaps your mother would be kind enough to join her in Switzerland?"

"Herr Haber, I hardly know what to say."

"Then say yes."

"Yes," I said, feeling suddenly as light as air. My family would be taken care of; my mother was going to Switzerland; and I would no longer be a governess. I would earn my bread by employing my gift and doing good to others.—Tears sprang to my eyes. I really *had* seen Marie-Caroline's inheritance into the right hands. "Yes, a thousand times."

"And the rest of you?" Franz turned to the three others. Nijam did not look up; her chin was sunk upon her breast in an attitude of deep dejection. Vasily's calculating eyes fixed on me.

Alphonse, glancing from one to the other, cleared his throat diffidently. "I should be happy to follow sir."

Nijam sent him a look of pure venom, but said nothing.

All attention was now on Vasily. "Your grace?" Franz prompted. "Your help would be invaluable; my cousin tells me the abbot in question is from the Russian Compound."

Much as I had wanted Vasily for the graveyard job, I was unsure whether I liked the idea of his joining us in Jerusalem. I felt I had pushed him too far—had tipped my hand too freely. He knew exactly the sort of conniving female I was, and I did not relish the thought of having to spend the next goodness-knows-how-long watching my back.

All the same, I had come to respect his abilities on a purely professional level. Vasily had something like my own knack with human foibles, but his knowledge of the world was far greater, and he moved far more easily among both the highest

330

and the lowest sort of people than I ever could.

I cleared my throat. "In reference to past events, your grace, I do hope we can let the water go under the bridge."

"Oh!" he interrupted, all urbanity, "I don't dwell on bygones, Miss Dark. I shouldn't trust me either if I were you. One thing I insist upon knowing for certain, however. Do you still plan to turn me over to the Okhrana? I seem to recall you suggesting something of the sort, the night of the cemetery job."

My mouth was dry. I sent Nijam a pleading look, but she gave me no help.

"Never again," I promised. "I was only bluffing, of course. I would have been *helpless* without you."

"In what way, precisely? You seem to have done pretty well in my absence."

"I couldn't possibly have dug up that coffin," I pointed out, and he burst into laughter.

"I like to think I have a *little* more to offer than a decent shovel arm," he said. "Very well: you have conquered. I will stay with you, Miss Dark, and help you to lay angry ghosts. It's interesting work, and I think I should like to keep an eye on you for a while."

"And *I* think," thought I to myself, "that perhaps you are not quite as conquered—nor so tired of virtue—as you claim to be." But of course I did not say it aloud.

"Miss Nijam?" Franz now turned to the window where Nijam had been brooding all this time in silence.

"I won't do it," she said flatly. "It's no use, Dark; you and I don't get on. And I don't believe in ghosts."

With that, she pushed away from the window and tramped towards the door.

"Nijam!" I cried, hurrying after her. She moved quickly, but I caught her in the courtyard. It was covered in snow today: the marble lady at its centre was clothed, for once, in a fluffy white muffler.

"Nijam," I panted, catching her hand. "Do you really have such an aversion to me?"

"Why does everyone think I hate them?" she said, frowning. "I have no aversion to you, Dark; I object only to working with you. I don't believe you see ghosts, and I've learned not to trust your judgement."

"It would be different if we worked together," I pled. "Please, Nijam. You're the cleverest of all of us. I will do as you advise, I promise."

For a moment, she almost looked tempted. Then she shook her head. "Chasing ghosts? Pardon me; we're calling them *dybbuks* now? It's sheer folly, and I won't be a part of it. Do you understand how difficult it is for a woman—and a *half-caste* at that—to be taken seriously in this profession, without believing in ghosts to boot?"

"I'm sorry you had to hear that, but—"

"Don't ask me again, Dark," she said forbiddingly. "I can't do it. I can't bear to watch Alphonse Schmidt letting that master of his walk all over him. Take care of him for me, will you? I'm going to find a cure; I'm going to get his memories back. If you want to do me a good turn, just don't let him get hurt before then."

I thought she was mad to walk away from the man she loved. How much time had they already lost? If she loved Alphonse, she should tell him so; she should take him as he was, and not as she wished him to be.—But no, there was that foolish scruple of conscience preventing her.

"You could ask the Infante," I suggested. "The melusines have mesmeric powers. Perhaps one of them could help Alphonse recover his memories."

"Can't be done," she said. "I wrote to Jaime, of course—but no. Alphonse's memories were stolen by a siren, and only a siren can reverse that sort of damage. A melusine can only suggest; and there's a risk of creating false memories. I won't do that to him." She smiled bitterly, and then put out her hand. "So long, Dark. I'll write when I know more."

She wrung my hand and went away. I suppose she had the carriage carry her directly back to Wiener Neustadt, rather than spend another moment in the same house with Alphonse Schmidt.

The door closed behind her and I let out a sigh, glancing up at the house rising on all four sides. Was it only two weeks since I had lived in this lap of luxury, disguised as a princess? I turned back towards the sitting-room I had left and startled a little to find that my thoughts had summoned Maria Charlotte herself. Despite the snowy day, she was wearing a dress of thin white lace, and when I approached to see what she was painting, I caught my breath to feel an almost painful sense of hope.

In her watercolour, the whole courtyard bloomed with summer flowers.

I was still watching her when I heard a door open and turned to find that Vasily had also entered the garden, in his soundless, catlike way.

"Haber is giving us lunch before sending us on our way to Jerusalem," he told me with a smile that did not quite reach his eyes. "Are you coming?"

"Thank you; I will." I sent one last glance towards the

princess, but she had already faded.

Vasily remained in front of me, blocking the entrance. His cold smile broadened a little, and his voice sank to a whisper. "You betrayed me three times, Molly Dark."

My blood turned to ice in my veins. I had lied to him about my tail; I had lulled him to sleep at Mimi's; and I had put him in the path of the Okhrana at the cemetery.—*He knew.*

"Please believe that I would never have left you in Nikolasha's custody," I began.

"Of course not," he said drily. "Listen well, my little mouse, for I won't repeat it. I'm not the sort of man to forgive lightly; so don't keep me with you if you mean to betray me again. I may no longer be a vampire, but I still have teeth."

I looked into the face of this extraordinary man, with whom I had somehow entangled myself. Guiltily, I remembered the way he had kissed me in the little sitting-room some weeks ago. I wondered, not for the first time, what he would say or do if I walked towards him now, and dragged him down by the lapels and returned that kiss; whether he would pull me closer, or push me away; and somehow the thought of either was equally unbearable.

My wretched face had warmed at the thought. I would not, I told myself—I *would* not run into the wilderness with the bad Grand Duke.

"No," I said. "I think we're of the same mind on the matter, your grace. Sometimes it's better to be apart from your friends, and nearer your enemies."

S.D.G.

Unhistorical Note

Today, Schloss Frohsdorf—the royal residence of the last Bourbon pretenders—has been rebranded as "Château Petit Versailles," an eye-wateringly luxurious getaway spot for oil billionaires just twenty minutes by helicopter from Vienna's international airport (or forty minutes for those cheapskates who prefer to travel by car). I plan to take a holiday there myself once this book storms the New York Times bestseller list, becomes a star-studded Hollywood movie production and wins the Nobel prize for literature. But while I'm waiting, I might as well fill you in on the history.

The French Revolution claimed the lives of Louis XVI, his Austrian queen Marie Antoinette, and three of their four children. The only survivor was the eldest child, Marie-Thérèse, who was released in a prisoner exchange arranged in 1795 by her cousin, Francis I of Austria.

It was Marie-Thérèse who ultimately purchased the Schloss Frohsdorf in which to live out her final days. Upon her death, the property passed to her nephew Henri, Comte de Chambord. The Bourbon royal family had continued to cling to power in France for some time after the revolution (since Napoleon, three of Louis XVI's younger brothers had worn the crown in succession) and Henri, the grandson of the second of these, was the last male-line descendant of the Bourbons. Henri lived at the Schloss Frohsdorf for much of his adult life with his wife, Archduchess Maria Theresa of Austria-Este. In reality, they had no children, although I have taken the liberty of naming their imaginary daughter, Marie-Caroline, after Henri's mother Caroline of Naples. After Maria Theresa's death the property, as well as the claim to the throne, was passed to their great-nephew Jaime de Borbon.

I'm afraid I made up the parts about the giant snake monsters.

I want to thank my wonderful beta and sensitivity readers for their time, patience, and attention: Peirce and Christina Baehr, Sahrish Nadim, Marie Lewis, and (last but not least) W.R. Gingell, for talking me out of razing this book to the ground and sowing its foundations with salt. My deepest thanks also go out to Molly Dark (of the Victoria, Australia Darks) for allowing me the use of her name, even though I gave it to a character who is her opposite in almost every respect.

Suzannah Rowntree
    March 2022

About the Author

Suzannah Rowntree lives in a big house in rural Australia with her awesome parents and siblings, drinking fancy tea and writing historical fantasy fiction that blends real-world history with legend, adventure, and a dash of romance.

You can connect with me on:
🌐 https://suzannahrowntree.site

Subscribe to my newsletter:
✉ https://www.subscribepage.com/srauthor

Also by Suzannah Rowntree

The Miss Sharp's Monsters Series
The Werewolf of Whitechapel
Anarchist on the Orient Express
A Vampire in Bavaria

The Miss Dark's Apparitions Series
Tall & Dark
Dark Clouds

The Watchers of Outremer Series
A Wind from the Wilderness
The Lady of Kingdoms
Children of the Desolate
A Day of Darkness

The Pendragon's Heir Trilogy
The Door to Camelot
The Quest for Carbonek
The Heir of Logres

The Fairy Tale Retold Series
The Rakshasa's Bride
The Prince of Fishes
The Bells of Paradise
Death Be Not Proud
Ten Thousand Thorns
The City Beyond the Glass